An Awkward Commission

DAVID DONACHIE

Allison & Busby Limited
13 Charlotte Mews
London W1T 4EJ
www.allisonandbusby.com

Hardcover first published in Great Britain in 2006.
Paperback edition first published in 2008 (ISBN 978-0-7490-8067-9).
Reissued in 2010.

10 9 8 7 6 5 4 3 2

13-ISBN 978-0-7490-0831-4

Typeset by Allison & Busby in Sabon.

The paper used for this Allison & Busby publication
has been produced from trees that have been legally sourced
from well-managed and credibly certified forests.

Printed and bound by
CPI Group (UK) Ltd, Croydon, CR0 4YY

To Jim & Les Davies
without whom this book would
not have been written.

CHAPTER ONE

The square was full of people, the ground covered in a putrid mixture of human and animal ordure, laced with blood and white viscous entrails that sucked at his boots. Try as he might, John Pearce struggled to make headway through the solid crowd, ogres that turned their hideous faces towards him with a terrifying grin or a wide open mouth, each yelling a different, indistinct message. In that mire at his feet he had to step over couples publicly copulating, the women sewing together their cockades of red, white and blue as they ground out their carnal pleasure with obvious glee. In the background stood the outline of a heavy wooden scaffold, the floor set high so that it was visible to all the dregs of Paris. On that wooden frame stood the lethal guillotine, the silver blade, caught by shafts of strong sunlight, dropping with a deadly thud at regular intervals, to be raised again and again, dripping blood, the whole accompanied by a constant, funereal drum roll, interspersed with exultant cries at raised, detached heads.

The winged horse came from nowhere and soon he was mounted, above both crowd and scaffold, looking down on the sea of faces that filled the huge stone-built quadrangle of the Place de la Revolution, and all the while that rhythmic thud continued. Very obvious was the snaking line of scarecrow-like victims that ran all the way from the scaffold steps back to the River Seine and along the bank of the sluggishly flowing river. There it broke up, one line extending across the Pont Neuf to the Conciergerie, stone walls ten-foot thick, grey and forbidding like a malignant womb, others to the prisons of Châtelet and La Force, each converging inmate waiting their turn to offer up their heads to the killing machine of the Revolution. Swooping down like Bellerophon astride Pegasus, he came face to face with his own father, moving along to his fate – not the man he had seen last, but the younger, healthy Adam Pearce who had raised him. He spoke, his deep, strong voice full of the passion for truth that had been his greatest asset, as well as the cause of his ultimate downfall.

For a brief moment John was a boy again, his hand warm in that of his only living parent, and the snaking line had gone. They seemed to be on a road of some kind, a brick *pavé* that led to a sparking citadel – all gleaming spires and snow-white walls – the very image of paradise shining in a never-reducing distance, perhaps the home he had never known, but always longed for. But that faded as the slow thud-thud-thud came again and he watched aghast as slowly and inexorably his father aged and withered, the hair going from black to grey, to white, the voice from power to a sickly wheeze, the body shrinking until he was reduced to a thin-haired and blood-drained head, held in the outstretched hand of a fat, leather-clad and grinning executioner, while behind and below him that vicious crowd screamed in a paroxysm of homicidal ecstasy.

It was the furious cry of a boatman that woke him, that and the summer sunlight streaming through an uncurtained window right onto his eyelids, though he had no knowledge of what was being shouted, only that fulsome curses were being employed. Pearce lay in the bed for a whole minute listening to that repeated thud before he could place it, and in doing so come to some knowledge of where he was.

The night before seemed as misty a memory as the horrible dream from which he had just surfaced; his dry mouth and leather tongue, plus the sour taste on his palate told him that he had been drunk, long before the lump of swollen flesh at the back of his throat gave him some idea of how much he had indulged in open-mouthed snoring. The thudding sound continued and it took time for him to realise it was that of a boat snubbing on the wooden jetty outside and below his window, striking the timbers each time it was lifted by a wave running into the deepest reaches of Portsmouth harbour.

Lifting himself to drink from a pitcher by his side, he groaned at the pain that seared through the top of his head, swallowing greedily to turn his tongue from fur to flesh, as some of what had happened the day before came back to him, that and all that had occurred these last few months: a whirlwind of the press gang, service at sea, storms, fighting the enemy less often than authority, and in doing so establishing the kind of friendships that a life of wanderings with his radical father had never allowed. What now of the confidence with which he had arrived in Portsmouth, sure in the knowledge that a promise he had made to the trio with whom he had been press-ganged months before would be fulfilled; that they would, like him, have the freedom to follow their own wishes rather than stay as enforced sailors in King George's Navy? He recalled the look of sheer pleasure on the Midshipman's face as he informed this fellow, attired now in the uniform of a lieutenant, that those he had come to free were no longer in the anchorage or aboard HMS *Centurion*, but had been shipped out on another vessel bound for the Mediterranean, condemned to continue to serve because he had dallied for a day or two longer than he should have in the arms of a beautiful, wealthy and indulgent woman.

Stood on the deck of the 50-gun warship, he looked on in dazed silence, at a loss to make sense of what had occurred, as the carpenters worked away to repair the damage inflicted in the recent action, fitting new bulwarks and deck planking where they had been blown in or scarred by cannon fire, others pedalling fast-turning lathes, carving out the newel posts and uprights that would make up the replacement staircase rails. All around in the Spithead anchorage lay the might of Britain's wooden walls, the great ships that were all that stood between tyranny and what the inhabitants of Albion took to be liberty.

All the while that midshipman stood there, silent but mocking, declining the idea that he might provide further explanation. The return journey across the anchorage seemed to add to that contempt, the hired wherry taking him past the damaged stern of *Valmy*, the 74-gun French ship that he, along with his companions, had helped to capture. Soon, no doubt, she too would be repaired, would be renamed under a British flag before being sent back to sea, there to challenge those vessels which had once been her consorts.

Ashore, Pearce had headed straight to a tavern crowded with soldiers, sailors and as many locals; dockyard mateys, costermongers, draymen and a sprinkling of fly types, ordering a flagon of French brandy and 'damn the expense', thus attracting attention to himself, for being now contraband, that was an expensive beverage. A fellow-drinker identified him as the hero of the recent action – he had seen him come ashore ten days before, the talk of a port that lived off the King's Navy and loved a victory. That had led to bumper after bumper to celebrate the first true triumph of the latest French war, drinks consumed with relish by a man who had no desire to think, only to forget. Now he knew he was in a narrow bed, but not precisely where, knew he felt like death, but was wholly alive, knew that he still had on the breeches, silk stocking and silver-buckled shoes bought for him by the generous Lady Annabel Fitzherbert.

Sitting up, he could see his new coat, of dark blue, heavy broadcloth, was crumpled on the floor, along with his black silk naval hat. A quick feel of his purse told him it was still inside his breeches and still near-full, which led him to suspect that he had got very drunk on the coin and generosity of others, which was shaming. Head bent, Pearce reacted too sharply to the creaking door, and sent a shaft of pain through his temples, which meant the person who entered addressed a man with his eyes shut tight and his head in his hands.

'There you are, sir, up an' about at last. We had you down to sleep a month after the state you came to us in.' The face, when he lifted his head and opened his eyes, was female, round, rosy-cheeked and affable, though the smile was without a single tooth, which gave the voice a lisping quality. 'Now it strikes me, you bein' the hero you are, that a proper breakfast is in order, that is after the necessary, of course.'

The 'necessary' turned out to be a herbal infusion of the inn-keeper's own making, though there was a telling dose of alcohol in the brew, rough to be sure, Arrack most likely, given it burnt the back of his throat. He had to drink it straight down, for the maker of the potion stood before him, fists on a pair of hips so substantial that they would have stood comparison to a three-tun barrel. Her eyes were narrow and she seemed determined to ensure it went straight down to the seat of the problem for, as the landlady said, 'Though the pain might be in your head, young sir, to be sure the seat of your malaise lies deep in the vital parts, in short, in your entrails, where the soul of man resides. The necessary, first, and perhaps a good evacuation, will see you renewed. Take my word for it, sir, for I have seen many a fellow in your condition and worse, my own late husband not least, in half a glass of sand you will be as right as rain and tuckin' into a fine beefsteak or two washed down with my own true porter, or I, Peg Bamber, am not the widow of a blue-water sailor.'

Peg Bamber had the right of it; not that a clearer head and a well-satisfied belly brought much in the way of true relief, for John Pearce was faced in clarity with the same dilemma which had plagued him these last months – how to get his mates, those men he called his fellow Pelicans, off the ship in which they had been sent to sea. Sitting in his shirtsleeves, looking out of the window by which he sat – for Peg insisted he eat in his room; 'Why, young sir, to enter the taproom is to invite a return to the state in which you came upstairs this forenight' – Pearce ran his eye over the bustling inner port. There were one or two vessels tied up to the shore, and over the nearest water a pair in dry dock, but the main part of the armada was some way out, with a stream of boats and hoys carrying people and supplies to and fro.

His friends, Michael O'Hagan, Charlie Taverner and young Rufus Dommet had been on that very water no more than five days before, no doubt anxiously looking over the ship's rail for a sight of him come to rescue them. He had failed them, just as he had so recently failed his own father. As elements of that dream with which he had awoken came back to him, he began to talk in order to mask out the feelings it induced.

'The name confuses, sir,' lisped Peg Bamber, when he alluded to the problem of the Pelicans.

'We were all press-ganged not five months past from a tavern. It was called the Pelican and stood by the banks of the River Thames.'

'London, sir, a hateful place, I am told, where it ain't safe to walk the streets.'

Pearce took another draw on the tankard of porter, sure he could feel in his gut the way it was doing him good, sipping as he explained the illegality of what had happened that night, but leaving out the fact that he himself had been on the run from the law and a King's Bench Warrant, and had only gone into the Pelican to escape pursuit and, if caught, imprisonment.

'In seeking to secure ourselves against the malice of others, and as a badge of our shared misfortune, we adopted the name of Pelicans as a soubriquet.'

'I have no notion of what a subrick is, sir, but I do know that pleading to me will get you not one whit forrard. The only authority that can gainsay your quandary is the Admiral himself.'

'Howe.'

'Why it's as plain as the nose on your face,' Peg insisted, lifting his plate and popping into her mouth the long slice of fat Pearce had trimmed from the edge of his beefsteak. 'You must ask the Admiral to fetch them back. A fast pinnace will have no trouble coming up on a seventy-four, as long as her course is known, even a naval widow knows that.'

'Admiral Lord Howe,' said Pearce patiently, wondering if Peg really knew what she was talking about. He might consider himself no tarpaulin, but he did know that spotting another ship at sea, even if you had a fair notion of its course, was hit and miss at best, and in twenty-four hours, even at a medium rate of sailing, she could be a hundred miles down-Channel.

'Black Dick Howe!' Peg exclaimed, finally getting his drift. 'Why, only God knows how a man can run a fleet of ships from Bath.' Seeing the look on Pearce's face, she added, 'The crabbed old bugger has gone to take the waters, young sir, and no doubt to try and get his old bones a'fit for dalliance, which is fanciful in a man of his years, and all the while we are at risk of an enemy sailing in to burn and make devilment. It is to be hoped he can post-chaise back here

13

faster than the French can cross the waters, the idle dog.'

'It was he who said the matter would be taken care of.'

'Then let us hope he remembers, though I has to say it ain't common in those of his advanced years. He's not more'n a lick and a spit off seventy, the old goat. Happen you should try Admiral Graves, who does all the work for Black Dick and, if rumour has it right, suffers the brickbats for it not bein' done quick enough.'

One of Peg's girls came into the room holding his coat and hat, the former having been steamed and pressed, while his hat had been brushed to remove what Peg called half the mud of the alleys in which he had rolled. The conversation that ensued as he dressed himself established who and what Graves was – second-in-command of the Channel fleet, and an irascible man with much to be irascible about.

'You will need to boat out to his ship to see him at all,' Peg added, with a loud disapproving sniff. 'He abides to the rule that it is sinful for anyone to sleep ashore, admiral to mid, which makes him the devil incarnate to folk who make their coin from accommodating and feeding the likes of your good self. Instead he fills the purses of bum-boat men and their floating harlots. Not that tars don't need comfort, sir, but...'

Pearce stopped the indignant flow by agreeing with her, then established that Admiral Graves was aboard his flagship, HMS *Royal Sovereign*.

'Shall I send a girl to bespeak you a boat?'

'Please, and I will settle what I owe in case I do not return.'

'A hearty bill, sir,' Peg exclaimed, opening her mouth to show pink gums. 'You treated the good folk of Portsmouth well this forenight, and paid for more sore heads than your own. I'll grant you the cure *gratis*, as is only fittin' for a hero, the second I have had under my roof this present war.'

'The second?' said Pearce, distracted by the thought of what might be a substantial bill, and the disturbing thought that he might not be able to meet it.

'Why yes, sir. I had a lad even younger under my eaves a month or two back, a midshipman as brave as you, sir, to judge by his tale. Young Mr Burns, for that was his name, took a ship from right under the noses of Jean Crapaud, out of the very harbour in which it was berthed if you please, and brought her back to her home shore…'

Peg Bamber stopped, non-plussed by the look of deep anger in John Pearce's face.

'I know Mr Burns, Madame, and I can assure you were the truth of his tale to be known he would be whipped rather than lauded.' Pearce, recalling the pasty face of Toby Burns, of the boy's utter uselessness and the bland betrayal he had perpetrated on himself and the very men he had come to Portsmouth to rescue, had to fight not to add more than that bitter condemnation. But he had to stop; it was no concern of this woman that Burns was a lying little toad, even if he could not suppress his feelings entirely. His voice, when he spoke, carried the strain of a man holding an exceedingly unpleasant memory in check.

'I thank you, Mrs Bamber, for your care and attention.'

The reply was a pretty curtsy, even in a woman of her size, and mouth closed and frame diminished, it was possible to see the quite comely girl she must have once been. But the eyes had a sudden glint, when she added, 'I'll see to your account, sir.'

Several guineas lighter, John Pearce left Peg Bamber's, making his way to the shoreline of the Common Hard, where the boat Peg's girl had engaged was waiting, drawn up on the shingle. It turned out to be a family concern, a conjugal affair, and once paid a shilling in advance for their trouble, the husband and wife saw it as part of their task to entertain their passenger with an unrelenting account of mutual frustration – about their abode, the job from which they made their living, even their intimacy – with each in turn looking to him at some point for support.

'A pig-sty, sir, that is where I live.'

'Then it be above your station, that's fer certain,' spat the wife, a thick-armed crone with an unlit clay pipe clamped in her teeth. She looked to be twice as strong as her spouse, who was weedy and wiry, with a pinched unhealthy face, albeit perfectly able to match her pace on the oar. 'Just like the stick you are. Yer not fit to be a crossing-sweeper.'

'I would have to sweep hard to clear your filth.' A look to the passenger followed, his eyes searching for sympathy from his own gender. 'An' no warmth, sir, not a drop of it, just a cold shoulder.'

'Would that you had something to warm a woman, you spavined dog…'

Pearce tried to shut out the sound of their bickering and looked away so that neither could engage him in their cause. That dream surfaced again, in all its horrible clarity, because these were the kind of folk for whom his father had argued passionately all his life. Adam Pearce had travelled the length and breadth of the country, his son in tow, trying to better the lot of the dispossessed. He would speak at the stump of whichever place they stopped to lambast the comfortable and extol the intrinsic worth of the poor, who only needed an education to be as fine as those who saw themselves as their betters. And John Pearce had, for he was too young to do otherwise, shared such opinions, even as he sought to avoid being robbed of the contents of his hat, usually copper, rarely silver, by the offspring of the very audience his father was addressing. Those sentiments had even survived a spell in the Fleet prison, for Adam Pearce had a carapace of social faith every bit as strong as that of the most committed adherent of religion.

It was not one his son now shared. Age and growing independence, added to what he had seen in Paris in the two and a bit years they had spent there, had cured him. Were the pair on the oars the same kind of *canaille* who had emerged from the eastern slums of Paris to ruin the Revolution – filthy specimens with brains that could encompass no other thought than greedy violence, the types who had torn down the Bastille stone by stone? And if that was a laudable event, joyously hailed even in Britain as an end to royal tyranny, what followed over the months and years became progressively less so. He had seen the likes of this pair covered from head to bare foot in fresh blood, running under flaming torches through the streets of Paris, bearing heads on pikes that they had hacked off from their dead victims, and screaming of how many more would die.

'Name, sir?' demanded the boatman. 'We's a-coming under *Royal Sovereign*'s counter.'

'Pearce, John Pearce,' he replied, looking up at the towering three-decker, and the mass of gilded carving that decorated her stern. Then he added a word that still sounded bizarre to his ears: 'Lieutenant.'

Once alongside, the fellow called over his shoulder to the entry port, a dark hole in the ship's side, framed by the climbing battens that would be needed to get aboard at sea. Here, they had fitted a long sloping gangway.

'Lieutenant Pearce seeking permission to come aboard, your honour.'

'Your honour?' called a voice from the interior. 'You ain't talking to me, that's fer certain.' Two sailors emerged, boat-hooks at the ready, one taking the prow of the wherry to haul it in, the other more rigid to steady the approach of the stern. 'Boat your oars, fellows, for if'n you scrape the paint it'll be my guts.'

'One of them's a woman I reckon, Clem,' said the other sailor.

'You don't say!' Clem shouted, looking hard at the female in the boat, all wild grey hair and wrinkled skin. 'Then make sure when I is soused and ashore, mate, that I stay well clear of her, for Old Nick hisself would blanch to be seen coupling with that.'

'One of these days, husband, I might find a tar with enough to please a woman, but I doubt this be the one.'

'I make you right there, Susie, my love,' her husband replied, in the softest and most defensive of voices, making it clear that civility came to them only when they were faced with an external insult.

On what now seemed a steady platform, Pearce stood up, wondering at a life like theirs, in which the next meal had been probably uncertain since birth, but he was soon obliged to think more of his own immediate safety as the wherry was pulled in, nearly knocking him off-balance.

About to step onto the gangway, he stopped dead when the sailor called Clem cried out, 'Right foot first, sir, where has you put your wits?'

He had to skip to get his right foot on the wooden platform first, and thus he avoided the opprobrium of condemning the whole ship to perdition through the act of ignoring a superstition. Up he went to enter the dim interior, to be greeted by a midshipman who raised his hat. Pearce did likewise, distracted as he glanced along the empty maindeck, then wondered at the look on the boy's face as he put it back on. Quickly he raised it again, half-turning to salute the unseen quarterdeck, mentally kicking himself to remember the things that an officer was supposed to do on coming aboard.

'I have come to see Admiral Graves.'

'Have you indeed, sir,' replied the boy. 'Do you have an appointment?'

'No.'

The boy sighed. 'Then I fear you are in for a long wait. Best bespeak the officer in charge of the anchor watch and see if he will allow you the use of the wardroom.'

'Obliged.'

'Follow me, sir.'

He was led across the gloomy deck to a wide stairway that led up to the quarterdeck. There they found the man presently in charge of the ship, likewise a lieutenant, in an unadorned blue working coat, who, on being introduced, immediately enquired as to the date of his commission. Admitting it to be only days old brought forth a puffed chest and the information that this man was his superior by three years. Only then did he ask his name, and a raised eyebrow went with the reply.

'Pearce, of the *Griffin*? The fellow who was spoke of in the local journal only last week?' Trying to look modest, Pearce nodded. 'Damn you, Tait,' the officer barked at the mid, 'you best learn, you pint-sized blackguard, to execute proper introductions.'

'Sorry, sir,' said the boy, abashed, though clearly he was equally confused.

'You will be.' With Pearce, all condescension disappeared. 'Allow me, sir, to shake your hand, for that was a worthy exploit, and it warms our cockles to look out over the taffrail and see the ship you helped to take. I would be less than honest, sir, if I did not tell you it stirs a little jealousy also, for we would all wish to have such luck.'

A vision of the bloodshed that had attended the capture floated into Pearce's mind, which sat uneasily with the concept of luck.

'The Admiral has much to attend to and a queue of supplicants, but I am sure your name will see you well up the list.' There was a pause them, before the Lieutenant added, 'But were you not a midshipman, sir?'

'I was, sir, but the King, at his levee, saw fit to insist that I be promoted, hence the newness of my commission. The commander of HMS *Griffin* was made a post captain at the same time.'

Pearce did not add that the Earl of Chatham, First Lord of the Admiralty, had objected to his elevation only to be over-ruled by his own younger brother, the King's absurdly young First Minister. He was later told by the lovely Lady Annabel that William Pitt was more concerned with the state of the monarch's health and the maintenance of his government than the propriety of promoting a man who lacked any of the qualifications that the post demanded. In a parliament riven with competing ideas and policies, Pitt commanded a tenuous majority, which required constant manoeuvring to sustain. War with France was not universally popular, indeed there were those who would make peace on the morrow if they could just gain power. The ministry of Pitt was based on Tory support, but that was not unanimous, yet the opposition Whigs were no more united, some sections inclining to the government view that the Revolution must be contained, the majority of that faction lining up behind Pitt's great rival, Charles James Fox, to challenge the government on every issue, from the war itself, to the prosecution of the conflict, egged on by the power-hungry heir to the throne.

Pitt's party was the one favoured by King George, who could not be other than opposed to a radical polity in Paris which had executed his fellow monarch, King Louis of France, a few months previously. But George III had been declared mad just three years before – which had created a political crisis – and it was feared by all that the affliction which had rendered him unfit to govern would return. The Prince of Wales and his Whig supporters longed for such a thing, for in a declared Regency, with the King's heir apparent as head of state, they, not Pitt's Tories, would hold the power. To the King's First Minister, indulging an unstable king with an inappropriate promotion was obviously a small price to pay for the security of office.

The advancement of Colbourne to the rank of post captain brought forth a gleam of near-avarice in Pearce's fellow-officer. 'Then I envy your Mr Colbourne, sir, his promotion, even more than I envy you.'

'He lost an arm, and I do believe he has to face a court-martial.'

'A formality, sir, nothing more.' Clearly, to this fellow, the loss of a limb or a ship counted for less than Colbourne's new rank. 'What is that when you are made post? Why, a man on the captain's list is a man made for life, with a flag on the horizon if the Good Lord spares you. I long for nothing more, sir, as I am sure you do too. Mr Tait, take Lieutenant Pearce to the wardroom as my guest, and tell the Steward that he is to waive the normal contribution we ask of visiting officers to our fund.'

Pearce was about to demure when the lieutenant added, 'It is the bane of life on a flagship, sir, the law of hospitality. We are obliged to levy a charge, for we are called upon to feed all and sundry as they wait for their interview, which would devastate our private stores without recompense. But you, sir, are an exception, a worthy guest. Meanwhile, I will tell the Admiral's clerk who's come a'calling.'

To enter the wardroom of a vessel this size, a hundred guns or more, was a revelation to John Pearce. It could not be said to be spacious, yet compared to that allotted to the common seamen, or what he had experienced so far, it was luxury indeed, with a long table across the room and small screened-off cabins to either side. Three marine officers and another lieutenant were playing backgammon, while others, close to flickering candles or the five transom casements, read their books or wrote letters.

'Forgive me, Mr Pearce, while I inform the Premier of your presence.'

Going to rear the boy rapped on a wooden door. There was another on the opposite side, a private space of proper cabins for the two most senior officers under the Captain. The disinterest with which he had been greeted on entering the wardroom, for visitors were so commonplace, evaporated as the First Lieutenant emerged from his quarters, a beaming smile on his face and a shout on his lips.

'Steward, fetch the best claret, we have a fellow on board deserving of a toast.'

Named, they gathered round him, trying to feed him cup after cup of wine, but Pearce, obliged by the welcome to relate every detail of the recent action, stayed as abstemious as was possible, knowing that he needed a clear head for what was to come. More troubling was the technicality of the questions he was asked about courses, wind strength, gun calibres and the effect of various weights of shot on the lighter scantlings of a French ship, all of which he struggled to answer out of sheer ignorance.

He wanted to tell them that his entire time at sea would not amount to much more than five months – that he had read his books but not enough. Yet he knew that such disclosure would be unwelcome, so he tried his best to satisfy their curiosity, drawing the elements of the action on the wardroom table with a finger dipped in his wine. It was with some relief that he was finally dragged off to see the Admiral, with an invitation from the First Lieutenant to be their guest that afternoon at dinner. Young Tait was again obliged to guide him, this time past two marine sentries who stood at the door to the anteroom of the Admiral's quarters, and once inside that, to introduce him to an officious-looking civilian at a desk.

'Your business, sir?'

The voice was bored and dismissive, but that was as nothing to the look of utter disbelief on the fellow's pasty face as Pearce replied. His voice had all the arrogance of the jobsworth, and when he spoke, it was icy. 'You have come all this way to importune the effective commander of His Majesty's Channel Fleet on the fate of a trio of ordinary seamen, indeed landsmen, who are, I must tell you, now sailing to be part of a fleet that will be commanded by another admiral, Lord Hood?'

'They are not ordinary to me, sir. They are my closest friends.'

'Then I wonder at your connections, sir, for it is uncommon for an officer to so term a sailor.'

'Perhaps more of that would make the Navy a happier occupation! Lord Howe specifically alluded to their case, sir, in the most positive manner, and were he here I am sure he would oblige me by fulfilling the promise he made. I have no doubt that Admiral Graves would be only too keen to carry out the expressed wishes of the actual commanding officer.'

The look that got, as the clerk stood up to reveal a body shaped like a pear, no shoulders and a fat behind, was tantamount to a denial; in fact it implied that pigs might fly. 'Wait here. I will ask Admiral Graves if he will see you.'

Half a minute passed before the man returned. 'I am to show you through, though it is only your name that gains you an interview. Do not hold out any hope that the Admiral will oblige you.'

'Then there is no purpose in going in,' snapped Pearce, who, though restrained in his consumption of the wardroom claret, had drunk too much to suffer any hint of condescension.

'None, except that it is in the shape of an order that you do so, one which the marines behind you would insist you obey.'

The Admiral sat at a round table, a slim man of some height, with a white wig over a long, greying face and a firm, jutting-out jaw. The table was covered in books and papers, all of them, from what Pearce could observe, official. He looked up at the man before him, standing to attention with his hat under his arm, with the quizzical expression of a less-than-pleased adult faced with a recalcitrant child.

'I wanted to look you over for a second time, Pearce, for I was at the reception when you first came ashore.'

'I'm sorry, sir, I do not recall. There were so many senior officers present.'

'I was happy to praise you then, but not now. I am here to tell you that your elevation to your present rank is nothing short of a disgrace. There cannot be a serving officer who knows the truth of your promotion who is not incensed by it. Six years' sea time is six years, sir, and the position you hold demands it, as well as the knowledge a man gains in that period, something you ain't got under your belt.'

'Then you will be glad to know, sir, that I have no intention of applying for a place aboard a ship.' That came out without thinking, and was acceptable, as well as being true. Had Pearce left it there he might have held some sway with the Admiral, but the devil was in him as it often was when faced with authority, and what sympathy he might have elicited went right out the casement windows as he added, 'Nothing would induce me to serve in such a body. Your Navy, sir, is riddled with tyranny and open corruption and I can only suppose that those with the power to chastise the men who run the institution are afflicted with a kind of

24

blindness. The trio I have alluded to were, like me, illegally pressed into the Navy by a blackguard called Barclay—'

'Ralph Barclay?'

'The very same.'

'I know of Captain Barclay.'

'Then you will know, sir, that he is not fit for the rank he holds. The man is a martinet of the worst kind and a liar to boot—'

He was interrupted by a snarl. 'You will withdraw that remark, sir, for you are taking liberties with the name of a respected officer in the King's Navy.'

'If he, sir, is respected, it says little for those he serves with, or under.'

'Get out.'

'I demand you accede to the wishes of Lord Howe and do something to get those men back.'

'You can demand all you like, Pearce, and I must warn you if you do not do as I say you will be demanding from the cable tier, and you will be in chains while you do so. Your friends can serve for a decade for all I care. I repeat my words: get out!'

As Pearce turned to go, the Admiral added his final insult. 'And get off my flagship with the utmost speed, for you presence defiles the deck.' Then he shouted, 'Marines, escort this blackguard to the entry port.'

CHAPTER TWO

'Mr Glaister's compliments, sir. He believes we have a sight of the French coast, and judging by the skyline, despite the recent blow, he feels we will make a perfect landfall.'

'Please inform Mr Glaister I will be on deck presently. And request him to signal HMS *Firefly*, although I daresay Captain Gould already knows.'

Crouched over the muster book of HMS *Brilliant*, Captain Barclay did not deign to look up at Midshipman Farmiloe, who, having delivered what he thought was a dramatic message deserving of attention, was obliged to turn about and leave the Captain's cabin in a rather crestfallen manner, though he did elicit a nod and a smile from the Captain's pretty young wife, busy at a piece of embroidery in which the name of the frigate was already completed. Several cushions with similar covers lay along the bench seats, giving, if not a feminine touch to the place, at least an atmosphere more gentle than that one would associate with such an austere commander as Ralph Barclay.

From above their heads came the sound of repairs, as they had, in the last twenty-four hours, come through a vicious and sudden squall of the type that plagued ships in the Mediterranean, the kind that threw vessels on their beam ends with scant warning, so forceful and unexpected was the wind. Ralph Barclay was now listing the damage, as well as the materials – timber, cordage and canvas – that was needed to make matters right, employing a small percentage of exaggeration that any examining clerk at the Navy Board would have to be eagle-eyed to spot. Given that he was personally responsible for everything of that nature on the ship, and could be obliged to pay from his own pocket for unjustified wastage, he was, in time-honoured fashion, taking the opportunity to create a handy excess.

Next came the muster book where he listed, alongside all the other things that pertained to the existence of his crew, the fact that two of them had broken limbs, and one a dislocation of the shoulder. The surgeon's report lay by his hand, which told him one break was clean, the other not, and an estimate of how long each would be under medical care. It was a tedious duty that should have fallen to a clerk, but the then impecunious Captain Barclay had sailed from England without one, keeping for himself a proportion of the pay for the office. Running his finger down the list, of tobacco bought, clothing items deducted from pay, and the cost of treating their venereal afflictions, he came to the pencilled name of Ben Walker, lost overboard two weeks before. The time had come to use ink, and to discharge that sailor as D.D., dead in the execution of his duties, with the storm as an excuse. Keeping him on the muster for a few extra days made up for some of the depredations of the rats that infested the lower reaches below decks.

This was carried out with the connivance of the purser, who stood to gain more than the captain by a little judicious accounting, for it would transpire that the late Ben Walker had bought quite a quantity of tobacco in the last two weeks, the cost of which, since it was the Purser's private venture, would go straight into his account. Provided their ledgers agreed, no one would spot a discrepancy, nor would an eyebrow be raised to the notion of a man lost at sea, given it was commonplace. For every man that the Navy lost in battle, they lost ten to shipwreck, accident and disease.

'Is not Mr Farmiloe's news of some importance, Captain Barclay?'

Ralph Barclay looked up and smiled, struck, not for the first time, by the picture of sheer loveliness Emily presented – one of perfect harmony with the life she lived. All awkwardness was now gone; the months at sea had inured her to whatever the elements or shipboard life could bring her way, and he was even pleased at what he called her fripperies – those bits of decoration she seemed determined to create in order to make more domestic their living quarters. Gone was the gauche and embarrassed seventeen-year-old girl who had come aboard at Sheerness, who in her ignorance had embarrassed both his purse and his authority: here was that creature grown to womanhood complete, though she had only added one year to her actual age. In short, she had become the perfect wife to a serving sea captain, and the twenty year gap between them – once a concern – seemed now to be irrelevant.

'It is vital, my dear, and I would have been most put out had it not come, but it does not do to show too much zeal in these things, as I have told you before.'

Emily Barclay, even seated, managed an ironic bob. 'The captain's majesty?

'Precisely. I am no enemy to enthusiasm, in its place, but...'

Ralph Barclay followed that pause with a smile, for that was one of the things that Emily Barclay had not understood in the early days, the way a captain must be seen in the eyes of those under him; stern but fair, remote yet approachable, a balancing act between tolerance and punishment that was difficult to achieve and hard to maintain. He felt he had managed it, despite some initial hiccups, and he had been helped by some good fortune in the article of prizes which meant the crew could expect an addition to their pay, which always aided contentment. It was not pleasant to recall the way that his wife had challenged him over that fellow Pearce, who he had been forced to punish, and then been obliged to get rid of. She would not do that now, she would know better; that justice must sometimes gave way to authority.

'Would you care to join me on deck, my dear?'

'Is there anything to see, husband?'

'I doubt it. Land will have been spotted from the masthead, and even in an hour, given the heat of the day, it will be no more than a smudge on the horizon.'

'Then if you do not mind, husband, I will visit the men who suffered injury in yesterday's storm.'

'Of course,' he replied, before calling to his steward. 'Shenton, my hat.'

As he closed the muster book, Ralph Barclay promised himself that, at the first opportunity, he would employ a clerk to do the work that he had just completed. It would have to be someone who understood the meaning of discretion, as well as the need for certain reservations with the absolute facts; no captain could afford to tell the Admiralty and Navy Board everything, and a certain security lay in the fact that, though they claimed to be zealous, those clerks were, in fact, only too human. He had had to decline his wife's offer to undertake the work, for he knew she, of all people, being so delightfully ingenuous, would not comprehend that particular requirement.

His officers removed their hats as he stepped onto the quarterdeck, each acknowledged by no more than a nod. First he looked at the slate, and the course that had been chalked on, knowing that the ship's master, Mr Collins, a man of an extremely insecure temperament, would be made nervous by his action. His frigate, HMS *Brilliant,* with the sloop HMS *Firefly* in her wake, was making some four knots on a steady south-west breeze that was coming in nicely over her larboard quarter. He cast his glance upwards, to where, amongst the taut sails, the topmen were working, splicing ropes that had parted in the squall and re-roving blocks that had come apart from the falls. Forward, over the waist, the sailmaker and his assistants were sitting in a line repairing a damaged topsail, their long needles flying through the thick canvas, the whole of the work on deck and aloft overseen by Mr Sykes, the bosun. Here was another cause for satisfaction, a crew that, due to his constant training and stern attitude, had become efficient at their work, and warrant officers like Sykes, who had seemed uncertain at first, now relaxed and competent. They were not at the peak of perfection – that took years at sea to achieve – but they were nothing like the rabble with which he had put to sea.

Likewise, in his First Lieutenant, he had an officer who understood what was required of him; that the deck be spotless, the cannonballs in the rope garlands black and chipped free of rust, the cannon tight to the ship's side, idle ropes perfectly coiled and the crew quiet and industrious, yet ready at a moment's notice to go from peaceful sailing to fighting readiness. That had not been so when he had set off from Sheerness, but good fortune had attended the cruise of HMS *Brilliant* in that respect too, ridding him of subordinates inclined to be contentious, and replacing them with men who understood the need to obey.

'Mr Glaister?'

The lanky Scotsman, with his thin, near skeletal face and startlingly blue eyes, replied to the implied question in a lilting, Highland tone. 'Masthead reports that our landfall is mountainous, sir, which leads me to suspect that if we are not dead set for the Roads of Toulon, then we are not a hair's-breadth off it.'

'Then, Mr Collins, you need to be congratulated.'

The master took the compliment, even though he knew how much of a hand his captain had had in the plotting of the course. So did every officer aboard, but praise from Ralph Barclay was rare enough to be prized, even when it was not truly warranted.

'Mr Glaister, I take it the work of repair will be completed before we can see the shore from the deck.'

'I will make sure of it, sir.'

Ralph Barclay picked up a telescope and trained it on the distant shore, though it hardly made it any more clear. 'Good, for if it is Toulon they will have lookouts on the mountain, and communications with the port, and some expectation of the imminent arrival of a reconnaissance vessel.'

'You mean they might wish to chase us off, sir?'

'It is what I would do, Mr Glaister, it is what I would do.'

Replacing the telescope in the rack, Ralph Barclay walked to the weather rail and began to pace up and down that space between the poop and the waist which all vacated, it being the preserve of the captain when he was on deck. His orders obliged him to reconnoitre the main enemy naval base and report back to Admiral Hotham and the fleet the state of readiness of the French capital ships in the port. If the commanding enemy admiral had any sense he would have frigates at sea to intercept such a mission. That they had raised the land without such a sighting implied that he had not. What did it mean? Was the Toulon fleet in the kind of disarray rumoured to have ruined French naval strength, with experienced officers fled from their posts for fear of the guillotine? Or was it a ruse?

'Mr Glaister. Break out a tricolour flag and raise it to the masthead.'

'Sir.'

'And keep our own pennant ready to replace it in an

instant. I would also like to shorten sail so that the repairs will be completed and the men will have had their dinner by the time the shore is hull up.'

'Should we clear for action, sir?'

'After the officer's dinner, Mr Glaister. As you know, my wife goes to great trouble to help the cook prepare a memorable meal. It would not do to upset her.'

He looked at them all then, in a sweeping glance that had everyone avoiding his eye. There was not a man jack aboard, before and abaft the mast, who was not as jealous as hell of their uxorious captain and his lovely lady. To see her on deck, common enough in benign weather, was to induce feelings best left ashore, some mere nostalgia for hearth and home, others more carnal, that mixed with resentment that Barclay should be so favoured. He was so much his wife's senior and did not reckon himself handsome or very attractive a person – something with which most of his crew, had he asked them, would have concurred, but he had her companionship in all respects in a way denied to the others aboard, if you discounted the Gunner's wife, exasperating to men who had not been ashore for months. The satisfaction to be gained from the knowledge of their emotions was one of which he could never get enough, for Ralph Barclay reckoned that he had lived a life that owed him some recompense for miseries suffered, slights endured and ambitions thwarted. Now he was enjoying the feeling of justified redress, as he turned on his heel and left the quarterdeck, his parting words: 'Mr Glaister, once you are sure all is in hand, please join me in my cabin. I need to hear your opinion on who amongst the ship's corporals is to replace the Master-at-Arms. Mr Lutyens informs me he will be unable to fulfil his duties for some six weeks.

* * *

'Mr Lutyens.'

Lutyens looked up from the large journal in which he was writing. Habit made him half-close it so that what was written could not be seen, silly really, for of all the people aboard this young lady would be the last person to pry; she was too well-mannered.

'I came to see if our injured are comfortable.'

'They will certainly be made more so by your presence, Madame. I fear they see in me a rough and indifferent mendicant.'

Emily waved away such a suggestion, in truth to cover a degree of embarrassment, for gossip from her husband's officers, as well as the odd overheard remark from the men, had it that Lutyens was a touch insensitive in the article of pain, much given to applying herbal treatments which he supposed to be relieving, but failed to dull as much as the method which sailors knew and trusted, rum or laudanum. And she was slightly put out by the way he had so immediately shut his journal, as though whatever secrets he had could possibly interest her. For once, she decided to let him know her feelings, though she made a great effort to sound good-humoured.

'I should sand your latest scribblings, sir, for if your finger slips from holding open the page they will be rendered unreadable.'

The feathery eyebrows on his rather fish-like face were raised at what was, regardless of the delivery, nothing short of a direct admonishment, something new from the Captain's wife. That would be an interesting observation to add to what he had been writing, which was in the nature of the changes in the crew since the ship first weighed. The journal contained everything he had learnt since coming aboard, part of his study into the workings of a ship and the people who sailed it. Above his head, in a secure locker, were the notebooks which he had filled on a daily basis before transcribing his interpretations into this journal, which would, one day, be the basis of a treatise which would make his name in the circle of savants to which he aspired.

In future, those wishing to understand the strange nature of shipboard life and the people who lived it would read Heinrich Lutyens on the subject, and be informed on such diverse matters as reactions to impressment, arbitrary and accepted punishment, the relations between a certain type of officer and the men they led, the tensions that existed in the wardroom, where he ate daily, as well as in the living and sleeping quarters of the crew. Perhaps more interesting was the nature of warship captaincy, with the additional bonus that with his wife aboard, Captain Barclay had added the study of the conjugal relationship between people of very different backgrounds, ages and perceptions of the world in what was, to say the least, a peculiar setting.

'Mr Coyle, who has the compounded leg fracture, is beyond that screen. I am sure he will welcome a visit.'

'Is he in pain?'

'Of course, and that will be increased if he moves in any way. The other fellow, with the broken arm, I sent to help the cook as even one arm is enough to throw wood into an oven. As you know, the Captain does not like men to be idle.'

It was indeed a strange world to a landsman, and despite his office Lutyens considered himself to be that, not least in the variety of souls that were contained within the confines of these wooden walls. Every vice was present, and each person was an individual to be studied for their tics and emotions, but more importantly for the subtle changes that emerged as the time spent in the confines of the ship grew. As Emily Barclay went through the screen, he did as she had suggested, opened his journal and sanded the half-dry ink. Then, reflecting on the changes in her, he went back over the observations he had made from the very first time they had met.

Such words as 'shy', and 'tense' leapt out at him, and he knew that at the time of writing they had been accurate. Then had come the day when she had stood up to her husband over what she saw as chastisement of an innocent man. From that day on, his observations had told of a changed woman.

'Mam,' said Coyle, seeking to ease himself up from the cot on which he lay, that made more awkward by an attempt to touch his forelock. He was a stocky fellow, with enough scars on his face to hint at a life of hardship.

'Please do not bestir yourself, Mr Coyle. The surgeon was most adamant on that point. I have only come on behalf of my husband to see how you fare.'

Coyle kept his face bland then, as still as his bad leg, for the notion that Ralph Barclay cared two hoots for his welfare was sheer bollocks and he feared that might show. That his wife might was possible; he did not know her well enough to say though she appeared a kindly soul, but he knew his captain both by reputation and experience. If he was respected for being a hard horse, he was not loved, and he had shown on this voyage that he would flog any man who crossed him even if the offence fell outside the Articles of War.

'I must confess to knowing very little of you, Mr Coyle, which is shameful given the time we have spent at sea. Now I have a chance to make amends. Would it be too much of a strain for you to tell me something of yourself?'

Again Coyle had to keep a straight face, for once his leg had been set in splints, and he had rested from a night of deep discomfort, he had suffered a long interrogation by the surgeon; where was he from, did he have any family, what had brought him into the Navy, where did he expect that such service would take him, all jotted down in one of those little notebooks that Lutyens was never without. Suspicious that the surgeon had the means to withhold relief from pain, Coyle had said more than he normally would to anyone. It was not that he was a secretive man, but life had taught him that it was best to keep what was personal to himself.

'Not much to tell, Mam. I was a soldier afore I came to the Navy, which is why I has my rating.' Seeing the look of curiosity, he added, 'Master-at-Arms aboard ship is often an office filled by an ex-soldier, seeing as we know about weapons and their use, for there be precious few tars of my acquaintance who know bug— 'owt about them, which can be mortal should we get into a fight. Half of them I teach are more like to shoot their foot off than maim an enemy, and as for wielding a cutlass, why they're more danger to their own.'

Emily Barclay had come below to comfort Coyle, to ask if he had any family, would he like her to pen a letter for him, always assuming he lacked the ability to write himself. The idea that came into her head then was sudden and thrilling.

'Would you teach me to shoot, Mr Coyle?'

He stirred in surprise and pain flashed over his face. 'You, Mam?'

'Why not? I am told you will be laid up for some time, but you will be capable of some movement.'

'Shooting muskets ain't for ladies, Mam.'

'Why ever not, Mr Coyle? Am I not aboard a fighting vessel?'

'The very idea. Why, Captain Barclay would have my guts at the suggestion.'

'Mr Coyle,' Emily replied, with a look on her face that brooked no argument, 'you must leave the feelings of Captain Barclay to me.'

It was late afternoon before HMS *Brilliant* got close enough to make out the state of the French fleet, and what young Mr Farmiloe, his lookout, saw in the outer roadstead and reported to him, made Ralph Barclay content, for the news was promising. The last thing he wanted was to send back a depressing despatch. Even if he could not be blamed for telling the truth, he knew that the person who delivered bad news in King George's Navy was sometimes somehow tainted by association. There were two dozen ships of the line, but none with their yards crossed and ready for sea. In the dockyard other line-of-battle ships were being built or repaired, and Farmiloe was sure that another one, the biggest of them all, was floating in the water of the inner harbour and being fitted out. They came about twice to traverse the harbour entrance, well out of the range of any fortress guns, forty-two pounders capable of firing a ball some two miles. That they made no attempt to essay the range made the thought of closer observation tempting, but Ralph Barclay surmised they were keeping their powder dry for that very purpose, in the hope that he would stray into their deadly orbit.

'Vessel making sail in the outer roads, sir.'

'Can you make out what it is, Mr Farmiloe?'

'Frigate, sir, but I can not see the ports to assess the number of guns as they are hidden by the mole.'

'Come to chase us off, sir,' said Glaister.

'Too late for that, I think, Lieutenant. More likely their admiral has a notion that we will engage and he can take or sink us. That now is the only way to stop us telling the fleet what we have observed.'

'That tricolour must have fooled them, sir.'

'Yes. Let's get it down and show them who we are, then close with Captain Gould, while I go below to write my despatch. And keep me informed of the progress of that ship making sail.'

There was no cabin to enter, for everything had been taken down when they cleared for action. The bulkheads that had formed the walls were now either hinged up and fastened to the deckbeams or down below, as was the cabin furniture off which they had eaten their dinner. A chair had been left for his wife to sit on, as he apprehended no immediate danger, and a small desktop escritoire on which he could pen his despatch, though he had to kneel on the deck planking to do so. His letter was addressed to the man he had last seen in Lisbon harbour, Vice-Admiral Sir William Hotham.

HMS Brilliant; *at sea, off Toulon, July 28th 1793*
Sir,
In pursuance of the orders given to me aboard your flagship, I have the honour to furnish you with the following information about the state of the enemy fleet.

He went on to list what had been observed in terms of tonnage, guns and a guess at preparedness before concluding:

I felt it my duty to send off Captain Gould as soon practicable so that you will have information on which you can base a sound judgement. I acknowledge that it is incomplete, but I will endeavour in the following days to secure a more accurate picture of the state of affairs in the port, and a clear idea of the exact state of readiness of the enemy's ability to mount operations prior to the rendezvous I anticipate you will make, here, off Toulon, in the coming weeks.

I am, sir, you most humble servant.

Sanded and sealed, he put the despatch in an oilskin pouch, then turned to Emily, who had sat silently while he wrote. 'Now, my dear, you can quit you chair and come on deck, for I believe we will soon have something to show you.'

'A frigate, sir, a twenty-eight, just clearing the outer anchorage.'

'Thank you, Mr Glaister.'

Farmiloe positively screamed from the masthead. 'Deck there, sail bearing due east.'

'Of what nature?' called Glaister, as both he and his captain grabbed a telescope and trained them over the rail.

Ralph Barclay positively spat at his First Lieutenant, angry at himself for not anticipating what should have been obvious, but quite prepared, in the time-honoured fashion he had observed from his first days at sea, to pass on his ire.

'Are you a fool, sir? It will be a warship, Mr Glaister, the fastest the French have, set to trap us!'

Glaister took the rebuke with equanimity, too well versed in the ways of the Navy to protest, indeed composing his face into an attitude of open respect. 'You did wonder at it, sir, which is close to anticipation.'

'I did, Mr Glaister, you are right.' Mollified by the Highlander's tone, Ralph Barclay spoke in a more friendly way. 'Though I think, like me, you will observe he may have come too precipitately upon his task. He should have waited until we engaged or sought to play catch me with that fellow coming out.'

'They have the wind, sir.'

'So do we if we run, Mr Glaister.'

The emotion, in the look that crossed his premier's face, was replicated in the bodily attitude of every officer and midshipman on deck; they saw only the chance of a fight, with the possibility of glory. That it could be madness made no odds, for glory brought with it rewards that could not be gained in any other fashion. It also brought with it the possibility, or in this case the near-certainty, of death and destruction, but that was as nothing compared to promotion, public gratitude and wealth. Ralph Barclay, who scoffed at the kind of captains who indulged in quarterdeck explanations, was obliged to address the matter, though he took care to look at Emily as he did so, for though he cared not one jot that his inferiors might consider him shy, he cared a great deal that she did not.

'I am as minded to engage the enemy as the next man, but at odds of two to one in vessels, and I am sure, more in weight of shot, I would not take it at the best of times. This is not such an occasion. We have a duty to the fleet and Admiral Hotham to stay in one piece and to continue to be observant.'

He turned away from his wife then to give his orders.

'Mr Glaister, bring us about, and order Captain Gould to close so that he can take on board my despatch. Mr Collins, I want everything aloft that she will bear. Let's show these French dogs what a British ship can do, well handled, one that will be back off their anchorage a week hence, to assess their progress. And rest assured, gentlemen, if we catch one of the enemy alone, we will show him what the Royal Navy can do in a fight.'

Closing with HMS *Firefly* so that his despatch could be transferred, and the subsequent shortening of sail to effect it, slowed down that flight, but Ralph Barclay was not bothered by that. The fact that the French ships were closing brought them into view, hull up, through a long glass. But before he could do that he must give his junior his instructions.

'Mr Gould, we shall run due west until nightfall, when I want you to set your course for Gibraltar. You are to proceed with all haste, sparing neither wood nor canvas, and keep a look out for the fact that Admiral Hotham may have already cleared the Straits. What you carry is vital to the future success of our nation's arms.'

Having delivered what he thought a rousing little homily, he took up a telescope and began to study his putative enemies. Carefully he noted the distinguishing nature of each vessel, sail plan, figureheads, how she lay on the wind, as well as the manner in which they were handled and which was the swiftest, making many a mental note that would come into play should he meet any of them again. Finally, aware that the whole of his crew were merely waiting for the order, he gave the command to set all sail.

That occasioned another shaft of pleasure, for his men were now fully worked up, so that the task of setting the sails, once a noisy mayhem, was now smooth and carried out in relative quiet, with only spoken commands and the Bosun's various pipes being required to complete the whole in very short order, as they headed towards the setting sun, sitting in the diminishing wake of HMS *Firefly*.

CHAPTER THREE

If John Pearce's interview with Admiral Graves had gone badly, that was as nothing to the one he sought to have with Lord Howe. Having, at a rate of eight pence a mile, taken a post-chaise all the way to Bath, he found that the old admiral had surrounded himself, in the form of clerks and aides, with a carapace of protection that would have done justice to an Eastern potentate. Only official despatches from the Admiralty or those from his inferior admirals in Portsmouth were allowed to disturb his days of eating, drinking, taking the restorative waters in the old Roman baths and playing cards in the Pump Room. A plea that the liberty of the King's subjects was at stake got Pearce precisely nowhere; a demand that a promise made required fulfilment also fell on deaf ears, with the addition of a stinging rebuke for presumption thrown in from a member of his protective screen.

'When will the Admiral go back to Portsmouth?'

'When the French make it necessary he should do so. Now be gone.'

There were two other possibilities, people who might intercede on behalf of his Pelicans; the Admiralty itself and William Pitt, the King's First Minister, who had offered his help in the matter of a place should he need it, though he had no certainty what it would be worth as a promise, any more than that of Howe. He was even more doubtful about it being extended to an entirely different matter, such as the fate of illegally pressed seamen. Even with time being of the essence, that required a careful assessment of his funds – money 'borrowed' from his wealthy paramour – for he could not afford another post-chaise all the way to London. A compromise was called for: speed to Marlborough, then a slower mode of transport – a stage coach – from there to Charing Cross, this by a man who was cursing himself for not buying a horse.

Both in post-chaise and stage coach he was mostly uncommunicative with his fellow passengers, alone with his own thoughts, none of which were pleasant, declining to even discuss the latest news from Paris, which was that the firebrand revolutionary Marat had been murdered in his bath. As he listened to this being discussed, he did feel the temptation to intervene when opinions composed of arrant nonsense were being advanced, for he knew the man through his father. The dwarfish Marat had been one of the people who had originally welcomed Adam Pearce to Paris, lauding him as a true son of the Revolution who had fallen foul of his own government merely for his expressed and printed opinions. That welcome had not lasted; the leaders of the Revolution had no more time for an honest radical speaker than King George and his ministers. Marat was a prime example of the breed; the scrofulous troublemaker could not bear the notion of being behind the mob. Like so many of the Paris *enragés*, he wanted to be ahead of them, leading them on to further excess and murder. To John Pearce's mind he deserved to die in such an ignominious way, given that he had demanded, through the pages of his journal, *L'Ami du Peuple*, death of so many others.

The trouble was, that in thinking about Marat, he could not avoid ruminating on other things. Though he knew it to be pointless he could not help but go over what had happened in Paris, gnawing at the notion that by some act unspecified he could have changed the outcome and saved his father's life. To force himself away from those thoughts only brought Pearce back to why he was in this damned conveyance in the first place; his own utter unreliability, and that led in turn to gloomy reflections on his future prospects, which were not dazzling, given that his upbringing, while making him an independent soul, had ill-prepared him for anything like a career.

The one occupation that was definitely out of the question was that he should follow in his father's footsteps and become a radical speaker and pamphleteer, a scourge of the powerful and titled. What had been much sought after in the year '89, after the Fall of the Bastille, was not welcome now. After four years the mood of the nation was almost wholly set against change, having seen from across the Channel what happens when the props which a polity needed to exist were removed. Worse than that, he had no other real skill that he could think of to turn to; an ability to ride, to fence, a superficial knowledge of the Classics and fluent French, plus reasonably polished manners seemed to be either in abundant supply or not at present required outside the possibility of becoming a schoolmaster. That was an idea he abhorred, just like the army, which anyway he could not afford; a commission cost too much. None of it mattered anyway, not until he fulfilled the purpose of the journey he was now on.

Arrival in London, and the prospect of a warm and affectionate welcome, provided another disappointment, as a rather arch footman at the Fitzherbert London townhouse informed him that her Ladyship had left for the country, having sent the few possessions he owned to be stored at Nerot's Hotel in King Street to await his return. A letter that had arrived had been forwarded there as well, for which he owed the household payment of sixpence, since it had come express. Standing on the stoop, for he was not allowed into the house, Pearce was aware that the footman, obsequious a matter of days ago – though markedly less so now – could be lying. Annabel might well be at home or at least in London, but he was also acutely aware of the fact that he could do nothing about it. Had he been but a dalliance for a rich and titled lady who had taken a fancy to a young, handsome, and heroic sailor?

Directions supplied, it was a slow walk through the streets again, once more contemplating failure, ignoring hucksters, lottery ticket vendors and entertainers, plus the dozens of beggars, some children, many limbless, that either accosted or called to him for succour, this while the sedan chairs of those who were wealthy enough to pay jogged by at speed, weaving through the tradesmen's carts and the coaches of the truly wealthy, which set up a cacophony of noise, as iron-rimmed wheels rattled over the uneven cobblestones. Recalling Peg Bamber's words about London being 'a hateful place', at this moment he had an inclination to agree.

Chokingly full of smoke in winter, when some of these beggars would freeze to death, it could be like a cauldron in summer, when the smell of rotting rubbish, human waste and decomposing flesh, both human and animal, attacked the senses. But all cities were the same; if anything, Paris was worse, with a nosegay an obligatory object when the temperature rose, even indoors. That peripatetic life, when growing up, had given Pearce a love of fresh air and open spaces, even of clean sea-breezes. Indeed, there had been moments aboard ship, when the weather was clement and the work satisfying, that he had enjoyed the experience, moments when he could forget how it was he had got there.

To enter ' ice's hotel was to put that behind him. Double

doors snuffed out the noise, while the smell of scented candles and the beeswax polish of floor and furniture took away the exterior stench. There were well-upholstered settles in the lobby, and deep armchairs, even a fire in the grate for those who had no notion that that it was a warm day outside. It was not all pleasant, the hotel clerk who received guests was even more condescending than the footman who had opened the door to him at Lady Annabel's. He wrinkled his nose and pointedly cast an eye at Pearce's boots, which had upon them the filth, in the form of mud, manure and the odd bit of straw, that came from walking through the streets of the capital. Name given, a letter was produced, which had on it the easily recognised seal of the Admiralty.

'Will "sir" be requiring a room?'

If I do, thought Pearce, aware of how the travel to Bath and back to London had nearly cleaned him out, it will be in a debtor's prison, but such a depressing thought was quickly followed by the next; that he needed to do something to get help and the only two sources he could think of who could provide that were close by. Letters from Nerot's would imply a standing he, in truth, did not possess, which could only aid his cause. As for the cost, John Pearce was subject to more than one devil that he had inherited from his father, for Adam Pearce had never let a lack of funds interfere with the need to lay his own head, and that of his son, on a decent pillow, sure that the next day, a good and rousing speech, and the hat passed round, would provide the money to meet the bill.

'I shall.'

The clerk, with a haughty expression, looked at the small valise with which this 'guest' had arrived, and sniffed again, though this time disdainfully, an expression repeated when Pearce informed him that he had some luggage already stored here, for unbeknown to him the clerk recalled the arrival of an extremely old and battered trunk, which the storekeeper had made a point of telling him was almost empty. This was clearly no well-heeled prospect, a point of which Pearce was well aware. Normally modest, he knew he had to say something to avoid being politely shown the door.

'You will have no doubt heard, sir, of the recent taking of the French ship of the line, the *Valmy*?'

'Who has not, sir, a most inspiring event,' opined the clerk, with a tone that almost implied his own involvement. 'The nation has once again shown the glorious abilities of our Wooden Walls.' Try as he might, having finished speaking, he could not hide a degree of curiosity. 'And a very valuable prize, I daresay. Am I to understand that you were part of that action, sir?'

His own chest puffed out, and speaking in a tone he would have despised in another, Pearce replied. 'Part of it, sir! I can tell you that without me no success would have been possible. Indeed King George himself, when I was called up to attend his levee at Windsor, made that very connection.'

The words 'King' and 'levee' were accompanied by a clicking of fingers, as the now-smiling clerk summoned a porter in a striped waistcoat and leather apron. A heavy key was produced and an instruction whispered, whereupon the porter lifted the small valise, with a care that suggested it contained the whole prize fund for the French warship, and headed for the thickly carpeted stairs. The clerk indicated that Pearce should follow, with the words: 'I hope you enjoy your stay with us, sir. It is most uplifting to have a hero under our rafters, and one who will garner a fine reward for his sterling efforts.'

Wondering if the word sterling was a pun on money, Pearce made for the staircase. The porter had waited for him, the paucity of the luggage and the notion that he was dealing with a well-heeled champion of the nation's arms had no doubt inspired his excessive garrulousness; he seemed eager to inform Pearce that the room he had been allotted was one normally reserved for folk of real quality.

'Fit for an admiral, your honour, and why not, if'n it be fit for a duke or an earl. Why, I have had folk in there, sir, who have needed a dozen local beds just for accommodation of their servants.'

Pearce was shown into a comfortable sitting room with tall windows, armchairs and settles, and a bedroom attached, while the porter made a great play of carefully placing his valise by the washstand, talking all the while in an ingratiating manner. Well versed in the art of extracting a tip from his guests he then stood and waited for this new one to oblige. He was even practiced enough to hold the smile on his face when he felt the paucity of what had been placed in his hand, bowing slightly as he informed John Pearce that he would fetch his luggage from the basement store room, 'in a trice'.

'I shall be back in a jiff, your honour, and I daresay you would like to remove them boots and have them cleaned, as well as welcome some jugs of piping water fetched for a bath?'

Grubby from travel, that was a very welcome idea. 'Thank you.'

'And wine, sir, will you be partaking of some wine? The hotel does a fine ordinary claret, of which I am happy to say we have a good supply. Not that it will be long before that is back on tap, those madmen have taken to murdering each other now, though I will add that you'll be safer in your bath than that sod Mirat.'

Too embarrassed to refuse, and too disinterested to correct his mis-naming of Marat, Pearce just nodded. 'I need writing materials.'

'In the bureau, sir. Paper, quills and a knife to sharpen

them, as well as fine sand. I shall fetch a candle, sir, for the wax.'

The porter departed, the face outside the door less pleasant as he contemplated the two pieces of copper in his hand, for he was a man accustomed to silver at the very least, and in the case of proper folk with a rate of servants, the odd half guinea. In the basement he moaned to the storekeeper that, 'This new fellow is no gent, but Ezekiel Didcot knows how to get his due. And I shall, be it in dribs and drabs of copper, I'll get my due.'

Didcot had left John Pearce wondering how he was going to pay for this, or rather how he could avoid payment, for he knew he lacked the means for such accommodation. Matters were not improved by his missive from the Admiralty, his lieutenant's commission, along with a bill for eleven shillings and eight pence due to the clerk who had drawn it up, to be paid at his earliest convenience. The enclosure also informed him that he needed to attend the building to swear allegiance to the King, his heirs and successors, as well as the need to confirm that he was not of the proscribed Catholic faith, this insured by his acceptance of the Thirty-Nine Articles of the Protestant religion.

By the time he had contemplated those, and decided they could be safely ignored, Didcot was back with claret and biscuits, followed by a row of servants with a bath and jugs of hot water, that soon transferred, and another bearing a battered old trunk. They departed, but Didcot did not, talking incessantly, which occasioned another raid on the guest's rapidly diminishing funds to see the porter out the door, backing out with the words: 'A warming pan for the bed, your honour?'

'No!' Pearce snapped, closing the door.

A muffled demand came through the panelling. 'An' dinner, sir?'

'I'll be eating out.'

There was a short letter from Annabel Fitzgerald in the trunk, which managed to be affectionate and distant in the same set of sentences, alluding to the pleasure they had taken in each others' company while making it plain, without saying as much, that it was now in the past. There was no invitation to call, merely a reference to the fact that, given his fame, and the way he was certain to be lionised, they would be bound to meet at the places frequented by those who moved in the best social circles.

'My dear lady,' he said quietly to himself. 'I suspect society is just as fickle as you. They will have forgotten the *Valmy* in a week or two.'

Pearce stripped off and lowered himself gratefully into the bath, but he did not linger, for to do so only produced ruminations on his predicament, none of which was comfortable. As soon as he was clean he was out and dried and into the clean clothing he found in the trunk. Then, taking the fine headed notepaper from the desk drawer and sharpening a quill, he dipped his pen and began to write. The hotel had provided wax and its own seal, which he used to secure the letters. He had to wait awhile, until his boots were returned, which obliged him to ignore the knocking on the door and wait till Didcot left them. As soon as the porter was gone he had them on, and went down the stairs and out through the lobby like a man with much on his mind.

Pearce arranged the delivery of his letters by a post boy for a penny, the addresses of the Admiralty and Downing Street being almost next door to each other, both also destinations that would not pay for the carriage. Taking a seat in the tavern from which he had engaged the boy, he ate a filling pie washed down with a very pleasant tankard of porter for a tenth of the price he would have paid at Nerot's, ruminating as he did so on what his missives would achieve. He had no faith that the letter to the secretary at the Admiralty would produce anything, and pinned what little hope he had on that he had sent to William Pitt, requesting an interview.

An hour later he turned up at the front door of His Majesty's First Lord of the Treasury, and was shown into an anteroom to wait, offered a glass of wine which he declined, something he came to regret as one hour stretched to two, then three and more, so that it was nearing ten-of-the-clock before he was ushered into Pitt's presence. Slim, pale, and still looking absurdly young for his office, William Pitt sat at a large table which seemed to fill most of a spacious room. With him was a solid, well-fed looking and florid fellow, and on the table the papers they had been going through, as well as several empty claret bottles, which they appeared to have consumed while doing so.

'Lieutenant Pearce, if I'm not mistaken.'

He's drunk, thought Pearce, looking at the bottles and catching the slur in the voice.

'Allow me to name to you a fellow countryman of yours, Henry Dundas.'

'Laddie,' Dundas said, using a diminutive, and in a deep, Scottish-accented voice, that was very reminiscent of his father. 'I knew old Adam well, sir, having crossed swords with him, verbally of course, many times. I commiserate with you in your loss and damn, as I am sure you do, the villains who did such a thing.'

Dundas too had had a drink, it was in the high colour of his cheeks, but he seemed less affected by it than Pitt. 'We shall have to be about our business, Will, we are due in the hoose at this very moment.'

'Then we will need a couple to help us through, Harry, so pull the bell for more. Will you join us in a glass, young Pearce?'

'No thank you, sir. If time is pressing, so is my business.'

'Which is?'

'I believe when we last met I alluded to the fact that I was illegally pressed into the Navy.'

'Did you? I do not recall.'

'Along with several other unfortunates. Indeed, I hope one day to the see the captain involved, one Ralph Barclay, in court for the offence.'

Dundas cut in, speaking from the side of the great fireplace, in the act of tugging on the bell pull. 'I would'na pin too much faith in a satisfactory outcome of something like that, laddie. We are at war, or did ye no ken?'

'Careful, Harry,' Pitt cut in, with a lopsided smile, 'your "laddie" is a proven fighter.'

Pearce replied to Dundas. 'And we, sir, I believe, have laws that war does not suspend.'

'One or two of which, I ken, you and your late father were wont to break, to the point of both prison and flight. Sedition, was it not, scurrilous writings saying that what happened to King Louis should have been repeated in the case of our Geordie?'

The smile that accompanied those words had an undertone of menace, as Pearce recalled his father's opinion of Henry Dundas, which was not a high or flattering one. Called the 'Uncrowned King of Scotland', he was the leader of a large group of Scottish MPs, a staunch supporter of Pitt and his government, and so skilled in jobbery and corruption that his name was wont to induce apoplexy in those who opposed him, which included a goodly number of fellow-Tories. Pearce also knew the pamphlet to which Dundas was referring had called for the peaceful removal of the King, an abolition of the monarchy, having been written long before King Louis' execution. Adam Pearce would never have proposed decapitation for any human being, even a tyrant, but there was no point in saying so, for if time was pressing, there was no time to debate the rights and wrongs of Republicanism.

'Be that as it may, Mr Dundas, I have several companions still illegally forced to serve in the Navy. Admiral Lord Howe promised to release them and has not done so. I tried to get him to act in Bath, but I failed to even get to see him.'

'An indolent fellow,' said Pitt, reaching for a half-full bottle and filling his glass. 'Only the insistence of the King secured his appointment. But then, the King did the same for you when he demanded your promotion, did he not? So we must not complain.'

A servant entered and placed two bottles on the table, this while Pitt emptied into his mouth what he had just poured. The corks had been removed then replaced so that they were proud of the neck.

'I need your assistance to get them released, Mr Pitt.'

'That's coming it a wee bit high is it not, laddie, importuning the King's Furst Minister for such a paltry purpose?'

'It may be paltry to you, Mr Dundas, but to me it is important.'

The shrug that he received in response was eloquent enough; what was important to Pearce was not important to men such as these. 'We must go, Will, or Fox will start debating the West Indian situation without us. Much hangs on it.'

Pearce spoke to Pitt in desperation, for he suspected that if he failed in this interview he would struggle to get another. What he said was impulsive, but it was the only thing he could think of. 'Sir, at the King's levee you promised me if you could ever be of service to me, I was to call upon you. I do so now.'

It was Dundas who replied, leaving Pearce to wonder who held the power in the room. 'It is beyond our office to interfere in the business of the Navy, laddie. Lord Chatham and the sea officers of the Board of Admiralty would, quite rightly, tell us to poke our noses elsewhere, and the serving sailors would be a damn sight less polite.'

'Then give me the means to free them myself.'

'How can I do that?' slurred Pitt.

'I have a lieutenant's commission. Get me a place on a vessel going to the Mediterranean, for that is where these companions of mine are headed.'

'Will!'

'Quite,' the First Lord of the Treasury replied, nodding to Dundas and hauling himself slowly to his feet to stand, swaying ever so slightly. 'If I made such a promise, then I shall redeem it, for I would not have it said that I am not a man of my word. Leave a letter with one of my secretaries, tell me what you need and where you are to be found, and I will see what I can do.'

'A letter from you demanding their release would carry much weight.'

The tone of Pitt's voice had a harder edge than hitherto. 'I seem to recall I am obliged to you for one favour, Mr Pearce, not two.'

'Be so good as to be off, Pearce,' insisted Dundas, 'for if we dinna attend the hoose those damned Whigs might try to force a vote.'

Pearce bit his tongue then, holding back the desire to know how two men as inebriated as these could possibly engage in debate. Had he seen them enter the chamber later, each with a bottle in hand and their arms around each other for mutual support, he would have wondered even more. But then, a look at both the government and the opposition benches, and the sound of the raucous and uncontrolled cheers and jeers which greeted their arrival, would have established that the two men, as far as being drunk was concerned, were in good company.

CHAPTER FOUR

His first call, the following morning, was to the Admiralty, where he faced, for the first time in his life, the creatures who guarded access to the building, the uniformed doormen. Unbeknown to this visitor they were notorious throughout the Navy, well-remunerated fellows who could barely be brought to civility by the arrival of an admiral, were generally indifferent to Post Captains – hardly surprising given they were better paid – so that their attitude to lieutenants was nothing short of rude.

'Can't do any oath swearing today, they be holding their levee,' insisted one, a gnarled-faced gnome who smelt strongly of stale beer and tobacco. 'Come back tomorrow.'

'I was not aware they held such a thing.'

'I daresay there be a rate of things you don't know, young fellow, which ain't much use when you'se at sea. Happens one day every week, and if'n you ain't got a written invite, you can't pass through this door.'

There were two things of which John Pearce, looking at this pair, was sure: that no amount of pleading would help, and that he lacked the only other thing – money – which might get him inside. So he mentioned that which he had posted yesterday.

'You sent in a letter, you say?'

'I did,' Pearce replied, 'to the First Secretary.'

'Why, I suspect he is a'reading it now, young sir, and

wondering what he did to deserve your condescension.'

The other doorman wheezed out a laugh, proving to Pearce the thought which had already occurred: that he was being toyed with. 'All I want to know is if it has been received and read.'

'Have you any notion of waiting for a reply?'

'I do not have time to wait.'

Nor, thought Pearce, do I want to part with a sixpence to read it.

'Hear that, Alfred? Our young pup has no time to wait. I reckon the Frenchies would be quaking in their boots to know this lad's a'coming to do battle wi' them.'

The other fellow was looking over his shoulder at the busy Whitehall traffic. 'Well, he best be off to his fight, for we've got no time to indulge him. I suggest that you move along, for I see Captain Orde approaching, who is on the list of invites, an' we has no mind to keep him waiting for the likes of you.'

It was only curiosity that kept Pearce there until this officer was greeted and passed inside, that and a feeling of certainty that he would witness what he did, the passing of coin from this Captain Orde to the two now utterly obsequious, forelock-tugging doormen, which only served to underline his need for money. His next call was to see about getting some.

'Mr Davidson will see you now, Lieutenant.'

Pearce rose from the chair which he had occupied this last half hour and followed the fellow who had summoned him into a large office, leaving behind him an impressive bustle of activity, of the kind that convinced him that he was about to deal with a serious man of business, for he had been listed in the newspapers as the agent handling the prize fund due from the capture of the *Valmy*. The first thing that struck him about Davidson's appearance was his apparent youthfulness; such an enterprise as the one he had observed surely should have someone of more age and gravity at its head. Yet the smile was disarming, the welcome genuine on a young, attractive face, but the news the prize agent had to impart, once he had identified himself and where he came from, was far from encouraging, all hinging on the fact that the French 74 had been taken through the efforts of two vessels, with two commanders.

'I represent Captain Marchand of HMS *Centurion*, while your superior officer, Mr Colbourne, is represented by the company of Ommaney & Druce. It is they who have questioned the distribution, which has a share allotted to Mr Colbourne as being that of a lieutenant, instead of as a captain.'

Pearce knew all about that dispute, and the way he had referred to Marchand by his post rank, while calling Colbourne a mere Mister was revealing; Davidson was far from being a non-partisan representative.

'He was captain of the *Griffin*,' Pearce insisted.

'Master and Commander at a stretch, though an armed cutter does not carry the rank, Mr Pearce, but not made post and on the captain's list. You must understand, to acknowledge that Lieutenant Colbourne, as he was at the time of the capture, shares in a captain's rank and entitlements would cost Captain Marchand several thousand pounds. At present, since Captain Marchand was under Admiralty orders he has three-eights of the total, with no commanding admiral to satisfy. Were he to accede to Mr Colbourne's demands, half of that would be forfeit, and the complications of dealing with the senior officer who wrote out orders for HMS *Griffin* would just add another layer of difficulty.'

Pearce knew that whatever the arguments, they had no

effect on him except delay. His share would be fixed whatever the outcome of the dispute. 'How long before it is decided?'

'A piece of rope is a fair guide,' Davidson replied, with an almost embarrassed shrug. 'Lawyers do not rush in these matters. I have known such cases take years to resolve.'

'I need money now.'

Seeing the enquiring look, he decided not to mention Nerot's Hotel, which had provided him with a good night's sleep, and that morning with a sturdy breakfast. But he had no trouble thinking of a reason that would make sense to the man on the other side of the desk, even if it was a stretching of the truth.

'I have expectations of a place and I need to buy the necessities an officer requires for sea service. Everything I owned went down with the ship.'

'You were a midshipman, my clerk informed me.' Davidson smiled as Pearce nodded, with a clear air of sympathy. 'I fear a mid's cut will scarce suffice to provide for the whole of your needs, sir.'

'It will go some way to offsetting the costs,' Pearce replied, without certainty, for he had no real idea of what he needed to go to sea, only that he might require money to pay for his commission and, more pressingly, his hotel.

'I have advanced money to those members of the *Centurion*'s crew who have requested it, but I am obliged to do so at a discount which reflects the burden I have to carry in advancing sums for which I have no sure date for redemption.'

'Offset, no doubt, by the interest you will earn.'

Davidson was quite sharp then. 'You will have seen, while waiting, that I carry substantial overheads which must be met somehow.'

'How much would I be due in those circumstances?'

Davidson reached behind him for a large and weighty

ledger, thumped it onto the table, and smiled at Pearce before opening it. Running his finger down a column of figures his brow furrowed. He went to another and did the same until he eventually stopped.

'Pearce, you say?'

'Yes.'

'I'm afraid I have you listed as a landsman, Mr Pearce, scarcely credible given the uniform you are wearing.'

The reply carried all the tension Pearce felt. 'Captain Colbourne rated me a midshipman.'

'Not apparently in the last muster book he sent in, from which I take my figures. Do you have anything in writing to that effect?'

'No.'

'And it is to be assumed that the last books went down with the ship?' As Pearce nodded, he tapped the ledger. 'Then, unless you can produce some proof I cannot do other than take from this. Mr Colbourne can, of course, change it, with the consent of the other party.' Seeing the look of Pearce's face he added, 'I can write to him asking for clarification.'

Pearce was thinking hard, sure that the last submission of *Griffin*'s muster book had been after his elevation, because Colbourne had been adamant he would not get any pay for a rank that officially carried none. In fact, it only mattered in the issue of prize money. Their relationship had been far from good, in truth at times it had been downright hostile. Had the man merely not bothered, or had he humbugged him, as he had done more than once before?

'Would it be possible to draw what am I owed and still seek the rest once my rank has been established?'

Davidson nodded again. 'It is not a sum to excite, I must say, but we are dealing with the crews of two vessels, and I must say your *Griffin* was heavily manned for her size.'

'A figure, if you please, sir?'

Davidson shuffled some papers in a drawer, finally producing a sheaf to be studied.

'The whole prize is valued at just over twenty-three thousand pounds, and a landsman's share comes in at just above twenty guineas. I could advance you the sum of sixteen pounds with safety.'

'Can I ask what Captain Marchand will receive?'

Davidson had the good grace to look slightly uncomfortable. He was a man unaccustomed to having in his office those on the lowest rung of the prize fund ladder, the common seamen, and was therefore unused to trying to explain a system so manifestly unfair.

'It is a sum you can calculate for yourself, Lieutenant. Should his case be found to be correct, and given he was sailing under Admiralty orders with no commanding officer to share his good fortune, he will receive over eight thousand pounds, less of course, his legal fees and my commissions. If Mr Colbourne is successful in his suit that will be halved.'

'I have heard sailors curse the system of distribution of prize money. Now I know them to be right in their condemnation.'

'There are many sailors, sir, but only one captain.'

'Have any of the *Griffins* applied for advance payment?'

Davidson looked down at the ledger to check. 'Not a one, and nor has Mr Colbourne applied on their behalf.'

Hardly surprising, Pearce thought. *The poor sods are trapped on another ship, and I doubt Colbourne cares two hoots about them.*

'What you offer is not enough to meet my needs.'

'Then, sir,' Davidson replied gravely, 'you must act as do other naval officers and pledge your pay as credit. Those who supply the Navy are accustomed to accept such sureties in lieu of settlement.' Davidson actually laughed then, not very much, but enough. 'Damn me, sir, without that sort of credit we would scarce have a man able to serve. Even admirals are accustomed to pawning their plate or borrowing in order to take up their duties.'

The money was paid out by a clerk, and it was a ruminative John Pearce, mentally composing a stiff letter to his previous commander on the subject of his rank, who walked back to the hotel, there to find a letter waiting for him bearing an impressive Royal Treasury seal and franked as government post. It was clear, as it was handed over, that he was not the only one to be astounded; the hotel clerk who gave it to him had learnt how to grovel somewhat to a man who clearly had the ear of those in power. He waited till he was alone in his room to read it.

Lieutenant Pearce,

I am, on reflection, conscious of the commitment I made to you at Windsor and with that in mind I have made representations to my brother regarding your needs, unfortunately to no avail. You will understand that, at present, as the First Lord of the Admiralty, Lord Chatham is inundated with requests for employment from extremely deserving officers with exemplary service records, submissions he is often obliged to decline for lack of an available place. To ask him to elevate your claim above theirs would be grossly unfair.

Having read the letter you left with my secretary I am unsure of your purpose. Is your primary concern the release of those companions you claim were, like you, illegally pressed into the Navy and now on route to serve in the Mediterranean? Or is it that you seek employment for yourself?

Recalling what he had penned the night before, Pearce was sure that he had made plain what he sought, both verbally and in writing. He had, as a backstop, asked for a place if that would provide the only avenue open to him to help his friends.

While I cannot comment on the merits of your case, I can

see that the proper place to make representations on their behalf would be to Lord Hood, the Commander-in-Chief on that station, who, as the senior naval member serving on the Board of Admiralty, might also be in a position to adjudicate on your assertions of improper behaviour on the part of an officer presently serving under his command. It would also be the case, that should you seek an opening, Lord Hood, as a serving C-in-C on active service, would be in a better position to offer you employment than even my own brother.

With that in mind, and in the hope that it will satisfy you, I have arranged for you to take passage on the packet carrying official despatches for Lord Hood, which sails, weather permitting, from Portsmouth every seven days. There is also private correspondence of a confidential nature, which you must undertake to carry, along with a recommendation from me regarding the granting to you of a place suitable to your abilities, which I can say with some confidence should have the desired effect. If Lord Hood can oblige me, given that he is a stout supporter of my government, owing as he does his position as a serving member on the Board of Admiralty to me, he will undoubtedly do so.

If you agree, please send the enclosed, pre-franked note by return, the information in which I will pass on to the First Secretary at the Admiralty, who can then have drawn up the requisite official instructions. Should you accept the offer contained herein, I consider, as I am sure you do, that my obligation to you is satisfied in all respects.

William Pitt had signed it with a flourish, affixing his official seal and a ribbon inside as well. The blank letter mentioned was indeed enclosed, that too government franked, and thus free to both sender and recipient.

Re-reading the letter, John Pearce was more conscious of the problems such an offer could create rather than the opportunities. To take passage on that packet was to take a journey into the unknown; he had no real idea how close what was proposed would take him to those he was committed to get free, nor how the man in charge would respond. Hood could tell him to go to the devil in very much the same way as had Admiral Graves. What would he do then? And what about the request that he be found employment, a course fraught with peril? He might be a lieutenant – or would be once he had sworn the requisite oaths and paid his fee – but he had little knowledge of how to undertake the duties that went with the rank. The notion that he might be reluctantly forced to follow that course brought home to him another fact; as he had pointed out to Davidson, he lacked the means to equip himself with the clothing and equipment necessary to even look the part, and look the part he must if he was to have the slightest chance of achieving his aim.

The faces of his friends came into his mind, as well as the promise he had made them. Pitt had met his obligation, surely he, John Pearce, could do no less and if he was required to pretend to be that which he was not, so be it. He must prepare for every eventuality, but how was he to fund such a thing? The face that replaced those of Michael, Charlie and Rufus was that of the clerk who had handed him Pitt's letter. The man now thought him superbly well connected, and probably copper-bottomed as far as capital was concerned, with a huge tranche of prize money coming his way. He knew he must play to that, so moving to the door, he rang the levered bell that would summon Didcot, and when the man came, taking care to tip him with a shilling, Pearce had him send out to a series of naval outfitters, requesting that they attend upon him at the hotel, where he would kit himself out for his journey.

Within twenty-four hours he had ordered his two dozen linen shirts, a working hat and coat to go with the dress one he already owned, and he had chosen a brass edged sea-chest to contain it all with the initials Lt. J. P. to be burnt into it by the local blacksmith, then gilded by a limner. There were three pairs of shoes, one dress with silver-plated buckles, boots for going ashore and an everyday pair of pumps that would not damage the deck planking, breeches and a raft of silk stockings, small clothes, handkerchiefs, a boatcloak, a comforter for his neck, oilskins and a foul weather hat, a medicine box, and a vanity one with combs, a mirror and, last but not least, a proper dress sword, all fitted under the personal supervision of one of the senior outfitting partners, who had no doubt taken care to check with the hotel that this customer could be relied upon to meet his obligations.

'Your goods to be delivered here, sir?'

'No, no. Send them and the chest straight down to Portsmouth, with instructions that they are to be taken to the Pig & Whistle Tavern owned by a Mrs Peg Bamber, near Portsmouth Point.'

The quizzical expression on the man's face spoke volumes, and Pearce had to steel himself to sound languid as he sought to justify such a destination, which was, quite decidedly, not one of the port's best. The Point at Portsmouth, crowded with drinking dens and hard by the beach on which were drawn up the local boats, was notorious throughout the land for drunken behaviour and licentiousness, but he did not know the name of another establishment and he could hardly ask.

'I am hoist upon a promise I made some time ago, sir, to a warm-hearted naval widow, never to reside anywhere else should I be in Portsmouth. If you knew the lady, you would also know why it would be an unwise undertaking to break.'

'I daresay the drovers will know where it is. And the account, sir?'

Pearce could not look the fellow in the eye as he replied.

'Just send that here. I shall not be leaving London for several weeks.'

Having seen the chest taken away, he made a point of visiting the blacksmith who had burnt-in his lettering, even going to the trouble of delivering it back to the outfitters, and paid him in cash for his work and that of the limner who had gilded it, for he could not, in all conscience, fail to meet his obligations to the two working men. Back at Nerot's he sat down and wrote two notes, one to Didcot, who could probably read, the other to be handed into the front desk, which simply told them he was vacating the room and that the bill, along with any others due, as well as Lady Annabel's old, battered chest, should be sent to him *via* the Admiralty. These he left propped on the bureau.

The last thing he did was retrieve from that old chest a small tin, which thanks to a tight seal had not suffered from water penetration when he had been forced to swim from the fight with the *Valmy*. Pearce opened it, smelling once more the earth it contained, taken from a Paris churchyard in which he had watched his father interred. One day he would go back to that place, and see if the request he had made that a headstone be provided had been met. Perhaps, in a time of peace he could have his father's remains disinterred and taken back to Edinburgh for burial in his native city, and maybe even he would tell the truth about his death; that, a sick man who suspected he was dying, he had put himself in place of another marked for execution.

Until then, this earth would remind him of that which had caused his father's death, whatever name he chose to expire under. The curse of a French Revolution that had gone from high hopes to chaos would remind him of his aim to see those who had taken it in that direction brought down. There was nothing else he wanted from that chest. The outer garments were those in which he had come ashore after the battle, cleaned of course, but still shabby. Second-hand and ill-fitting when purchased, they also bore the faded marks of that engagement, including the blood of friends and foes, and immersion in the sea water.

Ordering a sedan chair to take him to Whitehall and leaving behind him most of the things with which he had arrived, he departed the hotel, sword at his waist, heading for the Admiralty and the swearing of a series of oaths of which, like his father before him, he was deeply sceptical. With no time to waste, he tipped the doormen two shillings, which he soon learnt from the growling acceptance was not much more than the bare minimum they expected, just enough to get him into the building. That was followed by a long wait in a warm and crowded anteroom till the necessary official could be found to administer the pledges of loyalty to crown and religion. That completed and the requisite fees paid, he was given his orders, which were to proceed with all despatch to join the packet preparing to sail from Portsmouth.

His next port of call was again at Downing Street. Directed to the office of the Pitt's secretary, he was given a thick oilskin pouch with instructions, gravely imparted, that it was to be delivered into the hands of Lord Hood, and him alone. He was then, to his surprise, directed into a government carriage for the journey.

CHAPTER FIVE

'Well, O'Hagan, I had you beat there for a moment, indeed I had written off my wagered guineas, but the way you rallied in the last three minutes was magnificent.'

'Mr Taberly.'

Michael replied to the officer, though not with any clarity, for his lips were swollen and his jaw aching from the numerous punches it had been forced to absorb, and even nodding his head occasioned a degree of pain. He winced as Charlie Taverner pressed an alcohol-soaked piece of tow onto his cheek, a cloth which came away carrying traces of red. Rufus Dommet stood by with a bucket of sea water, said by many to be efficacious in the treatment of flesh wounds, though the squeamish youngster showed a marked reluctance to wash the streaks of blood off his friend back, arms and chest.

The opponent in the fight, a barrel of a fellow called Clipe, had been a very tough customer indeed, a really long-serving naval hard-bargain, immune to the kind of fighting wiles that were Michael's trademark way of winning a scrap. Clipe was the kind of man who ignored such subterfuge, who stood up rock solid to the heaviest blow, so it had therefore come down to a contest of sheer determination not to give in, a toe-to-toe slugging match. Taberly, the lieutenant in charge of his division, had been the only officer aboard HMS *Leander* to back him – all the others, commissioned and warrant on the 74-gun ship, had gone for the other man, who had a reputation which made him well worth a wager, thus the odds the lieutenant had managed to extract were showing him a handsome return. With crew it was mostly not money, but grog and tobacco that were used to bet; few of the original crew had any coin after weeks spent at anchor in Spithead, and the Griffins had been fetched aboard without being paid.

'I will see you are rewarded once I have collected my winnings, O'Hagan. There's a couple of gold coins coming your way, and I have the power to excuse you from duties for a few days to recover. See the surgeon, if he's sober and you feel the need, and if the sot seeks to charge you for palliatives and the like, I will pay.'

Taberly probably thought that Michael dropped his head in gratitude, but in fact he had done it so that the officer would not see the anger in his eyes, the desire to do to him what he had done to Clipe, whose partisans were around him trying to revive the poor sod. Charlie, who knew only too well what the Irishman was thinking, for he talked enough about it beforehand, dabbed harder with his piece of spirit-soaked tow than he should, which got him a curse in the Erse tongue. But he had done it for the best, for they had seen the grating rigged from the first day of coming aboard this ship, and Charlie knew that half the floggings witnessed had come from acts of common seamen talking without due respect to their officers.

The fight need never have happened; sure he and Clipe had eyed each other on first acquaintance, as those of a certain ability with their fists always do, but the man was no more of a fool than his Irish counterpart. Michael was big and broad of shoulder and had the air of confidence that went with skill. Clipe could see an opponent that would hurt him, even if he was the victor in a contest, and with the wisdom of someone with nothing to prove he had been warily friendly. But those denizens of the wardroom, led by the Premier, who seemed to take pleasure in seeing a man flogged, had grown disputatious regarding the abilities of certain crew members. One of the marine lieutenants knew Clipe from a previous commission, and the man had reputation enough to suggest that none could stand against him. It had been Taberly who had demurred, and suggested that there might be another aboard in his very own division who could more than hold his own.

After only fourteen days at sea, and not so much as a sniff of a sail, friend or foe, many of the occupants of the wardroom professed themselves bored, fed up with cards, word games and the tunes played on the marine officer's flute. A boxing bout, in the absence of dogs, bears or spurred cocks to set against each other, was just what the doctor ordered. Notwithstanding the fact that they were breaking half the rules laid down in the Articles of War, for both fighting and gaming were forbidden, they wanted a chance to engage in a spot of the latter too, as Taberly had explained to his chosen champion, experience a bit of stimulation.

Reluctance on behalf of the principal meant little; the Premier ran the ship, for Captain Tucker was an indolent, if compliant, commander who might stir for an enemy warship or an admiral's flag but not for much less. He kept to his cabin, his books, and his collection of rare butterflies and appeared on deck for no more than a quarter of an hour, twice a day. So when the First Lieutenant let it be known that a fight was required, the whole ship was pressed into the goading of the pair, for the crew, landsmen to top rating, were as fond of a bout and a bet as their superiors. So the following Sunday was chosen, and luckily the sea state was, for the waters off Cape Ortegal at the northern tip of Spain, relatively benign. With the boats over the side and towed astern, and replacement spars shifted, a space in the waist was chalked off for the contest, and it being a make and mend day, when after Divine Service and dinner the crew had few duties, most of them were free to line the gangways as spectators.

It was, in every respect, just like a boxing match ashore, except that no cheering could be permitted lest it bring the Captain out of his quarters for a look. Not that he could be in entire ignorance of the event, but it would not do to force from him a decision he would be obliged to make. It was the old blind eye; what he did not see, did not happen. The Chaplain had a watch to time the contest, and so a very good place from which to observe, while the ship's boys earned themselves a few pennies or favours by relaying the state of matters to those who could not be spared their duties, the Officer of the Watch and his two midshipmen assistants, the Quartermaster and his mates, conning the ship, the marine sentries on duty at the various fixed posts and the lookouts aloft who had to remain in place in case a Frenchman, coming in or out of the Gironde Estuary, crested the horizon.

'Well now,' Taberly concluded, rubbing his prominent chin. 'There will be no one aboard *Leander* willing to stand against you after that display, but I daresay when we join the fleet in a few days there will be others who fancy a bout. They, like the crew here, would not know of your skill, and it will be in our interest not to let on. Hell's teeth, it is only by chance that I myself did. An inter-ship contest could be formal and sanctioned, could even be fought ashore. Who knows, perhaps the admirals may take to such a spectacle, which will mean rich pickings for us if we triumph, for it would not surprise others that we back our own man.'

'Us,' hissed Rufus, as Taberly turned and moved away. 'What does the sod mean by us?'

'Pearce should see this,' said Charlie, as the lieutenant

appeared to crow as he began to collect his winnings from those of his wardroom companions, the glum-looking lot who had backed Clipe. 'If he had got us off, like he said he would…'

'Enough,' snapped Michael, ignoring the pain in his jaw. 'You have a way of blaming John-boy for all our ills, Charlie, without ever being sure that he is at fault. Sure, he could not have known what was going to happen any more than we did ourselves. We were given one hour to shift and no more.'

Charlie Taverner stood to his full height, the tricorn hat he had hung onto since being pressed set back at a tilt showing his fair hair. His normal good looks were spoiled by the petulant cast of his features. 'He's deserted us before, and surely he should have got back to save us from this.'

'But he did come back the first time,' said Rufus Dommet, his face bearing his usual look of innocence.

'If you look across the deck, Charlie,' hissed Michael, 'I think you will see where the blame for this lies.'

Turning, Charlie followed Michael's angry glare. Cornelius Gherson, a man pressed on the same night as them, though not from the *Pelican*, had been a pest ever since they had first made his acquaintance. He was standing on his own, the crowd having cleared, a hand held out in which he tossed several gleaming coins, evidence that some aboard had not beggared themselves with whores and illicit drink. The look on his absurdly handsome, babyish face was enough to inform the trio from where Taberly had got his information about Michael's prowess, for Gherson had seen him fight. It would have been he that saw the chance to make money, which seemed to be his abiding concern in life; he, the practised sneak, who would have hinted to Taberly that O'Hagan and Clipe would be a good match. Only a notion perhaps, for the sod would never admit to it, but just then the lieutenant moved toward Gherson and patted him on the back with a clear air of gratitude. The look and the sneer aimed at Michael then was like saying that the thought of his culpability was as true as Holy Writ.

'We should have let that bastard drown,' growled Charlie.

Michael slowly raised himself off the stool, easing each pain as he did so. 'Jesus, I don't recall havin' a hand in the saving of him then, but I reckon we all regret the saving of him later. As the Blessed Virgin is my guide, the devil is in him.'

'Perhaps we should teach him a lesson, Michael, have him learn that those fists of yours are not there for his profit?'

O'Hagan slowly shook his head. 'He's kissed Taberly's arse, Charlie, and lined his purse. If we touch him we would have to silence the bugger, else we'd be the ones to suffer, for he would not still his tongue.'

A sailor approached Gherson as Taberly moved away and asked him something, which elicited a nod and a hand out demand for payment. A wad of tobacco was proffered, Gherson's fee for letter writing, something of which he had let the crew know he was adept. On a make and mend day, those with family or a true wife would pass up part of their ration to get a letter penned to go on the next British vessel heading for home.

The notion that HMS *Leander* would join the fleet, as well as Taberly's hopes of a profitable contest, was dashed as soon as they opened up the Lisbon roadstead, for it was bereft of anything other than Portuguese warships, and Captain Tucker was bluntly informed by the naval resident that having replenished both wood and water, HMS *Leander* was to proceed with all despatch to join Lord Hood, who, in company with the Spanish Admiral Langara and his Cadiz squadron, was taking his fleet into the Mediterranean.

* * *

Lieutenant Henry Digby, aboard the 12-gun sloop, HMS *Weazel,* could not help but admire what he saw over the stern, even if it had been the same for several days. Under a warm sun and a cloudless sky, the two fleets of Britain and Spain ploughed their way across the deep blue Mediterranean. Leading the main column of 74's was HMS *Victory,* flagship of the commanding admiral, Lord Hood, courses, topsails and jibs stretched taut, with each ship taking station upon her at a strictly defined distance of a cables' length. Over to the south lay the second column, just as rigidly fixed on the flagship of the second-in-command, Admiral Hotham, and God help any vessel which strayed, for its number would be up the masthead of *Victory* in a flash, the instructions from the Captain of the Fleet to keep station, reinforced with a gun.

That the Dons were less rigid in their dispositions, less inclined to properly hold their station on their flagship, was only to be expected; they lacked the sea-going ability and discipline of their British allies. Digby knew if he climbed to the tops with a telescope, there to join the lookouts, he would see all around the fleet a screen of frigates and sloops like his own, set at distance enough to warn should an enemy warship be sighted on the horizon. The other task they performed was just as vital, to bespeak every passing fishing boat or neutral trading vessel, to glean information on what was happening to the north, on the great landmass that was France.

Thus they had learnt throughout the fleet that Provence and the Rhône Valley were in turmoil, from the boats that plied daily between fleet and flagship that the port city of Marseilles had declared against the Jacobins and sent packing, not without bloodshed, those who supported the revolutionary government in Paris. Like many others, Digby had speculated that Lord Hood might make for that place to support the rebels, only to realise when the course remained steady that their C-in-C had his eye firmly fixed on finding and beating the enemy fleet. That achieved, all things would be possible.

Somewhere ahead, off Toulon, would be HMS *Brilliant*, the vessel on which he had originally set sail from England. The thought of the frigate and her complement brought to him a slew of different emotions; the fact that service under Ralph Barclay had been less than pleasant, even if at the same time it had been far from dull. Digby had the suspicion that, in shifting him to Hotham's flagship in Lisbon, Barclay had got rid of him at the first opportunity, not because of any inability on his part, but because he felt that all his inferior officers had been foisted on him by the very admiral who was now heading towards a rendezvous off Toulon. It was a double irony that he had been shifted a second time, to the sloop HMS *Weazel*, though recalling the lack of warmth in wardroom of HMS *Britannia* towards him as a new officer, the very obvious fact that he had been treated as some kind of interloper, it was hardly surprising.

Never having been in a flagship wardroom before Digby had nothing with which to make a comparison, but it had been made plain to him on his arrival that he had cut across the hawse of the Premier, who had been manoeuvring to have a relative of his own appointed to the first vacant place, that of a lieutenant called Glaister who had been shifted to *Brilliant*. The rest of those present; naval and marine officers, the purser and the master, had taken their cue from the man who led their mess, and, while staying within the narrowest band of politeness, had done nothing to make him feel a true part of things; no invitations to play cards or backgammon, little in the way of enquiry about his career to date or the possibility of mutual acquaintances. It had actually come as a relief when he was told he was being moved to this sloop, presumably because the Premier, a powerful figure aboard any vessel, had preyed upon his captain, who in turn had persuaded Admiral Hotham that Henry Digby, even if he proved disgruntled, was an officer who had little in the way of influence, and one who could safely be ignored.

The problem on *Weazel* was the master and commander who captained her, or rather his addiction to the bottle. A choleric-faced fellow called Benton, he seemed never to be really sober, even when he appeared briefly on deck of a morning to check that his ship was still in sight of the fleet. The man was rude by his very nature, seemingly incapable of saying anything praiseworthy, more inclined to nit-pick and complain, his comments just on the very edge of that which could be challenged as outright denigration. Digby's predecessor had used what connections he had to get out from under Benton, something the present incumbent knew he probably lacked; had he possessed any worthwhile patrons, he would still be aboard Hotham's flagship.

'On the whole, I think I would prefer to be back in the frigate.'

'Sir?' asked the young midshipman standing close to him, a freckle-faced youth called Harbin, who made up in application for what he seemed to lack in brains.

Digby smiled, wondering if the boy thought him mad, talking to himself. 'I was just ruminating, young feller, on the merits of sailing in a frigate as opposed to this vessel.'

'*Weazel* is uncomfortably small, sir.'

'Frigates are certainly not spacious, either, but they are rightly called the eyes of the fleet, and often away from the prying interference of very senior admirals. That has to be worth something.'

The lookout called down, '*Victory* signalling, your honour.'

Digby raised his glass to look at the flagship, seeing the various pennants run up, that followed by a puff of white smoke from the signal gun. He needed no book to read them, having seen the flags before.

'*Agamemnon* again,' he said.

He swung the telescope round to look at the sixty-four, halfway down Hood's main column, and the men running through the rigging, seeking to take in reefs in the sails to slow her down, for the problem for Captain Horatio Nelson was not to keep up with the fleet, but to sail slowly enough to keep proper station, for his ship was a real flyer. A crash of marine boots told Digby his captain was coming on deck, and he and the boy with him turned to raise their hats as Benton, his face dark-skinned over ruby-red, took a telescope from the rack, and swaying more than the ship, trained it over the rail.

'I see our friend is entertaining us again,' he said.

'Sir.'

'One wonders at Captain Nelson sometimes, if his travails are quite as serious as he makes out, given that he's a man fond of attracting attention to himself. It would not surprise me to find he fails to keep station on purpose, just to ensure he is not forgotten. Still, Lord Hood seems content to indulge him. Personally, I think it a mistake to do so.'

There was a note of pique in that last remark, underlining several things; the first the rumour that relations between the two admirals were not of the best, the second that Benton was a partisan of Hotham, who was no doubt the man who had given him this sloop to command. Lastly that it was known that Lord Hood admired Nelson, a view not universally shared by every captain or admiral, and allowed him a latitude at captains' conferences he rarely extended to others.

'I went aboard *Agamemnon* with Admiral Hotham once, in Lisbon,' Benton continued. 'I cannot tell you of the state of the deck, nor the familiar way that his men address him. He might as well be a common seaman himself. And the man is a light head in the article of drink. Two or three glasses and he is quite intoxicated.'

The way Benton said that, Digby suspected that he saw such inability to imbibe as a greater disgrace than an untidy deck or some over-familiarity from the lower deck. More interesting to him was the relationship between the two men who led the fleet, surely something which could influence its effectiveness. On arriving in Lisbon and finding Hotham still there, it soon became common knowledge that Lord Hood had used high words to demand to be told why. To his mind the fleet he was sent to command should have been on its way to Toulon well before the day it actually sailed, something it did as soon as he could issue his orders. Hotham's protests were not only brushed aside, the man had been dressed down like the newest midshipman, and was boiling with indignation because of it, and it was said he had written home to complain. There was further delay at Cadiz, while Hood harried his Spanish allies and got them to sea.

So it was that HMS *Firefly* had found them not much beyond Gibraltar, with Captain Gould going aboard to give Admiral Lord Hood a message that went round every ship under his command in a day; that the enemy fleet had not been ready for sea as of ten days previously, but that it was working double tides to get yards crossed, sails hoisted and stores aboard. *Firefly* was ordered straight back to Toulon, with another sloop in attendance, with orders to ensure that the fleet was kept informed, especially if the French got any capital ships to sea, the whole incident inducing a palpable air of excitement throughout the fleet.

In calling aboard all senior officers to disseminate this information, it had been spread by the various barge crews as they returned to their ships. Likewise it was no secret, happily imparted to those same barge crews by the cabin servants, that Nelson has asked to be sent ahead, with as many frigates as could be spared, to join HMS *Brilliant* and help keep the French fleet locked up, if necessary to fight them as they tried to clear their harbour. Hood had been quite amenable to the idea, but the Dons, lukewarm allies at best, more accustomed to fighting against King George's Navy than sailing alongside, had been less enthusiastic, an attitude Hotham had apparently shared. In the face of so many objections, the idea had been dropped.

'Well, Mr Digby, how are you enjoying service aboard my ship. A different kettle of fish from your previous commission, eh?'

Which one was the man talking about, frigate or flagship? And he had to admit to being surprised by the friendly tone, so very different to that Benton normally employed, which meant that it took Digby a second or two to answer, and robbed his reply of any sincerity.

'Very much so, sir.'

The captain picked up the hesitation, and reverted to a tone instantly more familiar. His ruby-red cheeks deepened considerably. 'Captain Barclay got rid of you, though, did he not?'

'I'm sure he had his reasons, sir.'

'Take care that I don't discern the same ones, Mr Digby, whatever they are.'

With that, Benton left the deck, his gait betraying him just once as the swell showed a slight increase, causing him to stagger. Comparing the two captains, and on the principle of the lesser of two evils, Henry Digby could not but prefer Barclay. A hard, determined man, yes, but a competent sailor, if a touch impetuous and prize hungry. He, too, was a man with obvious faults, though over-indulgence in the bottle was not really one of them. For instance he found it too easy to be jealous, a fatal flaw in man who had a young wife with him at sea. There had been that affair with the pressed seaman Pearce, for one, which had caused such disquiet amongst the crew. He could clearly recall himself being unhappy about the punishment, just as he could remember the way that Barclay's wife had made her own displeasure plain.

It had proved to be a lesson in the limitations of command, and Digby had taken note of it. Not that Pearce was innocent in the matter of his own misfortune, for the fellow had an arrogance about him which was misplaced given his station. Idly he wondered where he was now; probably ashore, and damned glad to be so, but that did not last, for his thoughts quickly turned again to his old ship and his old commander, somewhere ahead, over the bowsprit, patrolling impatiently while waiting for the fleet to arrive.

CHAPTER SIX

John Pearce was sailing the English Channel once more, this time trying to learn as much as he could from the roly-poly owner of the postal brig. The captain of the *Lorne* was someone to whom he had taken an instant liking; from the moment he had come aboard he had been in receipt of nothing but kindness and consideration, which extended to the best available accommodation, a fuss about his comfort plus the provision of food and drink. Hailing from the Irish province of Ulster, Captain McGann was easy to like; everything that happened for good or seeming ill made him laugh, and that was wont to affect his whole being. His shoulders shook and his substantial belly heaved.

Things were bound to be amiss with any group of seamen who had spent a last night ashore; there were sore heads a'plenty from the young and unattached, allied to regret from those who loved their wives, and impatience from those glad to be free once more from domestic ties. Their captain was the very antithesis of those Pearce had served before, more like a father to the men who crewed his ship than a captain, a feeling that they returned in full measure.

A tactile man, dressed in the same manner as his crew, McGann was more inclined to cradle his sailors with a friendly arm than chastise them. It soon transpired – a fact Pearce learnt while the Blue Peter was still flying – that every one of them had sailed with him before; they knew his ways and he knew theirs, as well as their families, wives, children and even the mothers of the younger crew. *Lorne* was that rare thing, a happy ship, a truth made doubly obvious before they had cleared St Helens. The men of the brig went about their tasks without so much as a shouted order, for their captain spoke quietly, and followed every request to shift sail or haul on a rope with a sincerely added 'please'.

From those same hands – a talkative, friendly lot – Pearce learnt the respect in which McGann was held, told by each one to whom he spoke that their master was a man who knew the ways of the sea better than anyone afloat, and was at the self-same time a complete mandrill ashore, for he drank too much and had a conviction when inebriated, with no basis whatever in truth, that any woman who came within his line of vision was madly in love with him, and determined to drag him to the altar.

'Should you go ashore with him, sir,' whispered one older hand, 'which is likely at Gibraltar, then be like we is, prepared to either drag him away from some indiscretion, or fight off the beaux of whichever women with whom the silly sod has taken a liberty.'

'Yet he does not drink at sea? He declined to join me in more than one glass at our first meal.'

'Never, sir. He respects the sea too much and as he says, he is damned if he will surrender any of us up to its tempers for not being as sharp as is needed.'

To take such a liking to anyone so quickly was a strange sensation for Pearce, hardly surprising given the life he had lived. Too many times, growing up, he had trusted someone only to be disappointed, which had made him reticent in meeting people for the first time. Yet he had felt the need to be completely honest right off, with the captain hinting that having a 'capital naval fellow' on his deck would be good for all sorts of things, not least in allowing them to compare the different ways of rigging and sailing.

'You will find me a sad example of a naval officer, Mr McGann,' Pearce said, feeling the movement of the ship on his knees as they moved out into the Spithead anchorage. 'The uniform is a sham.' The response to his candour was that disarming, body-shaking laugh. Encouraged thus, Pearce told his tale, as well as his purpose, told how he had come by his rank, though he played down the action from which it had resulted, praising instead those who had fought with him.

'So you see, Mr McGann, it is not sea service but a stroke of luck and the aid of others that has got me to where I am.'

McGann swung the ship's wheel a fraction, reacting to a change in the current as it ran in from deeper water. The wind strengthened too, which called for a slight trimming of the yards.

'It is a singular thing, sir, such elevation, though I have a'heard of it happening afore, an' from the same king who showed favour to you. I know, too, that it is not given for light work, but for acts quite exceptional in the fighting line.' The man's chest and substantial belly heaved as he laughed once more, his eyes twinkling as he added, 'Mr Pearce, I suspect you are guilty of modesty.'

'It is some consolation to me to know that I am not too singular. The charge of modesty I deny.'

'Deny away, sir, for to do so gives you credit.'

'Needles coming up on the starboard beam, Capt'n,' called a hand who was aloft in the rigging, changing a block and so could see well ahead over the bowsprit.

McGann called back 'Why thank 'e, Harold, much obliged,' before speaking softly to Pearce. 'A fine lad that, as they all are. His father and I sailed together when I was his age, and we was true mates.'

'What brought you to this?'

'Good fortune, Mr Pearce, which has stayed true, not least in the willingness of those I know to stick with me, and those who knew me as a lad to teach me the ways of the sea and how to make my way around it. Sailed to the Carnatic and the Bay of Bengal more'n once, and I was allowed to indulge in a little private trade, buying spices, gold trinkets and the like that I could sell on my return. Husbandry gave me enough to put down a sum on a boat, and I engaged myself to the postal service when it was still a sinecure. By the time Billy Pitt bought it in, I had the *Lorne* and was set up to sign for regular service, Gibraltar and back, with the government. I was also lucky, as you were not, never to be taken out of a ship or ashore in a time of war, and so never suffered the indignity of being a pressed seaman.'

'Indignity describes it, Captain McGann, though it gives me no pleasure to say I have known worse.' Responding to the enquiring look, Pearce said, 'In time, sir, we will be in each others' company long enough for me to tell you all.'

'Have it as you will. I will not press you.'

The pun on the word press brought forth another hearty laugh, one so intense that the captain had to ask Pearce to hold the wheel steady while he recovered. With that in his hand, and feeling that the ship had a life through it, Pearce was once more reminded of the sham of his commission, and the haunting fear that once in the Mediterranean, he might be offered a place aboard a ship which he might have to accept just to stay on the station.

'I may press you, sir, for as I have already told you, my ignorance of the sea is great.'

'A capital play on the word, sir,' exclaimed McGann, heaving once more, and wheezing as he sought air. 'Capital indeed.'

'But true.'

'You wish to know more?'

'It matters not what I wish, it is more what I need.'

Short by a head though he was, McGann nevertheless managed to get an arm around Pearce's shoulder. 'Then this, sir, shall be your school for the time you are aboard, and I take leave to say you could find none finer, for there is not a hand serving on this vessel that would not be pleased to instruct, as am I. But, recall this, if you want to stay off the deck and out of wind, water and cold, that is your privilege.'

Pearce hardly hesitated a second. 'I would be happy to be your pupil, sir.'

'Then I too am happy. I ain't never taught a man 'owt, but that I have learnt something in return, sir. I look forward to having you on my deck, but just as much I anticipate with pleasure the conversation we will have when we are below.'

Lorne was constructed for speed through the water. She was of narrow build, carrying as few stores as possible, no cargo and damn stability, for the contract McGann had was not one to allow him much in the way of double ventures. His task was to get the mails to Gibraltar and back as speedily as possible, avoiding any attempt to intercept them now the nation was again at war with France.

'Twelve days is around the norm for the passage, though I have had it take twice that time in the winter months. Made it in under five days, one trip. Never known such a wind oblige for the whole journey. Blew hard and consistent from the north-east to push us down the Channel, then swung round to a fine, strong north-westerly off the Lizard so that the lee rail was never clear of the sea all the way south, with every man jack up from below to take pleasure in flying. Fourteen knots was our best cast of the log. Fourteen knots, Mr Pearce, have you ever heard the like!'

According to McGann, they were doing very well at the moment under a bright blue sky, a warm late-July sun and an gentle easterly breeze right astern. The log had run off six knots on the last cast, Pearce sure of this for it had been himself in the chains doing the casting, with the man accustomed to the task there to make sure he learnt to do it right and did not risk drowning by too much enthusiasm. Prior to that he had been aloft helping to run out the booms for the skysails, then going out onto those booms to haul the sails aloft, lashing them on and then loosing the ties and letting them fall, bare soles bouncing in the footropes, his shirt billowing out on the breeze, constantly admonished by the man next to him to, 'Clap on, sir, clap on. Allas keep one hand for the boat.'

And it had been a pleasure, so different from when he been aloft on either *Griffin* or *Brilliant*, different because it was voluntary, the pleasure doubled by making a real effort to do the tasks well, even more pleased by the way he was cheerfully egged on by the men with whom he was working. Those same fellows could not tie a knot or look to splice a rope without calling out to show how it was done. They could not haul a fall through a block without explaining why one line was on a single block, when another, for its weight, needed the gearing of a double. And he hauled with them when hauling was required, the tar on his palms like a badge rather then the disgrace it had previously been. John Pearce was enjoying himself.

Soon they were past the Lizard and, in darkness, they had made their southing to run well clear of Ushant. The weather was good, the sea steady, a long and comfortable swell that hardly disturbed the plates on McGann's dinner table. Their course was set and a trusty pair were on the wheel, with half the crew standing by as a watch, for like the Navy a postal packet did not shorten sail at night. Earlier that same day, he had been instructing Pearce in the use of a sextant, expressing no surprise that he had no prior knowledge of an instrument he owned, albeit one that had suffered from use in hands that had clearly, more than once, dropped it.

'Now once you got the sun reflected a'right, bring it down to the horizon, waving a fraction left an right, which tells you when it touches, and stops it dipping below the horizon.'

Doing that twice a day was something Pearce mastered; what he found impossible were the calculations necessary to make sure the time was correct, this before Captain McGann could adjust one of his chronometers, the difference between the one set to Greenwich time and the result giving the ship's position. Night-time sightings were a mystery and likely to remain so, 'Shooting Stars', as the his mentor called it, with seven different celestial objects to aim at, and the obscurity of something called a nominal point to commence matters.

McGann, who would not suffer another soul to touch them, took a cloth and gently rubbed one of his beautiful clocks. 'It be hard to think of life without them now, yet it is not more'n thirty years since Harrison proved their worth. Many's a sailor was lost and went to Davy Jones without them. And here we are running past the Scillies. Did you ever hear of an admiral called Sir Cloudsley Shovell?'

Pearce smiled and shook his head at the outlandish name. He had learnt very early on that McGann loved to tell a tale – what sailor did not – just as he had learnt that, unlike a lot of folk he knew how to do it without boring the breeches off the listener.

'This be in the year 1707 and it goes to show the worth of Harrison's invention, which came about as a result, though it took time, if you'll forgive the pun. Old Shovell was bringin' a squadron of ships back home, his course set for the Channel and Portsmouth, when one of his men told him he was sailing a risky course, that he would run foul of the Scilly Isles if he kept on. Bein' a choleric bugger, and sure of hisself, Shovell pulled a strop and had flogged the man that dared to question his orders. He then held to the course he had set and ran half his fleet on to the lee shore and drownded 'em. Thousands of sailors lost on a man's temper. They say he survived and was murdered for his ring, which serves him right.'

There was a moment when both men contemplated that, Pearce having an uncomfortable memory of struggling in a raging sea that was hammering a rock-strewn shore. It was not a pleasant image.

'I feel safe in the notion that I can master the instrument, Mr McGann, and the clocks present no problem at all, for a careful child could adjust those, but I fear the mathematics will stump me.'

That was no lie. His father had sought to teach him mathematics, but was only competent in the basics of adding, subtraction and multiplication. His Parisian tutor, the Abbé Morlant, with whom he had studied for two years, was steeped in the Classics, and knew nothing about such matters as geometry and spherical trigonometry, probably seeing them, though he was no zealot, as the work of the devil. Pearce continued to assert that, however interesting it was to be shown something new and instructed in matters outside his experience, it was only curiosity that made him attend to it; he had no notion to ever use it, a declaration at which McGann was quick to scoff.

'But you ain't got my drift, Mr Pearce. I am sayin' such things is best left to those that are brought up to it.' Responding to Pearce's enquiring look he shook with humour once more. 'Do you think all your braided officers know about navigation? Do you think they are all sure

87

which sails to set aloft to get the best out of a ship or where the rocks lie on a lee shore? Who is it that stows the hold and trims the barky so she sails smooth. It ain't the captain that's for certain.'

'I suspect they must know about navigation, even if your late and unlamented Sir Cloudsley Shovell did not.'

'There are those that do, and capital seamen they are, Cook and that fellow Bligh to name but two. I know it has become common these days to expect a commissioned officer to find his way about in all manner of things, but to my mind a wise man leaves such matters to the vessel's master. When I first went to sea as a lad, near forty-year past, I admit in merchant service, a ship's captain was just that, the fellow who saw to the running of the barky and made certain that each man was in the right place to carry out his given task, as well as to do it proper. It weren't too different, from what I have heard, in the Navy.'

'Is that not dangerous?'

'Not if you has the right people, good people, and unlike that daft Shovell bugger, you listen to 'em. A wise captain has a good master, a wise master has good mates. That Bligh I mentioned started life as a master's mate, and that was his rating on Cook's first South Sea adventure, which not many seem to recall. That's were he learnt his skills, not in a wardroom, or standing watch on the deck of a king's ship.'

'No doubt it was in those he learnt to ferment mutiny.'

'Happen, for there are those who claim he brought it on hisself. Be that as it may, there is no doubt he is a capital seaman, has to be to sail four thousand miles in an open boat, and I would trust him to keep me safe if he was setting my course. That is not summat I would say to every naval captain I have come across.'

'I am not sure what you are trying to say.'

'What is a king's ship for, sir?' A cautiously raised

eyebrow forced McGann to continue. 'Why it's for fighting, is it not?'

'Yes.'

'Then the job of a captain on a king's ship is to make sure that when it comes to the moment of truth, when the enemy is beam on and firing broadsides, that his ship is set for the response. That does not require him to get it in the right place, or set the right suit of sails to do so, for he will have folk on board who know a damn sight more'n he does about such things. But he must have men on his cannon who can fire and reload, even if the air be full of metal and wood splinters. He must be the kind that can lead when boarding and fight with a cutlass, pistol and pike. Now you have been modest on the question of the *Valmy*, but you have yet to smoke that Portsmouth is my home. Ashore I am a man who likes to take a drink, and that I has a fair pair of lugs with which to hear what you might term chatter.'

Seeing McGann tug at a fleshy lobe, emphasising that he did indeed have large and good ears, or lugs as he termed them, Pearce adopted a tone of voice larded with sarcasm. 'No doubt there has been a certain amount of talk in the taverns. If my experience is anything to go by, most of it will be nonsense.'

McGann's face filled with blood and his body began to heave, which increased as he confirmed what Pearce had said, so that his words were delivered with a degree of spluttering.

'I won't deny that a rate of it is. For one, that there was a midshipman in the *Valmy* capture who did prodigious deeds, and lost half his limbs in the doin' of it, 'cording to some. Depending on which tale you listened to, and how gone in drink was the tale-teller, he lost an eye, his right or left arm, and for certain at least one of his legs, and had musket balls and sword thrusts enough through his frame to make a fair imitation of a sieve for fine flour.'

Pearce smiled and shrugged. 'Few tales do not grow in the telling, Mr McGann, perhaps even that of your Cloudsley Shovell.'

As an attempt to change the subject, it failed abysmally. As soon as McGann could control his hilarity, he spoke again. 'Yet what do I have sitting at my table drinking cider, but that very same fellow, whole and hearty and scarce a scratch, which I do hope you ain't going to deny. Now filletin' the tale, and sorting truth from gossip, it seems that what you did was singular.'

'That word again. I'm beginning not to like it.'

'If'n it be the one that fits.' McGann stopped smiling, and for once his face was serious. 'I am happy to teach what I can, as is every man in my crew, as I know you have found, but there is scarce time enough to turn you into a Cook or a Bligh. So I have this advice for you. Learn what you can, but never forget that the prime job of a Navy officer is fighting, and in that region, you has better credentials than most.'

'Except I have no desire to be a Navy officer.'

'You will forgive me for goin' beyond the bounds of bein' polite, but what in hell's name do you have a desire to do, and don't go telling me again about rescuing your old shipmates. Now I am goin' to say that I took to you the minute I clapped eyes on you, 'cause there was no showing away about what you had done, and that is a feeling that has only grown on acquaintance.'

'It is, Captain McGann, returned in full measure.'

'For which I thank you. I am goin' to tread the path of discourtesy by alluding to the fact that you are without a father, God rest his soul.' That was not a sentiment Adam Pearce would have appreciated, but this was not the moment to say so. 'An' bein' without that you lack anyone to advise you.'

'Which you presumably intend to do?' said Pearce, his smile now absent.

'I see I have angered you, young sir, but if I have my intentions are good ones. What I am saying is this: if you doubt where your future lies you could do worse than the King's service. You're a fighter, lad, and a proven one, and I will hazard that with what is going on in the new war with the French, that Farmer George and Billy Pitt need fighting men more'n they need men that can get themselves to the South Seas and back again!'

Taberly got his fight, but it took place in Gibraltar, HMS *Leander* calling at the Rock to deliver duplicate despatches, and only because his captain refused to sail on into the Mediterranean with a full supply of wood and water, notwithstanding a dispute with the commanding admiral at Gibraltar, who wanted him back at sea forthwith. The excuse for delay was simple; with no British base in the Inland Sea, and no knowledge of whether purchase would be possible in places like Genoa and Leghorn, nor any faith in the Spanish alliance, a hold full of stores, four months' supply, was not only wise, but essential. That Captain Tucker, taking advantage of the current state of relations with Spain, could take his net for a day to a hot and arid country he had never visited, and possibly add to his butterfly collection species he had never before seen, was just an accidental dividend.

With only a patrolling naval presence at the port it was the army who provided a contestant, easy to arrange because soldiers, bored stiff on garrison duty, were so easy to bait, as well as being boastful coves who would never allow that the Navy might have a champion to outshine their own. And, as men who had their commissions through purchase, they generally had the means as well as the inclination to wager high, which suited a confident *Leander* wardroom. Michael O'Hagan had been excused duty in anticipation of Lisbon; on the journey to Gibraltar that had continued, his sole task to train with Clipe, and to hone what were rough skills into those that would tell. They were at it again now, in the waist, again clear of boats, in the space where the first bout had taken place.

'The pity, O'Hagan,' Taberly said, 'is that it will have to take place on our quarterdeck, for we dare not let the crew ashore for fear they will try to run, and there would be a damn near mutiny if we denied them a sight of your victory.'

Michael was looking at the rock, wondering where, on such a small outcrop, they could desert to. 'I might lose.'

Taberly's face was bland, the voice emotionless, but it was just as threatening, perhaps more so, than if he had barked his response. 'You would be best not even thinking in those terms. There will be a great deal of money riding on you, and I doubt that those set above you would take kindly to losing it. You might find that punishment in that quarter would be greater than any you could receive from a fellow boxer.'

'So,' Michael said, once Taberly walked away, 'it is a win or the grating every time I so much as fart.'

Clipe, his previous opponent, patted him with a heavily bandaged and padded hand. 'The army man will be big, Michael, they tend that way do bullocks, but that does not mean he will have skill.'

'Do you know, Clipe, I am gentle as a lamb, sober.'

'But I,' added Charlie, taking a wardroom donated towel to wipe him down, 'have seen you in drink, Michael.'

'Sure, I did my ditch digging by day, Charlie, and took my pleasure when the sun went down.'

There was a slightly sour note in Charlie Taverner's response. They might have both been pressed from the same tavern, but they had not been friends in the Pelican. Charlie, being a fly sort, a man who had once made his way in the world by fleecing the unwary, had more than once tried to do the same to Michael O'Hagan. Then there had been a small matter of rivalry over the 'affections' of one of the serving girls.

'I recall where your pleasure was directed.'

Michael brightened, then, lifting the gloom that filled him at the prospect of the coming fight. 'Ah the sweet Rosie, as plump as a Wicklow cow, an' twice as willing.'

'For those that could pay,' moaned Rufus, which brought a bitter nod of approval from his friend Charlie.

Michael hit the boy gently with one of his own padded hands. 'You could have had all the coin in the land, Rufus, but I doubt you would have satisfied Rosie. There's not enough of you.'

'I got what it takes,' Rufus protested, his face reddening in a deep blush. 'You mark my words.'

'What's important,' interrupted Clipe, 'is whether Michael here has what it takes to beat the army, for if he ain't, them bastards in the wardroom won't confine their fury to him.'

'Boats comin' off,' shouted a voice from the gangway. 'Dozens of the buggers, full o' red coats and blue.'

Taberly appeared again, this time with Gherson in tow, though he hung back. 'There's not a man aboard who has not been to the purser for a loan, O'Hagan. The whole ship is riding on you.'

He passed some of those men on his way up to the deck, Leanders and well as the Griffins who, like the Pelicans had been shifted aboard without so much as a by your leave. First to encourage was Latimer, an elderly sailor with a wrinkled, walnut complexion who had proved, aboard HMS *Griffin*, to be a wise old cove.

'We beat the French, Michael. Be a pity to lose to the bullocks.'

'Well said, Lats,' called Blubber, another Griffin, fat

and sweating in the heat. 'We's got money coming from the *Valmy*, Michael, and it's all on you.'

'You'se got money comin' should you ever set foot ashore and free, Blubber,' added Latimer, before patting his champion and pushing him on. 'Do your best, an' I for one will rest content.'

The decks were for visiting dignitaries, and there was no shortage of those. Army officers came aboard in their regimentals, Navy in their best blue coats and snowy breeches. The word had gone out amongst the traders and officials on the Rock, and they were there in numbers too, happy to chuck coins into a half barrel carried round by a midshipman, this to cover the cost of entertaining them with food and wine. The crew were given the shrouds and yards from which to observe the contest and they were now as crowded as the deck, and since the approval of the admiral had been sought and given, as being a welcome diversion on a tedious posting, there would be cheering as well. The most senior officers of both services, along with the *Leander*'s wardroom, sat on the poop.

The army man, Raef Braddock, was huge, giving a good three inches on Michael, with plenty of muscle as well as a face that looked as though it had taken enough punishment to last a lifetime; a flat nose where the bone had been too crushed to repair, heavy eyebrows that did nothing to disguise the thick scar tissue underneath, wooden teeth, which were removed to show pink gums framed by lips that had evidence of half a dozen poorly healed splits.

Taberly had done his homework, for he was no fool, and Michael knew that his opponent was a soldier always in trouble with his superiors, a drinker and brawler who was regularly given several dozen lashes at the wagon wheel, this proved when he removed the cloak he was wearing to reveal a back so

94

criss-crossed with scars even the hardest of the sailors gasped. The fellow was used to pain, and he and Clipe had opined that the wiles that had failed in the previous fight might be the best avenue in this one, for given this fellow's reputation, he lacked in brains what he had in sheer bulk. Just hitting him around the body and head might not suffice; Michael had to draw him out so that he could strike in places where a well-delivered blow would down him.

It was odd to O'Hagan, how sensitive to the mood of the crowd he had become. The air of confidence that their champion would triumph took a dent as soon as the soldier appeared, and fell further when he revealed his muscled torso and his lacerated back, so there was a flurry of late betting as some tried to cover themselves both ways. Behind him stood Clipe, Charlie and Rufus, the first to advise, the other two to wipe away blood and sweat. An army major checked his hands to ensure nothing was contained in them, like a piece of lead, while Taberly did the same to Braddock, then both men where brought forward to their marks, just far enough apart for them to beat each other. There the rules were read out; toe to the line, pull back for more than a count of three and the bout was forfeit.

Close to Braddock, and looking into eyes hooded by scarred brows, Michael, reckoned that Clipe had the right of it; he did not reckon he was facing a fellow who would back off from the line. The man would stand his ground and take whatever he was given, his aim to wear down his opponent to the point where he could deliver a killer blow. And looking at the hands, which were huge even to a man who had big mitts of his own, and the thick arms to back them up, he reckoned that the blow could be fatal.

'Ride his punches at first, Michael,' Clipe whispered, as if he had not said it a dozen times already. 'Sway back and see what he's about before you weigh in total.'

'Gentlemen,' said Taberly, holding up a handkerchief, 'are you ready.'

Both fighters nodded, and the handkerchief dropped, an act which killed off the murmuring that had been rippling through the crowd as the spectators waited for the first blows to be struck. It was Braddock who obliged, catching Michael in the upper rib-cage with a telling right-handed blow that hurt even as he rode it, which brought forth an encouraging yell from his support. The soldier tried to follow that up, with a left, only to find it parried, with Michael feinting to hit him and force him to back off. Braddock did no such thing, he stood rock like, so Michael hit him hard just to let him know he had a fight on his hands. That produced a gummy grin.

Those blows had set the crowd off, with both sets of partisans yelling encouragement as the fighters began to exchange. Braddock seemed content to keep hitting the same spots over and over again, there was no science in his assault, unlike Michael who tried to vary what he did, striking different parts of the body. All the while Clipe was shouting in his ear, 'Ride it out, ride it out.' That followed by, 'Find the spot, Michael, find the spot.'

The man he was coaching thought that easier said than done. Hit the Braddock's nose hard and it did not bleed, it was too smashed already for anything to break; strike his head and all he did was shake it and swing back a killer blow. Punches to the body seemed useless, the man did not even move at the heaviest delivery, so Michael decided to use time. No man could fight without using up his puff; he must conserve his, and let Braddock squander his own. Then he would get a chance to aim at the target that might bring a result, the point of Braddock's jaw.

Michael had experienced before that strange clarity which comes when fighting; the heightened awareness of everything around you as well as that immediately in front. He never took his own gaze off Braddock's eyes, for in shifting they began to tell him with increasing accuracy where the next blow would fall. He was aware too of his own balance, and how by adjusting it he could weather the storm of the man's aggression. More tellingly, he could almost feel the mood of the watching crowd, tell that the soldiers were exulting while his own supporters and backers were more muted. There was also the contemplation of losing deliberately, just to infuriate Taberly and his ilk, not to mention that gobshite Gherson, but that had to be put aside; too many of his shipmates had borrowed money riding on his success.

So he took more punches than he gave, which were painful though never hitting anything vital, dropping his head to blunt blows to that part of his body so that it now ached, as did his upper arms and shoulders, where by swaying aside he could deflect Braddock's intent. And he did strike back, mostly to parry what might be coming, but giving his opponent cause often enough to blink in surprise when he landed a real power punch. Time lost any meaning as thud followed thud, and sometimes the crowd were near silent long enough to allow the sound of bone on flesh to be paramount, for the longer it went on the less sure both sets of supporters were about the outcome.

O'Hagan was not, for in his fierce concentration he knew that Braddock was not only tiring physically, but he was also running out of ideas and that was sapping his will to continue. On more than one occasion Michael could have stepped forward and hit him hard enough to knock him back from his toe line yet he did not do so, and Braddock, who might be as thick as a first-rate's scantlings, was enough of a bruiser to sense that he was being played with and that added anger to the other dearth he had, of ideas. If the spectators were confused, Clipe was not; he knew enough, and had seen enough in his own fighting, to read the way matters were going.

'You will have him soon, Michael. Hold to your method.'

With both bruisers wheezing like prize bulls such whispered encouragement was hard to hear, but Michael was encouraged by the sentiment, even if he ignored it. He did not hold fast, he upped his pace and the power of his response, hitting harder and more often, making the man think, for he reckoned he knew better than Clipe how to play Braddock. If the man lacked brains then the notion was to confuse what few he possessed, to do what was not expected. His tempo was reflected in the power of his support, who were now screaming with blood lust, not sated by the amount already spilt, for around both men's feet what had been spots had merged by increase, foot movement and sweat into a mess that seeped into the deck.

The blow that finished matters came suddenly, but it was planned. Michael had lined up Braddock to protect one side of his body with a series of hard left-handed blows, for several minutes following that with mere feints to the right, that quickly followed by a renewed assault on the spot between rib cage and breeches that was now black with bruising, and which with each assault became increasingly painful. Three blows there, one parried, one successful, were followed by what Braddock again surmised was a feint. It was not, it was that all-out blow to the point of the jaw that O'Hagan had had in his mind from the very outset of the contest, that punch which sent a message to the top of the man's head that was lethal in its effect. And Michael got right that most necessary thing to deliver, his balance.

Tough Braddock might be, big and larded with muscle, but on the receipt of that punch he dropped like a stone.

CHAPTER SEVEN

With the shoreline in view, no great feat of navigation was required to bring HMS *Brilliant* to a rendezvous with Glaister and Farmiloe and the fishing boat they had taken in to look over the enemy, the sight of which brought everyone on deck. However, the news he brought, that a large element of the Toulon fleet was ready to weigh, did nothing for the comfort of the captain. Ralph Barclay, as he paced up and down the windward side of the quarterdeck, was torn between two alternatives. He could up his helm and head east hoping to intercept and alert his admiral – he had to assume Hotham was now on his way; or he could stay on station and keep the French in view, for the very obvious reason that, if they were to put to sea, there was no telling in which direction they would sail and that was something his commanding officer would want to know.

The latter required him to make immediate if long-range contact, and to maintain it in the face of any escorting frigates, and no doubt sloops and corvettes, which would definitely try to head him off. He would have to close at night to have any chance of maintaining his vigil, with the concomitant risk that at first light he might find that he had either lost them, or that they were close enough, both frigates and ships-of-the-line, to overwhelm him. Duty was one thing, risk to reputation another and it was that which decided him on the latter course, despite its attendant dangers. No one would condemn him for shadowing the enemy, or, should the worst happen, being taken by a superior force in an attempt to do so, and he would fight them before he would strike his colours. But if he ran east and missed Hotham, leaving him blind with an enemy fleet at sea, he would very likely face censure, for it was only a meeting of capital ships that could resolve the issue of who controlled the Mediterranean.

Challenged, he would have vehemently denied that his own personal standing in the Navy had anything to do with his choice – that he craved to be known as a bold and aggressive commander, yearned to be lauded for carrying off some stroke that would make him famous – like victory in a single ship action – the acme of achievement in his chosen profession. Nor that the previous act of running from his enemies still rankled, and was still, he was sure, to be seen in the attitude of his inferior officers. It was one of the benefits of captaincy; the decision was his, and no one on his deck had the right to question it.

He turned to face a quarterdeck full of people pretending not to keep him in the corner of their vision. The only man actually looking at him directly was the surgeon, Lutyens, but he had become so accustomed to scrutiny from that quarter that he hardly noticed. As he began to issue his instructions, it was to others that Lutyens turned, whipping out one of his little notebooks, eager to record their reactions to the news that they were to sail into an area which even to a lubber like him was clearly one of danger.

'Mr Collins, set me a course to close Toulon once more, though as far south as is consistent with the need to be able to spot their topsails once they have cleared inshore waters. Mr Glaister, I want as many bulkheads as we do not absolutely require out of the way, as well as all unnecessary furniture struck below. Make sure the gunner has enough cartridges filled for a running fight and that the small arms are ready for use with everything sharpened. I want every moment used to practise clearing for action and getting the guns run out. The time that takes has to be shaved if we are to have any chance should it come to a contest.'

The dirt on the man's face, streaked as it was, heightened the look in his pale blue eyes, one of eager anticipation at the prospect of action. Looking around Lutyens could see that expression was present in nearly every countenance, from common seaman to officer. He had seen it before, that keen anticipation of a contest, which seemed quite capable of ignoring the fact that it was of necessity bloody, and that in such an encounter men could die.

'The manger, sir?'

That, after weeks at sea and a number of Emily's dinners, was not as full as it had been. 'It will have to stay were it is for now, but if we face action what we have left must go overboard. We cannot risk the ship for a pig and a couple of goats.'

Barclay paused for a moment, to consider the next step. 'Mr Farmiloe, prepare the pinnace. Step a mast, and take aboard men to sail her, as well as stores and a water barrel which will hold enough for a week. That you will have to take ashore and fill as soon as the light begins to go. I leave it to you how you accomplish that. Once you have water aboard you are to hold to this station and keep a lookout for either the fleet or any ship sent ahead with despatches and orders.'

There was gloom in the boy's positive reply, for if there was a successful action, he would miss out, and perhaps on the rewards or any glory that would accrue.

'If your water runs low, you will have to replenish that again from the shore, and for food, you can live off the fishermen, who I am sure will be happy to sell you the contents of their cooking tubs. Take a copy of the signals for compass headings as well and keep a sharp lookout, for once we have discerned the course of the enemy, I will try to close with you and give you what I know of their intentions.'

He did not add that he would be back on this same station and facing censure if he lost them.

Below he was brusque, quite sharp in the way he told his wife that there would be no more formal dinners for a day or two, and that they would be obliged to live on the same food as the rest of the crew.

'Likewise I intend that the main cabin bulkhead is to be hinged up, and the pantry done away with, though our sleeping quarters will remain. You may wish to sort out some clothing for a few days, which should be practical. Everything that can be done without will go into the hold.'

Emily just nodded, and went into their sleeping cabin to comply.

'Shenton,' Barclay shouted, 'I want a couple of fresh shirts and a pair of clean breeches, then strike my chest below. Once that is done prepare the lady hole. Give it a good clean with fresh vinegar, and make it comfortable for my wife.'

HMS *Brilliant* was round and on her new course, and above his head Barclay could hear the running feet of the men manning the falls as Collins sent aloft sail after sail, just as he could feel the increase in the heel of the ship as that extra canvas worked on her trim. The pinnace, towed astern to keep her seams tight, for the weather was hot and dry, was being hauled in, this while Farmiloe picked his men, four at most, in case they needed to row, and took aboard biscuit and some grog, for men deprived of their daily beer would be crabbed without it, as well as some funds borrowed from the purser to purchase fish. He was back on deck again as the midshipman prepared to go over the side, into a boat that now had a mast and a furled gaff sail, with a block at the masthead to run it up and down as required.

'You have a timepiece, Mr Farmiloe?'

'I do, sir,' the boy replied, tapping his waistcoat pocket.

'Then use it, as well as the sun, to aid you in fixing your position and nurturing your stores. Always make sure you have the shore in sight at first light, but if you have not, at that time of day any drifting that has taken you off is easily corrected. Put one man to lookout to the east, for sight of the fleet, and another looking west for me. And Mr Farmiloe, keep moving. Do not be tempted to just drift, for that will do nothing to keep either you or your men sharp.'

Farmiloe wanted to ask what to do if no one came, fleet or messenger, but he reckoned that would not elicit an answer that included any instructions. Subject to the vivid imagination that went with his age he had a vision of drifting around in these waters forever, broiled by the sun, if he was not capsized by a sudden squall or taken by an enemy cruiser. Instead, he lifted his hat, tried to pretend that he was pleased by the responsibility being entrusted in him and prepared to go over the side. The voice that came then, did something to lift his mood.

'Mr Farmiloe,' called Emily Barclay, who had followed her husband on deck. 'May I wish you safety, and say that we all hope to see aboard again soon. Until then, if you have no objections, I will include you in my prayers.'

That made Farmiloe smile, puff up slightly, and produce a brave statement. 'Then I feel sure that no danger will threaten me, Mrs Barclay.'

'On your way, boy,' growled Ralph Barclay, 'and pay attention to your orders.'

'Aye, aye sir.'

The boat, on the lee side of the frigate, was bucking along lashed to the ship, so that he had to jump aboard, only saved from the indignity of ending up in the thwarts by the strong arms of Dysart, who did not wait for the nominal officer to issue orders to cast off. By the time Farmiloe had taken station on the tiller, turning it sharply to starboard, the sail was run up and the cutter was sailing away.

'Mr Glaister, when all else is completed fetch out the boarding nets and lay them along the bulwarks. I want them shipped as night falls and lookouts with muskets set at ten foot intervals on both sides of the ship. I have no notion to be taken by an enemy boarding party during the hours of darkness.'

Ralph Barclay went back to his captain's walk, feeling the warm southerly wind on his face, bracing himself against the heel of the now racing frigate, going over in his mind every scenario he could think of that might bring danger to his command, trying to foresee ways of countering them. That was when the thought came to him, that the French would not have seen the fishing boat and might not know that their state of readiness had been compromised. In his mind he formulated a plan to discomfort them; to either keep them in place or hurry them to sea before they were fully ready.

'Mr Collins, a change of course. Take us in closer to Toulon. Mr Glaister, prepare the signal flags for the message, "Enemy in sight", that followed by a Blue Peter to denote they are preparing to weigh, then repeated, and get some powder charges up to the signal gun, which we will be firing at regular intervals.'

The desire to seek an explanation was plain on the Premier's face, but he had the good sense not to ask for one, or to question whether the proposed signal would be understood. The order went out to trim the yards as the rudder brought *Brilliant* round on a more northerly course, which took her off her very best point of sailing and cut her speed.

'We just raised the tip of Mont Faron, your honour.'

The lookouts up there would have him soon, and there was no way to bluff, given that every feature of the frigate would be known to them. He anticipated that those enemy frigates would intercept again, seeking to drive him off, indeed he was somewhat surprised that they had not been set further out to sea for the purpose. Speculation about that produced several possibilities; over-confidence that they had driven him off station, or what he hoped was the cause, that they were too fearful of being caught in a single ship action by a well worked-up British opponent to close with him unless they could guarantee each other support.

'Dinner for the men as normal, Mr Glaister, the officer to take theirs at the same time. Once that is over we may fully clear for action.'

Below, Shenton was standing beside the cook, much to the man's annoyance, as he tagged the pieces of salted pork he was taking from a barrel, each required to have the mess-numbered metal tag attached. None could be given out until the captain's steward had examined it, his aim to find the leanest piece for the main cabin. If he was going to be forced to eat seamen's food, then he wanted the cut with the least gristle.

'That one,' he cried, as a slightly over-sized portion of leg came out, adding with a leer. 'And we'll want some scouse, Cookie. Can't wait to see Mrs Barclay's face when she has to pop that and a biscuit full of weevils into her ever-so delicate mouth.'

His last task was to pass over a bag filled with a mixture of suet and raisins, which would be boiled to provide a pudding. 'Don't go putting it too close to the burning wood, Cookie, it has a fair bit o' brandy mixed in.'

'And no doubt you'll be havin' more'n your share o'

that, Shenton,' moaned Devenow, a burly brute of a fellow, waiter for the day to his mess, one of the sailors forced to linger for his portion.

Shenton blew a soft raspberry. He was not cautious with Devenow, unlike most of the crew, his station as the captain's steward protection enough. The man was a bully who used his size and if necessary his fists to get what he wanted, usually a share of someone's grog ration, husbanding that to be consumed in a binge. This had seen him at the grating three times already this commission, for he was not a quiet drunk. Not that Devenow complained; he took his dozen without a murmur, and was never absent from duty for more than a couple of hours after that. He was, in many ways, one of the banes of Ralph Barclay's life, for he deeply admired his captain – in fact he had come aboard as a volunteer as soon as he heard of the commission – a feeling not reciprocated in the slightest measure.

'Goes wi' the station,' Shenton added, 'Has to be some perks to make up for being on the rough end of Barclay's tongue, day in, day out.'

'Like we ain't, brother,' growled Martin Dent, a spotty youth with a badly set broken nose, not long moved from being a marine drummer – really a ship's boy – to being a topman, one of the ship's elite. He could speak up because at his age all he would ever get from Devenow was a slap, and being a cheeky bugger he had had a rate of those in his few years, none of which had stilled his tongue. The sentiment was taken up by the rest of the people waiting with their mess kits, which manifested itself as an angry ripple of discontent.

'Belay that,' Devenow shouted, before glaring at Martin, who dared to glare back. 'I won't hear a word agin the captain. The man might be hard, but he be fair.'

That brought immediate quiet, with no one prepared

to challenge a statement they believed to be untrue, for Devenow would mark the speaker, and there would be a price to pay.

'What's Barclay about, Shenton?' demanded one of them, to lighten an atmosphere that had suddenly become tense.

'Why ain't you smoked it, matey,' hooted the steward. 'We's goin' to sail right into the port and take on the whole French fleet. Death for you, but glory and a Gazette for our beloved captain. Must be off, got to get his pistol primed and ready.'

'D'ye reckon he licks Barclay's boots?' asked Martin.

'Kisses his arse, more like, mate,' said the cook, before raising his heavy meat cleaver, and waving under the bully's nose, daring Devenow to gainsay him. 'And he's too spavined a creature to even consider the arse we all hanker after.'

Ralph Barclay did not enjoy his dinner; he found seamen's fare brought back unpleasant memories of a life spent in a midshipman's berth, that and wardrooms where he and his fellows had lacked the funds necessary for the luxury of private stores. But it had the effect of pleasing him, nonetheless, making him feel that he was at one with the men he commanded, which in turn decided him to do a touch of 'Harry in the night', to tour the ship like Shakespeare's King Henry and impart encouraging words to his crew. He was unaware that the smiles he bestowed on most of those he encountered induced feelings of deep distrust, that was until he came to Devenow.

'Is we goin' to have a fight, your honour?'

It seemed a strange question from a man who had more fights than most, usually with people he beat, though there had been one, which Barclay was not supposed to know about, who had bested him.

'Only one we can win, Devenow.'

'I have a fancy to board an enemy, capt'n.'

'Then I hope you get your wish.'

'If we do, your honour, rest easy that I will be at your right arm, an' God help the sod who tries to harm you.'

Even in the gloom of the t'ween decks, the lanterns picked up the sincere look in the man's eyes. Common seamen's fare did not extend to doing without wine, and Ralph Barclay had allowed himself several glasses more than normal to cover the taste, so that his temper was doubly mellow. Devenow's words touched him in a way they would not have done had be been strictly sober, indeed he might had told him brusquely to keep to his station, for outside young midshipmen and junior officers he had brought on in the service, he had never had what could be called a personal following, certainly not amongst the lower deck.

'Why I thank you for that, Devenow. And may I say, if you were to moderate your drinking, I daresay you might find that your station aboard ship would improve.'

'God help us,' said Coyle, the master-at-arms, still on crutches, but over-seeing the sharpening of the cutlasses and tomahawks, and close enough to hear the exchange.

Kemp, the rat-faced individual who had got himself moved to ship's corporal, and so was doing the actual grinding, replied. 'Amen to that.'

'Mr Glaister's compliments, your honour, came a voice from the gangway. 'There a sail been spotted due east, and the lookout thinks it is one o' them French frigates.'

'If it is only one, Devenow, you will get your wish.'

Back on deck, Ralph Barclay nodded to his wife, who was taking the sun with Surgeon Lutyens on the poop. He then took up a telescope and trained it in the direction indicated. In the heat of the early afternoon there was a haze in the air that made a clear sight of anything from the deck hard, but he held his station for an age until the first faint outline of the enemy vessel, a wisp of topsails and a wind blown tricolour pennant, came into view.

'*Lutine*.' He said finally, the bigger of the two he had faced before, which would mean quite a contest. 'Lookout! Any other ships in the offing?'

'None, sir.'

'Do you think he means to takes us on, sir?' asked Glaister.

'Possibly.' For once Ralph Barclay wanted to think aloud, to share his thoughts rather than husband them. He answered his First Lieutenant, but in a voice loud enough to be heard over a decent stretch of the ship. 'His task has changed, Mr Glaister. He cannot afford the luxury of us getting sight of what is at anchor in the Grande Rade. He must seek to drive us off before we get close enough to see that, unaware as he is, that we already know.'

'And us, sir?' the Premier asked, emboldened by this display of openness.

'Why, in order to carry out the plan I have in mind, we must get past him, either by fighting him or, since we have the wind, out-sailing him.'

'If we slip past him, sir, we hand him the wind.'

'That is true, Mr Glaister,' said Ralph Barclay, dropping his telescope and looking directly at his junior officer. 'Which is why I expect to fight him at some point. But I will add that I wish that point to be one of my own choosing. Mr Collins, ease the braces a fraction, I want some of the way taken off the ship, but I desire to give our friend yonder the appearance that we are sailing at our best.'

'You mean to try and avoid him, sir?' asked Collins.

'I mean to get close enough to Toulon, to the Grand Rade, to spot what ships are anchored there. Then I mean to put up our helm and run west with all speed with our signal flags flying. Our friend here, will be in our path, and as Mr Glaister has so properly pointed out he will have the weather gage, but he will struggle to tell anyone our message is a negative. We may manage to avoid him once, yet once he has the wind in his favour, I doubt we will do so twice. The notion is simple. The admiral commanding the Toulon fleet will be given something to think about, like is there a British squadron just over the horizon, enough perhaps to think twice about putting to sea.'

He did not add that the whole thing hinged on his taking or beating the *Lutine*, a message for which he could have got a cheer. That was forthcoming anyway, when he announced a tot of rum for every hand.

Those at quarters on deck were doing what had been ordered, manning the falls and easing them slightly so that the lower parts of the sails were not drawing properly. It was slight, but the increase in the wind playing on Ralph Barclay's back told him just how much speed they had lost.

'Not too much Mr Collins. Remember he has seen us before on a wind.'

'Aye, aye, sir.'

'Perhaps,' said Glaister, 'we should gather the hands, sir, while we still have time, and give a rousing speech.'

It was at that point that Ralph Barclay regretted his prior openness, realising that by relaxing his habitual silence he had raised the expectation that it would be the norm. It was with something of a tone more familiar to his premier that he snapped.

'What a strange notion, Mr Glaister. The crew will know what to do when the time comes, and if they fail in that they will answer to me. Now, I think we must complete what has gone before. Clear for action.'

CHAPTER EIGHT

'Topsails, Mr Collins, if you please.'

The orders were shouted, and the topmen began to clew up the courses out of harm's way, as well as everything forward bar the flying jib. It was not wise to go into action with all sail set, hanging low, the mainsails were prone to catch fire from either shot, or the flaming wads that were discharged with the ball leaving the enemy cannon. If such a stretch of canvas ignited, bone dry after a week without rain, it could spread to the whole ship, which meant certain destruction. As soon as they were out of harm's way, the hose from the fire engine was hauled aloft, and the crew on deck pumped hard to wet the topsails and make them less vulnerable to the same danger, though their elevation, high up on the masts, was the main protection. It had the added advantage of sending a message to his opponent, that he was preparing to fight.

There were some fine calculations for Ralph Barclay to make; he intended to get by this enemy frigate, now hull up, but that would not happen unless he could bluff his opposite number. Positions reversed he would be calculating when to wear on to the same course as *Brilliant,* so ensuring that the British ship had to fight a running battle, hoping they might decline for fear of too much damage. It would not be cowardice on the Frenchman's part, he would have done his duty, as well as the task to which he had been assigned and kept secret the state of the Toulon fleet.

Because of the sea haze, it was impossible, even for the lookout high on the foremast, to yet see into the Grand Rade, and a mere sighting in this case would not do. He needed to convince his enemies that he had learnt their strength from observation; anything else would not affect their preparations or their intention to weigh. With yards braced right round to take the wind, and sailing some twenty points free, the enemy deck was in plain view, and he paid close attention to the position they had taken up.

'I thought, Captain Barclay, that I would take a last breath of air, before going below to aid Mr Lutyens.'

Ralph Barclay spun round to face his wife, irritated that she had not asked permission to be on what was about to be a fighting platform, but then he softened at the sight of her.

'The Lady Hole has been prepared for you.'

'No, husband, I shall, as I did previously, help Mr Lutyens.'

'So be it. I would say you have a safe twenty minutes, my dear, and perhaps you should ask Mr Coyle, since he has been instructing you, to issue you some pistols.'

Emily waved towards the bows, then slipped her hand through his arm. 'I may be a novice in these matters, husband, but I do know this much. If the crew of that French ship get as far as the cockpit, I doubt if a pair of pistols will affect the outcome.'

Tempted to kiss her forehead, to make plain his own feelings, Ralph Barclay had to remind himself where he was, who was watching, and what they were sailing into. This was no time for public displays of affection. 'They will not, my dear. Though our friend ahead sees it as a possibility.'

'May I ask what you anticipate?'

'I am hoping he intends to sail by on the opposite course, and, by backing his topsails, try to get across my stern so he can rake us where we are most vulnerable. He may do so, only to find that he is trying to destroy us at long range. But he can just as easily bar our passage and force us to fight on his terms. Whatever he does, I will get beyond him.'

Easy to say, trickier to do. He needed to fully man his guns on one side, hopefully get off two salvoes to his opponent's one, but following that he had to get enough topmen aloft to let fall his mainsails, with the required hands on deck to sheet them home, this while his guns needed reloading. It was a circle impossible to square, especially against an enemy who would have other ideas, so he just decided that he had to stick to his plan and hope that it worked.

'I think I can best him, because he will have to change tack at least once before he can engage, and he will not know my aim is to get past him. The real danger is in having succeeded, thus giving the appearance of examining the French fleet, when we put up our helm to escape. In that case, as you will readily appreciate, the positions are reversed. He will be sure he has me in a bind, but I am equally sure his crew are not as well worked up as ours and that is doubly true in gunnery. I anticipate he will not be able to stand against our rate of fire even if he has the wind and that we will get past him a second time.'

'There will be casualties?'

'I fear that is inevitable, my dear, but I think more on the enemy deck than our own.'

Emily used her arm to squeeze his, and said, 'Then I pray that you are not one of them, my dear.'

That said she disengaged herself and went below, to join Lutyens, busy fiddling with the layout of his instruments, brushing the old piece of worn canvas covering his operating table, set out on a series of sea chests.

'Enemy preparing to come on to the starboard tack, sir,' cried the lookout.

'Mr Sykes, attend upon me if you please.' The burly

bosun came aft, hoping that the captain had not spotted some area in which he had been remiss. 'Mr Glaister will use the speaking trumpet, but I want that backed up by your pipes, so that there is no doubt about the orders.'

'Aye, aye, sir.'

'And Mr Sykes, the hands must move swiftly. Given we are likely to engage on our larboard side, the topmen will have to go aloft on the lee shrouds. Make sure they do not, by habit, head for the weather shrouds for if they do, half of them will fall to musket fire as they ascend. Are you happy with the arrangements so far?'

'Once the deadlights are shipped, which is being seen to now, I am, sir.'

Ralph Barclay imagined the effect of that. The thick boards across his casement windows, set to discourage boarding in what was the most vulnerable part of a fighting ship, would cut out any hint of daylight, leaving the only source of that the open gunports. Even more depressing was the fact that they could be smashed into deadly splinters that would race down the open maindeck, maiming and killing on the way, an image that nearly made him shudder. Instead he patted Sykes on the shoulder, by way of encouragement.

'Then all we can do now is pray to God that everything goes well.'

A stillness descended on the ship; everything that needed to be done in preparation was complete. Even the powder monkeys were idle, for all the guns were fully served with their cartridges, quills, flints, the gunners' powder horns full, their lanyards tested, the crews crouched and ready for the reload. Aloft and on the forecastle the marines were lined up, weapons at the ready. Ralph Barclay kept his eye on the enemy deck, relieved that once the act of changing tack was complete, the men manning the falls went back to their guns.

The two vessels approached each other, both with their cannon trained as far forward as the gunports would allow, the French captain probably aware that he would only get off one real broadside. How would he react in receipt of two? Did he know that British gunnery, through constant practice, was generally superior in rate of fire? These were all questions without answers, best not dwelt on. All Ralph Barclay knew was one fact; that it was this for which he had spent his life training, that today, though not his first sea fight, was a moment of truth, a single ship action against an enemy warship in which all the decisions made would be his. Could he lead men into an even contest and not only achieve his aim, but once he had worn to get back to sea, take on this same enemy and either take him or get free?

Suddenly that seamen's dinner, that salty pork, the scouse and the hard biscuit, not to mention the wine, did not feel so comfortable in his belly. There was a moment when, his mouth full of saliva, he thought he might be sick, and indeed a small amount of bile rose to burn his throat. But it passed as he steeled himself to give the order, which would come as soon as the gun captain furthest forward, sighting through the port, raised his hand to say he had the enemy in view. The silence, which would soon be shattered, was total; no one moved, no one spoke as the two frigates closed at a range of not much more than long musket shot. The gunner's arm shot up, and Ralph Barclay nodded to Glaister, who raised his trumpet and shouted, just as the first puff of black smoke emerged from the leading enemy ordnance.

'Fire as you bear.'

'Mark the time Mr Glaister.'

The rolling broadside erupted from both ships, the French balls screaming high as the enemy captain tried to wound a vital mast. That was not the way of the gunners of HMS *Brilliant*; their shot poured one by one into the side of the enemy, smashing bulwarks and cracking scantlings, which sent splinters flying in all directions. Kill or maim the gunners and you emasculate the ship lay behind the tactics, though few now furiously reloading could have put it in those terms. Handspikes were working too, to turn the trunnions so that they faced square on to the enemy, and Ralph Barclay, standing stoically as shot, musket balls and detached rigging whistled round his head, felt pride as the first gun on his deck fired before the last had been discharged, taking out ten foot of rail on the Frenchman, the effect of that flying wood obvious from the agonised screams which came across the intervening water.

Glaister barked out a new set of orders through the speaking trumpet, backed up by the faint whistle of the Bosun's pipes, reinforcing the message that the men should get to their sailing stations as soon as the twice discharged cannon were safely lashed off tight to the bulwarks. Above their heads there were several holes in the canvas, as well as an almighty crash as one French ball took a chunk out of the lower mainmast, thankfully only a wound, not enough to truly render it useless. The French captain must have seen what was happening, that his enemy's guns were being housed, and guessed what Ralph Barclay was up to. He put up his helm immediately and tried to use the wind to get his bows round to run inboard of his opponent and stop him dead, but the breeze, while durable, was not enough to oblige him and he found himself suddenly taken aback for he had not trimmed his yards to accommodate the manoeuvre.

All that was happening while *Brilliant*'s topmen got aloft and began to loosen the mainsails. What few men could be spared, those of the quarterdeck cannon, especially the carronades, kept firing, keeping down the heads of the enemy gunners, this while the few marines that Ralph Barclay could spare to man the mainmast cap played with musket fire of the French quarterdeck. The rest, along with the hands, had laid aside their weapons and were hauling on ropes to sheet home the mainsails, which had an effect on the ship as soon as it was achieved. HMS *Brilliant* picked up speed on the wind and took off with an inelegant shudder that strained her masts, leaving the captain to wonder if he had been too precipitate. But nothing carried way, and soon they were clear, with the enemy ship still trying to come round, still showing enough of her stern and the name *Lutine* standing out in gold, for a parting broadside. That would never answer given the increasing range.

'Mr Glaister. Note the time again. I want a report of any damage and any casualties. Then get a cask of beer up from below. The men will have a raging thirst.'

'Aye, aye sir.'

There was a crash as a lucky long shot removed a section of *Brilliant*'s taffrail, but that did not deter her captain from ascending to the poop to play his telescope on the enemy deck. It was certain that the Frenchman had suffered more than he, hardly surprising given his better rate of fire. What was obvious was that such a thing was no longer a surprise, and would be bound to affect the next phase of the action; but as of this moment, he could feel reasonably satisfied.

The cry of the foremast lookout, kept aloft throughout the action to give notice of clarity in the Rade of Toulon, ruined that, as he called down to identify another sail beyond and to the north-west, weathering Cape Sicié, its location and course, as well as the flag flying from the masthead, dashed any idea that it might be a friend instead of an enemy. Ralph Barclay was suddenly acutely aware that it was the *Poulette* and that he may well have strayed into a carefully prepared trap, while equally conscious of the fact that everyone on deck was looking at him for reassurance. The question was simple; his best chance, though a slim one, of getting out of this fix, was to wear immediately and hope that he could get clear of *Lutine* before her consort could close and make the odds insurmountable.

He could not bring himself to do it, for that would mean another attempt to avoid combat. He had to make sure his enemy knew their dispositions were discovered, so forcing himself to be calm, he said, 'We must hold our course, gentlemen, and carry out the task we set ourselves. Once that is completed we will deal with what follows.'

It was agreeably received, evidenced by the nods he got, not just from his quarterdeck officers, but from the quartermaster and his men on the wheel.

'One topman wounded by a ball in the shoulder, sir,' said Glaister, 'and another who tripped over his a cannon, and has a serious gash on his head.'

'Thank you,' Ralph Barclay replied, thinking that he had got off lightly, something that would not happen twice.

Further news came from aloft, to say that *Lutine* had altered course to the south, this with a clear view to cutting off his escape in that direction, while *Poulette* headed for the position she had just vacated. *Lutine* would not stray far, just enough to ensure that he had to fight to get clear, the task now to stop news of the state of the fleet from reaching Hotham. Again Ralph Barclay craved someone to talk to, another officer of equal rank with whom he could weigh the odds and discern, through conversation, how they could be dealt with. It mattered not that it would be a discussion about how to fight two ships, not if, for they would have to face one or the other, and with HMS *Brilliant* sailing into the wind, having handed his enemies the weather gage, they held all the cards. Once engaged, and under topsails, it would be a simple matter for the non-engaged French frigate to pile on all sail and close in, hoping to trap him between two fires.

It was not silent now. The carpenter was busy inspecting

the mainmast, and calling for battens and ropes with which to gammon it, not much in the way of adding strength, but it was best to do something rather than nothing. Sykes was directing those aloft who were attending to damaged rigging, while the quarter gunners and gun captains were fussing round their cannon, slowly reloading each in turn, for most of the crew were still on sailing duties. On the slate in front of him Ralph Barclay could see the two times that Glaister had had marked; one when action had commenced, the other when it had ceased with that ball through the taffrail, only seven minutes in all. It would have been better to destroy *Lutine,* for in that time, in theory, he could have put aboard her seven or more broadsides.

'We have the Rade in view, capt'n,' called the lookout, after some ten minutes, 'though it be misty, but I can see plain that it be full of ships.'

'Then we have done that for which we came. Mr Glaister get that signal aloft. Mr Collins, prepare to wear ship. I want a course that splits our enemies until we can see which of them can close at the greatest rate.'

HMS *Brilliant* came round sweetly, and with the sails sheeted home and the yards braced right round, they brought her as close to the wind as she would bear, her prow dissecting the sea between the Frenchmen. Ralph Barclay, with the wind in his face, looked from one to the other, trying, in that most tricky calculation of triangulation at sea, to make out who was nearest, for that was the one he must fight first.

It took time to be sure it was *Poulette,* racing to get astride his course, where she would stay, which would force him to come up on her facing broadsides, while he could reply with nothing but his bow chasers.

'Mr Glaister, confirm that the quarterdeck and forecastle guns are loaded, then bowsed tight against the ports, which will remain closed until it is essential that they be opened. I want every man who has no need to be on deck down below, and they are to return there once they have completed any task they are called on to perform and await further orders. Mr Collins, I want to come about on to the larboard tack now, but I want to keep changing so as to sow doubt in the mind of our friend yonder.'

That too was carried out smoothly, then repeated on to the starboard tack, forcing the Frenchman ahead to shorten and increase sail, this while Ralph Barclay was examining the number of gunports of the enemy frigate, which thankfully were only two more than his own. At least he had the satisfaction of having chosen the weaker of his two enemies. But what was equally obvious was that which he had hoped for was not going to be gifted to him, the notion that the man he had to face might be a fool and do something imprudent enough to allow him to get clear. The way the enemy sails were changed suggested a degree of efficiency.

'I think another drop of grog for the men might be in order. See to it.'

With that he went into what had been his cabin, and to the part of his desk which had been left by the stern casements, not lit by lanterns. From that he took the book which gave the private signal by which, on a daily code, one British warship could identify another. Then he stood up and, turning, looked along the maindeck all the way to where the manger had been. Now it was empty; the only living creatures left were men, and they were crouched round their guns.

'Shenton, a canvas sack and a roundshot to weight it, if you please.'

'Is it that bad, your honour?'

That snapped the veneer of enforced calm which Ralph Barclay had maintained, though he could not shout, given most of the crew were within earshot. 'It is not your place to question me, Shenton, but to do as I bid. Now get on with it!'

Unfazed, Shenton did as he was asked, this being a tone to which he was accustomed. Next Barclay removed the ship's books, the muster, log and those listing stores loaded, still below, and consumed. Once Shenton was returned he was sent off again to find the purser, with a whispered instruction to be discreet in telling him to gather his papers. That done, he took out the locked metal box that contained the ship's funds, the money a captain needed to purchase necessities where no agent of the Crown existed to grant him credit. These golden guineas and silver crowns, in several small leather pouches, he spread about his person, before going forward and below to talk to his wife.

The fellow who had gashed his head was sitting on Lutyens table, swathed in a great but untidy bandage, and Ralph Barclay was reminded that in the article of sewing and swaddling Lutyens was all thumbs. It was young Martin Dent who had the musket ball wound. The lad had his arm in a sling, and was grinning inanely, clearly having been in receipt of some potent spirit to facilitate the removal of the ball.

'Which shrouds did you climb, Dent?

'Sir?'

'You went up the weather shrouds did you not, your back close to the enemy sharpshooters, in spite of direct orders not to do so?' The sheepish hanging of the head was confirmation enough. 'Damn you, boy, if you were not wounded I would flog you.'

'With respect, Captain Barclay,' said Lutyens, 'It was probably habit.'

'Please keep your mind on your own concerns Mr Lutyens, and leave me to mine.' The tone of her husband's voice made Emily frown, but she got no chance to say anything because her husband took her arm and led her far enough away to talk without being overheard.

'I do not wish to unduly alarm you, my dear, but I fear we, that is the ship, is in a perilous situation.' Ralph Barclay experienced a moment of pride then; there was no reaction to his words, no gasps or fainting fits, not even a stiffening of his wife's body. He slipped her one of the pouches containing money. 'We may escape, yet if we do there will be a bill to pay that will end up on the surgeon's table. But if we do not, be assured that the enemy officers, once you have identified yourself as my wife, will show you every kindness should we be taken.'

He would like to have been certain of that, but who knew what kind of ruffian might come aboard in a Navy run by the sailors of the Revolution.

'Take this pouch and secret it about your person. It will provide you with the means to purchase some comfort if the worst happens.'

'And you, husband?

'I must be on deck, my dear, and I must, like every man aboard, hope that providence will spare me.' Seeing that she was finally showing alarm, he added quickly. 'Also, there is a very good chance we will get clear, and if I can do so without too much in the way of damage I might be able to outrun our foes. But I must first fight at least one of them to have a chance and in battle nothing is certain.'

'And if they succeed?'

The words that came out then were more bitter than the bile which had earlier half-filled his throat. 'If the case is hopeless, I must strike our colours to prevent the useless loss of life.'

With that he raised her hand and kissed it, before making his way back on deck. In doing so, he passed the huge bulk of Devenow, his face blackened from powder smoke. Just beyond him, he had a sudden thought, and turned to face him.

'I have a special task for you, Devenow. My wife is in the cockpit aiding the surgeon.'

'Then God bless her, your honour,' Devenow replied, knuckling his narrow forehead.

'We are about to take on odds of two to one and it is very likely that the enemy might try to board. If they do, and you can carry out this task, I want you to make your way to the cockpit and ensure that she is in no way molested. Will you do that?'

If the deckbeams had allowed it, Devenow would have raised himself an inch above his real height. 'I will, sir, even if I'd rather be at your shoulder.'

'You will be rendering me a better service in this, Devenow.'

CHAPTER NINE

What Ralph Barclay had feared was coming to pass. *Poulette* would do everything to stay across his bows to keep him engaged while the *Lutine*, with him fully engaged, closed for the kill. He had one hope; that having withstood the broadsides on his approach to the enemy blocking his escape, he could put up his helm and deliver such a devastating rate of fire that he could blast him out of his way. That possibility depended on what damage he suffered before he could get into a range to make a his superior gunnery really tell.

'Enemy shortening sail, your honour.'

He would have to do the same soon, and it was not just a fear of fire that prompted the need to go down to topsails. His forecourse, maincourse and the inner and outer jibs would present a juicy target to his enemy, and if they were riddled with holes, which they surely would be if he left them set too long, they would be next to useless in a stern chase and he would be gifted no time to bend on replacements.

'We will let him try the range before we do likewise.'

It was as if the *Poulette*'s commander heard him, for the side of his ship erupted, billowing smoke, and from that, arcing high in the sky, everyone of *Brilliant*'s deck could watch the black balls as they sped towards their ship. It was a shot at long range, but the man knew he had the wind to aid him, knew that even if Ralph Barclay wanted to reply with his bow chasers, that same wind would reduce the range of his cannon. The sea in front of the prow boiled as one by one the balls dropped, great spouts of water coming up to be swept over the forecastle, soaking the gun crews crouched below the bulwarks.

Glaister marked the slate and over a minute passed before the next salvo, which told the captain of the *Brilliant* nothing about the enemy rate of fire; with time to spare, and the range to close, his opposite number had no need to rush in reloading. Again the side of the French ship erupted, but this time all the shot did not fall into the sea. Elevation had been adjusted, the range had closed, and several balls hit the bows, which sent a shudder through the ship, to go with the noise of cracking wood as some of the flimsier parts of the timbers were rent asunder. There was a clang as the last to arrive struck the cathead and ricocheted into the anchor.

'Everyone off the deck with no need to be present.'

That order was slow to be obeyed, no one wanting to be seen as cowardly enough to rush, until Ralph Barclay repeated it as a snarl, leaving himself, his premier, the master, Mr Collins, the quartermaster and the two men on the wheel looking straight at what could well be perdition.

'Mr Collins, time the enemy shot, Mr Glaister, try the larboard bow chaser.'

That order was given, and the gun spoke, but the ball fell a good hundred yards short, which by Ralph Barclay's calculations meant they would have to face at least three more salvoes before they could even hope to reply, and that with little, if any effect. They came, aimed not at the bows now, but high at the rigging, trying to knock out his topsails and render the ship useless. Turning, Ralph Barclay looked at *Lutine* coming up, not quite hand over fist, for the wind did not truly favour her, but fast enough to show that escape would be nothing short of a miracle. Yet he had to believe that a miracle was possible. The enemy before him was succouring that hope by firing high at a hard-to-hit target, the masts, no more than six feet across at the widest point, where they went through the deck. The Frenchman was damaging the sails, but what Ralph Barclay had feared most was that the deck would be the target, which would have been likely to dismount his cannon, taking away what little hope he had of demolishing the Frenchman's own batteries.

Salvo after salvo whistled through the upper works, round and chain shot, holing the sails, parting ropes and sending blocks falling into the overhead nettings rigged to catch them, with Ralph Barclay well aware that he would have to order the topmen aloft soon, sending them into what could be maelstrom of shot if *Poulette* chose to fire a salvo of grape. He had no choice; he must get his courses up before they suffered any more, and following on that, he would need the rest of the crew on deck to man the falls and bring the ship round broadside on. The other problem was simple; having done that he would have little way on the ship, and that would allow *Lutine* to close much more quickly.

'Mr Collins, get the topmen ready at the head of the companionway. They are to go aloft as soon as the next salvo passes over, and tell them to be sharp, man. I do not want them up there for a second longer than is required.'

'How do we fare, sir?' asked Glaister

He was looking at the deck of *Lutine*, now close enough to see the figures by the wheel. Once she got within range she would swing round and *Brilliant* would be at the mercy of two broadsides and only able to reply to one.

The man was looking for reassurance, hoping that his commander had some notion of how to get out of this, but Ralph Barclay had no intention of lying to him. He had erred in his appreciation and actions, leaving the outcome in little doubt, for the French had outwitted him by setting *Poulette* well to the west, probably anchored behind the islands of Embiez in the next deep bay between Toulon and Marseilles, instead of just shielding the naval base. There would be no need for signals or lookouts; the booming sound of his cannon, as he trifled with *Lutine*, would do to alert her consort.

'I fear we are in the steep tub, sir. I think, Mr Glaister, you may have cause to regret not learning more French.'

'We will fight, sir?'

'Most certainly. The Royal Navy does not haul down its colours without the enemy knowing they have been in a contest. Now please go to the main battery and inform Mr Bourne of what is happening, and what we need, which is the very best efforts of his gun crews.'

'Another discharge due, sir,' said Collins, his voice low and hoarse.

The anticipated salvo screamed over their heads, one taking the top foremast yard full on and splitting it like a match ten feet from the end of the sail, only the chains holding it in place. That was followed by the yelling topmen, no doubt shouting to give themselves courage as they went aloft with the devil at their heels, up the bouncing shrouds, then stretching along the yard to haul up the main and forecourse. It was not done tidy, it did not need to be, it just had to be got out of the way. They took two salvoes while they were about their task, with one man losing his footrope to fall screaming to the deck, two others being blasted sideways to end up over the side.

'Get that fellow off the deck. All hands to man the falls, then the guns, and get a couple of hatch covers over the side to those men in the water.'

That was a forlorn hope, few sailors could swim, while the chance of landing something to keep them afloat, close enough to save them, was slim, and that was without knowing if they were wounded. Yet it was better to do what

127

he had asked just to reassure those still on deck .

'Quartermaster,' Ralph Barclay shouted, over the sound of yet another salvo, and as soon as the yards were freed. Slowly HMS *Brilliant* swung round, and while that was happening the already loaded guns were being loosed off, the gunports opened and the muzzles run out. 'Steady lads, I want a broadside and damn the timbers. You are all to fire as one on my command.'

It was an agony, waiting for HMS *Brilliant* to come round, the bowsprit swinging so slowly that Ralph Barclay feared it would never get there. He had his arm raised, this while every gun captain waited, standing well back from his piece with a long lanyard to the flintlock. He waited until the deck was level on the swell, but dropping, for what he was about to do would lift the whole ship slightly. His arm dropped and the side of the ship erupted, sending a shock wave through the timbers that the captain suspected would mightily strain the frame. It was worth the risk for the result was gratifying, as half the side of the *Poulette*, towards the stern, disintegrated. Over the water came the sound of clanging metal, that of guns dismounted and the screams that followed as the dislodged splinters did their work. Not that the men who had caused this mayhem paid any attention, they were too busy reloading, and in just over half a minute the first of Barclay's cannon began to fire once more into the smoke of their own guns, a black cloud which was billowing over them.

That was the point at which *Lutine* joined the contest, not yet with her full armament, but enough of her forward cannon to do damage, and this time they were aimed at deck level. Now it was the turn of HMS *Brilliant* to suffer from smashed bulwarks, that while the higher shot screamed across the deck at body height, cutting a pair of hands in half as it blasted apart the fire engine. *Poulette* was still firing, but not with the same venom, and once the smoke had cleared Ralph Barclay could see that the enemy quarterdeck was empty, with the wheel smashed, and not only the bulwark on their beam gone, but that on the other side as well.

'They cannot manoeuvre,' he shouted, pointing to the absence of a wheel. 'Mr Collins get some damned way on this ship.' Then to his premier. 'We must get broadside on to *Lutine* as well, otherwise she will destroy us.'

The proof of that statement came with the next salvo from that quarter, which did to *Brilliant* something similar to that which she had done to the *Poulette*, though it was the forecastle which was swept and not the quarterdeck. Two cannon forward were dismounted, their crews pulped either by the shot or their own weapon, one of which had been blasted on to its side, while the other was hanging on to its lashing by a single rope.

'Secure those cannon, get those wounded men below. Gunners below, reload and fire as you bear.'

Now it was *Lutine* on the receiving end once more, but that left *Brilliant* bows on again to what was left of *Poulette*'s main battery. There was no coordination, but the two French vessels were firing at intervals that meant the British deck was repeatedly swept, half the time by grapeshot. The trio of ships were now so close that musket fire was pouring in, not aimed, for that was impossible on a swell, but just as deadly if the man firing got lucky.

It was one of those that did for Ralph Barclay, a small ball of lead that seared across his brow, hitting enough bone to stun him. He dropped to his knees as Glaister rushed to him, the voice asking about his state like an echo in a distant chamber, as were the words to get the captain below. Two sailors, one of them Devenow, carried him to a now full cockpit, where Lutyens and his wife were working flat out to stem the flow of blood from wounds, or to stifle the cries of badly wounded men with doses of laudanum and rum. Already the tub by the surgeon's table had in it cut-off limbs.

Devenow called that the captain needed attention, and he ignored the head-shake from Lutyens, busy sawing off a man's leg. The bully sat Ralph Barclay on the edge of the operating table and insisted that he be attended to, all of this heard by the patient, but in a way that made him feel as if he was not present. There was blood in his eyes and on his tongue, and even his own voice sounded ethereal as he said, 'I must return to the deck.'

Lutyens' loblolly boy forced back his captain's head and poured neat rum down his throat, which made him gag. He was unaware of his own wife as she threw a thin strip of bandage round his head and pulled it tight, in an attempt to stem the bleeding, this while her partially recovered spouse was trying to get to his feet.

'Stay still husband, stay still!'

That voice penetrated, and he stood swaying while the bandage was applied and secured. His head felt like a ton weight, but he knew he must get back on deck, for a decision had to be made, one which fell to him as long as he could think straight, whether to strike his colours or keep fighting.

'Devenow, get me up there, even if you have to carry me.'

A strong arm was under his, and that aided him in walking, or rather staggering towards the companionway. Devenow had to practically lift him to get him up the two sets of stairways to the quarterdeck, but he did manage, and they emerged to a maelstrom of noise, death and destruction. Even through hard-to-focus eyes, Ralph Barclay could see his ship was in desperate straits, with half his guns dismounted or slewed away from the ports, bodies everywhere, the ghostly ships closing to board through the dense smoke.

The thought then was not of his ship but of his wife; if a fight started on this deck who knew where it would end, who knew what kind of undisciplined fellow would get to the cockpit first? Ralph Barclay staggered across the deck to where Glaister stood, hatless, his face blackened, and one arm hanging loose with blood dripping from his fingers, his sword in the other. The way his premier looked at him showed some appreciation of the horror he had witnessed; there was no thirst for glory in those pale eyes now, just as there was no one on what remained of the wheel. Aloft the rigging was in tatters, his topsails ragged while the mainmast above the cap was leaning, only kept in place by the backstays. The situation was hopeless, even if those gunners that could reload and fire where still doing so, the means of escape in both men and canvas was diminishing by the second.

'Strike the colours, Mr Glaister. Collins, the sack with the private signal book over the side, if you please.'

Glaister stared at him without moving, until Ralph Barclay took the sword from his hand, passed it to Devenow, and ordered him on to the poop to cut the colours down from the mizzen mast. Collins was on the side furthest from the Frenchman, dropping the weighted canvas sack into the sea.

'Cease firing,' Ralph Barclay yelled, an act which sent a searing pain through his head.

It was a feeble imitation of the sound he was normally wont to make, so feeble that it had an effect only on those closest to him. It was more the cheering from the enemy decks which told his crew that the fight was over and lost, that and the way their fire slackened. Then, apart from that cheering, there was relative silence; no more deadly balls or grapeshot, no more musket fire, and as the smoke was blown clear Ralph Barclay could see that he had acted just in time, for the deck of the *Lutine,* not more than ten feet from his own, was crowded with armed men just waiting for the ships to collide so they could board.

They did come together, the Frenchman having braced his yards round to make it possible, and the enemy crowded over, led by a fellow in a sky blue coat, but the command to cease fire had taken effect, and no one sought to challenge him. Making his way to the quarterdeck, he approached Ralph Barclay and bowed, as Devenow returned the sword to his captain's hand.

'Capitaine de Frégate Hypolite Monceau, a votre service.'

His opposite number touched the bloodstained bandage round his head. 'Captain Ralph Barclay, of His Britannic Majesties' frigate, *Brilliant.*'

'Parlez-vous Français, Capitane?'

'Non.'

'Malheureusement, je ne parle pas anglais.'

'Someone fetch Mrs Barclay.'

The two men, as well as the two crews, stood eyeing each other while they waited, the Frenchman's eyes lifting as Emily emerged onto the deck, her apron and hands covered in blood.

'Please, my dear, tell this fellow who I am, the name of the ship, and that I am surrendering my sword to avoid further bloodshed.'

As Emily spoke he held the weapon out, secretly pleased that it was Glaister's, and not his own.

The whole French fleet cheered as the trio of frigates sailed into Toulon, HMS *Brilliant* between her captors, the tricolour above the blue pennant that denoted the rank of the commanding admiral under which she sailed.

The *Poulette* was in a sorrier state than her capture, being steered by relieving tackles and commanded by *sous-officers*, its wheel and most commissioned members of the company having been swept away. If they noticed that the damage to all three was great it did nothing to temper their joy. That might have happened had they been able to see below, where they would have found that all three maindecks were now extended sickbays, that is where they were not occupied by those already dead.

Captain Monceau had been all courtesy, and it transpired he had been an officer in the old Marine Royale, though a lieutenant, not a captain. While he had insisted that the captured crew must remain below, with musket-bearing guards on the companionways, he had, before returning to his own quarterdeck, leaving a lieutenant in charge, ordered that the main cabin be put back into some semblance of order so that both Ralph Barclay and his wife could, once the wounded were treated, wash, change their clothes and make themselves presentable in some privacy. Prior to carrying out her own *toilette,* Emily cleaned and redressed her husband's wound, where a chunk of flesh had been removed from his brow just below the line of his hair.

The wardroom likewise had been restored, and in that lay Glaister with an arm broken by a musket ball and a couple of wounded midshipmen and master's mates. The cook was allowed to light his coppers so the men could be fed, and the Frenchman had shown no desire to interfere with the dispensation of their rum ration. Naturally he asked for the ship's papers, but showed neither surprise nor a hint of anger when he was informed that the private signals had been disposed of; that was a captain's duty in any navy.

Nor did he object when Ralph Barclay asked to address the men, and to talk to those wounded who could communicate. He, with Emily alongside, walked down a line of injured sailors laying on the deck, some with wounds that would heal, others maimed so they would never serve again. It was in the eyes that they saw those who would probably expire, that dull look of man prepared to give up the fight. Emily especially tried very hard to lift the spirits of those fellows in a way that her husband envied. Try as he might, his sympathy was tempered by the thought of how his actions would be received by higher authority. He had lost his ship, but to superior odds, and Britannia was inclined to make heroes of men who suffered such a defeat, seeing it as glorious. The Admiralty, however, might take a different view, and demand to know why his ship had been put at risk in the first place.

'The bill is heavy, Mr Lutyens?'

The surgeon was tired, his eyes red rimmed, for he had not stopped tending to those who needed his care. 'I will give it you in writing when I have time.'

'Captain Monceau has assured me that they have an excellent naval infirmary in the port. He will have us alongside the quay so they can be transferred with as little disturbance as possible.'

'With your permission I will go with them.'

'Granted, and my wife and I will visit as soon as they let us. Mr Sykes?'

'Sir,' replied a dispirited bosun, who was, at least, unwounded.

'When we get ashore the officers, warrants and men will be separated. I am putting you in charge of the seamen, and I have spoken to the purser and he has agreed to dispense what tobacco he has, though he must for his own sake put it against your names. That you must see to right away, before we dock, or the Frenchmen ashore will surely steal it.'

'Sir.'

'I have funds to purchase necessities, but they are

limited. It is my hope our captors will feed us without payment, but should they not do so, direct them to me. And Sykes, no man is to be allowed to volunteer to serve the enemy, no matter how bad conditions become.'

'Can I assure them of an exchange, your honour?'

'You can certainly encourage the belief that it might happen, but I think you know as well as I do, that our own Navy must have something with which to bargain.'

'Capitaine Barclay?' Ralph Barclay turned to see the lieutenant Monceau had left in charge. The man was looking at Emily, which was natural since she had to translate; what was less acceptable was the obvious delight he took in doing so. 'Would you be so good as to join me on deck, Admiral de Trogoff's barge is coming alongside, with the military commander as well, and he and his staff will want to be presented to you and your wife.'

Emily saw the pain in her husband's eye, for this was likely to be a humiliating experience, even if the French officers sought to make it as painless as possible. She took his arm and whispered in his ear.

'Remember, husband, you are a hero. You have fought hard and lost honourably. The Admiral and the other French officers, with the exception of Captain Monceau, are mere mortals.'

CHAPTER TEN

Dysart woke Farmiloe as soon as the birdsong began, picking up on the first sign of pre-dawn, eastern light, it being time to get back out to sea. The cutter was hauled up onto the beach, with a line to a pine tree trunk to make sure it remained there. It was Dysart who had insisted that staying at sea at night when, 'They couldn'a see their bluddy hands in front o' their faces,' was a daft notion, of the kind only an indifferent captain, 'Snug in his ain cabin, wi a wife tae comfort him', would have burdened them with.

Farmiloe had not assented the first night, but ten hours of darkness and fitful sleep in an open and uncomfortable boat, with one man tasked to stay awake as lookout, was obviously stupid when that same lookout could see nothing of any import unless the moon was near full and not covered by cloud. Quite apart from the aches where the wood had indented their bodies, the sole result of trying to stay on station had been to find that they had drifted miles off, and that it took two hours after dawn to get back to approximately the position from which they had been dropped off from *Brilliant,* and from which they were supposed to pick up Barclay's signal.

The advantages to being ashore were greater than just a decent night's sleep. It was possible to light a fire and cook their own food, and once they had found a source of water they could drink as much as they pleased, welcome after a broiling day at sea. If anyone local had spotted them, even if they had come to investigate, all they would observe was a group of sailors doing what such men did, for there was nothing to denote their nationality. Dysart was of the opinion that they would not care. Most folk, he asserted, were like those the world over; content to mind their own business if what seemed odd had no bearing on their existence and if they did seek to alert authority, it would be in daylight, when they would be gone from the beach.

Farmiloe woke slowly, lost in a lubricious dream of the type to which lads of his age were only too prone. That had him moving quickly, once he was upright, to relieve himself in the water lapping the shore, the gentle waves pleasant on his bare feet. By the time he was done, the rest of the men had been roused, and Dysart was using the increasing light to extinguish all trace of their presence; the now-cold ash from the fire and any impressions in the sands that spoke of human existence. When they landed again that night, it would be on a different part of the beach that edged a cliff-enclosed bay at least a mile long.

The cask of fresh water was loaded into the cutter, the mast stepped and they pushed off, sure of which course to set, that being the reverse of the previous night, looking for a fishing boat that might provide them with something with which to breakfast. There were, as usual, dozens of them out at sea, boats which had set off in darkness to get to their favourite ground and claim it for their own, each one with a permanently boiling tub of food, part of which they were happy to sell, for once they had a catch it would be replenished. After four days, and with no sight of their mother ship on the horizon to tell them if the French fleet had sailed, the atmosphere had become relaxed, almost soporific, with everyone taking a turn on the tiller, while the rest used the shade of the sail to stay out of the sun.

'Holy Christ,' cried Dysart, 'Look lively, there's a ship in the offin' an if am no mistaken it's *Firefly*.'

Farmiloe, grabbing the mast, pulled himself up and shaded his eyes, his voice, when he spoke, larded with anxiety. 'You're right, Dysart, and there's another ship with her, and we are not where we are supposed to be. Barclay will have me kissing the gunner's daughter.'

'Christ Almighty, Captain Gould doesn'a ken that, sir, so I shouldna go worryin' aboot it. All we has to do is tell him what it is we know an' he'll be cock-a-hoop. But I should get your shoes and blue coat on. Ye dinna want to be seen an a state o' undress.'

There was no sitting in the shade now; it was all hands to look dutiful, even if, with the course to close set and the mast hauled round to take the wind and hold it, there was nothing left to do. Low in the water and in a seascape dotted with fishing smacks, it took some time for the lookout on HMS *Firefly* to spot them, and that only when Farmiloe, in his blue coat and now stained breeches had stood on the gunwale to wave in a furious attempt to attract attention. Both ships backed their sails and rode on the swell as the cutter closed, the first voice they heard that of Davidge Gould calling over the side.

'Is that you Mr Farmiloe?'

'It is, sir.'

'Where is Captain Barclay?'

It was a garbled account that came out, but it was complete by the time they came alongside, not knowing how relieved was Gould, who on being told of the approach of the cutter, and seeing the midshipman in command of it, had half feared that HMS *Brilliant* might have been taken or destroyed. He was moved to near elation when told that not only was the French fleet preparing for sea, but that the youngster had a list of the ships and their armament.

'Mr Farmiloe, to my cabin at once. I must write a despatch for Lord Hood.'

'He has taken command, sir?' asked Farmiloe, before blushing at the look engendered by that statement of the obvious.

Gould wrote swiftly, listing the enemy ships from Farmiloe's notes, wondering why with this information on such a powerful fleet Ralph Barclay had not sought out the admiral to alert him. But then he reminded himself that in the time they had spent sailing together he had never quite fathomed Barclay, so it was no surprise he did not do so now, all he knew was what he would have done, while acknowledging that he had certainty of the relative proximity of the fleet.

Hood was making good progress, but it was not as swift as it could be, mainly owing to the inability of the Spanish to keep station on their British allies if the latter put on a press of sail. But with news like this, Hood, always by reputation aggressive, would almost certainly have sent ahead a couple of line-of-battle ships, the swiftest sailers, to close Toulon with all despatch, ships strong enough to look into the port and brush aside any frigate that tried to stop them. Much as he was dying to ask the boy now drinking his wine about Ralph Barclay's motives, that was a conversation he could not have with a midshipman, lest he let slip in his enquiry that he found those actions questionable.

'Mr Farmiloe, finish your wine and go below to the mids' berth. You know where that is, I trust?'

The answer was a reluctantly acknowledged yes, he and *Brilliant*'s mids having got drunk on a visit at Lisbon. Their hosts from *Firefly* had been liberal with the wine, before the entire party went ashore and caused as much mayhem as young bucks do when they are full of drink and in a foreign port. Several ladies of Lisbon had had their skirts tweaked, and those local youths who had tried to stop them had been forced to retire after a good bout of fisticuffs, carrying off those that were too knocked about to walk. It was happy memory, marred only by the punishments inflicted by their superiors for upsetting the nation's Portuguese allies.

'Get yourself some clean linen off one of my lads, and a pair of breeches that do not stink of fish. And for God's sake wash that face of yours, it is filthy.' That made Gould look really closely. 'It is time, too, that you started shaving.'

Farmiloe rubbed the soft blond down on his chin, pleased to feel the odd stiff bristle.

'You are to go aboard my consort HMS *Tormore,* and carry this despatch to Lord Hood.'

'Thank you, sir.'

Gould had thought about sending one of his own mids, but that, he reasoned, would be unfair. It was Barclay who had discovered the state of affairs, so it was only fitting that one of his youngsters should gather what credit was going for making it known to the C-in-C.

Back on deck, the cutter had been emptied and sent astern, her crew standing about the deck. Gould emerged from his cabin and gave the orders for HMS *Tormore* to close. When Farmiloe appeared twenty minutes latter he was rubbing a freshly shaved chin, and dressed in a clean shirt and stock and a fresh pair of breeches, this while ropes were being thrown from *Tormore* to haul her alongside, with Gould in deep conversation, over the bulwarks, with her commander. Farmiloe was handed the despatch, safely sealed in an oilskin pouch, with Gould peering again at his face, nodding with satisfaction to see a clean chin.

'Try and stay presentable till you meet the admiral, Mr Farmiloe, for if you turn up in his cabin as filthy as you did in mine, he'll masthead you. Now say goodbye to your men.'

Dysart was the only one who spoke, the other three just knuckling their foreheads. 'Look after yersel, laddie, which ah have tae say, nature has not geared you for.'

The smile took the sting out of the words, and Farmiloe patted him on the shoulder to show he was not offended. Then he leapt up and jumped aboard *Tormore*, which cast off immediately.

'Bosun,' Gould shouted, pointing at Farmiloe's men.' Get the ratings of these fellows. I will alter the watch and station bills to accommodate them until we make contact with their own ship.'

'An' here's me,' moaned Dysart, 'thinkin' we were goin' to get a wee bit o' ah bluddy breather.'

Captain McGann did no more than touch at Lisbon, dropping off mail for the British Resident there, picking up the return post, establishing the fact that Hood's fleet was long gone, first to Cadiz, then to Cartagena in the Mediterranean to rendezvous with the rest of the Spaniards.

Gibraltar he raised in seven day's sailing. The first sight of the great rock, and the narrow channel it controlled, not forgetting the proximity of the Spanish mainland to the north, made it easy to understand its importance. Nothing could sail in and out of the inland sea without risk from the ships based there.

Dressing in his best uniform to go ashore, hands smelling of turpentine where he had rubbed them to remove traces of tar, Pearce felt a slight sadness, for he had enjoyed the voyage and the company aboard the postal packet. Even in such a short time he had learnt a great deal about everything to do with the sailing of a ship, for McGann had undertaken no change or action with which his passenger was not involved, and he and his crew were patience personified when it came to explanation. He now knew a buntline from a clewline, and which on the *Lorne* ran to which belaying pin, a becket from a grommet, how to find his latitude, though a precise fixing of his longitude was a very hit and more likely miss affair. He understood something of sails and their functions, as well as the fact that less aloft could often produce more speed, that any sail plan was a balance of the force of the wind on the canvas it touched and the run of the sea through which they were travelling.

There were a thousand other small facts to add to what he had already learnt aboard Navy ships about what was a very complex instrument of movement, one that looked so simple from afar. McGann had talked about the sea they sailed through as though it was a living, breathing thing. He seemed to know every current from the Channel, through Biscay to the coast of Iberia, where the water was slack and when, and what tides at what time would make for a swifter passage and, just as important, those that would impede him. He talked of variable winds caused by the heat of the land and the cold of the sea, of the general irregularity of the breezes however steady they seemed, which called for constant attention to sails and course if a ship was to get the best out of it. In truth, he imparted so much, that John Pearce doubted he would remember it all.

'I wish you God speed, and the hope that providence will keep you safe.' Peering a little closer at the roly-poly captain, Pearce reckoned he saw a wetting around the eyes, and was touched. 'And I hope that you will think kindly of me and my lads.'

'Always, Mr McGann,' Pearce replied, truthfully.

They were all on deck now that the packet was moored, waiting to shake him by the hand, and Pearce had to admit that the parting made him, too, a little lachrymose. It came to him then that *Lorne* had been like a home to him, a brief one but a place that had given him that rare thing in his life, a feeling of belonging. His sea chest loaded into the boat with the containers of post, and being rowed ashore, he reflected on that, wondering if he would ever be settled, if he would ever cease to move around and one day put down roots. Given the task he had set himself, it looked unlikely that such a thing would happen in the immediate future.

The Rock of Gibraltar, the peak surrounded by a single cloud, was a crowded place, not only by its indigenous inhabitants and the Navy, but by soldiers permanently placed here for defence, a fact made obvious to Pearce in the short walk he took from the landing stage to the Port Admiral's house. The place bristled with gun emplacements and redoubts, red coats and blue. Taken from Spain in 1702, the Dons had never renounced their claim to it as their territory, and had indeed tried to retake it more than once, the last attempt just over ten years previously. Ownership had become, to them, an obsession. Looking out of the Port Admiral's window, he could see the narrow isthmus that connected the Rock with the shore, open now, but so enfiladed with cannon that it could be turned into a death trap at a moment's notice.

'Damned odd seeing old Langara sail by in company with Hood,' said the lieutenant who had been detailed to look after Pearce, this while the admiral's clerk perused his orders. 'Couldn't anchor, of course. Would never do to let a Don admiral set foot on the blessed rock. We might never shift the sod.'

'Did HMS *Leander* dock here?'

The man nodded. 'A week ago, or was it eight days, to make up her water. Captain got a cold welcome from the admiral, and a sharp command to get back to sea and catch up with Lord Hood, but he would not do that without he had made an excursion to the mainland. Ask me, they only touched to arrange a boxing bout with the army. Brought with them a fine bruiser of a fellow, a Irishman who might make his mark if he took to it proper. He was not just good, he was clever with it. The Leanders cleaned out the bullocks, who naturally backed their trooper.'

'This Irishman, did he have a name?'

'O'something or other, don't they all? Can't quite recall to be precise. Seemed a bit slow at first, but he was just biding his time. Got going once the army fellow had tired and knocked him out cold. Not that he got off light. Took him an hour to finish it and he took punishment in the process. I doubt he was much use for duty once they were back at sea.'

'You watched it?'

'The whole island did, and thank God I knew one of *Leander*'s officers, for if I had not I would have backed Braddock.'

'Who is?

'The army's man. What a lump he was, still is I suppose, and hard with it. I don't think I have ever seen a back with so many lash scars.'

'This Irishman, was he a big man, with dark curly hair, blue eyes in a square sort of head?'

'That describes him. Do you think you know the fellow?'

The calling of his name killed any reply. He turned to see the admiral's writing clerk, holding his orders. The pouch containing the despatches from Pitt was still in his pocket.

'The admiral's instructions. You are to go aboard HMS *Tartar* which is at present preparing to weigh to join Lord Hood. Since your duty is to carry despatches to him from London, the admiral would be obliged if you would undertake the same duty for him.'

Agreement was mandatory, but when he and his sea chest arrived aboard HMS *Tartar* Pearce was given some understanding of the word preparing. Certainly the frigate was about to sail, she was fully loaded with what stores she needed, but there seemed no immediacy to the notion. Indeed the officers who greeted him to the wardroom, barring one on anchor watch, were preparing to go ashore and since the new arrival had no duties, they insisted he accompany them, a night out that introduced John Pearce to the fleshpots of the Rock.

Everything about the place was designed to cater for the military, and it was hinted to Pearce that should he, later on, have any unusual proclivities, they could be satisfied, that the frigate's officers knew where to go for shows with naked ladies and bestial displays with animals.

'The Dons might be Papists,' said one, 'and cursed to suffer eternal damnation, but by damn, they are more loose than any Anglican I have ever met.'

He was quick to assert that food and drink were sufficient, and paid no special attention to the young *senoritas* that came to sing songs in Spanish at their table. Nor did he, at first, pay any attention to a row brewing behind him, that was until he heard the unmistakable, though clearly drunken voice, of Captain McGann. When he turned, it was to see the tubby little man, flushed with drink, dressed in his best finery, a velvet coat and a lace ruff, the whole under a big, feather-edged hat, swaying before an army officer whose face was as red as his coat. There was no sign of any of his crew.

'You fail to understand, sir,' McGann slurred, 'that the lady has taken a shine to my person.'

'And you, blackguard, have failed to take account of the fact that the lady you refer to is my wife.'

'A trifling distinction, sir, and no doubt an error the lady regrets.'

The lady in question was attractive certainly, but no real

beauty, although she did have her gown cut low to reveal an ample bosom that was perilously close to McGann's nose. She looked mortified and was tugging at her husband's arm to pull him away. Pearce swung round, stood up and closed with the trio, taking McGann's arm and spinning him round.

'Captain McGann, how pleased I am to see you. Pray come and join us. I am with a party of naval officers.'

'Pearce, just the fellow,' McGann cried, pulling so hard that both men now faced the beetroot-red army officer. 'Please explain to this poltroon that he is encroaching upon my preserve. That he best be off and leave me to this lady who, I might add, would, I'm sure, be most happy to have you attend our forthcoming nuptials. She's a fine-looking filly too, wouldn't you say.' A swift elbow in the ribs hurt. 'Bet you'd like to bed her yourself, you young rogue.'

'Damn...'

The redcoat got no further, as Pearce spoke in a conciliatory voice. 'Pray ignore him, sir. You can see he is seriously in drink, and I am told by his crew that this is a state he often gets into, and that he will wake on the morrow full of mortification at his behaviour.'

That was when the army officer slapped McGann hard, knocking his hat off while shouting, 'He will not, sir. If I have my way he will wake in the morning to take a lead ball in his brain.'

Pearce should have continued to play the peacemaker, should have accepted that McGann, in being struck so hard, was only getting his due, for he had been rude to the point of absurdity, and being drunk was hardly enough of an excuse. What prompted him instead to thump the army officer back, and knock him sprawling over a table he was, afterwards, at a loss to explain. Except that in the short voyage he had become close to this older man, who had even gone so far as to play the father with him. It was unfitting that a younger, fitter fellow should strike a person of McGann's age.

Suddenly all the *Tartar*'s officers were at his side, this while every redcoat in the room was reaching for some weapon with which to fight. Bottles began to fly, that followed by fists, and soon the entire tavern was in turmoil, women screaming, those singing *senoritas* at the highest pitch, as folk with no attachment to either service got involved. Pearce was in the thick of it, throwing punches right and left, painfully fending off a blow aimed with a chair leg, wondering how he had got into this when a hand on his collar dragged him back, ranks closing in front of him. He spun, fist up, to find himself looking at McGann's crew, two of whom were lifting their captain off the wooden boards.

'We lost him your honour,' shouted young Harry over the din of the fight. 'Sneaky bugger that he is.'

'Get him out of here, now,' Pearce shouted, 'before he gets himself killed.'

The Premier of the *Tartar* had detached himself from the mayhem, and was shouting at him as McGann's men complied. 'You get out of here too, Pearce, for if that bullock comes to you'll be obliged to duel with him in the morning. Get back to the ship and stay there.'

'Run away?'

'Yes, and that Mr Pearce, is an order. Now go.'

HMS *Tartar* sailed at dawn the following morning. If Mr Freemantle, the captain, who had come from his cabin to supervise the act, wondered why all of his deck officers were showing facial bruising, and were moving exceedingly stiffly to boot, he did not enquire. He merely gave the orders and they were obeyed. In the wardroom, Lieutenant John Pearce, with nothing to do in the way of duty, was enjoying a leisurely breakfast, listening to the creaking of the timbers as they began to strain against wind and tide, happy, for more than one reason, to be on his way again.

CHAPTER ELEVEN

Ralph and Emily Barclay found themselves accommodated in a comfortable three-roomed apartment in the higher reaches of the Grosse Tour de Mitre, a moated, medieval tower overlooking, from the ramparts, the Grande Rade and the inner roadstead called the Petite Rade that made Toulon a perfect naval anchorage. Slightly further off they could observe what the French called the Vieux Darse, the heavily fortified harbour large enough to support an entire fleet, that also housed dry docks, the arsenal and all the buildings from admiral's quarters to that of the lowly saw pit worker. Servants had been provided, and all their possessions and papers, including Emily's cushions and unfinished embroidery, had been brought to them and Lutyens had given Emily the means, clean bandages and some evil smelling white spirit of German extraction to keep treating her husband's now healing head wound.

His officers, midshipmen, the master and his mates, along with the fat little purser, were in the guardroom, less salubrious quarters on the ground floor, while the crew, at least those not wounded, were in the lower chambers, not dungeons exactly, but what had been storerooms two centuries earlier, when the Tour de Mitre had been of some use as a defensive bastion. They were neither damp nor cold at this time of year, but the chambers were certainly not comfortable, and as an added affliction, were much prone to invasion by vermin. Included in that was Shenton, who had complained bitterly at the denigration, as had Railton, the gunner, though on behalf of his wife, the only other woman on the ship apart from Emily Barclay. At least that had produced a result; Mrs Railton had been moved to help the surgeon. Looking past the ships readying to weigh was the infirmary, where Lutyens, with French help, was trying to nurse back to health those who had not expired in the recent action.

The bill was heavy, over thirty-five dead already, with those who cared for the survivors shaking their heads over a dozen more, all listed on a sheet of paper laying on the elegant Louis XV table alongside the report Ralph Barclay had written on the action. There were men he knew on that list, as well as names on which he had to stretch his memory to recall a face; Lemuel Hale, his coxswain, a man who had served with him for many years – even when he had no ship – who had been a reliable informant on the furtive actions of the crew, seemed like a personal loss. Ridley, one of the Bosun's mates, he could not recall ever having spoken to. The quartermaster and his men on the wheel had expired as a group while he was being attended to below. Had he been on deck, he might have gone with them, which brought, for a brief second, the thought that such a glorious death might be preferable to captivity. A midshipman had perished as well, which would occasion a sad letter to his family. There had been a sprinkling of French coves in the crew, taken from a corsair he had captured, but he had sent them off as part of a prize crew, which was just as well for them, for they would not have been greeted kindly by their fellow-countrymen if captured.

The enemy had endured a heavier cost, perhaps twice as many deceased and, of course, a corresponding number wounded, which was something. The quarterdeck of *Poulette* had suffered especially, and though not told directly, Ralph Barclay had been in receipt of enough hints to know that there were several officers wives who were now widows, and several children who would grow up without a father.

'Naturally Captain Barclay, we would ask for your parole, but once given I can see no reason why you and your wife cannot come and go as you please during daylight hours, provided you are escorted. I regret, that unless invited out for a specific purpose, you must suffer a curfew that debars you the hours of darkness.'

The speaker was Capitaine de Vaisseau, le Baron d'Imbert, a long serving and aristocratic officer of the French Navy, an English speaker who exuded both a charm and a courtesy that his British counterpart had thought gone from this country following on from the Revolution. Of medium height with a face marked by smallpox, he was not handsome, but wearing his wig, his braided uniform and his manners he was like a creature from another age. Indeed Ralph Barclay had been amazed to find such people still serving, but it seemed that Toulon, so far from Paris, had yet to be cleansed of royalist officers. The commanding admiral was le Comte de Trogoff de Keressy, and on first meeting him and his officers, all displaying the same qualities as d'Imbert, it had seemed as if the upheavals of 1789 had never happened. While it was a good thing on the whole, it had one downside; a fleet of ships commanded by men of experience, instead of those politically elevated, would be a harder opponent to face.

'You are most kind Captain d'Imbert. I will, of course, need to see to the care of my men.'

'Naturally, monsieur. As is the practice your sailors will be put to some form of labour, and thus justify their being fed. With the wounded, there is a boat available to take you across to the infirmary at any time of your choosing. I am also commanded to ask if you and your wife will consent to join Admiral le Comte de Trogoff for dinner today?'

'Delighted, sir,' replied Ralph Barclay, with an enthusiasm that was mirrored by a look of doubt on his wife's face.

'Then I will take my leave,' said the Baron. 'A carriage will be sent for you at six this evening. Should you wish for anything, please do not hesitate to ask one of the servants.'

As d'Imbert exited, Ralph Barclay spoke in a rather sly fashion. 'And to think, my dear, I was worried we might get our throats cut.'

Emily's reply was quite terse. 'It seems we will be filling our bellies instead, husband.'

'You object?'

'I wonder at the propriety. To break bread with those you have so recently been trying to kill?'

'Let us call it chivalrous, the notion, which I wonder survives, that once a battle is over, we revert from the barbaric to the civilised. Were the positions reversed, I would entertain the French officers, and I suspect, you would be happy to do so as well.'

'Forgive me, husband, I did not understand.'

'No forgiveness is required.'

'We will be visiting the infirmary?' asked Emily.

'The crew's quarters first, then the wounded.'

As Emily went to change into something more fitting, Ralph Barclay went out onto the ramparts, and stood as if he was examining the fleet before him. Really he was ruminating again on his own recent actions, most tellingly that despatch laying on the table and how it would be perceived by higher authority, his mind swaying from a positive outcome to disgrace and back again. Walking to another part he could see HMS *Brilliant* just inside the Vieux Darse, tied up to a quay by the long buildings that housed the fleet workshops. Already there were shipwrights aboard, working to repair the damage, with a heavily craned flatboat alongside taking out the damaged topmast, prior to seating home a replacement. He knew that very little harm had been done below the waterline, so it would not take these workers long to get her ready for sea. She would be renamed, of course, and he felt his heart miss a beat as he contemplated that; it was not a feeling for the ship, but for himself, for no fellow officer of his could ever see her without recognition, also remembering at the same time the name of the captain who had lost her.

They called on the officers first; Glaister with his broken arm in a sling, Lieutenant Bourne, the second, who had a bandaged head where a splinter had narrowly missed giving him a mortal wound, the youngsters quiet, having lost any temptation to lark about as they contemplated the fate of being captured seamen of low standing. Compared to the Barclay's accommodation the guardroom was a dark, cool affair, for being so low there were only barred, narrow embrasures to let in air and light. Likewise, the furnishing was plain, unlike that on the floor he had; a pine table and chairs, with straw-filled mattresses on cots ranged around the walls.

'We are all anxious to know what will become of us, sir?' asked Glaister.

'I will try to find out tonight, Mr Glaister. My wife and I are to dine with Admiral de Trogoff.'

It was a tactless thing to say, evident on the faces of those imprisoned in the room, but Ralph Barclay did not observe it.

'It is an invitation we cannot refuse, Mr Glaister,' said Emily, who did.

'I have no idea,' Barclay continued, vaguely aware of a chill in the atmosphere, 'what the arrangements are for naval prisoners, or should I say officers. Are they the same as in King Louis' time? Let us hope they are gentlemen, and that some action had occurred in which Britannia has been triumphant, for then we will soon be exchanged.'

It was nonsense and all present, except the youngsters, should know it. Many a captured officer in previous wars had spent years incarcerated in a dingy fortress far from any coast, forced to eke out an existence without funds, unless someone from home had enough to send them money to buy from their gaolers. Escape was near impossible; how could any prisoner cross a country like France, even when it was a monarchy, with its numerous customs posts, active Gendarmerie and a need for fluent French. Given the nature of the Revolution, and the suspicion it clearly generated, that must now be even more difficult.

'I must go see to the crew,' he said to his juniors. 'Believe me, you are better off than they.'

'I have set some of the men to catching the rats that are already in these chambers, and others to block off the points of entry.' Sykes was walking the Barclays around the basement, triangular storerooms that had once housed powder, grain and water enough to withstand a siege, with the captain and his wife exchanging encouraging words with a crew that sat listlessly round the walls. 'What we cannot do, Captain, is stop the scorpions, which are bad, seeing as we are sleeping on the ground.'

The thought of that, of a crawling creature which could invade at night and go where it pleased, even across the face of a sleeping individual, made Emily shudder. She would have had an even more telling reaction if Sykes had gone on to tell of the other vermin they faced; beetles, cockroaches, centipedes and the odd snake.

'Has anyone been stung?'

'No, sir.'

'I will speak to the surgeon about it and our captors. Any man suffering from a sting should be sent to the infirmary right away. I will see if I can get you some timber to knock up cots, and tubs for water to put the legs in. Nothing discourages vermin like water. At least you will be out of here during daylight hours.'

'We are to be put to labour?'

'The French will not feed you otherwise.'

There were enquiries about the food they had been given till now, which Sykes stated was adequate without being what the men were accustomed to; general health with an admonition to take advantage of the ample anti-scorbutics that were available in this warm climate to ward off any hint of scurvy. Sykes was given some funds, with strict instructions to use them sparingly, money with which to bribe the guards to provide additions to the rations they were receiving, most particularly tobacco which was disappearing at a prodigious rate.

'And set the men to work making traps that can be left to do their work when you are not present.'

'None of the men asked about their future, husband,' said Emily, when they were in the boat being rowed across the Grand Rade. 'Is that not odd?'

'You will find, among the common seamen, that they accept their fate, my dear. After all, what have they got ashore that is so much better. Besides, they too have the prospect of an exchange. If Hotham can take a French ship, he will send in a cartel to arrange it, their sailors and officers for ours.'

'And us?'

'It will need an officer of equal or superior rank.' Ralph Barclay patted his wife's hand then. 'But fear not, while we are in their care we will be treated with all courtesy, I am sure.'

* * *

'Marseilles has risen, and I am told the sentiments in the town are much the same. If there are radicals here they are not of the Jacobin faction which has taken power in Paris. There are meetings going on nightly, with most of the wealthier citizens of Toulon, and certainly the delegates to the local assembly, insisting that they should join with Marseilles and declare the whole of Provence free.'

'Who told you this, Mr Lutyens?'

They were walking through the naval hospital, past open windows which let in much air and sunlight, something *Brilliant*'s surgeon had insisted upon for his own patients, much to the bemusement of his French counterparts, who agreed, only on condition that they were closed before dusk to keep out insects who would be attracted by the lanterns. Lutyens, who had first examined and pronounced himself satisfied with the state of Barclay's wound, had waited until Emily stopped to speak to the young topman, Martin Dent, before quietly imparting this information to her husband, out of her earshot.

'The men who run this infirmary, Captain Barclay, two naval surgeons of long standing, and gentlemen with strong opinions.'

'And you believe them?'

The surprise was every evident on Lutyens' face, one that appeared fish-like when his eyes were wide and his sharp nose raised in enquiry. 'Why should I not?'

'I fear exaggeration, sir. If this sentiment to free themselves from the Parisian yoke is so strong, why have they not acted?'

Lutyens waved his hand though an open window at the crowded anchorage. 'I think the presence of several thousand sailors might have some bearing on the subject, though I am told that even there opinion is divided.'

'It only has merit if such a thing is prevalent amongst the

officers, Mr Lutyens. Even in a revolutionary navy, officers command the ships.'

'If, as you say, sir, you are dining with Admiral de Trogoff tonight, it might be an avenue of conversation worth pursuing. I, am sure like you, have no notion to remain a prisoner of the French, which we would not be if Toulon declares its detachment.'

That made Ralph Barclay stop in his tracks, for he had not followed through to the natural conclusion of what Lutyens had been saying. If the locals did cast off the revolutionary shackles, they would cease to be the enemy. They might give him back his ship, repaired, and what remained of his crew, a prospect so enticing he could hardly bring himself to believe it possible, or speak of it. An immediate problem presented itself; recalling the preening fellow who had come aboard *Brilliant* he had the sure knowledge that Admiral de Trogoff did not speak a word of English, and a conversation about what was being mooted was hardly one he could have through a third party. But Emily would be with him; would she agree to be his interrogator? The trouble was that his wife had a very proper notion of what constituted good manners, something of which she had reminded him of on more than one previous occasion. This might well fall outside that.

'I think, perhaps Mr Lutyens, it might be worthwhile if you put the same proposition to my wife, who after all speaks the language, while I continue my tour.'

'I hardly feel it is my place…'

Barclay interrupted him. 'Mr Lutyens, I doubt you have any more desire to remain in captivity than I? All I am asking you to do is touch on a subject that would be a delicate one for me to advance.'

Barclay strode off to the next cot, while Lutyens moved back to where Emily was still talking with Dent, who had said something to make her laugh, which was engaging. For a moment he held back, watching her standing in a shaft of strong light, head slightly back, the bonnet she had put on to avoid the sun tilted back to reveal a happy face, and it occurred to him that he had rarely seen her so amused in the months they had been at sea, just as it pleased him to see it now. She really was a charming creature, so charming that in another place and in other circumstances... That was a train of thought better left.

'I see Martin had been jesting with you, Mrs Barclay.'

'He has indeed, Mr Lutyens, for he has been telling me how he intends to escape disguised as a girl, and the image of that tickles me somewhat.'

'He can try when he mends, I doubt a lass with her arm in a sling, and a spotty face, would pass muster.'

'Muster, Mr Lutyens,' crowed Martin with a wide grin. 'Is you getting all nautical on us?'

'Over-exposure, disrespectful pup, to the likes of you. Now, if I may borrow Mrs Barclay, I have something to ask her.'

'Thank you for visitin' Mam. It's kindly.'

'I shall visit again Martin, and we can discuss dresses and the art of applying powder and rouge.'

'Might we walk in the gardens for a moment, Mrs Barclay?'

'The rest of your patients...?'

'Will wait a few moments, I'm sure.'

There was a bench made of logs on a sort of terrace, under a large elm tree, where recovering invalids could take the air, and it was a curious Emily Barclay who allowed herself to be directed to it and invited to sit. The heat of the sun would have been oppressive anywhere else, but there was a gentle breeze coming in off the azure Mediterranean that made the situation pleasant, which Lutyens alluded to. Seated himself, and having made that observation, he seemed content to gaze out to sea, staying silent.

'Do you regret taking this commission, Mr Lutyens?' Emily asked, removing her bonnet.

'A strange question, is it not?'

'Hardly, sir. Are we not captives of out nation's enemies?'

Lutyens smiled. 'I had no notion of being a prisoner, Mrs Barclay.'

'I think we knew each other well enough now to be on Christian name terms.' A furrow on that beautiful brow followed, as she added a telling point. 'At least when my husband is not present. He is, as you know, a man who holds to certain standards.'

'I am honoured that you think so Emily. I think you know my given name is Heinrich.'

'Just as I know that your father is the Pastor of the Lutheran Church in London, a place of worship frequented by the Royal Family.'

'How do you know this?'

'Lisbon was a place of much gossip, Heinrich.'

'His church is hardly frequented by royals,' Lutyens replied, with a defensive air. 'The Queen attends occasionally, the King rarely, and their children only when commanded to do so.'

'You have no idea how your presence aboard has excited speculation since your parentage became known.' He had a very good idea, but declined to say so. 'That someone so well-connected should serve at sea at all, never mind in such a lowly vessel as a frigate. I was wondering, now that we are where we are, with no ship, you might tell me why?'

Lutyens had no intention of telling her, even if she was the one person aboard he would have opened up to, if that was part of his purpose. But what he was about he was determined to keep to himself. He had deliberately sought out a ship like HMS *Brilliant* for its size, as being a location where the crew was of a number that he could get to know and examine, not their physical beings but the nature of their minds and the processes of their thoughts, something that would have been impossible on a fully manned ship-of-the-line. He still had his notebooks and the journal into which he had transcribed his conclusions, and how could he tell her or anyone that being taken by the French, being able to observe the effects of captivity, added more meat to his aim, to write a treatise on the life and minds of sailors, both officers and men: how they put up with a life commonly known to be harsh; what made them so eager to fight; did their nature differ at sea and on land.

The frigate had turned out to be even more than he had hoped, with pressed men aboard who had insisted they were taken up illegally, volunteers who cared little for which ship they served on and others, the late Hale and the still alive Devenow, for instance, who seemed strangely attached to Ralph Barclay, strange because he was not to the surgeon's mind a man who inspired affection. Emily Barclay had been an added bonus, as he watched a meek and uncertain young girl, well bred with a natural kindness, find her feet in a relationship with a man twice her age in a milieu so different from that to which she was accustomed. And that had made doubly interesting observation of that singular creature, a naval captain, who had the power of life and death over his crew. Close observation had shown him currents of thought and action that began to make sense of that strange breed, the men of the sea, which he would write up as a paper, one he knew, presented in the right quarters, would elevate him above the status of mere surgeon.

'Is it not common, Emily, for men to crave adventure?'

'Would it offend you if I said that I do not see you in that light?'

'I would say, my dear lady, that you would struggle to offend me, and since I have patients to see to, and your husband to satisfy as to their care, I must ask you the question that is the reason I brought you out here to this charming prospect.'

His explanation was simple and honest, which had Emily furrowing her brow again. 'I cannot see that I would have the right to withhold consent, Heinrich, for would I not be acting on behalf of every man who served under my husband, as well as he?'

'You would, of course, for if what is being talked about comes to pass they could all be free.'

CHAPTER TWELVE

HMS *Leander* had joined the fleet by the time Midshipman Farmiloe came aboard the flagship, his news occasioning an immediate conference of the senior officers, both Spanish and British, with the youngster, invited to stay for questioning, surprised at the sheer quantity of admirals. Hood's first captain, in essence the executive officer of the fleet, was Rear Admiral Sir Hyde Parker. Vice Admiral Hotham had in the same capacity another Rear Admiral of the Blue Squadron called Cosby, with the actual Rear Admiral of the Fleet, Samuel Cranston Goodall, accommodating on his ship Rear Admiral Gell, and that was without the Spaniards who, in terms of flag officers, out-numbered their allies two to one. To Farmiloe's unformed mind, as he listened to the introductions, it all seemed a tad unwieldy. There was a civilian taking notes, but it was a telling indication of where he stood in the hierarchy that the actual captain of HMS *Victory* was not invited to attend; his job was to sail the ship.

'So gentlemen, according to Captain Gould's despatch our enemy has immediately available to him some seventeen ships- of-the-line, with some thirteen in various states of refitting or repair.' Samuel Hood waited until that was translated for his Spanish counterparts, his heavy eyebrows lowered over a nose that dominated his ruddy, cratered complexion. 'Thus it seems obvious that delay is not in our interest. The French fleet will only grow stronger. My view is that we should let them sail in order that we take on and destroy them.'

Admiral Hotham spoke then, toying with an apple in his hand. 'I do not think we should be precipitate. It would not do to charge on with such flimsy evidence.'

Hood's eyebrows closed even more, and a crooked finger summoned Farmiloe forward. 'You made several casts across the bay, boy, is that correct, and reported accurately to Captain Gould, so this list of ships is comprehensive.'

Farmiloe replied more like a croaking frog than a human being, so nervous was he, with Hood admonishing him to, 'Take your time, young feller.' He acknowledged what he and Glaister had done, sailing close in a fishing boat which had seemed risky at the time, but now, related to these elevated personages, seemed tame. He added the names of ships they had been able to make out, but faltered when asked by the Spanish translator how they looked.

It was Hyde Parker, a substantial, rosy-cheeked man who looked very comfortable in his slightly corpulent state, who clarified matters. 'I think our friend is asking if they looked capable of giving battle.'

'That I could not give you an opinion on that, sir. I lack the experience.'

'Properly said, lad,' Hood interjected, his look aimed at his second-in-command. 'Properly said. We would not want anyone giving views which were based on faulty assumptions.'

A little blood suffused Hotham's cheeks, and he put the apple to his mouth to cover for what had clearly been a rebuke, but he declined to take a bite, putting it, untouched, back on the table. As he did so another civilian entered, a black-coated fellow with hands deeply stained with ink. He went to Hood and spoke quietly, words that Hood repeated to the room.

'We have just had a signal from one of our frigates, to say that a Poleacre is approaching under full sail from the north. The message is unclear, but it seems to be flying a flag of truce.' That set off a buzz of conversation in two languages, with Farmiloe wondering, and fearing, that it might mean peace. If it did there was little future for him in the Navy; advancement only came with war. 'I suggest gentlemen, that we go on deck and see what we can make of this fellow.'

One by one they trooped out, taking their hats from one of Hood's servants, until the admiral's day cabin was empty, except for Midshipman Farmiloe, agog, as he had been on entering, at the space a flag officer was allowed on a ship, even one the size of *Victory*. A day cabin, a dining room, sleeping quarters, his own privy, it was luxury indeed to a boy accustomed to crowded mids' quarters. Slowly he approached and ran his fingers over the highly polished oak of the round, paper-strewn table. Then he moved to stand behind the point from which Hood had presided over the meeting. There was devilment in his next act, to sit in the C-in-C's chair, and to see that within arm's reach, Hotham's apple was still on the table. Like most midshipmen, always hungry, the temptation was too much and he grabbed it, taking a bite out that filled his mouth with fruit and had juice running down his chin.

He then felt a shock go through his body when the voice said. 'If'n I were one of them there admirals, you would be on your way to the masthead by now.' Jumping up, Hood's chair went over, as Farmiloe exchanged looks with a check-shirted servant of an uncertain age, who was at least grinning. 'Best get on deck lad, though I'd get shot of that there apple before Hotspur Hotham sees you. He is partial to his grub, that one, more partial than he is to activity. Mind it will do more good in your gut than his.'

Farmiloe was out of the cabin in a flash, slipping past the

marine sentries. He stopped on the companionway to finish the apple, stuffing the core in his pocket. Then he went on deck, to see a raft of admirals, the captain and at least four lieutenants all looking north through extended telescopes.

'Captain Knight,' said Hood. 'Ask your lookout to identify that flag at the masthead, would you.'

The captain of HMS *Victory* did not shout himself. The order was quietly passed to a lieutenant, and it was he who called aloft. The reply that came back set off another buzz of dual-tongued speculation.

'Looks like a fleur-de-lys, your honour, the old standard of the Marine Royale.'

Which it proved to be when it came close enough to be seen from the deck, a blue flag dotted with the French royal device in gold, very obvious against the dark red sails of the Poleacre.

Hood spoke again. 'Captain Knight, a gun if you please, just in case he has not made out my flag.'

That flew at the foremast, the pennant of a Vice Admiral of the Red Squadron. The gun had an effect, the French ship altering course slightly to close the flagship, and now, on the after deck, they could see several civilians in tightly buttoned coats, with scarves tied round their heads to keep on their hats.

'Marines and your premier at the entry port, Captain Knight, please.' Then he laughed, which was a deep rumble. 'To either give these people a salute or shoot them.'

Hood led the way back down to his cabin on the maindeck, with one young and nervous midshipman, who followed because he had no idea if they were finished with him, wondering if a certain admiral would miss his apple and demand to know where it had gone. Suddenly that core in his pocket felt visible, and Farmiloe cursed himself for not getting rid of it while he had the chance.

* * *

'Marseilles is entirely in our hands, messieurs. The Jacobins have been sent packing, their infernal guillotine has been broken up, and those who support the madness in Paris have left the city on their coat tails.'

'And the reaction, Monsieur Rebequi?' asked Hood.

The Frenchman, who claimed to be a deputy to the National Assembly in the Girondist interest, spoke with enthusiastic certainty, his face showing the excitement he obviously felt, this while those who had accompanied him, and spoke no English, looked on anxiously – for he had not translated his words for their benefit – and shifted uncomfortably under the keen gaze of this clutch of Spanish and British officers. He had managed to tell the assembly that he personally was uncomfortable under a Bourbon flag – he was a Republican through and through – without in any way saying if he had voted for the death of King Louis.

'So far, Admiral, none, and I do not anticipate that there will be any. The forces the Jacobins can put against us are in disarray, an ill-disciplined rabble. More important, we have had representatives come from Toulon to say that the sentiment there is of the same nature as in Marseilles, though action is harder for there are elements of the fleet who are against revolt. Lyon is in open revolt and the right-minded are stirring in Nimes and Montauban.'

'And what, monsieur, would you have us do?'

'Land men and materiel, Admiral, and take possession of what is the major city in Provence, and is too a substantial port. We have gathered an army of ten thousand men, with the aim of marching to the aid of the Lyonnais, and we will grow stronger on the way. Stiffened with what you could provide...'

'There is nothing between you and them?' asked Hotham, as Rebequi left the rest of his sentence up in the air.

'A rabble, unfit for combat.'

'I do not have what you seek, monsieur.' Farmiloe, standing well back against a bulkhead, saw the speaker's face fall, and that was replicated in the worried looks of his companions, who read his reaction. Rebequi had about him the air of an orator, with drama in his voice and gestures, so it was easy to see the change from enthusiasm to doubt, as Hood continued. 'I have, at best, if I strip every ship in my fleet, some fifteen hundred marines, and I assume Admiral Langara to have something of the same number.'

A look at the Spanish translator brought forth a nod. 'Three thousand men are not enough to hold a city like Marseilles, regardless of how much your enemies are in disorder, and I cannot march them away from their ships and into open country. It is too dangerous.'

'Sailors?'

'Please be so good as to translate for your companions,' Hood insisted, 'they are growing increasingly concerned.' The Frenchman complied, which did nothing for the mood, if anything it deepened their gloom.

'There is also the fact that, from information we have just received, the Toulon fleet is preparing to weigh. Let us say that I agreed to partially aid you by taking charge of the port. To secure Marseilles would require me to take my ships into a situation in which they would not be able to manoeuvre, in fact one in which they could be blockaded, cut off from the sea by your country's warships and the land from the forces of the men you call Jacobins. I could not even contemplate putting such a notion to this conference.'

'Then what are we to do Admiral?'

'You must put aside any thought of going to Lyon. Instead hold as best you can with what you have, and let your enemies assault you, not the other way round. If they are, as you say, a rabble, then they will break against your defences with a greater loss than you will suffer.'

Hood looked at his fellow admirals as he continued, as if to seek their silent support. 'I, with my Spanish allies, must sail on to Toulon. If the fleet is at sea we must meet and defeat it, if not we must keep it bottled up in the harbour. Once that is achieved we can look at other possibilities.'

Rebequi protested. 'It is an opportunity not to be missed, Admiral. The whole of France could be yours.'

'I, monsieur, must first hold the whole of the Mediterranean, for I am, as you can see, a sailor.' Hood then turned to face the civilians, even if they could not understand him. 'Believe me, messieurs, if I could help you I would, but though it may not sound this way, our interests coincide with yours. The city of Marseilles, indeed the whole of southern France, can only be held if the Toulon fleet is reduced to impotence. Monsieur Rebequi, please be so good as to translate that.'

A loud cough came from a doorway, and Farmiloe craned to see that same fellow who had caught him eating the apple. Hood nodded to him and said, 'Gentlemen, a turn on deck if you please, so that my servants can set things for dinner.' In a louder voice he added, 'Which will naturally include our newly arrived guests from Marseilles.'

Hood was left alone, looking at something on the table, as Farmiloe began to edge out in the wake of the others. The voice stopped him dead. 'Mr Farmiloe?'

'Sir?'

'What the devil are you doing here?'

It was as if all his blood had suddenly decided to fill his boots. 'I was unsure if I was still required, sir.'

'You heard what I said to the Frenchman?' Farmiloe nodded, and Hood crooked a finger, adding, 'But did you understand it?'

'I think so,' Farmiloe squeaked, moving towards the table, and what he now saw was a large map showing the coast of France from the Spanish border to Italy.

Hood's next words were larded with irony. 'Then you are wiser than your years, boy, for there were flag officers in this cabin a moment ago that did not.' His finger hit the chart. 'Look here!'

Farmiloe followed his finger, as Hood outlined the wide delta of the rivers Rhône and Durance, with the city of Marseilles further down the bay, this while a raft of servants were arriving with the leaves and supports of a large dining table.

'Flat country to one side, some protection from marshes, but multiple lines of assault down the river valleys. The place is surrounded by hills but they have long crests and are some distance from the actual port. I have no faith in this ten thousand men of theirs. If the armies opposing them are rabble they cannot be much better. They may well be forced to retreat and do as I suggested, yet the defence of such a city and port would require a much larger and better trained army, which, as I pointed out to our Frenchman, I do not have. I could secure the place from the sea but to what purpose? The task of a British fleet is to fight and win at sea. Are you hungry?'

The question threw Farmiloe, as he was concentrating on a map and a problem he barely understood, terrified he would be asked a question, but not that one.

'Yes, sir.'

Hood replied with a good humoured growl. 'Never knew a mid that wasn't. Tell my steward to set a place for you. Might tickle your ambition to see the comforts an admiral enjoys.'

Another midshipman came through the open doorway between two bits of table. 'Captain Knight's compliments, sir, but HMS *Tartar* has made her number and is flying a signal to say she is carrying despatches.'

'Signal *Tartar* to close. Captain to come aboard. Mr Farmiloe, you might wish to introduce yourself to the mid's berth, but keep your ear out for the dinner drum.'

John Pearce had never seen a fleet at sea, and he had to admit that he was mightily impressed by the sight as HMS *Tartar* ran between the two columns. The towering masts and huge dun coloured sails, as well as the strict order in which they held station, actually induced in him the strangest emotion, one he recognised as a swelling of pride. In a more rational moment he would have scoffed at such a feeling, but he was, for all his scepticism, a Briton, and to see these huge leviathans actually at sea, and to have some feeling for the power they projected, was stirring.

'Lieutenant Pearce,' called Captain Freemantle, 'we have been called aboard *Victory*. Please be prepared to accompany me.'

'Sir.'

'And I would get one of the wardroom servants to secure your sea chest. You may not be staying with us much longer.'

Orders rang out to get Captain Freemantle's boat alongside, as his coxswain hurried the oarsmen to their stations. Pearce went below to collect his despatches, and to pack his own chest, taking too long about it so that a mid was sent to tell him, in a voice in which Freemantle's irony was copied, that, 'the captain was awaiting his pleasure.'

Freemantle was pacing back and forth before the open gangway, his clerk beside him carrying his muster book and logs in a sack slung over his shoulder, and his greeting was in the same vein, one which had all the other officers on deck, those who had brawled with him in Gibraltar, grinning. It was the same grin that they had displayed when, out at sea, Captain Freemantle had called Pearce to his cabin and quietly roasted him for getting his officers involved in a brawl.

'Good of you to join us, Mr Pearce', as the clerk went over the side. 'Now please lead the way into the boat.'

That made John Pearce gulp, for he knew he was no master of the art of getting into an open boat in a running sea off a moving vessel, knew that he could very easily make a complete ass of himself. But there was no alternative; he was junior, he must go first. Looking over the side, he saw that the man ropes were well secured by the stanchions fitted to the timbers, that the cutter was bobbing around on what was not even remotely a rough sea, being held steady from the ship's side by men who stood and swayed easily as the waves ran under the boat.

He called to the coxswain, 'You there, catch if you please,' and with that threw his oilskin pouch into the man's hands, for he had no notion of trying to descend with that to encumber him.

'Please feel free to take your time, Mr Pearce. Admiral Lord Hood is, as I am sure you know, all patience.'

The laughter was suppressed, but it was there. Captain Freemantle was not a shouter, but his biting sarcasm, his chief weapon of command, was more wounding. Pearce turned to face him and taking hold of the man ropes put a foot out to locate one of the battens that ran down the frigate's side, his foot waving about uncertainly until it finally made contact. He had seen people do this, men used to the act, who leant back to a point where their bodies appeared near-horizontal, men who did not need to look down every second to see where their next foot was to go. Slowly his head disappeared, but not until he heard Freemantle quip.

'Damn me, Mr Pearce, I hope you board an enemy quicker than you exit a friend.'

It was not far to the cutter, ten feet when it crested a

wave, fifteen in a trough, though it seemed a mile, and it was made doubly uncertain by the fact that the battens were wet, caked in salt, and slippery. Pearce knew he was too upright, but he lacked the confidence to ease backwards and let his arms hold him, so that it took him an age to actually get aboard. Sat in the thwarts, he saw Thomas Freemantle skip down with ease, till he took his place beside him.

'I think coxswain, now that our guest is comfortable, we may cast off.'

It was only when he was halfway across the gap between the huge bulk of HMS *Victory* and the insignificant-looking *Tartar* that he finally looked at Captain Freemantle. He saw that his jaw was set tight, and the slightly humorous look he normally wore was absent. He had heard enough in his week on the frigate to know that Lord Hood was a proper tartar himself, indeed he had been obliged to listen to endless puns of the ship's name and admiral's reputation. Odd then that he was quite relaxed, while the captain was clearly nervous.

In the great cabin, the same Lord Hood was being subjected to a moan from the only man, it was said, who dared to address him so, the same fellow who had let Farmiloe eat Hotham's apple.

'Is I to fetch another leaf from the hold or what?'

'Do be silent, Sims,' growled Hood.

The admiral's steward ignored that, his voice becoming even more crabbed. 'I has set the cook a dinner for twelve, and no sooner have I done that then you add another half dozen. Now, not content with landing me with a mid and a captain suddenly come up on the horizon as though they sniffed the grub, I am told there is two officers in the bugger's boat, not the one. That there table will need resetting for the third time. No, if'n there be anyone else a comin' let me know, an' I'll extend it.'

'One of these days, Sims, I am going to extend your neck,

which will have the added virtue of stilling your damned tongue.'

The steward exited, tetchy still, his voice fading. 'Should have stayed ashore, a man your age. Had everything, comfort of your own hearth and high office, an you goin' an chuck it all up for a cruise.'

Up above his head he could hear his dinner guests moving around, being entertained as they were in Captain Knight's cabin, sipping their pre-prandial drinks. He should have gone there with them, and left that grouchy bugger Sims to get on with his tasks. Then he smiled; the man had been with him for three decades, they knew each other inside out. Many's a time his steward had pointed out to him where he was doing wrong, something no one else, certainly not his inferior officers, seemed brave enough to contemplate. Command was a lonely station, for all the privileges. A honest voice was worth a mint, even if it did come from an untutored pest.

Marine boots crashed outside the doorway, and his clerk appeared to announce, 'Captain Freemantle, sir, and Lieutenant Pearce.'

'Captain,' Hood said, peering at Pearce, who was holding his oilskin pouch over his belly.

'The lieutenant has the despatches from Gibraltar, sir, which he had given your clerk, as well as a set which has come from Downing Street.'

'Indeed?'

'To be given in to your hands only, sir,' Pearce added. 'Mr Pitt was most insistent.'

'Then do that thing, Lieutenant,' Hood replied, as they were passed over. The drum rolled out on the quarterdeck to announce dinner, and those feet above his head began to move. 'I will read these later. You will, of course, join us for dinner.'

'Much obliged, sir,' said Freemantle, with palpable gratitude. Pearce said nothing; he was not so sure, looking at the table and the number of place settings, that an invitation was to be welcomed.

Farmiloe, shaved again, got clean linen only because the dirty shirt he had to swap was so much better than that for which he exchanged it, a well washed and worn affair that had nothing left of cloth under the armpits. The villain who had dunned him, a fellow midshipman of the same size, had at least let him black his shoes, polish his buttons and brush the salt streaks out of his coat. The breeches would just have to do, and anyway they would be under the table. He was surprised to bump into to another mid from *Brilliant*, called Toby Burns, and that was when the drum roll caught him, so he had to run up to the maindeck and the admiral's cabin. By the time he got there, half the guests were seated, and that got him a dark look from Hood, who indicated that he should take his place at the far end of the table next to the marine captain.

That he did, looking down the snow-white cloth, covered in crystal and silverware, to the other end, where sat the Marseilles civilians, the leader of whom, the fellow called Rebequi, had been given a place of honour just past the admiral's on the host's right hand. There was a lieutenant talking to those citizens, obviously put there because he knew the language, and sideways on there was something familiar about his bearing.

But it was not until he looked up the long table and their eyes met that Farmiloe felt real shock. Burns had been enough of a surprise, but now he was seeing, in a lieutenant's uniform, dining at an admiral's table, a man who only a few months before he had seen lashed to a grating.

CHAPTER THIRTEEN

Since the hour off Marseilles was the same in Toulon, the Barclays found themselves sitting down for dinner at the same time as those aboard HMS *Victory*, one either side of Contre-Admiral le Comte de Trogoff, albeit ashore and in a well appointed dining room at the quayside chateau that he used as his headquarters. The windows were shuttered to keep out the heat of the late afternoon sun but there was still sufficient light to sparkle off the plate and crystal glasses, as well as illuminate the dark portraits of previous incumbents studded around the walls. De Trogoff's junior admiral, St Julien, was present, as well as numerous captains and marine officers. The difference from the meal happening at sea was the presence of ladies, not least Emily Barclay, dressed in her most becoming jade gown, her auburn hair piled high and held by a matching silk band. In the company of gallant French officers she had attracted a great deal of admiration, in all of which she took pleasure, much to the chagrin of her husband and those naval wives and mistresses who felt neglected. Ralph Barclay was doubly cross that he could see the attentiveness, but could only guess at what was being said in the way of compliments.

Admiral de Trogoff, in his powdered wig and flabby, florid countenance, was too mature and rotund to make for much of a suitor, not that such impediments debarred him from the attempt, for he kissed Emily's hand with a lavish, almost slavering courtesy. His second-in-command was a different kettle of fish altogether and Ralph Barclay examined him closely. Rear-Admiral Etienne St Julien was a darkly handsome cove with shiny, carefully curled hair worn in the latest revolutionary fashion, and he was quite unabashed in using his seniority to discourage any other officer who wished to pay court to Emily Barclay in the time before they actually sat down at table, seemingly equally adept at ignoring the furious looks he was getting from the lady who had accompanied him.

Decency and language had obliged the host to place Captain d'Imbert on Ralph Barclay's left, which was just as well, given that de Trogoff had little inclination to speak with him, more concerned to stop St Julien monopolising Emily to his right. St Julien's paramour, on the far side of her escort, had no choice but to talk to her other neighbour, since her man was likewise engaged.

'Your countrymen seem to have a deep interest in the opinions of my wife, monsieur.' If d'Imbert picked up the pique in Ralph Barclay's tone he did not respond to it, smiling as though such a thing was natural, which to him of course, was the case; it was French gentleman's duty to pay court to beauty. 'I fear an English flag officer would feel an obligation to converse equally with both his guests, rather than just one.'

'I would take it as a compliment were I in your position, Captain Barclay.'

'Would you indeed?'

'It is mere gallantry, and of course rivalry, and I am obliged to add that the subject warrants the attention.' The smile disappeared from his disease-scarred face. 'How I wish it was ever the case, but I fear our pair of admirals would compete over a used dog bone.'

Earlier conversations had established that le Baron

d'Imbert was the senior captain in the fleet, a man who would have been an admiral himself by now if the Ministry of Marine in Paris was not overseen by Jacobins. Another officer of the old Marine Royale, he came from that strata of French society which had seen it as *de rigueur* to be competent in English, something he had perfected when serving as a young captain in the American Revolutionary War, so that his voice had in it the twang of the old colonies.

'They do not see eye to eye?' Ralph Barclay asked.

D'Imbert smiled. 'I believe that is what an Englishman would call understatement. I doubt they could agree on the hour if called upon to do so.'

Ralph Barclay had a glass of wine halfway to his mouth, but it stopped there, for this hinted at proof of what Lutyens had said at the infirmary. 'Would you feel it impertinent of me to enquire as to some of those differences?'

'Not at all, Captain,' d'Imbert replied, with a bitter tone. 'Why be discrete about that which is common gossip in the markets and on the fish quay. Our friend St Julien yonder is a staunch republican, a committed supporter of the Revolution, a Jacobin and a creature of Paris, eager to get the fleet to sea and meet an enemy he suspects is on its way from England. Admiral de Trogoff, on the other hand, sees the fleet as a weapon to be preserved, that to lose it would be a disaster, and in contrast to St Julien, he has a conscience about his oath to his late sovereign as well as a deep distrust of those now running the country.'

'Is he a royalist, then?'

'That might be too deep an emotion for a man not given to such definition. Let us just say that he is uncomfortable serving those who presently hold power.'

'So he does not hanker after a restoration?'

'If I understand the word hanker correctly, which I admit I may not, then it describes his attitude very well. It does not, after all, suggest any sense of real engagement. But in his defence it needs to be pointed out the consequences of open disagreement with Paris would mean a great deal more than merely being superseded. He could lose his head.'

'I must ask you Captain d'Imbert, what your own feelings are?'

'Let us say that I, like most of my fellow officers, prefer order to chaos…'

'Captain Barclay,' Emily called across de Trogoff, producing an unwelcome distraction to which her husband nevertheless had to respond. 'Admiral St Julien has invited me to take a carriage ride with him into the hills outside the town. He says there are fields of lavender that stretch for miles, which I may pick to my heart's content.'

Her husband looked past his wife at the coiffed St Julien, wet-lipped and smiling, his hooded eyes quite unabashed in the way he held the Englishman's gaze. Ralph Barclay smiled at him, and touched the white bandage on his head before replying, in a gesture designed to ensure this popinjay knew he was a fighter. 'Tell the Admiral, my dear, that *we* would be delighted.'

The emphasis was enough to make Emily blush slightly, and she sounded hurt. 'I do hope you did not think I would go with him alone?'

'Not for a moment, Mrs Barclay, but I suspect that the Admiral would not object if you did.' Then he turned to d'Imbert and said, not without irritation, 'Gallantry, you say?'

'I fear the Revolution has destroyed more than the ancient monarchy of France. Manners have suffered as well.'

Ralph Barclay was not a patient man, never had been, and that knowing look from St Julien made his next question a sharp one. 'What support does the junior Admiral have?'

Captain d'Imbert hesitated then, for it was obvious that to

reply to such a direct enquiry was to commit an indiscretion much greater than anything he had said hitherto. The truth of that was in the keen look on Ralph Barclay's face and the Frenchman toyed with his glass of wine while he ruminated on the consequences, with his fellow guest holding his breath for what seemed an age.

'It would be impossible to be precise. It depends on how many of the sailors would follow their officers.'

'The officers then, would back Admiral de Trogoff?'

'Let us just say that their opinions are likely to coincide.'

'The warrants?' The look of incomprehension d'Imbert gave him then made him add, 'The ship's standing officers. The masters, gunners, bosuns and the like. You know as well as I do that on any warship they are the men, the steady types, that the crew will listen to. If a drastic course of action is proposed you cannot carry the crews without you carry such people.'

'I would say only this, Captain Barclay. Those who are true seamen, and have served for a time, will not follow St Julien. But you must understand, the fleet has been expanded, and those brought in by the needs of war are not of the same calibre.'

'Capitaine Barclay,' said Admiral de Trogoff, 'Pardonnez-moi...'

The beneficiary of what came next had to wait until d'Imbert translated words that were full of apology for ignoring his guest of honour.

John Pearce sat in idle contemplation as Lord Hood read the private despatches, that followed by the letter from Pitt, recalling the look he had exchanged with the young, fair-haired midshipman, wondering if he had shown any shock to match that which he had observed. He hoped not, for in his imagination he had, many times, conjured up a vision of meeting those who would recall him as a pressed landsman. That Farmiloe would do that he did not doubt; the boy had been with Barclay the night he had been forcibly taken up, so his name was imprinted on Pearce's mind, and it was not one to conjure up kind thoughts.

'Are you privy to what is in these papers. Lieutenant?'

'No, sir, except that Mr Pitt told me some of what he intended to write regarding my needs, based upon submissions I made to him.'

'About your being pressed?'

'That, and other things.'

'He makes much of the mode of your elevation to your present rank, and the reason?'

'If he included that, I was not aware of it.'

'I would have objected in the strongest terms had I been available to be consulted. The granting of commissions is the prerogative of those who run the Navy.'

'Mr Pitt seemed anxious not to upset the King.'

Hood nearly snarled his reply to that. 'It does sovereigns good to sometimes be disappointed.' There was a moment when he looked as though he was going to quote a few examples, but the annoyance cleared from both his face and his voice. 'Let us concentrate on the matter of your alleged impressment for now. I would wish to hear what happened, in your own words.'

Rehearsed so many times, they did not sound half as convincing spoken as they had in his head, and he left out the fact that he was running from a King's Bench Warrant at the time and had only ended up in the Pelican to avoid that pursuit, for mention of his father to a political admiral like Hood would not aid his cause. Instead he emphasised the fact that pressing men for sea service was illegal in the Liberties of the Savoy, in which the Pelican Tavern was located.

'I will not enquire as to why you were in such a place.'

In saying that, Hood was making it plain what he knew; that the Liberties were a part of London where those in fear of arrest for debt or a minor crime took refuge, a few streets betwixt the River Thames and the Strand, part of the grounds of the old Savoy Palace, from which bailiffs and tipstaffs were banned.

Pearce nodded towards the open letter on his desk. 'I did not reside there, my presence on that night was pure bad luck. It was the same for one of my friends, but two of them did live there, as well as an old fellow, now dead as a direct consequence of being taken up. Whatever reason they had to be in the Liberties does not detract from the fact that they were illegally pressed.'

'The truth of that is yet to be decided.'

'Not in my mind!'

The response was too sharp, too fierce, and that showed in the glowering look with which it was greeted. 'I think you will find, young man, that speaking to me in that tone will not do anything to aid your submission.'

Pearce made sure of a more emollient pitch, when he replied. 'Forgive me, sir, but I hope you will appreciate how the event still rankles. And if you wish for the truth of what I say, you have a midshipman aboard, a member of HMS *Brilliant*'s crew, who was there on that very night, and took part in the operation.'

'Farmiloe?' Pearce nodded and Hood called out for someone to fetch the youngster, after which he shuffled the letters, then said. 'While we are waiting, the action with the *Valmy*. I sailed before that happened. Tell me about it.'

Pearce reckoned this to be no time for modesty, but he managed, without sounding vain, to tell of the action, of how he had found himself forced to make decisions, of those he had made and the result. As Hood listened, Pearce had

180

the impression he was not entirely concentrating on what he was hearing, that he was thinking of other matters, which was unusual in a naval officer hearing a tale of battle.

'The result you know, sir. I was whisked off to Windsor, the King was excitable, and insisted on my promotion. Lord Chatham objected, his brother did not. I, for one, have no idea if it was deserved, only that it exists.'

'I saw you in deep conversation with those Frenchmen from Marseilles.'

Slightly thrown by the change of subject, Pearce took a second to respond. 'They were worried for their lives, sir. Monsieur Rebequi does not enjoy their full confidence, and they are not as one in their views. He, for instance, is a member of the faction called the Gironde…'

'Please don't confuse me, Pearce. Girondes, Feuillants, Jacobins. To me these Frenchmen, and their damned factions, are all as one.'

'Like Whigs and Tories?'

'Nothing like, as well you know, young man.'

Pearce could not resist baiting him, thinking his fellow-countrymen, this admiral included, pious in their condemnation of the French. 'It took them some time, I grant you, to get round to beheading a king, but you cannot deny that we in Britain, in chopping the head off the first King Charles, set them a precedent of near a century and a half.'

Hood would not be drawn into a discussion about the judicial murder of monarchs, British Stuarts or French Bourbons. 'I believe we were talking about your dinner companions?'

'Most would call themselves Republicans, but with, I think, no great depth of conviction. Some even mentioned a declaration for the brother of the late King Louis as a way to ward off the revenge of Paris. As I say, they are worried.'

That only got a raised eyebrow. 'They have every right to be, Pearce, and it is of some regret that I can do nothing to aid them. Let us hope the Revolutionary Army is in as much disarray as they claim. You speak good French, obviously.'

'I lived in Paris for over two years, and my father, naturally, as a Scot, having a warm feeling towards an old ally, made sure I had a grounding in the language before that.'

The big eyebrows went up. 'Indeed. Might I enquire what took you there?'

It was with an air of defiance that Pearce answered. 'My father took me there!'

'Pearce,' Hood said, his look uncertain, clearly seeking to make a connection in his mind. 'Paris?' That he did so was obvious by the sharp nod that followed. What was strange was the fact that he did not say anything more.

'Mr Farmiloe, sir,' said his secretary.

'Show the boy in.'

Expecting more questions about Toulon, Farmiloe's heart sank when he saw Pearce sitting at the admiral's table, and the look the man gave him did nothing to ease his disquiet. If he had been a discomforting presence aboard HMS *Brilliant*, he was a damn sight more so now. In the intervening hour, he had had plenty of time to recall everything he knew about the fellow and the trouble he had caused, though they had had little direct contact.

'Mr Farmiloe,' said Hood. 'This gentleman claims that he was illegally pressed into the Navy. He also says that you were present at the time. I wonder if you would care to shed any light on that?'

A boy would have to be deaf, dumb and blind to be unaware that what Barclay had done was not officially permitted. It had been a topic of discussion in the wardroom and that had filtered down to the gunroom, with much ribbing aimed at him about being hung, drawn and quartered for being part of it. Well aware that the blame for transgressions had a way of spreading, the other topic of conversation had been the response to an accusation, so it was without hesitation that Farmiloe replied.

'I was with Captain Barclay, sir, and obeying his orders.'

'So you do not deny that Mr Pearce here was pressed?'

'No, sir.' Farmiloe paused then, trying to remember after all these months what it was Barclay had actually said on that night. He could recall the captain being in a foul temper, but then that was not unusual. 'We were short on our complement and had orders to weigh. Captain Barclay made it plain that we needed hands, and that failure to get any would seriously compromise the ability of our ship to function. With the extra hands we were able to depart Sheerness the next morning.'

'You are not aware that I saw Captain Barclay the very day this impressment is alleged to have taken place?'

It was with genuine shock that Farmiloe responded. 'No, sir.' Pearce merely looked inquisitive at the use of the word alleged.

'The location of this was?' Hood enquired.

'The Thames, sir, above Blackfriars Bridge, where we expected to find at least some of those we took up were bred to the sea.'

'But not all?'

'There was no time to enquire, sir. Captain Barclay insisted we act quickly and take whosoever we could lay our hands on, albeit they were to be of the right age and fit enough to serve.'

'Tell me, Mr Farmiloe,' said Pearce, earning himself a dark look from Hood, who clearly felt he had no business interfering. 'Do you know anything about the Liberties of the Savoy?'

'No,' Farmiloe replied, unable to add a "sir" to that.

'They are in the part of London from which I was pressed.'

'I don't know London. That night was the only time I have been there.'

'So you had no idea,' demanded Hood, taking back the interrogation, 'that the place from which you were taking these men had a protection under the auspices of the Duchy of Lancaster?'

'No, sir, I did not.'

Again Pearce cut in. 'But you found out subsequently, I suspect?'

Hood barked at him this time, his heavy eyebrows nearly joined above his nose. 'Mr Pearce, please be so good as to leave this questioning to me. It makes no odds what people knew subsequently, all that matters is what they knew at the time.'

Farmiloe was looking at the deckbeams above his head, and Pearce, examining the boy, suddenly felt a tinge of sympathy for him. He was a midshipman; if his captain told him to do something there was no way a lad like this would question his orders. The real culprit was not present, and it was cruel to make Farmiloe suffer for the sins of Ralph Barclay.

'Mr Farmiloe, I apologise to you. But please understand that the memory of that night, to me, is something that I cannot recall without anger. It is then hardly surprising that it can be misdirected.'

'Thank you,' Farmiloe said, genuinely relieved, for he was certain he was going to carry the kid for that night, certain that he would be sent home in disgrace.

'Thank you, Mr Farmiloe,' said Hood, going back to the letters on his desk. 'That will be all.'

There was silence for a while, as he re-read some of Pitt's

letter, his brow furrowing in a way that implied some of what he was reading was unpleasant. 'So, Mr Pearce, you are in need of a place?'

'I am in need of a solution to the problem we have just been discussing, sir. If I, and my companions already named, were illegally pressed, and are anxious to get release from service at sea, then you are in a position to grant that wish.'

'I can do nothing until I have questioned Captain Barclay.'

'Who is where?'

'Off Toulon.'

'Which is where the fleet is headed, is it not?'

Hood sat back in his chair, and when he spoke his voice was flat, though the words he used were as pointed as they could be. 'It seems to me, young man, that you have a very unfortunate manner. I think my rank entitles me to a little more in the way of polite address.'

'That would only be because you are used to the company of naval officers.'

That was nothing short of damned cheek, but Hood did not respond. His voice remained even. 'Which you have been commissioned as. Whether such a thing is right or wrong it is nevertheless true.'

'One of the advantages of not seeking advancement, Lord Hood, is the fact that I can talk as I wish.'

Hood sat forward then, and lifted Pitt's letter. 'It says here that Mr Pitt would be most obliged if I would consider you for a place. You may or may not know that I am part of his government, appointed to my naval office by the very same man who tells me he has a commitment to you. He makes it plain how much meeting that means to him, which makes his request a hard one to deny.'

Pearce nearly blurted out the truth; that such a thing had only been added as a desperate attempt to make sure he got to where he was now, that if Hood acted as he should then such a request had no relevance. What stopped him he did not know, only that the admiral's attitude perplexed him, and that it was better to keep to his chest what cards he had to play with, rather than squander them.

'So,' Hood continued, 'I think in those circumstances a little less arrogance would be in your interest.'

'Can I ask about your meeting with Captain Barclay prior to my being pressed?'

Hood smiled. 'No, Lieutenant Pearce, you may not. Now please be so good as to depart, as I have more pressing business to attend to, dealing with our friends from Marseilles.' Then he added, 'I apologise for the play on words, it was unintentional.'

CHAPTER FOURTEEN

Midshipman Toby Burns was sitting on the south-facing part of the mainmast cap, digesting his dinner. He liked it up here when the flagship was sailing on a steady wind, with no one needing to trim sails and only the change of the lookouts plus the odd ship's boy skylarking to disturb his peace. Most of his contemporaries liked to stay below, snug in their berth. Since he had never liked it there, nor had much regard for the company either on this ship or HMS *Brilliant*, he stayed out of the place as much as he could. The sun was shining, he was delightfully warm, with a welcome breeze this far aloft to ensure he was not baking in the late afternoon heat.

Aboard as a supernumerary, being carried as a passenger until he rejoined his own ship, he had no duties except to daily attend the schoolmaster's lessons, something which the Premier of HMS *Victory* had insisted on as a cure for outright idleness. Earlier hints that he might undertake some duties, which would have relieved some of the ship's designated midshipmen, had been politely declined, an attitude which would have produced an ill-reaction were it not that the fellow concerned was something of a hero.

The unexpected arrival of Midshipman Farmiloe had no seeming effect on that status, although to see him aboard the flagship was a shock. But it had served one purpose for, though there had been caution – he and Farmiloe had not been close – there had been no outright reserve in the greeting, which confirmed how he was seen aboard the frigate; in short, he was still a hero in the places that mattered, the gunroom, wardroom and captain's cabin. At one time he had worried that one or two of the common seamen might have a different opinion, but then he had reasoned that no one who mattered cared what they thought, or would listen to what they said.

It was therefore a great shock to look down at the quarterdeck, and realise that the fellow who had just emerged from the after companionway, and in raising his hat to the officer of the watch had revealed his face, was the one man who could blow that undeserved reputation out of the water and damn him as a useless coward. What the hell was Pearce doing in the uniform of a lieutenant, and clearly being greeted as such?

Burns got himself behind the mainmast double-quick, so that when John Pearce looked up all he saw was the flash of a disappearing blue coat and white ducks. Given permission to walk the forecastle, he made his way along the gangway that ran alongside the Spar Deck, to where he could contemplate in peace what had happened in the admiral's cabin, not least the suspicion that despite the plain fact that he had established the illegality of Barclay's actions, and the men he wanted released were part of the fleet, Hood had seemed disinclined to do anything about it. Above his head, Toby Burns slipped back to the front of the mainmast, well hidden by the thick oak, desperately trying to think what to do.

It was not just his status as a hero that was at risk; the way he had left Pearce and his friends had been seen by them as a stroke of downright duplicity, even if he was obeying his captain's precise orders at the time. Pearce had made it plain that he would exact revenge for that, and in the imagination of Toby Burns that took many forms, none of them pleasant. Suddenly that sun was not so warm and the boy shivered with fear. Seeing where his nemesis had gone, he made his way back to the deck by the shrouds, to use a backstay might attract attention, his mind concentrating on where he could hide. HMS *Victory* was a large and crowded vessel, yet he knew, long before he got back to it, that the safest place for him was in that part of the ship he liked least, the midshipmen's berth.

'Farmiloe!' he whispered urgently, for they were not alone. 'You'll never guess who I have just seen.'

The other mid, stripped to the waist, did not look up as he ham-fistedly tried to repair a hole in the near-threadbare shirt he had exchanged prior to the admiral's dinner. 'Pearce.'

'The very fellow. What the devil is he doing aboard?'

'More to the point, what is he doing outranking us, Burns?'

The other midshipman, having pricked a finger for the third time, threw the shirt to one side and finally looked into the anxious face of Burns, wondering if any more spots had erupted since he had last seen him a couple of hours before. They had never really got on, although the acquaintance had not been of a long duration, weeks rather than months, for Burns had seemed a bit of a milksop aboard *Brilliant*, always moaning, dodging his duties and rather unfitted for a life at sea, slow to learn anything and even slower to apply what he had garnered. There was a certain amount of envy too; the fact that Captain Barclay, whose wife was the milksop's aunt, had sent him away with a prize and a positive despatch that would do his future career no harm. This had not endeared Burns to any of the other mids or master's mates aboard the frigate, in what was seen as a clear case of nepotism.

'I fear he has come to see your uncle put in irons,' Farmiloe added.

'My uncle?'

'Captain Barclay.'

Toby Burns was well aware of how his departure had been seen by his contemporaries, for he had been the youngest mid aboard; they had seen as corrupt what he had reckoned to be a reward for nearly losing his life, and if not that, at least a release from the misery of service. Going back to serve on HMS *Brilliant* was not something to which he was looking forward – service life was not as he had imagined it to be before enlisting – and he had tried to wriggle out of doing so with various claims of illness while at home. But the reasons that had seen him leaving home the first time, when he still harboured romantic notions of a naval career, still applied. His parents, having seen to his elder brothers, did not have the means to underwrite a career that went with their station in life. The Navy took aboard and educated its future officers for free, therefore Toby, the youngest in the family, must make his way in that profession.

'He is not really a proper uncle, Farmiloe, I have told you that a dozen times.'

'I fail to see how he is not, when he is wedded to your Aunt Emily, who is cousin to your father, though only the Good Lord knows how such a match came about.'

Toby Burns knew why; his grandparent's substantial house was entailed to the distant Barclay relatives through a previous connection. Emily marrying the captain had secured tenure for the whole family, not least his own mother and father, who, by living with those relatives, could keep up the appearance of some social standing with little or no income.

'What do you mean, putting Captain Barclay in irons?'

Farmiloe told him what had happened in Hood's cabin, but he did not open up, did not trust Burns enough to say that he had known very well that what they were about was illegal, and that had nothing to do with things called Liberties. The laws on impressment were strict, only men bred to the sea were to be taken up. It made no odds that the law was observed more in the breech, breaking it and being had up was serious, and he feared that he might be caught in the backwash of Barclay's actions.

'Anyway, Burns, you were with him when you went ashore, so you must have a better idea than I of how he got his rank.'

'I didn't go ashore with him or the others. They were pressed in soundings.' Farmiloe looked at him then with marked curiosity, as Burns went a deep red, which made the numerous spots on his face flare. 'I had orders from Captain Barclay that if such a thing were to occur, I was not to interfere.'

'Pearce was pressed again?'

'Have I not just said so?'

'Then his being a lieutenant is doubly mysterious.'

'I must stay out of his way, Farmiloe. I fear he will not remember me kindly.'

There was a terrible temptation for Farmiloe to say something like, 'no one ever will, mate,' but he bit his tongue. 'Don't look to me for aid, Burns. I don't think he has any regard for me either. You seem to forget I was there the first time he was pressed.'

Sick of traversing the forecastle, tired of gnawing at his problems, he made his way down to the wardroom, entering a place so capacious it made the accommodation of a frigate look like a hutch. With eight lieutenants, the usual number of warrants and three marine officers it needed to be substantial, though it was clearly not roomy enough. The table set across the stern windows was near full, and as he entered, heads turned, and all eyes were upon him in examination, that was until one officer spoke to an open door at the very stern, which brought forth another.

'Mr Pearce, is it not?' The nod got the introduction. 'Ingolby, first of *Victory*. Allow me to welcome you to our quarters.'

'Thank you.'

'You will, of course, realise that we are cramped, so I have had your dunnage sent down to the orlop deck, where there is room in the sick-bay to accommodate you. That is for sleeping only, of course, you are at liberty to use this place as you wish.'

'That is very kind of you.'

'Can I offer you some refreshment?'

'I think Lord Hood has seen to that, Mr Ingolby.'

'Quite.' Ingolby paused, looking not embarrassed exactly, but uncomfortable. 'I fear, sir, that you will be inundated with questions regarding the *Valmy*, since your reputation precedes you.'

About to ask how, Pearce stopped; even he knew that on a ship it was near-impossible to keep anything secret. He had had the same problem aboard *Tartar*, the need to recount every detail of the action to satisfy the insatiable curiosity of naval officers who dreamed themselves of such an exploit.

'I have impressed upon the wardroom not to hound you, for having received a *Gazette* with the mails, every one is agog for a first-hand view, though it does not exactly chime with what we have heard about you.'

'Much praise, I suspect, of Captain Marchand?'

'Why yes.' Ingolby replied, before smiling, as though he guessed what Pearce was driving at; that the *Gazette* would have been taken from Marchand's despatch and he was not a man to be modest or even truthful. 'I have suggested perhaps that we wait until supper, where I hope you will join us for cheese on toasted biscuit and some wine. Perhaps, until then, a tour of the ship?'

'Thank you.'

The master allocated him one of his mates, he, in turn, seeking out the warranted officers, all men of some age and experience, who were only too happy to tell all. Pearce treated them with respect, for to have their posts on this vessel made them very senior people indeed. These were men who had spent a lifetime in the Navy, had worked their way up from one ship to the next, the number of guns rising with each move, their appointments made by the Navy Board, a body with whom they would readily communicate if they felt their pride or their professionalism to be in any way questioned or traduced.

In an hour of walking he learnt that HMS *Victory* was two hundred and twenty-six feet plus a bit long, figurehead to taffrail, just under fifty-two feet in beam at the widest point, carrying a total of 104 cannon, 44 twelve pounders, 28 twenty-four pounders, and on the lower gun deck 30 massive thirty-two pounders, plus a pair of sixty-eight pounder carronades, know as 'smashers' on the forecastle, the whole displacing three thousand five hundred tons and carrying a total complement of 850 souls. Veteran of a couple of battles and the relief of Gibraltar in 1782, she had served as a flagship to several admirals and was held to be one of the finest ships afloat in King George's Navy. The last Pearce took with a pinch of salt; it was known, even he knew, that a ship's standing officers never, ever, uttered anything but praise for the vessel on which they served.

He was back on the main deck, having been in the bowels of the ship amongst futtocks and hanging knees, when the party from Marseilles, having concluded their discussions with the admirals, were shown to the entry port, and he was able to bid farewell to men who seemed happier than when they had last talked, buoyed by promises that Pearce suspected were more hopes than realities; that once the French fleet was either taken, destroyed or rendered ineffective, Hood would return to help them fight off the armies of the Jacobins.

While talking, he was being subjected to deep scrutiny by a pair of midshipmen crouched on the steps of a companionway, having raised their heads just enough to see him. But they had to move, as the bosun's whistle sounded to call all hands on deck. Above their heads the signal was being raised on the mizzen mast, flags that told all ships to wear in succession, that order taking effect with a discharge from the signal gun, their destination Toulon.

'Lieutenant Pearce,' said a secretary, 'Lord Hood has requested that you attend upon him.'

'Sit down, Lieutenant Pearce.' As he complied, Pearce was aware that Hood was using his rank, something he had studiously avoided in their earlier interview, and the realisation made him suspicious. 'As you will observe, my secretary is staying with us to take notes on our conversation and I have asked the Captain of the Fleet, Rear Admiral Parker, to join us. I take it you have no objection?'

'That would depend, sir, on the nature of our conversation.'

'I can assure you it is in the nature of being official, Lieutenant.' Pearce just nodded, besides, there was no alternative. 'You sat with our recently departed French guests at dinner?'

Parker, sleek and well-fed, entered the cabin, and at a nod from Lord Hood sat at the table, as Pearce answered. 'Have we not covered that fact, already?'

'We have, and I daresay over the food and wine they told you as much as they told me in conference.'

'That,' Pearce insisted, 'I would not know, since I was not present at your final conference.'

Glancing in his direction, he saw the look of surprise on Parker's face – mere lieutenants did not talk back to flag officers in such a way – before Hood addressed his Fleet Captain, though he was still looking at Pearce. 'You will find, Sir Hyde, that this young man has a unique way of responding to authority. It might be of benefit to us both if I point out to him that he will have no way of persuading me to grant him any favours if he continues in that vein.'

'I would point out to you, Lord Hood, that all I seek from you is a just resolution to a clear case of law-breaking.'

'And I would respond by saying that you are not the judge of what, and what is not, illegal.'

The threat, delivered without the admiral raising his voice, was potent nevertheless. Show more respect or you can whistle for any action in the matter of your impressment. The obvious thing to do was to knuckle under, to behave as any officer of his lowly rank would, and practically grovel to even be allowed into the great man's presence. Was it his bloodline, his Celtic blood or his own contrary nature that meant he could not do it? Yet he knew he had to somehow soften the atmosphere, and the only thing he could think of was a touch of flattery.

'Lord Hood, I am of the mind that your sense of justice will outweigh whatever you see as impertinence. And I would add that I do not mean to be that, merely to state the obvious. If you wish me to tell you in detail what was discussed I am happy to pass it on.'

'I doubt there would be much in the way of difference, though I would like to know what they told you about Toulon?'

'Only that they had received representatives from there, who were keen that the whole of Provence should declare

195

against the Jacobins. They asked for help, but they were told that none could be spared. It was more important to march on Lyon.'

'Meaning?'

It was not really a question. 'That they would have to act on their own.'

Hood nodded. 'Did it not strike you that their information on Toulon was limited?'

'I was given to understand that they were not entirely convinced by the confidence of the Toulon representatives. Marseilles being a commercial port has no organised body of sailors to question the actions of the town's leading citizens. Apparently, and as luck would have it, Marseilles got rid of its zealots a year ago when the government cried danger. Five hundred of the more radical citizens went to fight on the Rhine and have not returned, so the internal threat is diminished. They are not sure that was the case in Toulon.'

'Which leads us to what conclusion?' asked Parker.

'I'm sorry, I don't follow you.'

'Is it not obvious, Lieutenant Pearce,' Parker insisted, 'that we need more information.'

John Pearce was suddenly ahead of them; the allusion to his speaking French as well as he did, even perhaps his reputation, and that was without the fact that given his situation he was an officer they could part with, without loss to the fleet. Parker opened his mouth to speak again, only to be stopped by Hood's hand.

'I think, judging by your expression, Lieutenant, that you have a fair notion of what is coming next.'

'You want someone to go ashore and find out the true state of affairs?'

'Correct in nearly every respect except one, Lieutenant Pearce. We want you to go ashore and find out if Toulon is as ready to declare against Paris as Marseilles.'

Had Hood deliberately drawn him into impertinence, just so he could openly state that there was a *quid pro quo* for any action on Michael, Charlie and Rufus, never mind Barclay.

'Is that going to be an order?'

'That shows the degree of your ignorance, sir,' said Parker

'In what way?'

'Lord Hood cannot order you to undertake such a duty, any more than I could myself. He may request that you undertake it, but you, as an officer, have the right to decline this commission.'

Pearce smiled, but it was a grim affair. 'Without a stain on my character?'

'I would not go that far, Pearce,' Lord Hood, added. 'But I could ask any lieutenant on the ship to volunteer for the duty, and they would jump at it, even if their knowledge of French was limited.'

'They seek to impress you, Lord Hood, I don't.'

Even as he said it, Pearce knew he was bound to accede. Not to do so would nullify his sole reason for being in the Mediterranean. Refuse and he would likely find himself on a ship bound for home, for Hood would have despatches going back to England, and to refuse was not, either, an option. He would be put aboard whether he liked it or not.

Hood slid a piece of paper across the table. 'You would have to go in to Toulon by boat, and take a chance on not being intercepted. Then it would be necessary to find one of these men, at one of these addresses, which you must memorise before you leave.'

'The men who went to seek help from Marseilles?'

'Correct. They are delegates to the local assembly. It is to be hoped that they could then put you in touch with a sympathetic naval officer, who would be able to say what is the sentiment of the fleet, its commander, officers and sailors.'

'When do you expect to raise Toulon?'

Accepting that as tantamount to agreement, Hood replied. 'At first light we should have made contact with the vessels sent ahead. I would say, if the conditions were right, no moon to speak of and some cloud cover, we could put you ashore tomorrow night.'

'A pity.'

'Why?' demanded Parker.

Pearce just shrugged. It seemed to be tactless to say he was hoping to avoid supper in the wardroom.

Chapter Fifteen

The naval uniform had to be discarded and even on a ship with a complement of 850 souls, finding anything approaching a civilian garment that both fitted and designated him as some kind of gentleman, was no easy matter. Appearance was important – he could hardly claim to be Hood's representative dressed as a common seaman. In the end he had to settle for a black coat belonging to Hood's second secretary, the fellow with the ink-stained hands, one that was long enough, but too tight on the chest and under the armpits, and since it looked ridiculous with a sword he exchanged that for a shorter weapon, a midshipman's dirk. The hat was easier, tricorns being plentiful amongst the warrant officers' shore-going rig. Funds were provided by Hood's secretary, a decent purse of golden guineas, which apparently came from the secret fund and required no signature to account for their use.

The fleet made contact with Gould and HMS *Firefly* by mid-day but he had little to impart, having seen it as his duty to avoid contact with the enemy, and stay on the station in case a sighting was made or a signal came from HMS *Brilliant*. Hood had no such scruples; he made straight for the approaches to the French naval port and was close enough by the time he had his dinner to be sighted from Mont Faron. If they were still at anchor he wanted them to see his fleet in the offing, and if they had weighed to find out for himself.

The information from his lookouts, once they had got close enough, was satisfying. Admiral de Trogoff, pre-warned by his own patrols, had already began to warp his ships back into the Petit Rade, a place where they would be secure from attack by such things as fire ships. The only worry was that no sighting had been made of Barclay or his frigate.

Stood bareheaded on the ramparts of the Tour de Mitre, in the late afternoon, Ralph Barclay and his wife watched as the capital ships were towed by their boats through the channel that led to the Petit Rade. He could just see the topsails of his fellow-countrymen on the horizon, where he knew, as much as he wished it otherwise, they would stay. The offshore fleet needed sea room in case of a turn in the weather; being closer to shore would be, in the event of a southerly gale, fraught with peril. To come in even closer was worse; below his terrace they had already got the furnace going behind the battery of forty-two pounder cannon, to make red the shot that would be doubly deadly for a wooden vessel, not only smashing wood, but starting fires as well. Across the bay, at the bastion near the infirmary, they would be doing the same, indeed the shore of the whole outer roadstead was dotted with forts. Any ship sailing into the Grande Rade would be caught between multiple fire from guns heavier than their own, and that with no hope of getting at the enemy vessels in the inner anchorage.

'What will happen husband?'

There was just a tinge of hope in Emily's voice, hope that comfortable as their captivity was it would soon be over. He hated to dash that anticipation, but the truth could do nothing other than that. 'The French will anchor a ship across the entrance to the channel below once all the rest are through, put a spring on her cable till she is broadside on, and effectively shut off the Petit Rade. In an extreme situation, they would sink her there.'

'I meant as regards our ships, not theirs.'

'Little, I fear. Hotham will blockade, staying just on the horizon to keep the French bottled up. Admiral de Trogoff must wait for a wind strong enough to blow our fleet off station, and then, if he wishes, he can put to sea on that same wind and either offer battle of try to evade them.'

There was no point in adding an even more depressing fact; that Toulon had been studied by many naval minds over the years, who had concluded that it could only be taken by soldiers, and then it was not a matter of siege and assault but of attrition. To even have a chance of attacking the port and the town any aggressor must first subdue the batteries surrounding the Grande Rade, but that only brought them to stout walls and even more cunningly placed artillery. The defences had been designed by the Marquis de Vauban, Louis XIV's master of the art of fortifications, to discourage an attack from the sea, his aim to make the naval base a nut too tough to crack. Success in such a venture was not impossible, but given the time it would take and the force it would require, Toulon could not be captured before the arrival of a relieving army, so that those invading would have to fight a land battle at the same time as trying to press home a siege.

'What would you do if you were a Frenchman?'

'I would only know that if I knew de Trogoff's orders.'

Ralph Barclay declined to add anything about the Admiral obeying them, which was, if Captain d'Imbert was right, questionable. Thinking of that brought back the memory of that dinner, St Julien unashamedly paying court to his wife, and he had to suppress the feelings that induced, the belief that Emily had thoroughly enjoyed the experience. Certainly she had failed to do what he, or rather Lutyens, had asked; any information about the state of affairs in the port had been gleaned by him, not her.

'If he can get the rest of his 74's fit for service he would have an advantage in numbers, but that counts for little if his crews are not worked up, as ours must be. You will have observed aboard *Brilliant* that men need time to get to know their tasks and each other. If that is true of a ship, it is even more so of a fleet. New to operations, sails take longer to set and take in. Gunnery, the most vital element should it come to a fight, would be slow and poorly aimed, and that against men who have had months of training. If he has orders to get to sea, I would suspect he would try to avoid battle rather than invite it for that very reason.'

'Not very noble, husband, but I must say, for all he has a title, the Admiral did not strike me as overly endowed with that quality. He seemed a timid little man.'

'Unlike his second in command, perhaps?'

Emily did not respond; she knew how he felt, just as she knew to do so, to protest that it was just a bit of raillery, a pleasant diversion from being cooped up in a frigate with the same faces for months, would cut no ice and only lead to an argument. Instead she pointed up the long arm that enclosed the inner anchorage, to the point. 'Is that our men returning?'

Ralph Barclay nodded as he looked towards the town and the Vieux Darse, where his crew had been put to work shifting quarried stone. Led by Sykes, escorted by an armed guard, the dusty and weary Brilliants were trudging back to their underground accommodation. He had visited them at their labours, to find them under the supervision of overseers with whips. A protest had had these removed, but it was a moot point as to whether National Guardsmen with muskets and prodding bayonets were any less an evil. Emily, already indoors, was tying on her apron before gathering the unctions and ointments gifted her by Lutyens. She had taken it upon herself, each evening, to treat what sores and blisters the men had, and to insist on a transfer to the infirmary of any whom she deemed incapable of further exertion.

Ralph Barclay had accompanied her on the first two nights, but he wearied of endless attempts at reassurance, had a limited ability to look into sad, exhausted eyes concerned about the future and a limited fund of words to maintain the hope that all would be well; that either the war would end or that rescue or exchange would arrive in the form of a British fleet. The men might know that had happened this very day; let Emily be the one to confirm it, for he feared being asked the very same question she had posed, one to which, in terms of time in captivity, there was no answer.

'Will you not visit Glaister and the others? They at least should be made aware of what has happened.'

'Of course,' Ralph Barclay replied, with some force, to cover for the fact that he had completely forgotten about them.

With the sun beginning to dip behind the hills to the west, the men on the ground floor had tallow stubs lit in the sconces, which did nothing to make pleasant what was a vista of dank stone walls and a bare earth floor. The news of the fleet lifted the gloom, cheering them immensely, which left their captain wondering how long that would last, though he indulged in a little necessary dissimulation when it was put to him that an exchange might now be arranged, given that officers stood a much better chance in that matter than seamen.

'I am sure,' he said, without any personal conviction, 'that as soon as Admiral Hotham knows of our plight, he will send in a flag of truce for just that purpose.'

'I thought Lord Hood might come out of his cabin to wish me luck.'

Pearce said this as he prepared to lower himself into the

waiting boat, bobbing below the entry port and crewed by men from *Victory*, now heaved to, each one in dark clothing with blackened faces. Ingolby, the premier, responded with an embarrassed cough and an intimation that, 'The admiral, no doubt, had more important things on his mind.'

The man to whom this was addressed saw it differently; that for instance, the admiral saw him as expendable. The cloak he needed to hide his clothing was already in the cutter, he would use his hat to cover his face, for if he did get ashore, blackened features in daylight would attract attention. The midshipman in charge, a youngster called Trevivian, gave the order to shove off and, once clear, the men began to row in steady rhythmical fashion while above their heads the orders were issued to get under way. The dying sun lit them as they came out from the lee of the flagship, and being the Mediterranean, that soon turned to a full night in which the moon had yet to rise. Not that it was totally dark; above their heads the sky was carpeted with stars and it was only when a cloud obscured them that the men in the boat could feel any sense of security.

'They won't see us from the shore, your honour,' said the midshipman, in a voice with a strong West Country burr. 'We will be like a black dot, the trough of a wave to the eye if we stay mid-channel.'

The plan was to land him on the eastern shore of the Grande Rade, between a fort called La Malque and a hill called Pointe de Brun, which might, or might not, be home to another battery of cannon. To try to venture into the inner anchorage would be too perilous; crowded with shipping, it would be awash with guard boats. They would have those too in the Grande Rade, but in theory they would be less numerous and, given the area they were obliged to cover, easier to avoid.

Sitting silently, the only sound the heavy breathing of the

oarsmen, allowed Pearce's imagination to run riot; he saw in the glimmer of the starlight endless chimeras that he took to be boats, even worse, when the cloud cover increased and in stygian darkness, his eyes played more tricks, which induced a longing for this boat journey to be over and for him to be on dry land. He had no doubt that he could pass himself off as a Frenchmen, and in a naval port his accent would not attract any attention from sentinels who must be from all over the country. But that feeling of certainty only applied ashore; at sea with a bunch of British tars, any close inspection would be fatal, which had him saying out loud, as the moon appeared for a brief moment, before slipping behind a cloud again, 'What in the name of hell am I doing here?'

'We all wonder that, sir,' said one of the oarsman. 'That be what we all feel, your honour, for if we is caught by the Johnnie Crapauds, it'll be the galleys for the rest of our days.'

Pearce shuddered, not willing to add to his inadvertently spoken complaint, that for him it would be a firing squad, or if the wrong people were in charge in Toulon, a guillotine. As if to make real what was imagined, a gap appeared in the clouds, and a voice cut through the darkness, demanding the private signal for the night, and unshaded a lantern to show the bows of another cutter with a man standing peering into the gloom by the side of a small cannon. The *Victory*'s oarsmen immediately raised their sticks and the cutter glided to a halt. Pearce had formed in his mind the words 'j'ai oublié le mot', when another voice called out, 'Suffren. La response?'

'De St Tropez.'

Bobbing up and down slowly, oars still out of the water, Pearce and his rowers sat holding their breath, easier for him than those who had been exerting themselves. The lantern was shaded again, with everyone in the British cutter looking at the sky, at slowly moving clouds tinged with silver edges, praying it would not clear. Pearce, without consulting Trevivian, gave the men an order to row hard and damn the noise, sure that each of the two boats who had exchanged the identification would assume the noise came from the other.

'Christ, that was a stroke of luck.'

'Remember those words on the way back to *Victory*, Mr Trevivian. Suffren and St Tropez.'

'What do they mean, sir?'

'You a sailor and you have you not heard of Suffren?'

'I'd be obliged if you would tell me of him, sir.'

'He was an admiral and a hero in the Marine Royale, his full title being le Bailli de Suffren de St Tropez, hence the signal.' Then, thinking of the boy's accent, and to make safe the journey back, he had him practising saying that and the French for 'I have forgotten the words,' all the way to the shore, only to conclude that he would perhaps get away with it if the guard boats thought him Swiss.

'They got an accent then, these Swiss folk?'

'I've only met one as far as I know, Mr Trevivian, a lady called Madame de Stael.'

'A madam! God forbid, sir, I should sound like some bawdy house trollop.'

Pearce laughed. Thinking of Germaine de Stael in her Paris salon, the décor as glittering as the company, he wondered how a woman who prided herself on the sharpness of her mind and the acuity of her wit would take to being likened to a trollop. There was no salon now, no dazzling company. To avoid losing her head, rich and witty Germaine had been forced to flee to England, like so many others.

Thinking of her took Pearce back to a happier vision of Paris, in the days before those who had brought down the power of the monarchy lost control of the Revolution. It had been an especially sweet time for him, a youth growing to manhood, taken everywhere by a favoured guest, his father. He recalled the city in high summer, could remember the festivals held in the Champ de Mars at which all the folk of Paris could mingle, to exchange greetings as citizens, regardless of previous rank, to kiss in amity and exchange flowers. The thought of kisses led on to those he had bestowed and received, and of those women in salons like that of Germaine de Stael, who had espied and seduced a young, handsome fellow, in the full knowledge of their compliant husbands. Happy times, indeed!

The prospect of beaching brought his mind sharply back to the present and the knowledge that landing in the right place, the eastern arm of the Grand Rade, would be achieved more by chance than sure knowledge, given that Trevivian had used as guides what sightings he could get of the north star and the twinkling but distant lights from various points around the arms of the bay. Another break in the cloud showed that such methods had sufficed, as the cutter grounded on soft sand. They waited in silence for a full minute, to ensure that there were no foot patrols to worry about, before Pearce was carried ashore for, as Trevivian insisted, 'It would not do, sir, to be seen ploughing along pretending to be a local with squelching boots.'

His passenger gave him one more go at the password, took the lantern he would need to help them locate him, then set off up the beach, sniffing the night air, catching on it a whiff of pines, thinking that here he was again, an alien ashore in France for the fourth time since the start of the year. Those pines lay a short way inland, thin trees set well apart at ground level but with enough of a canopy above to blot out any light from stars of the moon. To keep going was to stumble and almost certainly trip and fall, so Pearce sat down, dirk by his side, pulled his cloak around him, and, using the tricorn as a pillow, fell asleep with his back to a tree. Those same trees blotted out the rising sun, so it was well up before he fully awoke from what had been fitful slumber, his first thought that he had not fetched with him anything to drink, and that as a consequence he had a raging thirst.

Pine needles over sandy soil would provide no relief, so Pearce began to walk towards what he could see of the sun as it filtered through the canopy. Rising ground directed him to the left and after some ten minutes of walking he emerged into open country, cultivated fields, with the town of Toulon rising into the foothills of Mont Faron visible to the north. Looking to the south he saw smoke rising from a hill, which he suspected was the redoubt on the Pointe de Brun. A dusty, rutted track ran from there, parallel to the woods, so, cloak off and rolled under his arm, with the dirk inside and readily available, he strode out and away from what danger that represented.

Hot in his ill-fitting coat, the discomfort of thirst increased, so Pearce was glad to spy a small village at the base of another hill. There were a few houses only, one of which had a table outside under an awning of reeds, and an owner who was obviously an ex-sailor, for even with only one leg he had the rolling gait and the dress to confirm it. Rough wine was not the thing to quench a thirst, that came from a bunch of juicy grapes, which accompanied his bread and cheese. That the silver he paid with was not French brought forth no comment from the lame proprietor, though the look spoke of curiosity. But nothing was said; Pearce surmised that the fellow, like so many of his countrymen, was grateful to be paid in coin of any kind rather than *assignats*, the increasingly worthless paper currency of the Revolution.

Carrying a second bunch of grapes, eating them slowly, Pearce made his way towards the walls of the city, stone ramparts buttressed by an earthen *fosse* to absorb cannon shot. This presented a problem, the gate being guarded by armed National Guardsmen, who, with the *Rosbifs* ships newly come, would probably be in a high state of alert. Watching from the shade of a nearby stable, he saw several people, civilians and soldiers, present papers, passes that let them through. Those that did not, the costermongers and farmers carrying produce into the town to be sold at the market, were obviously well known and greeted as such.

Must he rob someone for their pass? Could he get through that gate without one? Still popping grapes, Pearce pondered that as he watched, thinking that confusion might work just as well. It seemed an age before an opportunity presented itself, as two carts, one entering one exiting through the narrow opening, became entangled, leading to a loud dispute between the drivers. At the same time a group of besmocked children appeared on the road, being shepherded along by nuns, the whole party obviously heading for the gate. It was a risk, but it was one he had to take, for nothing could be achieved lest he was on the inside of the fortifications, so, placing a hand inside the wrapped cloak to take hold of the dirk, he walked out as the last of the children passed him and, as they approached the gate began to shoo them along.

Preoccupied with trying to untangle the carts, the sentries gave him a level of attention which was compromised not just by that, but by their need to raise their hats to the nuns, an act which actually surprised Pearce, given that such obeisance to religion would have seen them slung into prison in Revolutionary Paris. Still shooing the children, calling out at them to, 'Allez, allez, mes enfants', Pearce looked right at one of the sentries, and shrugged, mouthing, 'Les

209

jeunes,' with a weary expression. He carried straight on, any curiosity deflected by the deepening argument behind him, as the two carters' exchange erupted in a crescendo of mutual recrimination. By the time the sentry turned back to look, Pearce was nowhere to be seen.

The buildings inside the wall were widely spaced with little sense of order, laying as they did between what was an outer fortification and the old town defences, the gates of which, unmanned, led to a mass of narrow alleys off a wide quay. This ran around an inner harbour, lined with high warehouses, with bastions at the outer edge on either side of a seagoing entry port, one just big enough, Pearce reckoned, for a major warship to pass through. Since he could see one huge vessel still under construction, surrounded as it was by scaffolds, it had to be.

But that only held his attention for so long. As he walked towards the mid-point of the quay, he saw the stern of another ship, a frigate, crawling with men on both the deck and in the rigging. And there, right in front of his eyes, large in gold lettering, was the name *Brilliant*.

CHAPTER SIXTEEN

Pearce stopped dead, his mind working furiously to make sense of what he could see, dismissing the thought that the ship could be a French frigate with the same name, since the word brilliant translated as *éclat*. He knew that proper deep sea navy men could look at a ship, even at sea, and tell her name from her lines or her figurehead, just as he knew very well that it was a skill he did not possess. Also, he could see that a lot of the timber work was new, pale against the painted and weathered remainder, which confirmed the thought he found he was strangely reluctant to contemplate; that a ship on which he had served, however reluctantly, had been taken in battle. He might hate Barclay with a passion, but there had been good men on that ship, men who had, in their own way, defied the captain; what had happened to them?

John Pearce had never had an electric shock, all the rage when he had been growing up as the latest thing, a cure for all ills, for there had never been the money for what his father damned as quackery. But on hearing the voice of Robert Sykes, bellowing out an order to someone to 'Shift his arse', he reckoned that Dr Graham and his experiments could not have delivered better. He had to stop himself immediately facing towards that voice, in fact he forced himself to turn away and look out over the debris-filled waters of the inner basin, though experiencing partial relief, for Sykes was one of the 'good people' he had just been thinking about.

'We ain't aboard ship now, Sykes, so you can go an' stuff yourself.'

Kemp, thought Pearce, you little rat-faced shit, as Sykes replied. 'You was a lazy sod aboard ship, Kemp, an' you ain't changed.'

'Why is we toiling so hard anyways?' Kemp demanded in that well-remembered whine.

''Cause, idiot, if'n we don't work, we don't get fed.'

To walk away was agonising, but essential. If *Brilliant* had been taken, judging by the extent of the repairs having put up a fight, there was nothing he could do about it and that applied to the crew slaving for their captors as much as the ship. What had happened to Barclay, a thought that brought forth a flash of sympathy as he recalled the man's wife? Closer to him were Martin Dent and the Scotsman Dysart, but most of all was the last of his fellow Pelicans, Ben Walker, the remaining member of that band that had formed on being pressed. Ben had elected to stay aboard rather than join his companions, and go back to a life avoiding arrest for a crime he would never name.

On the open quay it was hard to find a spot from which to observe, certainly one close enough to avoid being seen, so when he did turn to look, well past the prow of the frigate, the faces were indistinct, made more so by the straw hats the men had fashioned to keep the sun off their heads. Height was a clue, for Ben Walker was slight, but he could not make out anyone who looked or moved like him. Imagining a bold rescue, he looked towards the armed guards who were eyeing their prisoners if not exactly guarding them, more content to rest their backsides on bollards and smoke their pipes. That was a thought that had to be killed off; what could he do, one man? Perhaps the mission he was on might provide the answer, perhaps he could attain liberty not just for Michael, Charlie and Rufus, but for Ben Walker and the crewmen of HMS *Brilliant* as well.

There was more purpose to his stride as he moved on, past endless knots of folk noisily debating politics, with passions clearly running high judging by the flying accusations. He was seeking the first address he had memorised, accosting a number of citizens to ask directions, finally locating it in an alley that backed onto the quay past the naval basin, the loading bay at that side, with name above, firmly closed. Suspicion made him walk past the dark, recessed door of the chandler's warehouse, in case anyone he had questioned decided to follow him, curious to know why a man clearly not a local was asking, for Toulon was obviously in a highly alarmed state, and likely to see spies everywhere. He waited at the far end of the alley for a whole minute, until he was sure, before making his way back and ducking into the small entrance, setting off a bell as he opened the door. The first thing to hit him in the dimly lit emporium was the smell; the hempen odour of new, coiled rope, a faint whiff of tar and turpentine overlaid with the kind of dusty ambience that spoke of long years of trading.

'Monsieur?'

The voice came from the top of a well-built but worn set of wooden stairs, and behind the man who spoke was an open door to what looked like his *bureau*, the walls being lined with sheaves of tied papers. A lantern set to light the steps showed he had jet-black hair, eyes that looked to be the same, and the kind of shaded chin that denoted a fellow who was obliged to shave more than once in each day.

'I am seeking the proprietor, Monsieur Mancini.'

'I am he. Can I be of service to you?'

'I hope so, monsieur, since you have, I believe, recently returned from Marseilles.'

Mancini, without haste, half turned for a second, but he

was facing John Pearce in another, this time with a pistol in his hand. Slowly, as it was cocked, Pearce removed his own hand from the rolled up cloak, realising that it must have looked as if he was armed likewise. Besides, against a pistol, and given the distance between them, that midshipman's dirk was of no use to him.

'That is unnecessary, monsieur.'

'Is it?'

'I do not represent authority.'

'Your speech marks you out as a stranger. I have always made it my business never to trust strangers, especially those who may come from Paris.'

'I am a stranger, but from further field than any part of France. And I would point out that if I had come here to challenge you, a delegate of the local assembly, about what happened in Marseilles, perhaps to arrest you for it, I would not come alone.'

'What could I have done that would justify arrest. I am a Ship's Chandler, monsieur, as the sign outside my door tells you, as well as being a representative of the people. Is it so strange that one trader from a port should go a few leagues along the coast to confer with another.'

'Only if that place has thrown out the Jacobins, raised the flag of revolt and only if that person made overtures about the same thing being applied to the whole of the coast, including Toulon.'

'Go on.'

Ever since this mission was first mooted Pearce had been thinking of what to say on meeting someone like this fellow, who was bound to be suspicious, bound to feel endangered by their views and actions in a country where hundreds of people were dying each day for nothing more than the supposed colour of their blood or the depth of their purse. None of the words were of any use now, in a situation where only the unvarnished truth would do, for he had no doubt that this man would shoot him if, for an instant, he thought him an enemy.

'You will have seen the British fleet out at sea, monsieur. I come from there. Yesterday I dined on the flagship with the men from Marseilles with whom you went to confer. They came aboard to ask the British admiral to take charge of the port and city. I fear they departed empty-handed.'

The muzzle waved slightly. 'Name them?'

'There was a National Deputy called Rebequi, several traders like yourself, Messieurs Moreau and Pascal, plus a lawyer called Monsieur Trallet. I can assure you they were discreet about you. They gave your name, along with that of two others, to Admiral the Lord Hood. He passed it on to me.'

The pistol twitched again. 'And those names are?'

Pearce shrugged. 'You will forgive me Monsieur Mancini, if I feel I have said enough. I will not reveal the other names, even to you.'

'You are?'

He wondered if the reply sounded false; it certainly did to him. 'Lieutenant John Pearce, of His Britannic Majesty's Navy.'

'And what is it you want?'

'My admiral needs to know the state of sentiment in Toulon, monsieur. He was obliged to decline the appeals of the delegates from Marseilles, but that is something he might not do if he received the same from the citizens of Toulon. I am here to see if such a request is possible.'

Mancini tried not to react to that and failed, his black eyebrows rising and half a smile appearing before being wiped away. Once he had composed himself he came down the stairs slowly.

'Lieutenant, please be so good as to put aside that bundle

215

you are carrying so that I can clearly see both your hands?' Pearce obliged, and stayed rock still as Mancini walked behind him. The doorbell tinkled again as the man looked out, no doubt checking that the alley was clear, a second time when the door was once more closed.

'I think I must take you, monsieur, to someone who speaks English, someone who can ensure you are who you say.'

'I am at your service.'

'We will walk close together, I will have with me this pistol, which be assured I will use if threatened. And if you are who you say, all I will have done is shoot an English spy.'

'Might I ask where we are going.'

The reply chilled Pearce. 'Certainly, monsieur. We are going to the Naval Headquarters of Admiral the Count de Trogoff, the commander of the fleet you see anchored in the inner roads.'

Walking back along the quay, in bright and hot sunlight, the coat John Pearce had borrowed now felt like a sweaty restraint, preventing the kind of free movement that might allow him to act. Not that attacking and overpowering Mancini was an option. Quite apart from that pistol, he was still on the face of it the link to those in Toulon who might ask for British assistance. That is, unless he had gone to Marseilles as a spy. These and other possibilities coursed though his mind on what was a short journey. They passed the sentries posted outside what was a handsome building of a previous age and entered a shaded hallway with a grand double staircase in the middle rising right and left to the upper floors. A liveried footman appeared, and Mancini, without taking his eyes off Pearce, whispered to him, words which sent the man up those stairs with the kind of gait that made no sound.

'Who are we going to see?' asked Pearce.

'I told you, monsieur, someone who can talk to you in your own tongue.'

'Is that necessary?

'Very, for if you cannot speak it well enough to satisfy him, your next journey will be to the dungeons.'

The footman came as far as the landing at which the staircase split and nodded, then waited for them to ascend before leading them up and on to a tall, first floor doorway. Mancini was announced, Pearce was not. The man at the large french windows, wearing the pale blue undress uniform coat of the French Navy, turned to face them. Stocky in build, he wore a powdered wig over a square, weathered face, and having looked at Mancini, he turned his brown eyes onto Pearce.

'This fellow claims to be a messenger from the British admiral. He also claims to have met those in Marseilles with whom I went to treat. He says his name is Lieutenant Pearce.'

'The name of the admiral is?' the sailor asked in English.

'Vice Admiral Lord Hood.'

'Of which squadron?'

Pearce had to think about that for a split second, but then the colour of the pennant flying on the foremast provided the answer. 'The red squadron.'

'Describe him to me.'

'Taller than you, monsieur, with a florid face, heavy eyebrows and a large nose.'

'His flagship is?'

'HMS *Victory*'

'A fine vessel.'

'According to those who sail in her, sir, the best ship afloat. Might I ask to whom I am talking?'

'Capitaine de Vaisseu, le Baron d'Imbert. What you say implies that *Victory* is not your ship?'

'It is not. I came from England with despatches.' Reverting to French, Pearce added, 'The admiral, noting that I spoke French with the delegates from Marseilles...'

D'Imbert threw a glance at Mancini, who nodded.

'...decided I would be able to carry out this mission without endangering myself.'

Mancini, still locked in eye contact with d'Imbert, told the captain in a rapid fire way, what Pearce had told him, the names of the Marseilles delegates, and how he had come into his emporium.

'One last question, Lieutenant,' d'Imbert asked in English. 'What ships have you served on?'

Pearce looked past him out of the open french window. He could not see the frigate from here, but it gave emphasis to what he said. 'One of them is being repaired in the basin below your window, Captain, HMS *Brilliant*. If you wish, I am happy to name some of the crew.'

'The captain?'

'Ralph Barclay, and when I was aboard he was sailing in the company of his wife.'

D'Imbert smiled suddenly, and said, 'His very beautiful wife. Please, Lieutenant, sit down, while I call for some refreshments, very necessary on a hot day.' While pulling on the silk cord to summon a servant he also spoke quietly to Mancini, who departed as the servant entered. Wine ordered, the servant too departed, and d'Imbert sat down opposite Pearce.

'I have asked the Corsican to go talk to his fellow traders, and arrange a meeting.' Seeing the look of curiosity on Pearce's face, he added, 'We call Mancini that for he is of Corsican descent, as are a number of the citizenry along this part of the coast. It also allows us to talk of him openly without giving away his name.'

'So you are engaged in a conspiracy?'

'I would prefer to say we are engaged in a righting of great wrongs, whatever other people may choose to call it.'

'Admiral Hood is curious to know the balance of forces in Toulon, who is for the Jacobins, and who is against.'

'I will tell you what I told Captain Barclay.'

'He survived?' Pearce asked, as the wine arrived, a cold white from what must be an ice room, judging by the mist that coated the bottle. D'Imbert answered as it was poured, wise enough to do so in French

'Fortunately, yes, having put up a brave fight.'

Pearce wanted to ask how many lives had been sacrificed in that brave fight, but it would not serve. He was here for a purpose, and to that he must stick, so, once the servant departed, he proposed one of the scenarios that had been discussed aboard *Victory*. 'Do you require Admiral Lord Hood to land a force of marines?'

'No!' d'Imbert insisted. But then he seemed to reconsider, and added, 'That is not what I think we would want at this moment, for two reasons. First it would excite those of no opinion to resist, and that, added to those who favour the cause of Paris, might tip the balance against us.'

'How many support the Jacobins?'

About to answer, d'Imbert stopped as the door burst open. Pearce turned to see a tall and handsome officer, with a sensuous face and shiny curled hair, dressed in the gold-fringed coat of an admiral. 'I heard you had a visitor, d'Imbert!'

The captain stood up, clearly angry. 'I think good manners, Admiral St Julien, mean that even senior officers are obliged to knock before barging into a room.'

'Shit on your good manners,' said St Julien, in a way that implied such crudity was normal. 'Are you not going to introduce me?'

It was Pearce who responded, and quickly, using the name, if not the priestly designation of his Parisian tutor, and adding a sharp bow. 'Auguste Morlant, monsieur, at your service.'

D'Imbert proved he was no fool; he picked up the name and ran with it. 'Monsieur Morlant has farms in the Camargue, livestock farms, and he has come to see if he can do any business with us.'

'What business?' St Julien demanded, in a voice larded with suspicion.

Wondering where the hell the Camargue was, Pearce, thinking rapidly, replied. 'Supplies of meat, beef and pork, for the fleet, properly salted from my own pans and at good prices.'

It was d'Imbert's turn. 'Monsieur Mancini, the chandler, made the introduction, and I felt it was only polite to listen, though we have good and reliable vendors already.'

'Don't you mean the Corsican chandler,' replied St Julien, with a sneer, which had Pearce wondering just how much he knew.

'I would remind you, sir, that Corsica is part of France.'

'But is Mancini, Captain d'Imbert?'

Throughout, St Julien had not taken his eyes off John Pearce, ranging over the too-tight coat, the hat now on his knee, even his breeches and shoes. It was if he was trying to commit everything about him to memory, and it was damned uncomfortable as scrutiny.

D'Imbert's voice had an edge to it. 'I have rarely met a man as loyal as Mancini, sir. His lineage may be Corse, but his heart is French.'

St Julien threw back his head and laughed. 'It's his head he ought to be worried about, d'Imbert, him and his fellow representatives. Don't think that I do not know what is going on.'

'I am at a loss, sir, to know what it is you are talking about.'

There was no humour now, as St Julien's gaze finally shifted from Pearce to d'Imbert. 'I am talking about what happened to those who play at treachery, Captain. In these times it is inclined to have bloody consequences.'

Glaring at them both in turn, the admiral spun on his heel and went out through the door, not bothering to close it.

'It is not pleasant to serve under a man who is a pig.'

Spat out in French, Pearce reckoned the word *cochon* to be much more descriptive than pig.

'I know, Captain d'Imbert. I have served under one.'

The Frenchman looked as if he was about to ask who, then thought better of it, for it was not germane to their present problem. 'We must go and see Admiral de Trogoff.'

'Who is, I trust, sympathetic.'

'There are many who would happily ask your Lord Hood to protect the town, Lieutenant, but only Admiral de Trogoff has the power to speak for the Toulon Fleet.'

As they exited, and began to walk along a wide corridor, Pearce asked, 'How did St Julien know I was here?'

'The footman would have told him. They are all easy to bribe.'

'Will not those same footmen tell if they see us visiting the Commander-in-Chief.'

The captain replied with an elegant shrug. 'Very likely. There are few secrets in this building.'

CHAPTER SEVENTEEN

Pearce did not find Admiral le Comte de Trogoff impressive. Small and plump, he was physically uninspiring and as evasive about his own opinions as he was fussy about his person, being a constant visitor to the long mirror set on the wall between a pair of french windows overlooking the harbour. Whenever d'Imbert tried to pin him to a definite answer, the man equivocated, saying on the one hand, in very vague terms, that such an outcome was desirable before shifting his ground one hundred and eighty degrees to espouse an equally feeble view on the opposite. Trogoff professed loyalty to his late and murdered King, while faintly praising those who had overthrown him for bringing his county into the modern age, only then to ask himself if it was not his duty to support whichever regime was in power, leaving Pearce to conclude that if his naval tactics in any way 'mirrored' his political wavering, then Hood, if it came to a battle, had nothing to worry about. Compared to the certainty of Rear Admiral St Julien, it was not encouraging.

'There are many things to consider,' de Trogoff insisted, fiddling with the lace jabot at his neck, 'and we must, at all costs, avoid bloodshed.'

Voiced in a worried tone, it seemed very obvious that the blood he was thinking of was his own.

D'Imbert replied to that frustrating attitude in an even voice. 'We have Marseilles as an ally, other towns in the region are in turmoil and if we in Toulon can do likewise the rest of Provence may follow.'

Trogoff was explicit for once. 'May! All the difficulties are in that one word, d'Imbert. Such uncertainty. And what happens then, eh? Do you think those madmen in Paris will just sit on their thumbs. Rumour has it that troops are already on the way to Marseilles. Some call them a rabble. I would remind you that such a horde defeated a coalition of all Europe at Valmy, another that fought and won on the Belgian border at Jemappes. It is not just the *sans-culottes* who are the fanatics, their generals are cast in the same mould.'

'Both armies who have since been beaten, and I would remind you, sir, that when defeated, a number of those fanatical generals you talk about are inclined to go over to the enemy.'

The admiral's eyes suddenly gleamed with fire, and he cried. 'Yes they do, in order to keep their heads. Look at General Dumouriez, at the victories he won. Then he loses a battle and what? What kind of regime is it that rewards military failure with death? No one has any faith in their Revolution, certainly not I. If I take my fleet to sea and fail, what then? Am I to be dragged in a tumbrel to certain extinction?'

Realising he was speaking loudly enough to be heard through a six inch plank, and certainly though the open windows, Trogoff dropped his voice. 'They have ruined France.'

Pearce bit off the temptation to point out that France was pretty much ruined before they had come along, though he would concede matters had been made worse. Instead he took his cue from d'Imbert, speaking calmly.

'Should you declare against the Jacobins, Toulon is, I am led to believe, an easy place to defend compared to

Marseilles.' Trogoff looked at him, blinked, then went back to face the mirror, seemingly unaware that his troubled reflection was visible to his visitors. 'It is secure from the sea, for there is no fleet to threaten you if you accept support from Lord Hood. I do not have the experience to cast an opinion on the land defences, sir, as I am sure you are aware.'

Trogoff's chin was on his chest now. He was not really replying to John Pearce, more speaking to himself. 'We have nothing to fear from the east, and if we can hold the heights and the reverse slopes of Mont Faron we are secure in the north.' Finished with the positives, he turned to address his visitors with the negatives, stating that to the west, both town and port were vulnerable. His right fist smacked into his left hand, and his slightly protruding eyes seemed to jump from his head. 'Toulon cannot be held without an army!'

'What if troops were available, sir?' asked d'Imbert.

'Are they?'

'That we do not know. The only person who can answer that question is out at sea blockading the port.'

'The Lord Hood?'

'Precisely.'

Trogoff looked at Pearce, who, with little choice, had to return a look that implied he did not know. It would not do to let on that Hood had declined the same request from Marseilles on the grounds that he lacked the forces to hold it.

'Perhaps a parley between you and Lord Hood,' suggested d'Imbert. 'Under a flag of truce?'

'No, Captain. St Julien would insist on being present. What could I say with that fellow at the table? Nothing.'

'Then someone must be sent to speak to Lord Hood, someone with the power to make agreements on your behalf.'

'Agreements?' That one word was said with a furious

224

waving of his hands, clear evidence that it alarmed him. 'No, no, d'Imbert. Not agreements. Possibilities perhaps, speculations, but not plans.'

'But you do agree that an officer of sufficient rank should talk to the British?'

Stood, hands on hip, in a place where he could catch a glimpse of his refection, de Trogoff answered. 'I think if an officer saw it as his duty to investigate such a thing, he would require no orders from me to do so. Do you not agree, d'Imbert?'

The admiral could not see his captain. If he had, he would have been less than pleased by the look of despair which crossed d'Imbert's face. 'I take it you would not wish to be informed, sir, of such a mission?'

'What good would my knowing of it do? Why, if that were uncovered, it would only give ammunition to St Julien and those who follow him.'

'Then if you will forgive me, sir. Lieutenant Pearce and I will take our leave.'

De Trogoff walked up to d'Imbert and came close enough to put a hand on his shoulder. 'Have a care for yourself, Captain. In these times, as I have already said, heads are at risk.'

'How did he ever get a command?' asked Pearce, as they made their way back to d'Imbert's room. 'The man sounds as if he was born straddling a fence.'

The captain flashed him an angry look. 'You are, sir, talking of an admiral in the French Navy, and moreover one who finds himself in a very difficult position, one much easier to criticise than comprehend.'

Pearce waited until the door was closed behind him before replying to that, suspecting that pain on hearing the truth was as much to blame as annoyance. 'I mean no disrespect, sir, and I am sure there are as many brave officers in the French Navy as the British.'

'There were, Lieutenant, there were. Sadly, most of them fled.'

Without meaning it, d'Imbert had answered the question. Trogoff had been promoted to command because there were few others who had not crossed the Rhine to join the émigré forces under the late King's youngest brother, the Comte d'Artois. That de Trogoff, though titled, had not done so probably had more to do with the man's endemic confusion than conviction, but with d'Imbert, Pearce felt that it must have been a sense of duty and obligation that had kept him in service, when common sense indicated that flight was the safest option for a man with a title.

'I take it Admiral St Julien is angling to replace him?'

'Lieutenant, if we do not act, St Julien will take charge even if our present commander does not wish it. Admiral de Trogoff does not appear to see that his head is on the block even if he does nothing, for St Julien will denounce him as a traitor as soon as he feels strong enough to do so. He will then send him to Paris and certain execution. Can I ask, what were your arrangements to get back aboard *Victory*?'

'A boat will come for me tonight, in darkness, on the eastern edge of the Grande Rade.'

'There are gunboat patrols out there.'

'We got through last night. That is where I landed, just to the north of the Pointe de Brun.'

'Then we must go from the same place tonight,' said d'Imbert in a leaden voice, 'and I must come with you. I must find out from your admiral just how much help he can give us.'

Going over to the window, he indicated that Pearce should join him, pointing out the Tour de Mitre. 'That is where the crew of your old ship are housed, officers and men. Perhaps you would wish to see Captain Barclay?'

Pearce was looking down across the harbour, to where his old shipmates were still toiling in the baking sun. 'That is a pleasure I can set aside, sir, until other matters are resolved.'

'Your captain…'

'Barclay is not, sir, my captain!'

'He asked me about our fleet, what they would do, if asked to proclaim against Paris.'

'You spoke to him of this?'

'I did, and I agree with what he said. If we can get the trusted men on our side, the sous-officers, then it matters not what St Julien does. The majority of the sailors will listen to them.'

'And if we can't?'

'There will be that bloodbath, Lieutenant Pearce, that Admiral de Trogoff so fears. Now, I must go and see Mancini and his friends and tell them of what I plan to do. They have much power in the town, and assure me that the whole population, bar the odd hothead, is ready to revolt. If they are right, then it puts the odds in our favour, but we must act in concert with the local population to have any hope of success.'

Still looking at his old shipmates, Pearce said. 'I have a favour to ask.'

'Which is?'

Taking out the purse Hood's secretary had given him, he emptied a number of gold coins into his hand. 'I would like you to take this, and ensure that those men working on the quayside, the prisoners from HMS *Brilliant,* have enough to drink and eat.'

The Frenchman looked down at the golden guineas. 'That will only last so long.'

'If we are successful, Captain d'Imbert, it won't have to last more than a few days.'

'A noble gesture, Lieutenant.'

Pearce did not reply; how could he say he had been imprisoned at one time in his life, had been forced to bribe warders just to get enough for he and his father to eat; that he had more in common with most of those men now than he had had when he served with them on board the ship.

The shaded lantern was where Pearce had left it, but finding it in the gloom of a twilit wood was not straightforward, which made more anxious an already nervous d'Imbert. The waiting that followed, for the boat would not enter the Grande Rade before it was safe to approach in the dark, did nothing for the Frenchman's mood, bringing forth an angry curse when Pearce suggested that he stop his pacing back and forth, since it was doing no good.

'How long now?' d'Imbert demanded, having already made the point that, if they did not come soon, they must abandon the attempt. The suspicions of St Julien would not be assuaged if d'Imbert was missing come the morning.

The lantern had been lit well in advance, so that Pearce had no doubt it was working. He unshaded it a fraction to look at his watch, and although it was not yet eleven, he decided to act as if it was the hour, just to appease d'Imbert. So they walked out from the doubtful protection of the sparse pines, and arranging their bodies that there was no spillage, he shone the lantern out to sea for no more than two seconds.

'You do understand Lieutenant, that should one of our guard boats see that light, they will probably come to investigate.'

Pearce replied quite sharply, because d'Imbert was getting on his nerves. 'Then I expect, sir, since you brought with you a brace of pistols, that you will discourage them.'

'Fire at my fellow countrymen, maybe even men who have served under me?'

'I doubt you will have time, sir, to ask for their record of service. I suggest at the point at which they call out in French, that you shoot at them before we both run like the devil.'

'I fear I have annoyed you, Lieutenant Pearce, but I would like you to understand that I feel uncomfortable in the role I have undertaken. I am not a natural conspirator.'

'Which implies you think I am?'

'I don't know what you are Lieutenant Pearce.'

Under his breath, as he unshaded the lantern a second time, Pearce murmured. 'Then that is two of us.'

'A light,' d'Imbert exclaimed, in a voice so loud it proved he was a stranger to deception. Commanding silence, Pearce unshaded his lantern again, opening and closing the door three times, that answered by a faint double pinpoint of reply.

'That's Trevivian.'

The midshipmen must have had them row hard, for it was no more than ten minutes till the cutter arrived at the moonlit beach, the men jumping out to carry the officers aboard, despite Pearce's vocal protest that it was unnecessary.

'I am more minded of your dignity than you are, sir,' he called, in his drawling burr. 'Might I ask who is the gentleman with you?'

'No, Mr Trevivian, you may not.'

Once settled in the thwarts, and the cutter pushed off from the soft sand of the beach, the midshipman referred to the lucky escape they had enjoyed the previous night, clearly concerned that having made the journey two more times, their luck might not hold.

'I fetched muskets on this outing, sir, though I will not permit their use if you think it unwise.'

'Never fear,' said Pearce, 'Your muskets will be superfluous. I think our passenger will know what to answer if we are challenged.'

* * *

Lord Hood was roused out from his cot, Pearce insisting that what needed to be discussed must be seen to straight away, so both he and d'Imbert were ushered into the presence of a rather irate admiral, who, being clad in a floor length dressing gown, lacked the distinction that went with his rank. Rear-Admiral Hyde Parker, likewise summoned from his slumbers and similarly clad, looked more suited to that garb than he did to his uniform.

'Might I introduce to you, sir, Captain the Baron d'Imbert.'

'Captain,' said Hood, his response lacking the degree of courtesy that Pearce thought warranted, so little that he spoke to the C-in-C quite sharply.

'This officer, sir, has undertaken a hazardous journey to get here and is engaged in a mission that, if discovered, will cost him his life. I think that however inconvenient you find it to be roused from your bed, it behoves you to recognise that.'

'How long is it, Parker, since an admiral could flog a lieutenant in our Navy?'

Parker smiled, as he replied, looking even more self-satisfied in the process. 'It must be over a hundred years, sir.'

'Then we need to see it revived,' Hood growled, before, in addressing d'Imbert, his voice changed completely. 'My apologies, I have been quite rightly corrected, even if the manner of it as well as the source, is inappropriate. You must be sharp set after your journey. Can I offer you some food?'

'A glass of wine, perhaps, sir,' d'Imbert replied. 'I doubt my stomach would accept food.'

'Mine would,' said Pearce, only to be told quite brusquely that his could wait.

He then listened to the preliminaries, as d'Imbert sought

to imply that his mission was exploratory only, and to allude rather than underline that there were competing factions in Toulon, Jacobins versus Girondists, and even those who sought a restoration of royal power, this while Hood played with various notions of what could, and could not be done, none of which came close to answering what was needed. Such play-acting might have gone on forever if d'Imbert had not noticed Pearce take out and make a great show of looking at his watch.

'Admiral Hood, you will forgive me if I am a touch abrupt. Lieutenant Pearce has just reminded me that time is too short for us to engage in diplomatic niceties. Admiral de Trogoff will need to know what you can do immediately, what is possible in the future, and when that may come to fruition. You will know without my telling you that Toulon cannot indefinitely hold off a siege, which must surely come at some time, without soldiers to man the defences. Are such soldiers available, and if they are, when can they be brought here?'

'There is much to consider, Captain d'Imbert.'

'And no time to do it,' interjected Pearce, though he added, 'If you will forgive me.' The Frenchman looked pained, so Pearce added, 'Captain d'Imbert will not say so, because he feels it demeaning to admit such a thing, but his life will be endangered if he does not return before daylight. If that is not possible, it alters everything. Indeed it might mean the Captain would be better abandoning his duties and staying aboard *Victory*.'

'Lieutenant,' protested d'Imbert, holding up his hand, for what he evidently thought of as a heavy-handed ploy. 'This is not the way such matters are decided.'

'I do think,' Pearce insisted, 'that the time we have precludes sticking to the normal rules. The captain will also not say that his commanding admiral is inclined to prevaricate, is an indecisive commander by his very nature and will only act on certainty, not chance. He has mentioned that Admiral St Julien holds different opinions, but not that he is viscerally opposed to anything that smacks of surrender and will do all in his power to prevent it, even, if he thinks he can get away with it, to the point of arresting Admiral de Trogoff for treason. I believe the only thing that stops him from doing so immediately, is that he is not sure that he can carry the crews of the ships.'

'Have you quite finished, Lieutenant?' asked Hood.

'I speak only out of concern, sir, that you do not understand the currents with which you deal, and I would say, that with my experience, I know more about the forces that shape revolutionary politics than anyone in this cabin. Those who must risk their lives by declaring for the cause of freedom must know they are going to be supported, otherwise they will do nothing.'

'I think you have said your piece, Lieutenant Pearce, now if you will let me, I will answer Captain d'Imbert's concerns.' With that he looked at the Frenchman, 'and of course those of Admiral de Trogoff. Would you like those in writing?'

'Yes.'

The under-secretary who had been forced to lend his coat to Pearce was fetched, dressed in his shirt sleeves and breeches, his attention at first on the state of his only covering garment. A bark from Hood had him seated, quill poised, as the admiral spoke.

'You will not know, since the news only came to me before I retired for the night, that Marseilles has been invaded by the army of a General Carteaux, this after he defeated those marching on Lyon, an action I must tell you I strongly advised against.'

'Then it cannot be held,' said d'Imbert, this while Pearce was thinking what a sly old fox Hood was, keeping that information to himself until it could be used with some impact.

Hood nodded his head in agreement. 'It cannot. I fear for the people who live there, for I cannot imagine that there will be much in the way of forgiveness.'

The Baron dropped his head, and it was obvious he was silently praying, which Hood respected by holding his tongue until the man was finished. 'But our concern is Toulon. I will undertake, on a request for support, to immediately land the marines, to the number of fifteen hundred, to secure the heights of Mont Faron and the approaches through Ollioules to the west and I am sure Admiral Langara will do likewise. I will also land sailors to shift what guns you have in the Arsenal, and set them to building the redoubts and gun emplacements necessary to hold off a besieging force well away from the town walls.'

'That will not suffice, sir.'

'I am aware of that, Captain, and because of that knowledge I will send for troops. First from Spain, though you must understand that I have to speak with Admiral Langara as soon as I can get him aboard. Then there is Naples. I will despatch a senior officer to request from the Kingdom of the Two Sicilies help to defend Toulon. I expect such a request to be met with a positive, given that they will be helping to secure the future of their own territories, albeit at some length from their borders, but also because, as you know, Queen Carolina is Austrian and a sister to Queen Marie Antoinette.'

The quill scraped behind, while d'Imbert sat rock still, leaving everyone else to wonder what he was thinking. Hood, it seemed, was the only one who knew. 'I see that you reckon that insufficient, too.'

'Even in numbers, Admiral, I have little faith that Spaniards and Neapolitans can hold any perimeter we decide upon. Spain is no longer the military power it was even fifty years ago, and as for Naples…'

He gave an elegant, and eloquent shrug, to say they would be near useless.

'I agree, which is why, before you leave, you will be given sight of a letter I intend sending by my fastest frigate to London, asking that troops be sent with all despatch to help us maintain not just Toulon, but to open a campaign to secure the whole of southern France.'

'Does England have such troops?'

'Britain,' replied Hood, with a half smile at Pearce, like most Scots inclined to bridle when the combined nation was not properly named. 'Our country has them available now. They are designed for service elsewhere, though you will understand discretion debars me for saying where. But I doubt they have sailed yet, and will not do so for at least a month. I am going to suggest to the government, of which I am, as the senior Sea Lord, a member, that they would be better employed on the coast of Provence.'

'Numbers.'

'Enough to hold off and destroy by attrition an army besieging Toulon, and once that army is forced to raise the siege, enough to pursue them and detach the rest of southern France from the Revolution. All we have to do, acting as allies, is to maintain the place until they arrive.'

John Pearce was impressed, thinking how different Hood was from de Trogoff; decisive, a man who could think through a problem and not only see but expound solutions, in short, a fighter and a leader who did not need to hold a conference to act.

'I would be happy to take these terms back to Admiral le Comte de Trogoff. I cannot guarantee he will find them sufficient.'

'And I cannot see what more I can offer. I would also

add that General Carteaux's army, once it has finished in Marseilles, will march on to Toulon regardless of what action you take, and as of this moment you have nothing with which to halt it.'

'I know that, Milord.'

'And you Captain, what is your opinion?'

Hesitating for half a second, d'Imbert was quite emphatic when he spoke. 'I will recommend that he accept your terms and act upon them, sir.'

'And the town?'

'Once they hear that Marseilles has been invaded, they will have no choice but to accept. There will, as you say, be retribution for what is perceived, let alone for what has been done.'

'Good. Lieutenant Pearce, be so good as to return his coat to my under-secretary, and your hat I will see gets back to its owner.'

'Sir.'

'Then get yourself into uniform. You will accompany Captain d'Imbert back to Toulon.'

'Why?'

Hood's eyes flashed. 'First, because I say so, and second because the terms of surrender I have outlined have to be presented to Admiral de Trogoff by a British officer, or at least someone dressed as one, and you are the person I have chosen for the task.'

'Sir, I have not slept for two nights.'

'You will have time to sleep, Lieutenant, when there is nothing to do. Now you will do as you are ordered.'

CHAPTER EIGHTEEN

The news had obviously come from Marseilles about what was happening there, and if half the shouted stories were true, the army of the Revolution was already in the city and spilling blood in quantity. Those on the Toulon quayside not arguing politics and speculating were going about their affairs with worried expressions, for the Revolution would not spare anyone thought of as traitorous, nor any person that a neighbour or rival chose to denounce. Pearce had seen it before, in Paris and the towns that led to Calais, that haunted look of being under threat from sources unknown.

In the early morning light, the old saw, 'sticking out like a sore thumb', was much in his mind as, one hand clutching his dress sword, he made his way along the quay. The white facings on his dark blue uniform coat, the brass buttons polished to gleaming perfection by a wardroom servant, were too obvious to be missed, especially set against the pale blue of d'Imbert's French uniform. Hardly anyone they passed failed to notice, which led to an extra examination and excited conjecture that obviously related to his presence ashore. He had no doubt that the news that a British naval officer was visiting Admiral de Trogoff's headquarters would spread around the town like a brush fire, adding to an already febrile and potentially perilous atmosphere.

Passing the same footman who had shown him to d'Imbert's rooms the previous day, he guessed that Admiral

St Julien would quickly be made aware of his presence, and it was clear from the lift of the eyebrows that the fellow recognised him, which killed off any notion that it was not part of some conspiracy. The grip on that sword tightened, and he made a point of asking his companion, once they were secure in his offices, if he still had those pistols.

'Nothing will happen to you here, Lieutenant, I assure you, for I can say you have come to us under a flag of truce.'

The Frenchman rang a bell, ordered that coffee and fresh rolls be fetched and that the Commanding Officer should be told that a plenipotentiary had come from Admiral Lord Hood with a letter addressed personally to him. Then he asked an equally important question.

'Admiral St Julien?'

'Is not at present in the building.'

'Good,' d'Imbert replied. 'Please let me know as soon as he arrives.' To Pearce's questioning look, he added, 'St Julien has several ladies by whom he is entertained. I suspect he is with one of them now, and since there is no alarm and every officer in the fleet knows what to do if there is, he will not rush to return to his duties.'

'Shameful,' said Pearce, unbuckling his sword and stretching out on a chaise, 'does he not know there's a war on?'

Under strain as he was, d'Imbert nevertheless managed a smile. 'I suspect, Lieutenant, that both you and I would both rather be engaged in what he is about, than what we are doing at the moment.'

'Right now, Captain, I think I would turn down even that in favour of sleep.'

With that Pearce closed his eyes, and fell into an immediate slumber, one that was not affected by the smell of coffee, freshly baked bread, the clinking of d'Imbert's crockery, the shouted exchanges and screams of encouragement and fear from the quay below his windows, or the endless stream of clerks bringing in the muster books, stores manifests and logs of the ships in the harbour, all of which they had checked, but which had to be passed and signed off as accurate by a senior officer.

D'Imbert woke him after an hour of truly deep and reviving sleep, which, once his eyes had cleared, revealed a worried-looking Frenchman holding a sheaf of reports in his hand, which he shuffled through as he spoke. 'Marseilles has definitely fallen and the guillotine is already at work. Rebequi, the fellow who led the delegation who came to see Lord Hood, has apparently thrown himself into the harbour rather than face such a death. The soldiers are raping, killing and stealing at will. Anyone prominent is being hauled to the scaffold for immediate execution.'

'Admiral de Trogoff knows this?'

The question was so obvious it did not have to be stated. Why had he not seen de Trogoff? It was a weary d'Imbert who told him. 'The admiral first sent to say he was at his toilette, which you will guess is not of short duration, but after an hour passed I enquired again. Now he has sent a second message to say he is indisposed, and would like to read Lord Hood's letter rather than meet you.'

'In short, I might ask him to respond to it?'

'I fear that is true. While you were asleep I sent a trusted man to inform Mancini and his friends of what Lord Hood proposes. I have added my own view that those in the town prepared to act must be ready to do so at a moment's notice, certainly before the day is out.'

Pearce had grabbed one of the rolls, and was chewing at it as he spoke. 'You do not see that as too hasty?'

'What do you think St Julien will do once he hears that a British Naval officer has arrived here in uniform, this after Marseilles has been taken and put to the sword by Carteaux. The man is far from stupid. He will surmise that portends a resolution, one that is unlikely to favour him and he will seek to act accordingly, which is what I would do. If he gathers his adherents, organises and arms them, they will form a formidable obstacle, perhaps an insurmountable one.'

'From where will the arms come?'

'Not from our warships, I am sure. The captains will prevent that. I have put guards on the Arsenal, but I have no guarantee they will bar a Rear Admiral from entry if he demands access.'

'Will Mancini act?'

'I hope so. The delegates to the local assembly are in session now, but no news has come that they are close to a conclusion. My fear is that the Toullonais will wait to see what the fleet does, while the fleet waits to see what action they take.'

'You must take command of this, Captain, of both townsfolk and the sailors.'

The reply lacked much in the way of conviction. 'I am obliged to obey the orders of my superior officer, Admiral de Trogoff.'

'Sophistry,' Pearce insisted. 'You are telling me you are prepared to accept the commands of one admiral, while I have no doubt you would readily disobey the commands of another.'

'Let me go and see de Trogoff. I may be able to get him to act.'

'And if he does not?'

The Captain turned his back on Pearce then, once more to look out over the Vieux Darse, to the ships being built and repaired, and the long lines of low buildings that made up the greatest dockyard in the Mediterranean, the pride of the French Navy since the days of Henri IV. His voice, when he finally spoke, was full of the despair of a man forced to contemplate going against all the tenets by which he had lived his service life.

'Then I must do as you say, and I hope that you believe

that my own fate will have nothing to do with whatever actions I encourage.'

'I know that, Captain,' Pearce replied, with genuine sincerity.

Pearce was left to his own devices and looking out over that same view that had so troubled d'Imbert, his eyes were once more drawn to the Brilliants, toiling away of the opposite side of the basin. If things were going to come to a head, if there was a possibility of fighting and bloodshed, they, under an armed guard, must be informed, for if they were not they could easily become victims. He was the only one who could warn them. He knew he should tell d'Imbert of his intentions but since he had no idea how to contact him directly, he was obliged to pass on the information to the footman whose loyalty was questionable. That hardly mattered; what could a footman do?

Back out on the quay, hurrying along, he was again the object of much speculation; these were folk who knew the dress of the different navies, and the wheel of rumour was working flat out, promising death from any number of sources. Not all the looks were hostile, most were alarmed or suspicious, but there was the odd fellow who shook his fist, though the hand on the sword deterred them from a more potent reaction. Unbeknown to John Pearce, that was the effect it had on Ralph Barclay, looking out at the morning view from the ramparts of his tower prison.

'Damn me, a British naval officer,' he shouted.

'Captain Barclay!' exclaimed his wife.

'My dear,' her husband replied, for once unabashed, 'there is nothing on heaven and earth that will condemn me for uttering an oath at the sight below.'

Emily came out into the open air, and followed his pointing finger, her hand up to shade her eyes from the sun, she fixed her gaze on the figure in the dark blue coat hurrying down the southern edge of the quay. 'That, my dear, is a British officer.'

'You are sure, husband?'

'My dear, allow that I know a lieutenant's coat when I see one.'

'I merely question whether he could be from another service.'

'No, he is one of ours.' Ralph Barclay insisted, turning to look out over the rest of the harbour, and seeing no change in the disposition of the shipping. 'The question you should be asking is this, what's a British naval officer doing parading about, unescorted, in a French naval base?'

'The simplest solution, husband, would be to ask him.'

'Which I was just about to suggest,' he replied. 'Perhaps you would care to accompany me?'

'I am not sure, given you have no idea of the nature of his presence, if that would be wise.'

'That is clever of you, my dear. Though I can see no danger, that does not mean that none exists.'

Ralph Barclay was in his coat and alerting his escorts within a minute, struggling to balance his uniform hat on his still bandaged head, this as his wife watched this unknown officer make a beeline for the crew of her husband's ship.

The men guarding the Brilliants were not like the townsfolk, or those sailors that had pointed at him from the decks of the vessels under repair. The man in charge, with the insignia of a sergeant on his cuff, stood up as soon as one of his underlings nudged him, the look of confusion on his face evident even at a hundred paces. The musket came half up and he called to the rest of his party to attend, so that by the time Pearce got close he faced a line of suspicious-looking men with weapons ready to be used.

'I am here under the parole of Captaine le Baron d'Imbert. I have his permission to talk to the prisoners.'

Said loudly, it had several of those prisoners looking up, but with the sun behind him and his fore and aft hat shading his face, they would struggle to identify him. The French sergeant responded with a deeply sceptical look, which matched his words. 'The good capitaine was here only yesterday. He brought them wine, food and coin, but he said nothing to me of a second *Rosbif* officer.'

The other *Rosbif* officer had to be Barclay, but that was irrelevant. 'I think you must ask yourself why I am here without my own guards. If you do not believe what I say you must send to naval headquarters and ask Captaine d'Imbert yourself. I wonder how he will take to you questioning the word of an officer, even a British one?'

Now all the Brilliants were standing, work forgotten, staring at the scene, as the sergeant chewed on his tobacco like a ruminating bovine, wondering what to do. The man before him had walked up unescorted, and behaved with a confidence he would be disinclined to challenge, considering the way he had used d'Imbert's name.

Seeing his wavering, Pearce added, 'I only wish to talk with them, in the same manner as their captain.'

'Then you will not mind, monsieur, that I keep a musket trained on you, one, which I must tell you, is loaded and primed.'

'Not one bit, but do make sure that your finger does not twitch.'

With that, Pearce turned to face the Brilliants, raising his hat as he did so, and watching the faces as one by one they recognised him. Costello, a dark-skinned bosun's mate who had been kindly in his own rough manner, cried out first, but it was the open-mouthed bosun he addressed.

'I bid you good day, Mr Sykes.'

'Pearce?' he replied, in deep disbelief, his eyes lowering and lifting from silver shoe buckles to uniform hat.

'The very same, Mr Sykes.'

'Christ almighty, Pearce, what are you doing here?' demanded Costello.

'And in that uniform?' wheezed a less than enamoured Kemp.

'And in that uniform, sir,' Pearce insisted, for Kemp was one who stirred unpleasant memories, a man to distrust, and one who was too free to use his starter on a man's naked back. But he was not looking at the rat-faced sod, he was examining all the faces for sight of Ben Walker.

'Like hell I will. Hell will freeze before I "sir" you, 'cause you ain't no officer, and that's no error. Dressed in that garb you'se asking for a flogging round the fleet.'

It was with a certain dread that he asked. 'Where's Ben, Mr Sykes?'

The bosun just shook his head in the way that implied that Ben was no longer alive. Pearce jerked his head back towards *Brilliant*. 'In the battle?'

Sykes shook his head again, about to explain, but in doing that his gaze was directed over the questioner's shoulder and it stayed there, this while Pearce was looking around for other faces, Martin Dent, Dysart, and Costello's best friend, Ridley. The shout from behind him took him by surprise, but that was overlaid by an immediate recognition of the voice.

'Lieutenant!'

Pearce turned to see Barclay, with two armed escorts, striding towards him, steadying a headpiece that refused to stay square on his head. Again the shade from his own hat hid Pearce's face, and he waited until Barclay was really close before lifting it, saying as he did so, 'Sir.'

Barclay reacted as if he had been hit by a hammer, stopping dead, his jaw moving but no sound emerging, his eyes full of the kind of look that Pearce imagined a man would have seeing a ghost. The words he added had a sweet quality, that did nothing to ease Barclay's confusion.

'Lieutenant Pearce, at your service, Captain Barclay.'

'You!'

'I do believe it is I.'

'Impossible!'

'Perhaps, Captain, you would like to pinch yourself to see if you are awake.'

That made some of the crew laugh, a sound which had an effect on Ralph Barclay, always sensitive to the possibility of ridicule. His mouth closed and his jaw clenched, the prelude to a burst of angry condemnation.

'How dare you, swine, wear that coat. I will not ask how you got here, but I suspect treachery has something to do with it. Explain yourself!'

'I am sorry, sir, I have no inclination to do that.'

'I am ordering you to explain yourself.'

'He's for it now,' Kemp said, an opinion that, judging by the murmuring, was shared by quite a few of his shipmates, some of whom must have wondered at the way Pearce was smiling.

'What a conundrum, Captain Barclay. You decline to see me in the rank I legitimately hold, which if I accept your premise makes me a civilian. As the former I have good reasons to decline the order, as the latter I can tell you to go sling your hook. Which is it to be?'

'I'll have you flogged for this.'

'Will you? I had it in the cabin of HMS *Victory* just last night that it is over a long time since lieutenants could be flogged by captains.'

'*Victory*!'

'Yes, I think I upset Lord Hood, but then I seem prone to that when faced with senior officers.'

'Hood is here?'

'Not precisely, but he is out at sea.'

'Why would Lord Hood have anything to do with the likes of you?'

'Now that is a question, in these last two days, I have asked myself more than once.'

Barclay's frustration boiled over, and he turned to the marine sergeant, watching the whole exchange with mystified curiosity. 'Arrest this man, he is an impostor.'

Seeing the confusion on the Frenchman's face, Pearce said, 'What a pity you don't speak French, captain. Not that I think he would obey you even if you could.'

Barclay looked around, as though salvation could be found from a dilemma that had no obvious solution. Finally he stared hard at what he clearly considered to be a walking insult. 'If I had a weapon Pearce, I would strike you down.'

'You remember my name,' Pearce replied, still in a sarcastic tone. 'That is something.' Then both his voice and his look hardened. 'As for having a weapon, I wish you had, for it would give me the opportunity to kill you.'

Barclay screamed. 'Explain what you are doing here!'

'Sorry, sir. I am under the personal command of Lord Hood, carrying out a mission for him which I am not at liberty to discuss. And even if I were not, I would decline to discuss it with you. Please be informed Captain Barclay, that as soon as the opportunity presents itself I intend to challenge you to a duel, and since I have some confidence in my ability with any weapon you care to choose, I can happily anticipate that the encounter will result in your demise.'

He then turned his back on Barclay, and indicated to Sykes to come close. The words he whispered had to be brief, but Sykes was quick to understand. Then Pearce turned to thank the French sergeant, who accepted a coin for his trouble, smiling, and totally unaware that the man giving it to him had just told the burly bosun that if a shot was fired anywhere in the harbour or the anchorage, he should immediately attack and kill his guards.

When he turned again it was to see Barclay's back as he strode back towards his prison, at a pace so furious that his escorts found it hard to keep up.

Ralph Barclay was still boiling with anger, his limbs shaking with that emotion, as he mounted the stone stairs that led to the top of the Tour de Mitre, and the questioning look that he received from his wife did nothing to mollify that. His hat was thrown at a chair and he was just about to open his mouth and tell her how much he had been traduced and by whom, when he realised that to be forthright was to open himself to a number of questions that he would not like to have to answer. Pearce had been the cause of trouble between him and his wife – indeed there lay the source of their first real quarrel – and he was not sure that she would, as she should, take his side. So it was with an almost Herculean effort that he steadied himself and answered the question that had yet to be asked.

'An impostor, my dear, and do you know those damned Frenchmen would do nothing about it. I shall complain to Captain d'Imbert.'

For once Emily did not chastise him for his language, too curious. 'An impostor? So he was not a British officer?'

'He was dressed as one, but no.'

'A Frenchman then?

'Not that. I am afraid he was exceedingly rude to me, and I had to threaten him with chastisement. I am happy to say that I put the blackguard in his place.'

'If he is not a Frenchman, who then is he?'

Cornered, Ralph Barclay gave an answer he was sure was true. 'A traitor, my dear, that is who, one that I hope will hang for his actions.'

CHAPTER NINETEEN

Like most seaports the lanes leading off the quay were narrow, high and heavily shaded tunnels that testified to the value of the land that edged the water, down which the wind would whistle at increased strength during any kind of blow. Pearce, striding along, was hardly aware of them or anything else, including the groups engaged in noisy and impromptu political debates. He was still savouring his encounter with Ralph Barclay and thinking of the various ways in which he would kill him, so the two quartets of cudgel bearing ruffians who emerged from the pair of alleyways immediately in front and behind took him completely by surprise. They were upon him so quickly he could only half-draw his sword before a blow on the forearm stopped the motion. By that time his arms had been pinioned, he had a knife at his throat, and he was being dragged out of sunlight into the shadows, with a rasping voice in his ear telling him not to try to resist.

If any of the numerous folk on the quayside saw what was happening no shout was forthcoming. Bundled into a dark alley he was pushed along, bouncing painfully off the walls, something to which his captors were indifferent. One had gone ahead and was now stood before a low door that had a step down to a dingy interior, into which he was thrown. He landed on a bare earthen floor, the door slamming shut behind him, followed by a voice from out of the gloom.

'So you are, as I suspected, a spy.' The voice was St Julien's, and with the oil lamps turned up that was confirmed. The admiral was in a plain black coat, looking, with his curled hair, quite the Jacobin.

'I am a British Naval officer,' protested Pearce, pulling himself onto his knees, aware that his captors, too, were inside and all around him, dark rough-looking men, but probably sailors. 'As you can see from my uniform.'

St Julien put a hand on his shoulder to prevent him rising to his feet, leaning over himself, his dark eyes flashing, black hair glistening in the light from the oil lamps, the heat of the now crowded room filling Pearce's nostrils with a whiff of a strong, rather feminine scent.

'You were not that yesterday, in d'Imbert's office. You were a Camargue livestock farmer. How do I know you are what you say you are today?'

'I am Lieutenant Pearce of His Britannic Majesty's Navy.'

That expression now sounded as feeble as a schoolboy excuse.

'Naval officer or farmer, you have come here for what purpose?'

'You cannot expect me to respond openly to that, monsieur.'

'Of course I do, though I suspect I know the answer.'

'Then why ask?'

St Julien hit him then, a swift backhanded blow that sent him onto his back. As he rolled, he landed up against the legs of one of the men who had abducted him, tasting blood in his mouth.

'Pick him up.' Two men took his arms and hauled him to his feet and now he and St Julien were face to face. 'You arrived this morning at the admiral's residence in the company of d'Imbert, who I suspect is in league with you in an attempt to persuade Admiral de Trogoff to betray his country. In order to get him to do that certain proposals would have had to be made, perhaps some signals agreed. I want you to tell me what they are, as well as the names of those you have dealt with here in Toulon, be they supporters of the Bourbons, or those traitors who have the nerve to still call themselves Republicans.'

'No.'

He was hit again, this time on the temple, and being tightly held there was no way to absorb what was a heavy blow. Hurt, Pearce shook his head, which St Julien clearly took as another refusal, providing an excuse to land another punch.

'I do not have time to toy with you. Right now I have every right-thinking French sailor, the men who believe in true liberty, gathering at the Place d'Armes in their thousands, and once I go to them I will lead them to seize the Arsenal. After that we will take over Toulon and root out the turncoats who intend to betray us to the English, naval and civilian. What is happening in Marseilles will be as nothing to what I will do here.'

'The answer is the same, Admiral.'

'I could hand you over to these fellows,' St Julien said, indicating those that surrounded them, 'and they would have great sport with you, I am sure. But that would take too long, so I must move quickly to a method I find personally unpleasant, but one that I feel is justified when the fate of my country is at stake. Fetch me a nail, a big one.'

Dimly aware of the movement, Pearce was forced to concentrate on the long sharp nail, at least six inches in length, which was placed in St Julien's hand, even more when one of the others brought forth an oil lamp, removing the glass sleeve that kept out the draft, to expose the naked flame. A pair of pincers were handed over as well, and St

Julien first placed the head of the nail in the jaw of the pincers, then the point in the now guttering flame.

'Distasteful as I say, and I hope you believe me when I say that employing it will cause me much grief.' Pearce was transfixed with the fine tip turning the flame from gold to blue. 'When this turns red, my friend, I am going to put it first in one eye and then, if you still refuse to answer my questions, I will heat it again and jam it in the other.'

Pearce was sweating, and it was not just from the heat of the room. Fear was adding to that, for he had no doubt that St Julien was telling the truth, except in one respect. His proposed victim was convinced that he was going to enjoy his torture, the evidence of that was in his silky, almost happy voice.

'Shall I call you Lieutenant?' St Julien asked, as the nail tip began to redden. 'Perhaps since I am about to render you useless, it would be a kindness. So, Lieutenant, before you forfeit one eye, what are the terms by which Admiral de Trogoff will be persuaded to act against his duty? Who are the people in the town who support such a move, and just how much is d'Imbert involved?'

The sweat was running down Pearce's brow and into his eyes, making him blink. He could feel the shaking in his knees as he anticipated the pain that he would soon experience, and was sure if his captors let him go, he would fall. His resolve was weakening too; was it worth refusing to speak? What was his silence for? The Navy? His Country? Trogoff and d'Imbert? The latter would tell him to give up what he knew; that was a Frenchman who would not see another man suffer to save himself.

The pistol shot, muffled by the thick oak of the door, stopped even that train of thought. It certainly made St Julien jerk his head to the entrance, and in the act of doing so remove the nail from the flame. Pearce observed this as his knees gave way, for those holding him had let go in alarm, something that increased as the door burst open, and a musket, taking no aim, fired into the group around him, producing a thud and a curse rather than a scream, one that told Pearce one of his captors had been hit. As that musket was withdrawn, two pistols appeared, to be discharged as well into what was now a panicked mass.

Pearce, now back on his knees, grabbed hold of St Julien's legs and hauled hard, bringing the admiral crashing down and sending the oil lamp flying, vaguely aware of another burst of gunfire and a great deal of yelling and screaming. But he was concentrating on the admiral, still with that heated nail in the pincers in his hand, as that was jabbed towards him.

The smell of singeing material was instant, and so was the searing pain as the nail penetrated the cloth of his coat and entered his upper arm. With his right hand he hit St Julien in a downwards blow that jammed the Frenchman's head into the ground, then he fell forward and finding the jaw he bit him as hard as he could, an act which had the nail removed. Scrabbling to get some purchase he then tried to knee him in the groin, which was only partially successful, and an attempt to follow it up was thwarted by hands grabbing him and pulling him back.

The despair that flooded through him was relieved when Mancini shouted at him, telling him to stop, telling him that he was free.

His arm aching like the devil, Pearce stood in his shirtsleeves, watching the confrontation between the two admirals. St Julien was defiant, bruised and scarred, not from what his recent captive had done to him, but to the rough handling he had been subjected to on the way to de Trogoff's headquarters, that added to by the many stones thrown at him by those who supported Mancini and his friends, which to Pearce's surprise, now seemed to be most of the inhabitants. Outside and below the open windows a noisy crowd had gathered, and it was obvious from the shouts floating up that they wanted St Julien strung up on the nearest warehouse hoist.

'You have acted outside your orders, Admiral St Julien,' said de Trogoff, but without much in the way of anger.

'I acted out of conviction, monsieur, which is more I think than you had in mind.'

That made de Trogoff slap his desk hard with one hand, but it seemed to stem from petulance rather than fury. 'You will address me properly, Admiral. I am your superior officer. You presume to issue a declaration accusing me of treachery, a call to support the Revolution as it is interpreted by those who have taken over the government of France, that followed an instruction to sailors of the fleet to stay ashore, leaving their ships when we have an enemy ready to carry out an assault.'

'Are you not planning treason?'

'You Admiral St Julien are engaged in it. If you are not, why gather so many sailors into a mob?'

'There is a need to protect the Revolution.'

'It is you and your Jacobins who threaten the Revolution!'

'I refute that.' St Julien looked around the room, with a sneer. 'And I ask myself why we are discussing this in the company of such people, and allowing a mob to gather outside, some of whom are openly calling for the return of a King. If I was in command...'

'Which you are not!'

'If I was in command, the National Guard would be dispersing them at the point of their bayonets.'

'Capitane d'Imbert,' asked de Trogoff. 'How many sailors have gathered in the Place d'Armes?'

'I would estimate the number at some five thousand, sir, but there are also a leavening of civilians and National Guardsmen amongst them, not many, but some.'

St Julien cut in. 'There are honest men in Toulon, then?'

De Trogoff ignored him, and with a worried look asked. 'Are they a danger?'

'They are leaderless, sir, and at the moment mainly without weapons. Without Admiral St Julien they have no idea what to do. I am happy to say that no officers obeyed the admiral's order to abandon their duties and join with the mob.'

'And the sous-officers?'

'They, sir, have stayed at their posts aboard ship, and done their best to persuade the crews to stay neutral. Also, I have set some trusted men to man the guns on one of the repairing warships in the inner harbour. Those guns are trained on the entrance to the Arsenal.'

'There you are, St Julien,' de Trogoff said. 'All that hot air to no purpose. The question is, what are we to do now, and most importantly what are we to do with you?'

'I would suggest a secure confinement, sir,' insisted d'Imbert. 'We cannot let the mob have their way.'

'How noble, d'Imbert,' St Julien sneered. 'I hope you have enough men to get me to a place of safety.'

It was the captain's turn to be sharp, and there was no petulance in his reply. 'I am extending to you, Admiral, a courtesy I doubt you would extend to me, but then I was brought up to believe that no man should be killed for his beliefs.'

'You should be prepared to die for your honour, and one day you shall, but it will be for your perfidy.'

Pearce finally spoke up. 'Admiral Hood should be told what is happening.'

That made de Trogoff shift uncomfortably in his chair.

'Are we absolutely sure what is happening? I am not certain you understand the currents of politics in the part of the world, Lieutenant.'

'I understand them very well.' Pearce insisted. 'They differ little from those of Paris in that he who acts boldly usually carries the day, and there is support for you if you do so. That shouting outside the window is not in my imagination. The town has made its voice and its aspirations known.'

'There are a dozen different opinions out there.'

'All anti-Jacobin, Admiral. The only question left is for you to make known where you stand.'

If he had hoped for a response Pearce was disappointed. De Trogoff just sat in his chair, half slumped, clearly overloaded with his responsibilities, while outside and in the harbour thousands of people waited for a decision which only he could make. It was a full minute before he spoke.

'Five thousand in the Place d'Armes, you say, d'Imbert?' The nod had the admiral's chin on his chest. 'We cannot imprison that number, nor can we have them free to do what they will.'

'Then, sir,' d'Imbert replied, 'we must send them away from here. Get them out of Toulon.'

The response was not a question. 'Send them away. Yes.' Then de Trogoff looked up, a gleam in his eye. 'But will they go?' No one had the answer, but de Trogoff did. 'They will go if you, St Julien, will lead them.'

'Sir,' d'Imbert protested, only to be silenced by a hand, as de Trogoff addressed his second-in-command.

'I have no mind to lock up an admiral of the French Navy, it is not fitting, nor am I prepared to hand you over to another authority and risk seeing you strung up like a common criminal.'

'I suggest it might set a precedent?'

The threat was obvious; hang me and one day the same

could happen to you. That the threat struck home was obvious, and Trogoff blanched at the thought of swinging himself. If he had doubted his course of action before, that evaporated, and his manner seemed more positive.

'Admiral St Julien, if you give me your parole that you will lead these malcontents away from Toulon, and keep them from any wrongdoing on the way, I will accept your word and let you go.'

As if on cue, the noise outside rose, and the threats to hang the Jacobin were the loudest. Even under his darker skin, and for all his bravado, it was clear that the junior admiral was fearful. His eyes were drawn to the window as he spoke. 'I accept.'

'You must depart at once and leave your servants behind. I will send them on to you with all your possessions.' Then de Trogoff, knowing the man's proclivities well, added, 'And of course anyone you wish to keep under your protection.'

St Julien grabbed a quill and a piece of paper off the desk and scribbled down a couple of names, which he handed to de Trogoff, who said, 'I hope, Admiral, that we meet again, in happier times. The rear of these headquarters are guarded by marines, and clear of those clamouring for your head.'

It was obvious that they had not originally been put there for his benefit, so St Julien just snorted, and without another word left the room, leaving the man who had troubled to ensure a route for his own escape, to crow. 'A neat solution, don't you think, gentlemen.'

It was d'Imbert who replied. 'A solution, sir. Only time will attest to how neat it is. Now, when will you go to meet Lord Hood.'

'I will not meet Lord Hood, d'Imbert.'

'You must, sir!'

The little rotund admiral was all unction as he replied. 'There is no must about it, d'Imbert. I am resigning my command as of this moment. I will not have those Jacobin swine in Paris say I am a traitor. Besides it is up to the town delegates to do what is necessary. Let them be sullied by that.'

'And our ships?'

'If you wish to surrender a fleet of France to an Englishman, then you do it.'

'You will receive Lord Hood if he comes ashore, will you not?'

'I have had my servants packing all morning, Captain. If the townspeople invite the English to come ashore and protect them from the forces of the Revolution, I will be in my carriage on my way to Italy. Once there, I will decide if it is wise to carry on to the Rhine, to the encampment of the Comte d'Artois.'

'And if we succeed in detaching Provence? The loss of Marseilles might not be permanent.'

'Succeed in detaching France, d'Imbert. Nothing less will do!'

Looking out from his tower, still fuming at his treatment by Pearce, Ralph Barclay, bandage removed to show an ugly scab, was watching things unfold with increasing confusion. He had observed numerous crowds of jeering sailors making their way into the town, to be greeted by gestures from the inhabitants that were far from friendly. If there had been mayhem before, it was clearly getting worse. Was what he and d'Imbert talked about actually coming to pass? He could also see the back of the mob outside de Trogoff headquarters, but he could not make out what it was they were baying for – perhaps the admiral's head. He knew from his own experience that such gatherings were fickle. No lover of the mob, he was far from convinced that what was afoot boded well, and so he had ordered a boat to take him over to the infirmary, which had the virtue of being further away from whatever trouble was brewing. If things turned out well, such a move would cause no harm; if it was threatening, then, as he explained to his wife, the infirmary, furthest from the centre of things, was the best place to be.

'Should we not then inform those in the guardroom?' asked Emily, talking to his back as she donned a cloak to keep off the sea spray.

'Glaister?' he asked.

'Who else?'

'Will the guards let them come with us, my dear.' That was when Barclay turned and saw the look on her face, and as quick as a flash, for it was not a pleasant one, he said, 'They will be obliged to stay, and I have had the thought that so must I. It would never do to desert my officers.'

'And me?'

'My dear, it was your safety that first raised my concern, and I have to admit, though you will find this hard to credit, that in thinking of you, I had momentarily forgotten about those in the guardroom, which is something of which I am now ashamed. You must take the boat, alert Mr Lutyens that something is afoot, and tell him to take what precautions he can in case it turns threatening.'

'I would rather stay with you.'

'Madame,' Ralph Barclay said, in a kindly tone. 'That is an order, and as my wife I expect you to obey it.' With that he stepped forward and kissed her on the forehead. 'Now put on your bonnet, and go.'

Back on the rampart, having seen Emily's boat pull clear, once more watching the mayhem across the Petite Rade, the knock made him stiffen, but the door opened to reveal Glaister and Bourne, looking perplexed.

'Our guards, sir. They unlocked the door to our room and then left their posts. What should we do?'

Ralph Barclay went out to the gateway, looked along the neck of land that ran towards Toulon, and saw that his crew were no longer working, but sitting idly, with no sign of anyone driving them to do otherwise. That added to his confusion, but on one thing he was determined. Whatever was taking place, it was no job of his to get involved, and since they were in no danger, it would be best to let them stay where they were, as any movement of such a body of men back to the tower might alert forces with which he would rather not have to deal.

'We stay put, gentlemen, but you may fetch your fellow prisoners up to these ramparts, so they can at least see what is happening.'

A request to Lord Hood had been drafted, the leaders of the town, like Mancini, ensuring it came from the delegates of the local convention, not the Navy. Pearce went out with them, to stand at the back and watch the formalities take place, a formal request for protection. Then Hood presented his terms; that a British governor would need to take charge of all civil affairs, and that official must have all the powers he would need under martial law, though he would operate through local functionaries in any decrees he implemented. That all French ships in the harbour must immediately strike their flags and be for use by the British Navy as they saw fit, an instruction Pearce was ordered to take back to Captain d'Imbert, now the senior French officer in the port.

This he did, expecting the man to object, but d'Imbert did nothing of the kind. He merely invited Pearce to step outside where he led him to the flagstaff that had served to relay orders to the fleet. There he hauled down the tricolour flag of the Revolution, and fastened on the Fleur de Lys of the royal house of France. As he raised it, a signal gun fired from just along the quay, and on every ship in the harbour the tricolour was struck, and the same flag flew to the masthead.

'You see, Lieutenant Pearce, we have declared for the King. We are now part of the coalition against the madmen of Paris. Lord Hood must now treat us as allies. Far better that, than surrender.'

'Well Mr Sykes, I find you at rest, I see.'

Sykes, sitting on a bollard, looked up at Pearce, and examining his face, saw the swellings where St Julien had hit him.

'You been in the wars?'

Pearce nodded, but made no mention of his arm, which was hurting like the devil.

'I still don't know what to call you?'

'For the moment John Pearce will do.'

'So what's happening, John Pearce?'

'If you would care to come with me, I would like to take you aboard a ship.'

'Which ship?' Sykes asked, with the suspicious look of someone being told something too good to be true.

'*Brilliant*.'

'The Frogs have surrendered?'

'No. It seems they have decided to join us. It's not the same.'

Looking towards the Tour de Mitre he saw Barclay hurrying towards them, a knot of other men, including two officers, behind him, though he was unaware that it was once more a sight of his coat that had made the man depart his refuge.

'*Brilliant* will be ours again, and I would like you aboard before the captain.'

Sykes followed his gaze and shook his head. 'Sorry, Pearce, but I reckon from now on you don't have to live with the bastard. We do.'

'As you wish.'

'One thing,' Sykes said, as he stood up. 'We've got a few in the infirmary, which is on the other side of the bay. It would be kind of you to let them know what has happened.'

'I will do that happily.'

'You best move, afore you has to carry out what you said, and kill Barclay. Might be a trifle hard, with him surrounded by his officers.'

'Barclay can wait, Mr Sykes. Not for long, but he can wait.'

CHAPTER TWENTY

'Hello Martin.' Young Dent swung round so quickly he was wincing from the pain in his back by the time he faced John Pearce. 'I am looking for Mr Lutyens, can you tell me where I can find him?'

Martin eased his bandaged shoulder then indicated the open french windows. 'He's out on the terrace. But what is you doin' got up in that garb? Never mind that, what in Christ's name are you doin' here?'

The throbbing pain in Pearce's arm had grown worse, and much as he knew he would have to explain himself, that was more pressing. Half turning he showed the singed hole where St Julien had stabbed him with the nail 'Later. I need the surgeon to look at my arm.'

Martin grinned and tapped his cheek. 'You been fightin'?'

'I'm afraid so.'

'Don't know why,' Martin said, grinning as he tweaked the nose that Pearce had broken. 'You'se a right bugger for a scrap, I seem to recall.' Pearce smiled, nodded and went out to the terrace, with Martin shouting after him. 'I'm happy to see you, matey, never mind how you got here.'

The shout caused the two people sitting on the rough bench to react. Lutyens, who was facing his way, twisted enough to catch sight of him. Emily Barclay, had to spin round completely, which had him removing his hat and bowing in a gesture of habitual politeness. The surgeon looked confused, the same as all the others he had met in Toulon, except on his singular countenance the effect was more marked. Emily Barclay reacted with shock, which was still on her face when he had completed his bow, and she stared at him in silence, her eyes ranging over his face; the even features, the direct, faintly amused and daring look remembered from the first time she had clapped eyes on him, which his bruised swellings did nothing to alter. When he spoke, even his voice was familiar.

'Mrs Barclay, my compliments. Mr Lutyens, I am happy to see you again.'

She blushed, the reddening of her cheeks adding to her attractiveness. It was the surgeon who spoke, pale blue eyes like saucers, his wispy near-ginger hair lifted by the breeze to stand up from his head. 'Pearce?'

'The very same, Mr Lutyens. Like the proverbial bad penny.'

'Your dress?'

Pearce spoke for Emily Barclay, not Lutyens, his voice pitched just the serious side of absurdity. 'It is entirely genuine, though there are those who question if it is deserved. A most fortuitous set of circumstances have given me a lieutenant's rank.'

'I cannot wait to hear you tell your tale.'

'That must wait, sir, since I require your services to treat a wound.'

Lutyens was off the bench in a flash, coming between him and Emily Barclay. She stood and said, in a slightly flustered voice, grateful for an excuse to get away. 'I will leave you to your duties, Mr Lutyens, and visit the wounded.'

Lutyens touched the wound, causing pain, which reminded Pearce that he was a cack-hand individual in that respect. Not incompetent, just disinterested in the discomfort of others.

'A red-hot nail, jammed in. I fear it went quite deep.' He spoke again before the surgeon could. 'Don't ask how.'

'Take off your coat and let me see.'

That had to be eased off as the pain was now quite acute, and as Lutyens was unable to get a good look, Pearce's stock and shirt were also removed. Emily Barclay, passing a window, looked in to see the half naked Pearce just before he sat on the bench, so much more like the seaman he had been than the creature in the blue coat. Her mind was racing with the same questions which had bothered everyone else: what was he doing here, ashore in a French port? But there were more: had it something to do with the turmoil from which her husband had insisted she take shelter? Would Lutyens tell Pearce that she had already visited the wounded on arrival, and thus reveal that her departure had been mooted by a lie and embarrassment? Why should she be embarrassed?

While thinking round these notions, her eye drifted to the blue coat, which Lutyens had thrown across the back of the bench, and a train of thought surfaced that she would have preferred to suppress. Emily Barclay recalled the high dudgeon with which her husband had returned to their apartment that morning, as well as the observation that had sent him out in the first place; the long distance sight of a man in the coat of Royal Navy lieutenant. She could recall quite clearly what he had said on his return; that the wearer had turned out to be an impostor, a blackguard and a traitor he had threatened with chastisement. Lutyens was tending to a man dressed in the same garment, but one salient fact, nor the conclusions it engendered, could not be contained. John Pearce might be all those things her husband had said, but he was certainly a man that Ralph Barclay knew well. If it was he, then why had her husband not said so?

'Devenow.'

'Mam?'

'The men who rowed me over here, I think they are taking refreshments in the kitchens. Please be so good as to call them for me, I wish to go back.'

'The only fear of infection,' said Lutyens, peering into the angry red hole, and the blistering that the nail had caused, 'comes from a quantity of your linen being carried into the wound. Was your shirt clean?'

'Fresh this morning.'

Lutyens shouted. 'Devenow, fetch the spirits of wine and my medicine case.' Seeing the arched eyebrows on his patient, at the use of the name, Lutyens added, with a slight cackle. 'The captain insisted I use him as an assistant, some kind of reward for his services in the battle. If they fail to arrive we can assume he has drunk the spirits at least.'

The bottle was fetched, an amazed look was added, then the bully disappeared, as Lutyens rubbed alcohol over the wound. 'I'm afraid I can do little for you. The hole is neat, and the burning nail has cauterised the flesh on entry. A little extract of lead will help with the bruising, and the blisters I will treat with my German herbal tonic. Do you recall it, that most efficacious brew called Melisengeist? Then we will just have to apply a bandage and check it daily to see if it shows any sign of suppurating.'

'No amputation?'

Meant as a joke, it fell flat with Lutyens. 'I have had enough of those to last a lifetime.' What followed was a garbled account of what had happened to HMS *Brilliant*, confused because Lutyens was no master of naval terminology or tactics, and also because he had been below in the cockpit throughout. But he did manage to convey how bloody it had been.

'Death or glory seems to be habitual in the King's Navy.'

'Are bad pennies?'

'Even more so, from what I have observed.'

'Was the letter I wrote of any use?'

'Immense,' Pearce replied, unsure if it was true or false, but the question reminded him of the help the surgeon had offered aboard *Brilliant*, quite unbidden, for which he was grateful. It also brought back the image of Lutyens father in his black coat and priestly collar, an older and more serious physical specimen of the son. 'Your father could not have been kinder.'

'What did he say of me?'

His patient winced as Lutyens applied the bandage, seemingly able to jab the wound with every turn. 'No doubt what he has said to you many times. That you are wasting your talents on your chosen path.'

Pearce had been surprised at what Lutyens had given up to go to sea; not a promising career but an established one as a leading medical practitioner in the capital, who through his connections had a list of patients that would have been the envy of most of his contemporaries, with fees to match. To abandon that for the lowly life of a naval surgeon was bizarre, indeed.

'He told you of my previous work?' Pearce nodded, and with a worried look Lutyens asked. 'I wonder if you would oblige me by keeping that to yourself. You will, won't you?'

'I owe you that, and more.' Seeing Lutyens embarrassed, he changed the subject. 'I was interested to see the Captain's wife here, and I must say looking as bonny as ever.'

'Her husband felt that the town was getting dangerous.'

'It will be safe now, Mr Luytens. In fact I expect before tomorrow is over that you will find the British fleet anchored just out there in the outer roads, and you may choose to stay here or go back aboard *Brilliant*.'

'So the men will be freed?'

'Naturally.' Pearce replied, wondering why Lutyens looked disappointed.

'And you?'

'I have to go aboard another vessel, called HMS *Leander*, to visit some old friends of mine.'

Lutyens tapped the coat, which now lay across the bench. 'Not till you have told me how this came to pass.'

The arrival of the British fleet occasioned a massive discharge of guns, as every fort and bastion felt it had to salute Hood's flag, and every ship in the fleet saw the need to reply. Stood on HMS *Victory's* quarterdeck, surrounded by flag officers, Pearce kept a telescope trained on *Leander*, coasting in under topsails in the middle of Admiral Hotham's division. Bourbon flag flying, the French had moved from its blocking position across the entrance to the Petite Rade, but either because of caution or good manners Hood made no attempt to enter the inner anchorage, happy to keep his ships in the outer roads. But a stream of boats did make their way to the shore, full of the fleet marines and those who would command them, this while yet more came out from the port, carrying dignitaries and French naval officers, who would conclude the terms of the agreement.

Mancini and his fellow delegates were piped aboard, as was d'Imbert, who threw him a warm look, all there to discuss how Toulon was to avoid the fate of Marseilles. With so many boats employed shipping troops ashore, Pearce had to wait to ask for one to transport him to *Leander*, so he was still aboard when Ralph Barclay arrived to see the admiral. After a glaring exchange, Knight took his fellow captain to his own cabin, later sending for Midshipmen Farmiloe and Burns for what Pearce supposed was probably a happy reunion. Finally, with a meeting in Hood's great cabin in full swing, and an injunction preventing any officer not on a particular service to stay out of both town and port, a boat became available, and he was rowed across to the now anchored seventy-four, where he went through the ritual of asking for permission to come aboard, readily granted by a fellow lieutenant called Taberly, the Officer of the Watch.

'I am seeking some men with whom I served before.'

'The wardroom is at your disposal, Mr Pearce.'

'Not officers, seamen. Those who were taken aboard at Spithead from HMS *Centurion*. They were from the armed cutter *Griffin*.'

'Seamen?' said Taberly, with an arch look. 'How singular that you call them friends.'

Pearce was quite cold when he answered. 'I find that when you face death with people, their rank ceases to have much relevance. If I were to give you their names…'

'I have my own duties to perform, Mr Pearce. Besides, you will have to seek permission from the Premier, who is at present in his cabin. I presume you can find your way there.'

Pearce decided he did not like Taberly, and it was plain from the look on that fellow's face that the feeling was mutual. So he nodded and made his way aft, then down to the deck below, but instead of making for the wardroom he just carried on to the lower deck, to the crowded quarters which were home to the crew and the ship's main armament. The sight of an officer made quite a few men stiffen; the presence of a blue coat in this part of the ship, outside a battle, was to order some unpleasant task carried out, to ensure none of the Articles of War were being breached, or just to nose around looking for something not right, in other words to cause trouble.

Bent over and hat off, for the deck beams were close to his head, Pearce made his way down the central walkway.

The mess tables were down, one between each cannon, with its six-man section taking their ease, happy to be at anchor, with little to do, talking, no doubt speculating on when they would get ashore and what they would find there in the article of women and drink. Some were dicing, but not for any money he would be allowed to see, others carving or mending clothing, the rest just idling, with one or two sleeping, heads on their tables.

It was Charlie Taverner's hat he saw first, that item of clothing so dear to him, always tipped back to show his fair hair, which he felt marked him as how he wanted to be seen; not a sailor, but a bit of a gent. There was Michael O'Hagan's back, broad enough to blot out two others in the mess. Fat Blubber, spotting the uniform coat, made sure his mates were aware of the approaching danger, which killed off their conversation and had them all looking at the table top. It took no flash of insight to guess, at that point, this was not a happy ship. The men had been like that aboard *Brilliant*, chary about catching the eye of authority. After the postal packet and his time on HMS *Tartar* with the sarcastic Captain Freemantle, he had seen how a happy ship was run, knew on such a vessel the crew were pleased to smile at an officer and expected the same in return. No eye met his as he stopped by their table. As well as those already identified he recognised old Latimer, Rufus Dommet stuck in the corner and the merchant sailor, Littlejohn, who had been pressed with them into *Griffin*.

Pearce put his hat on the table, and spoke quietly. 'Well here's a sorry bunch of tars, I must say, not willing to offer a seat to an old shipmate.'

Rufus Dommet could not keep his head down, he being a person who combined youth and endemic folly, but neither could he speak, his mouth working silently and his finger jabbing towards the visitor.

'Somebody pinch me,' said Latimer, the next to look up, his dark weather-beaten face even more wrinkled than usual by disbelief.

'John-boy.'

Pearce held out his hand, looking into the bright green eyes of O'Hagan, and to the fact that the brows on his square face seemed to be swollen and that he too was bruised. 'Michael, it is very good to see you. Indeed it is very good to see you all.'

'You took your time getting here,' said Charlie Taverner, but there was joy in it, not malice. 'Pull up a barrel and park yourself.'

'Now my old eyes might be playing tricks, Pearce,' said Latimer, 'but that ain't no mid's coat you'se 'a wearing.'

'It's not, old friend, but it is mine by right, gifted to me by Farmer George himself.'

'You're on a ship?' asked Michael, so far more reserved than the others.

'I am not. I am here to get you free, and I can tell you that it has been a damned hard job to make the journey.'

The rest of the crew, four hundred men barring those on deck, were made curious by the sight of an officer sitting jawing with common seamen, all seven at the table hugger-mugger, gasping and occasionally laughing as he told them a tale. Enough of them braved the possibility of censure to move closer, and as each part of Pearce's story was told, the salient point was passed around the deck. But there was one person who hung back from this, and eventually decided to go aloft and tell someone in authority of this strange apparition, which led to the arrival of a midshipman with a 'request' that Mr Pearce attend, immediately, upon the Officer of the Watch. Looking past him, standing, though well back, Pearce saw Cornelius Gherson.

'I see Corny has not lost his gift for duplicity.'

'He never will,' said Charlie, glaring at the man.

'Sir!' insisted the midshipman. 'If you cannot command the men to silence, I must.'

'What happened in Portsmouth, John-boy,' asked Michael, ignoring how much the midshipman was angered by his temerity in continuing to converse. 'Why did you not come back as you said you would?'

'A woman, Michael.'

There was a pause, with Pearce waiting for the bitter condemnation that was bound to follow, but the huge Irishman just put back his head and laughed, spluttering, 'A woman. Holy Mother of Christ, how often have I fallen by the wayside for that sin. A woman by God, sure I hope she was a decent filly.'

He could see that the others wanted to speak, some to follow Michael and laugh, Charlie with the peaked look of a man who could not decide if he was angry or jealous, but the presence of the midshipman, plainly seething, ensured silence.

'I will get you free lads, I promise.'

The midshipman actually growled. 'Mr Taberly is waiting, sir.'

The name brought a strange look to Michael's face. The laughter evaporated as quickly as it had emerged, and whatever thoughts he had were mirrored in the glum faces of the others.

'That might no be as easy as you think, John-boy.'

Pearce half stood, picking up his hat. 'Yes it will. I have Lord Hood on my side, as well as the law.'

'I demand to know what you, sir, were doing on the lower deck of my ship, sitting on a barrel, talking to those men like some fishwife without permission to do so.'

'I told you Mr Taberly, they are friends of mine. What's

270

more, three of them were illegally pressed, and it is my intention to get them ashore and free.'

'Illegally pressed,' Taberly demanded, as though the notion itself was nonsense.

'O'Hagan, Taverner and Dommet are their names. I will not trouble you with the actual circumstance, but I can assure you of the absolute truth of what I say.'

'You can assure away, sir, but I can likewise assure you that those men will serve in this ship, probably until the peace.'

'Forgive me, sir, but you are not the captain, who is the man who will make the decision.'

'I can speak for him, Mr Pearce, and a great number of the crew, especially as we are here in Toulon and the fleet is at anchor. Seek to remove O'Hagan and there will be a riot.'

'A riot?' asked Pearce, totally thrown.

'Every man aboard *Leander* expects to make a bit out of his prowess. As soon as possible we will challenge every ship in the fleet to put up a bruiser, maybe even one from the French, I hazard that few will match O'Hagan, which will line the pocket of every man who backs him, and his shipmates will.'

'Like in Gibraltar?'

'Exactly,' Taberly replied, his face eager. 'That made us a pretty penny I can tell you.'

'It did nothing for Michael O'Hagan. I have seen how his face has altered.'

'Rubbish. He had light duties for a week, he gets special food, though, annoyingly, he shares that with his mess, as well as a cash reward for his efforts.'

'It does not occur to you that he might prefer not to fight.'

'Prefer not?' demanded Taberly, in a shocked tone.

'What the devil, sir, are you talking about? Seamen do not state their preferences, they do as they are bid and hope to do it well enough to avoid being punished. Or are you one of these tender-hearted fools who indulges common tars? They need the lash, man, to do their duty, if not on their backs, in their minds.'

'I would like to see the Captain.'

Taberly sneered at him. 'I very much doubt if the Captain would care to see you.'

'He can see me now, or when I come aboard with an order from Lord Hood to release the named men. I would prefer it, and I am sure he would too, to offer them up without instructions.'

Taberly took a step back and put his hands on his hips, examining Pearce as though he was some freak show exhibit. 'You really are the most extraordinary fellow, Pearce. I have never heard of you and I doubt anyone has. You have a commission a few weeks old and yet you come aboard my ship, looking as if you've been brawling in the gutter, bandy about the name of the Commander-in-Chief as though his sole purpose is to do your bidding, and even threaten the captain with discomfort. I think you have taken leave of your senses.'

Pearce wanted to slap him, but instead he smiled. 'It is you who are the fool, sir, you who will face the wrath of your captain when I explain to him, as I most certainly will get an opportunity to do, that you failed to see the seriousness of my request.'

'What I fail to see, sir, is what you are doing on this deck, which I would be obliged if you would leave.'

'I will be back.'

'Then you'd best come with orders, sir, for I will ensure that every officer on *Leander* knows of you, and that any attempt to return to this deck without official sanction will be declined.'

Pearce turned to go, but spun round for a parting shot. 'You best tell the ship, sir, that if they want a boxing bout, they best find another champion. O'Hagan will not fight, for I will tell him to refuse.'

Taberly had no idea how close he came himself to being floored, when he replied with a humourless grin. 'Refuse. Men in my division do not refuse. I do not think O'Hagan will dare, especially when the option is to fight or take a turn at the grating.'

Still seething, John Pearce returned to HMS *Victory*, to find the whole Toulon delegation still there, including a worried-looking Baron d'Imbert, his concerns, once voiced, weighing heavily.

'I persuaded Admiral de Trogoff to stay on the grounds of his own personal safety, and treat with Lord Hood, but it will not surprise you to know that St Julien, in order to save his own skin, left without bothering to take with him his Republican followers. So we have near five thousand of them, officers and men, sitting in the town, and the Lord alone knows what to do with them.'

'Did you not say there were no officers in the crowd at the Place D'Armes.'

'I lied, Lieutenant Pearce, for fear of the effect it would have on my admiral. Now I fear for the effect it will have on yours.' A voice summoned him to the great cabin, and d'Imbert gave Pearce a weak smile as he moved away. 'I must go in there and propose a solution.'

CHAPTER TWENTY-ONE

Ralph Barclay had to wait a long time to see Lord Hood, which underlined to him his place in the pecking order, this driven home to him when Captain Knight played host to several captains who had been admitted, amongst them the captain of HMS *Agamemnon*. He was a man for whom Barclay had an almost visceral dislike, Horatio Nelson being the antithesis of what he considered to be a competent officer. Added to that were two facts that rankled even more: though just ahead of him on the captain's list, Nelson had been given command of a sixty-four gun ship, while he had a small frigate. The other was more telling: Nelson was known to be esteemed by Lord Hood, which Ralph Barclay was most assuredly not. Then there was the other point which mystified him; Nelson thought of him as a friend, and treated him as such, but then the man was like that. Quite a number of his fellow captains found him to be a bit of a sycophant.

'I have orders for Naples,' piped Nelson, in that voice which Ralph Barclay described to others, including his wife, as girlish. 'They are being drawn up as we speak. I must impress upon the Court of the Two Sicilies that a failure to support the Toulon enterprise will do them harm in the long run.'

Naples! Him! Ralph Barclay thought, looking down at Nelson. Hood must be mad! Surely he should send someone of stature, not to mention height, instead of this pint-sized poltroon!

'How interesting, Captain Nelson. You will be able to exercise your diplomatic skills.'

Nelson laughed, or as Barclay would later describe it, giggled, totally missing the sarcastic tone. 'I am damned short on those, I can assure you. But I am informed that the representative at Naples is a competent fellow.'

'Hamilton.'

'You know him?'

'I know of him, who does not? He tied himself to that trollop who sat for Romney, the one with the auburn hair, Emma something or other. Only God knows how many men she lay on her back for before she snared the old fool. Imagine, a relative of the Duke of Hamilton, a childhood friend of the King, in his sixties, and he goes and marries a whore.'

A servant topped up Barclay's glass, but Nelson declined. 'I was not aware of this, I must say.'

'I am surprised, sir. Where have you been?'

'Norfolk,' Nelson replied, in a hurt tone. 'Five years of unemployment, which I know is an experience we share.'

Ralph Barclay actually growled, though not at Nelson. Those five years on half-pay, lying to tradesmen, fobbing off his creditors, denying things to his sisters they saw as essential, were not something of which he cared to be reminded. At least they had ended happily with marriage and a ship.

'Well, let's hope that old Sir William has not lost his marbles completely.' Ralph Barclay waited for the response to his jest, but none came, which led him to conclude that amongst the other things Nelson did not know was that Sir William Hamilton was a noted collector of Roman antiquities. 'I am sure you will enjoy a visit to Naples,

275

Nelson. I have heard the ladies are very willing in that neck of the woods. Captain Augustus Hervey apparently sired several bastards in those parts in the late fifties.'

'I shan't linger,' Nelson replied seriously, equally quick to miss the salacious look which had taken hold of the face of his companion. 'Once my mission is accomplished, I shall be straight back here. Why would I not when there is going to be some fighting?'

'Captain Barclay.' Turning, he saw the C-in-C's letter writer. 'Lord Hood will see you now.'

'Good luck in Naples, Nelson. Don't get up to any mischief. Remember, every man is a bachelor east of Gibraltar.'

Nelson blushed at that, and added a slightly forced smile, it being something he had said, too loud and drunk with it, at a dinner in Lisbon.

'Captain Barclay,' demanded Lord Hood, in a voice that lacked any welcome. 'What is it you wish to see me about on a day when I have hardly a second to spare?'

'I wish to give you my report on the action of HMS *Brilliant*.'

Ralph Barclay took a chance to nod to the others in the cabin, admirals Hotham, Parker and Rear Admiral Goodall.

'Surely you mean the loss?' said Hood.

'We have her back now, sir,' Barclay said, placing the despatch on the table, 'and most of her repairs are completed. I have taken the liberty of raiding the French storehouses so I can confidently say that she is, in all respect bar one, ready for service.'

'Bar one?'

'I lost hands in the battle, sir, which leaves me short.'

Hood, busy reading the despatch, just grunted.

'I hear it was a hot action, Barclay,' said Hotham. 'And damned difficult odds.'

'Damned hot, sir, and I so very nearly got clear, but the wind was dead foul.'

It was Parker's turn to speak. 'I have to say, Captain, that questions have been raised about the probity of this encounter.'

The response had been rehearsed a hundred times in the last few days of captivity, so came out smoothly. 'Sir, I saw it as my duty to ensure that the French did not weigh, to sow in their minds the notion that this very fleet was close enough to bring them to an action should they do so. When you read my report you will see that I had the necessary signals flying to convey that message.'

'A bluff, Barclay,' said Hotham in a rather forced manner.

'Precisely that, sir. I feared that if they got out on a wind they could head in any direction.'

'And if they had?' demanded Parker.

'It was my intention to shadow them, sir, then communicate the course to the cutter I left on station.'

'Very proper,' said Hotham, throwing a glance at Hood, who was still digesting the report on the action.

The possibility of censure existed, it always did in King George's Navy, regardless of what one did, but he looked to Hotham for support. Hood, he knew, had little time for him; they had clashed in London before *Brilliant* weighed, and it had been obvious that he still saw him in the light of his past connections. Barclay had been a protégé of the late Admiral Sir George Brydges Rodney, a man he considered a genius, while Hood reviled his one-time superior as a fount of misplaced greed and outright corruption.

The problem for Ralph Barclay was in the 'late'. Admiral Rodney was dead, and nothing so blighted an officer's career as being attached to a senior who was a corpse, for he could do nothing to advance his followers from the grave, and that was the source of elevation. Without interest in the world a man was nothing, regardless of which profession he chose to follow and in the Navy it was especially paramount. He and Hotham, though it had not been stated openly, had come to an understanding in Lisbon. He had done the admiral a favour, without asking for anything in return as a sign of his attachment. So for Ralph Barclay, Hotham, hopefully, had replaced the late, lamented Rodney.

'Hands, Barclay,' said Hood finally. 'I seem to recall having a discussion on that topic before.'

'Yes, sir, at the Admiralty.'

'Ah yes. You implied I was a liar.'

'I doubt that, sir,' Hotham insisted, shock on his carefully barbered face. 'Captain Barclay is not that sort of officer.'

Hood looked from one to the other, and smiled to himself as he dropped his eyes back to the papers in front of him, the letters from William Pitt, the main thrust of which was the tenuous nature of his government's power. No one knew better than Samuel Hood the skeins of interest and how they operated, and by speaking as he had, Hotham had just told him that he was prepared to act as Barclay's protector. That complicated matters, for in the private correspondence that had come with Pearce it had been made plain that his Second-in-Command had powerful friends in Parliament, like the Whig Duke of Portland, who led a faction inclined to support the war against France. These were people that Pitt was trying to seduce into joining his government and the addition of such support was no light matter, for that bloc of votes, in effect splitting and emasculating the Whig opposition, would make his position as the King's First Minister unassailable.

Concomitant to that, although not stated in writing, was

the obvious fact that Sir William Hotham, because of that connection, was a man to be handled with care. To upset him, to have him writing home to his friends in complaint, which might give them cause to rebuff Pitt, was to risk the future of the government he supported, as well as his own position as C-in-C in the Mediterranean.

'But the discussion was about hands, was it not?' Hood insisted.

'I was very short on my complement, sir,' Ralph Barclay replied.

'So short that you indulged in a little illegal impressment?'

'Sir?'

'We had an officer come out from England, a Lieutenant Pearce—'

'Surely he is not truly of that rank, sir?'

'Please do not interrupt me, Captain.' Barclay nodded an apology, his mind spinning as to where this conversation was leading. 'As I said, Pearce. He is a lieutenant, made so at the insistence of the King himself.'

This was a time for Ralph Barclay to stay silent. To express his thoughts to a room full of admirals, that the King must indeed be mad, was professional suicide.

'And for outstanding bravery, Captain Barclay. Now this man says you pressed him and others illegally.'

'There is no truth in that, sir.'

'So Pearce is a liar?'

'I did press men before we weighed, but I took them to be seamen. If this Pearce, whom I scarcely can recall, says he is not of that profession, then all I can say is that it did not appear to be the case to those I sent out hunting.'

'You did not go yourself?'

'No!' The negative response was out before he thought it through, and he suspected it to be a mistake. But withdrawal was impossible.

Hood smiled to himself again. 'Perhaps we should bring you face to face with the fellow, and see who is telling the truth?'

'With respect, sir,' said Hotham, 'this is hardly a subject for a fleet with the defence of Toulon to deal with.'

Hood looked at Hotham with something less than affability – they did not get on – but his mind was registering the fact that his second-in-command would not only protect Barclay, but might go to some lengths to do so, just to establish his own position. If he could receive private correspondence so could Hotham. It made him wonder at what bargain they had struck, but since he would never know he gave up speculating. All he knew was that politics would insist that he accede to whatever Hotham demanded, if the man was prepared to push Barclay's case; he was not about to jeopardise the government of which he was a part for a brand new lieutenant, who was also the son of a man who abhorred everything that he held sacred.

He passed Barclay's despatch to his junior, feeling a bit like Pontius Pilate. 'Then we must think of another way to resolve it, Admiral Hotham. I would welcome any suggestions you have.'

'These orders are, I assume, from Admiral Hood?' The secretary shrugged, in a way that angered John Pearce. 'I wish to question them.'

That got a lazily raised eyebrow. 'Question them?'

'I had the impression that we both spoke English. What is it about that which I just said you find confusing?'

The tone of mockery was unwelcome, that was obvious from the response. The secretary was clearly used to respect, hardly surprising given his lofty office – the C-in-C's man of business and fleet prize agent. A hand was held out, into which Pearce placed the folded paper, to be opened and read.

'These orders come from Admiral Hotham.'

'Hotham?'

'Allow that I can recognise the hand of his letter writer, as well as the admiral's signature.'

'Why would Admiral Hotham be giving orders to me?'

'I have no idea. All I do know is you are being given a commission, and I have rarely known that to bring anything to a fellow of your rank other than joy.'

'I don't want a commission.'

The secretary sat back, exhaling air in the manner of a person who had too much to do, and no time to be bothered with this intrusion. 'You have the right to refuse, of course, but if you wish to do so, the place to make that known is aboard HMS *Britannia*, not here.'

'I wish to see Lord Hood.'

'Lord Hood is busy.'

'Ask him!'

He could not help but feel he was the witness to a performance. An under-secretary was summoned – the same fellow who had lent Pearce his coat – who went into the main cabin, only to emerge after a few seconds to whisper in his superior's ear.

'Admiral Lord Hood is busy seeing to the defence of Toulon. He has no time to see you, Lieutenant Pearce.'

'If I wait?'

The secretary enjoyed his riposte, which came with a thin-lipped smile. 'If you decide to do so, I should fetch your shaving kit.'

At least he got to see a naval officer aboard *Britannia*, not Hotham but his Flag Lieutenant, a good-looking fellow eager to explain to a less than enamoured caller the thinking of his admiral.

'Your complaint against Captain Barclay requires

investigation, but you will readily appreciate that this moment is hardly the time to undertake such a thing. The task given to HMS *Weazel* is neither hazardous nor likely to be of much duration, and her own lieutenant has, like so many other fleet officers, been ordered ashore, leaving Captain Benton unsupported. Since you had no employment, and none of the skills necessary to likewise work on the defences, the admiral felt that you would be better employed cruising than kicking your heels aboard ship.'

Reiterating that he did not want a commission brought forth a concerned look from the man he was addressing, a fellow of his own age with the air of a practised diplomat. Now he looked worried.

'Lieutenant Pearce, if I may speak to you man to man, and outside my duties as Admiral Hotham's Flag Lieutenant?' He paused, waiting for a frowning Pearce to nod. 'I am aware of your case against Captain Barclay, but I am also conscious, as I suspect you are not, that you will require the goodwill of the senior officers on the station to bring it to any sort of conclusion. He is a post captain, and while it may be true that what he did was questionable…'

'Illegal!'

'…there is not another captain or admiral on this station who has not at some time in his career done the same. While they are honest men, they are also serving sailors who have found themselves in a like situation. It would not be surprising, therefore, that they would have a natural inclination to support Mr Barclay.'

Pearce was genuinely surprised. 'You're saying that I am wasting my time?'

'No, Lieutenant Pearce, I am saying that refusing Admiral Hotham's orders will not endear you to him, and he is one of those to whom you must plead your case. I doubt HMS *Weazel* will be gone for more than a week, by which time things will have settled here, matters will be in hand, and time can be given to consideration of your complaint.'

'I seem to spend my entire time seeking to please admirals.'

'Believe me, Mr Pearce,' the Flag Lieutenant replied, in a deeply serious tone, 'that is a far better idea than upsetting them.' Sensing that his fellow-lieutenant was weakening, he added, '*Weazel* has orders to sail at dawn. I would suggest to you that it would be a good idea to get aboard and introduce yourself to Captain Benton.'

'I am concerned for my friends.'

'Which does you credit, sir, but what possible harm can come to them? The French in Toulon are now our allies, the revolutionary armies are occupied subduing Marseilles and are not expected here for weeks. The worst that can happen to them is that they will be sent ashore to throw up earthworks for the gun emplacements being planned for Mont Faron.'

Pearce was torn. Taberly had expressly forbidden him *Leander,* so he could spend no time with his fellow Pelicans. Hood, he suspected, would not see him, neither would Hotham, so his suit would languish, and he was not a person who enjoyed the prospect of being idle, with nothing to do but gnaw on and be frustrated by that. He imagined, once more, duelling with Barclay, but reverted to a decision he had already made; his determination to see the man disgraced before that took place. He could, of course, go ashore, given that he had an almost proprietary interest in the place, but would he be welcome and of any use if he was? The port was likely to be a dull place socially until things settled down, and any idea of looking at the region was out of the question given the impending arrival of a Jacobin army.

As long as Michael, Charlie and Rufus were safe, a week would make no odds, and this sloop, he now knew, was bound for a cruise round Corsica, an island and a people of which he had heard much from James Boswell, one of his father's old verbal sparring partners. Boswell had described it as a wild, romantic place, full of strange sights and an even more peculiar people. If he did not see it now, he probably never would. He was also tempted by another reason, which related to the conversations he had had with Captain McGann; was he up to the job of running a ship? The gaps in his knowledge were extensive, but he felt he had made a reasonable fist of his tasks aboard *Griffin*. Add to that what he had learnt aboard the Postal Packet and this would be by way of a test; a strange ship, and unfamiliar crew, and he would be, it seemed, the only officer under the captain. It was a chance to put one in the eye of people like Hood, who questioned his right to his rank. Even more appealing was the way it would infuriate Barclay!

Had it been a proper place he would have declined it regardless, but it was only a temporary posting till the present incumbent was free to resume his duties. 'I will accept, but I have one request.'

'Which is?'

'No boxing bouts.'

The Flag Lieutenant struggled with that. 'Boxing bouts?'

'Yes. I want a strict instruction to the captain of HMS *Leander* that he is in no way to arrange or condone such a thing.'

The man before him was enough of a diplomat to evade the truth with ease; not lie, for he had no idea of what answer Admiral Hotham would give to such a request. 'I will see that it is brought to the admiral's attention.'

'You may also wish to bring to the admiral's attention the fact that such an event took place, and included gambling, at

284

sea while HMS *Leander* was off the coast of Spain, which, if I am not mistaken contravenes the Articles of War, and should be the subject of a court martial.'

On entering Admiral Hotham's cabin, his Flag Lieutenant was faced with an enquiring look from the two officers present.

'Well?' asked Ralph Barclay.

'He has accepted.'

'Well done,' said Hotham. 'That gains us time.'

'He had one request, sir, a strange one.'

The young man explained, first to a raised eyebrow, then to a look of disbelief, until finally Hotham exploded, his face going bright red. 'Damn the fellow. Does he want to bring every captain in the fleet to court martial?'

His Flag Lieutenant did not reply, thinking the answer was probably, yes.

CHAPTER TWENTY-TWO

Pearce knew he had erred within ten minutes of being aboard, not because of any incompetence on his part, not because HMS *Weazel* was so small, but by the behaviour of the ship's captain. Benton was slightly drunk, and he looked like a fellow who was no stranger to that state, with reddish, watery eyes and that facial colour that spoke of badly corrupted blood under his skin. Pearce had seen too many of the type in his travels to come to any other conclusion; the taverns and pot houses of Britain were full of Bentons, usually addicted to gin, rather than that which the captain was drinking now and sharing with his new officer, which Pearce reckoned must be the cheapest form of blackstrap wine, the kind that left a sour taste on the tongue.

'I am not pleased they took Digby, Mr Pearce, I want you to know that. He was just getting used to my ways.'

'Digby?'

'You know him?'

'Only if he served aboard HMS *Brilliant*.'

'He did,' Benton replied, in a voice that had gravel, and little affection, in it. 'Barclay got shot of him at Lisbon, and he was not the type to fit in on the flagship. Admiral Hotham likes his officers to be true gentlemen with the means to support that station. Digby lacked both the means and any interest from a patron, so I got him.'

Responding to what was a less-than-pleased tone, and

recalling what Digby had been like aboard *Brilliant,* kind, if a little confused and uncertain, Pearce replied, 'I thought him a competent officer, sir.'

'He was far from that when he arrived, Pearce, but he benefited from being with me.' The bleary eyes fixed on his new officer over a gulp of wine. 'I assume you are another no-hoper, new to your commission, sent to try my patience.'

'Very likely,' Pearce replied, which had the virtue of both being true and surprising Benton enough to make him shift back in his chair.

'Well, be warned,' Benton growled, recovering somewhat, 'I expect the highest standard of behaviour on my deck, as well as competence, and if you don't have it now, you'd damn well best acquire it. We weigh at first light, our orders to sail round the island of Corsica, home to a couple of French sloops left there to support the military garrison.'

'We will be landing?'

'No, Mr Pearce, we will not.'

Suppressing disappointment, and wondering if he had chucked himself into danger, Pearce asked, 'And if we find these vessels, sir?'

'We are to report on their location and inform Lord Hood.' Benton shouted then, in a voice that must have been heard beyond the bowsprit, 'Harbin!'

That brought to the tiny cabin a freckle-faced youth, a compact sort of youngster who, once outside the cabin, produced a winning smile and a proper welcome aboard. He was instructed to take Pearce round the ship, as though such a thing would take more than two minutes. Pearce met the Purser, Gunner, Carpenter and Bosun, but most importantly, remembering McGann's injunction, the ship's Master, a grey-haired fellow of round and ruddy country complexion called Neame, who seemed old to hold a warrant for such a small vessel. He was introduced to two other mids and the master's mates. In doing so, he was eyed by but not named to the crew, all of whom looked at him with something approaching indifference. It was an act of course; every man jack was curious about this new blue coat, for he was a fellow who could make their lives a joy or a misery.

His quarters were cramped, a screened-off space in a tiny wardroom, hardly surprising, but they were the best aboard excepting Benton's. Digby's servant had seen to his dunnage, and he immediately changed from his best coat and hat to more workmanlike apparel. He then inspected the ship unaccompanied, not with any great eye for faults, just to show that he was prepared to go aloft to check on the rigging, and to ensure that the two decks were tidy enough in the matter of ropes and other impediments not to be a danger to those using them.

He then invited those who shared the wardroom with him, the master and the purser, to partake of some wine, a dozen of Hermitage he had bought from one of the numerous bum boats which had surrounded *Victory*, for this very purpose. Through a thin bulkhead forward, they could hear the mids and other warrants talking quietly, probably trying to assess this new arrival. Through a thicker one behind, they picked up the snores of the captain.

'A decent drop,' said Neame, smacking his lips as he downed his first tankard. 'Better than the captain is inclined to serve.' The purser, Mr Ottershaw, merely nodded, but the satisfaction at that which he was consuming was plain on his face.

Said with caution, Pearce reckoned the master was testing him, and he pulled a face to imply agreement. 'He treated me to some of his wine, Mr Neame. I must tell you I am in no hurry to force another invite.'

Neame leant close, talking softly. 'I doubt you'll get one in a hurry, Mr Pearce. Captain Benton much prefers his own company, excepting that of a bottle.'

'Another drop, sir,' Pearce responded, smiling into the perspiring faces of two men who had relaxed a trifle. Two bottles saw the whole story out. Benton was a protégé of Hotham, his uncle, a yellow admiral who had served with the man they termed Hotspur Harry when he had been a midshipman.

'He is a debt being paid, sir,' whispered Ottershaw. 'I am told the uncle resents being an admiral without benefit of flag, he feels shunted aside, never to be employed, and quite unable to grasp his own incompetence.'

Neither said it outright, but enough hints were given that said lack of proficiency was a family trait, that Benton's drinking was because he knew it to be so, that he had scraped through his lieutenant's examination only because Hotham rigged the panel and he knew that he would make post only by a miracle. Pearce had relaxed enough to state quite openly that they best not look to him for a rise in standards, that his commission was of short duration only to cover for the absence of Mr Digby. The mention of that name changed their attitude; they thought Digby a decent, useful officer, and so did the crew.

'I will strive for the decency, gentlemen, for the rest I will rely on you, Mr Neame.' He pulled another Hermitage from the wooden box at his feet. 'Now, what do you say we share some of this with the mids and the warrants? I find it is the best way to get to know people.'

By the time the men were roused out to weigh, word had got round that this new premier was no hard horse, in fact that he was more likely to be a Digby than a Benton, so there were no sour looks to contend with as the capstan bars were shipped and the anchor hove short, nor when the topmen went aloft to loose the sails. Pearce issued his orders to Mr Neame, and gave responsibility to Harbin, whom he had been told was a keen – though sometimes too keen – midshipman. As the sun rose, the gold of its colour reflected the mass of freckles that covered the boy's face, and he responded to the request to alert the captain with a grin that showed a set of teeth that seemed too numerous for his mouth. All went rigid as Benton came on deck, and what the rising sun did to his flaccid complexion was far from flattering.

'Ready to weigh, sir.'

Benton turned and looked towards HMS *Britannia*. 'Have you observed, Mr Pearce, our number flying from the masthead of Admiral Hotham's flagship?'

'No, sir,' Pearce replied truthfully, following his gaze and ignoring the furiously nodding head of Neame. 'I have not.'

'If you had, Mr Pearce, you would see that we are ordered to proceed to sea. I only hope it has not been aloft for long. I would hate to be rebuked by Admiral Hotham for your inability to see his signals. Now be so good as to get us moving.'

'Mr Neame.'

Topsails were dropped and sheeted home, the rudder creaked as the quartermaster used the forward movement induced by a land breeze to bring *Weazel* over her anchor, and sweetly it was plucked from the sandy bottom, to be fished and catted.

'Mr Harbin.'

'Sir?'

'Issue the orders to swab the decks, and alert the cook that he needs to get his coppers lit, since with the sun rising and a warm day, there will be no need for flogging dry.'

He turned to look for Benton, to see if that would be acceptable, but the captain had gone.

He had to deal with Benton, but in his quarters, for it seemed the captain had a mortal fear of fresh air, or such a love of wine that he feared to be separated from a supply. The man took his breakfast alone and that extended to his dinner. He did come on deck before that, but only for a short time to ensure that Pearce was not sailing them in the wrong direction. But after a brief look at the slate and the course, and a glance at the sail plan, he grunted his satisfaction, ordered that the details be sent to him in his cabin, and retired there. In contrast, Pearce was relishing the sun and the wind on his face, the azure blue of the sea, with dolphins off the bows and the fact that the contact with his inferiors seemed easy. The gunner, particularly, was a chatterer, a crook-faced fellow happy to converse with this new officer about weight of shot, the size of powder charges, elevation and ballistics, in a way that assumed Pearce knew what he was talking about, all the while rubbing with a loving hand one of the twelve nine-pounders that were *Weazel's* armament.

'As you know, sir, a set of long nines like these won't do much at range, well short on a mile with a five-degree elevation and a four-pound charge, but they are enough to put a ball through a foot of scantlings at half of that. Was you, beggin' your pardon, Mr Pearce, to get us close they would answer well.'

Recalling his service aboard *Brilliant*, and the insistence of regular exercise, he soon established that it was not something into which Benton put much effort. Even after less than a day, he was tempted to ask what the captain did do, only to deduce from the replies what he knew already to be true; that a captain, provided he properly kept his logs and did not seek too much in the way of bookish deceit with his muster and stores, could do very much what he pleased.

'Mr Digby suggested, your honour – with not a thought that it gave us work – to keep them blacked and handsome. Half hour each day, sir, late afternoon, he wanted, but the captain wouldn't have it. Can't do it now, I reckon. With our marines gone ashore, we is short on hands to man the breechings, so if you're thinkin' that way, it might be best left until we has all the labour we needs.'

That left Pearce not knowing if the gunner was for exercise or against it, especially as, at that moment, the fellow leant over and kissed the royal insignia on the top of the cannon he was caressing.

The bosun and carpenter were not as relaxed as the gunner in commissioned company, the latter particularly ill at ease, for the sloop was no spring chicken and even after a refit at Buckler's Hard the scantlings moved in a heavy sea and apparently wept significant amounts of water.

'It was hard pumping in the Channel, your honour,' he intoned in a miserable voice, 'and even worse in Biscay. We've got a right good sea state now, but you mark it, if it comes on heavy we will struggle to keep down the water in the well.'

Talking to the bosun about the distribution of the crew, the state of the sails including the spare suit, ropes, spars and blocks, Pearce began to appreciate the complexities of running even a ship this size; not the sailing or navigation, but getting the best out of the men, for McGann had insisted that was where the true merit of command lay. Though he could not, himself, consider going that way, he could grasp why many a ship's captain saw the lash as the route to discipline, it being so much easier than the effort of gaining personal respect. Thankfully, given the short-term nature of this commission, it was not something to which he had to give much concern.

Corsica, on a decent wind, was less than a day's sailing and before nightfall they had looked deep into the long sandy bay of San Fiorenzo to the north, with Mr Neame, on Benton's orders, making a sketch of the main features, especially the fortifications, which consisted of some odd round towers dotted around the coastline, that and of the ability of the place to provide holding ground for large warships, which saw him out in a boat with a tallow line, checking the seabed.

'Why the detail, Mr Neame?' asked Pearce, when he came back aboard.

'Don't take a genius to figure that, sir. Happen we get the heave-ho from Toulon, we'll need another place to anchor and victual. Mr Benton has orders to look out for that. Did he not say so?'

'No, Mr Neame, he did not.'

The master grinned. 'Didn't let on to me either, Mr Pearce. I had it from the master of *Britannia*, who's an old shipmate. Went to see him for a wet after we anchored in the Toulon roads. The Dons won't hear of us using Port Mahon on Minorca, which we had afore, case they can't get shot of us, and we has to have a place to shelter and revictual to keep to the Med.'

Once more, John Pearce was forced to admit that Hood was clever. It was not a betrayal to seek an alternative to Toulon, just wise to have a backstop in case of disaster.

Neame's jovial note changed, to one of resentment. 'Mind, when we gets back, captain will take my drawings aboard the flagship, no doubt sayin' they're his own.'

They set a course west to weather the western arm of the bay, a bleak and forbidding promontory of rocks and black beaches, and with the northerly holding true the next morning they were able to skirt the much more formidable Calvi, a port below a high citadel and a fortified town on the western promontory of a deep but shallow-watered bay surrounded by high mountains. One of the sloops for which they had been tasked to look out for lay snug and safe under the shore-based guns, though down to bare poles and not ready for sea. Benton was on deck for that, taking a close look at the place through his telescope, remarking that from the view of the numbers on the ramparts, it had a sizeable garrison, which would make it a hard place to capture, should the need arise. Against that, at the foot of the bay, lay a long sandy beach ideal for landing troops, which the master was busy sketching.

'Mr Pearce, I think we must test the defences if Neame's efforts are to be of any use. Please take us inshore a trifle.'

Sails trimmed and rudder down, the ship swung in towards the midpoint of the entrance to the bay, where the darker hue of the water indicated increased depth, though a leadsman was casting in the chains to ensure that they did not ground. HMS *Weazel* began to lose some of her way as the wind, on the beam, was eased by the high hills and it was not long before a pair of the shore-based cannon essayed the range, sending great plumes of water shooting up well ahead of the bowsprit. It was only luck that had Pearce looking deeper into the bay, where he saw a buoy with a rope attached, and what seemed like a set of flags at intervals halfway to the shore, the furthest of which they were inside. There was, as well, a pennant-carrying cutter, the cloth streaming out to show the strength of the wind. Could those flags indicate a range less than the maximum, working on the principle that even the best trained eye had difficulty with distance at sea?

'Would they fire short to draw us in, sir?' Pearce asked, then added, when Benton glared at him. 'May I draw your attention to that buoy, sir, and that cutter.'

Benton obliged, and the sight had him dropping his telescope. 'Bring us about!'

'All hands to wear ship!' Pearce shouted.

The proof of the notion was proved as soon as the men ran to the falls, to bring the ship back onto a reverse course. They too were being observed through telescopes, and by gunners who knew to the inch their range. The ramparts of the citadel were wreathed in smoke as the entire battery fired, and they could see a dozen huge black balls arcing through the air, to straddle the ship, sending up enough water to windward to soak everyone on deck.

'Mr Pearce,' cried Neame, pointedly ignoring his captain, 'let us use the wind.'

He did not understand and he was acutely aware of the fact, but neither it seemed did Benton. Fortunately, Neame did not wait for orders; he had the hands sheet home as soon as the northerly breeze would give them better forward motion. Pearce now comprehended the calculation, that any movement was better than the static position of coming right round to sail out of the bay, this proved by the shot that he was sure landed in the waters they had just vacated. They were now sailing towards that flag-holding buoy.

'Permission to sink that cutter, sir?' he asked Benton. The nod in reply was slow in coming, or at least it seemed so, even if it was only a couple of seconds, till he could shout, 'Man the starboard cannon.'

The guns were run out all right, with flintlocks fixed on, and the sight of their muzzles was enough to send off as fast as they could row the men oaring the boat. But they did not fire because the gunner had no charges filled, and by the time he did and the powder monkeys had got them to the gun captains, it was too late, the only positive being that the artillerymen from Calvi had ceased to waste powder and shot, as they were now beyond their reach heading for the eastern part of the bay.

'Bring us about again, Mr Pearce,' said Benton, 'but out of range this time.'

The way it was said seemed to imply that going closer inshore had been his fault. He half thought of protesting, but reckoned it not to be worth the effort.

* * *

Was it Benton's fault that there were no cartridges ready to fire the guns? Pearce did not know, but he was determined it would not happen again. Another, more forceful conversation with the gunner, reinforced the notion of how much he loved his cannon, but created a distinct impression that he loved them too much to see them discharged and was the type to see the proper place for powder as in the barrel, where it could be easily accounted for. He moaned that fixing the flintlocks had scratched the blacking, and asked that his gunner's mates could be put to making them pristine again; so much, Pearce thought for getting close and blasting away.

'But surely we must be ready at any time for a fight? What if that Corvette in Calvi was properly rigged and had decided to pursue us?'

'We is as ready as we need be,' he replied, bending his crooked face to one side. 'Stands to reason, sir, that if we see an enemy, we has time to do the necessary well afore they close.'

'Mr Digby approved of this?'

'Mr Digby never enquired about cartridges, seeing we was with the fleet, what would be the point?'

Pearce had to struggle to control his impatience, and he suspected, even with his lack of experience, that the man he was temporarily replacing would have been just as upset. Hate Ralph Barclay he might, but his example was the one to follow; regular exercise with the odd discharge so that his gunners knew their tasks.

'Please have powder ready for the guns at all times. Who knows, we might wake up one morning to find that an enemy has got close enough to sink us.'

'The captain?'

'I will deal with him.'

'What weight of charge, your honour?'

Unable to say what or why, Pearce just answered, 'The maximum!'

He left the gunner mumbling about muzzles being blown asunder, as he made his way back on deck and lifted himself onto the bulwark, hanging on to a backstay. Beneath him the sea was blue and clean, and he wondered if they would ever anchor so he could have a swim. Off the starboard beam lay the green-brown island, rocky promontories now mixed with long, blonde and sandy beaches, backed by rising ridges of crag-topped mountains, with a faint smell of myrtle and pines to mix with the tang of salt on the wind, just as Boswell had described it to a young and impressionable boy.

He longed to go ashore and see if he could find anyone who knew or could remember James Boswell. According to the man himself, Dr Johnson's biographer was something of a idol on Corsica – he had become an intimate of the local leader, Pasquali Paoli, and helped him in his attempt to eject the French from the island. But then Adam Pearce had always described Boswell as a man who cast himself in a good light. He also insisted that Samuel Johnson, whom Adam had met many times, had never said half the things Boswell attributed to him.

'Mr Pearce.' He looked down to Mr Neame. 'I was wondering, sir, if you was going to put the hands through practise with boarding weapons. It is the day for it according to Mr Digby's list.'

Pearce smiled. 'Am I allowed to join in?'

'Well, I ain't never heard of an officer doin' so, but I don't reckon it would be a cause for mutiny if he did.'

'So be it, Mr Neame. And let's have the mids on deck and I will teach them how to properly use a sword.'

That passed a pleasant hour, as they passed an empty bay with a town called Porto at its base, and because the forecastle was small, instruction had to be given in relays, which had the effect of bringing him into close contact with the crew, his only stricture to stop them indulging too heavily in the use of their weapons; pikes, cudgels, dummy tomahawks and cutlasses made of wood, but still enough in weight to cause harm. With the mids, he showed caution with a sword in his hand, for he had been taught by experts, his prowess acknowledged by those with whom he crossed wooden blades. Not that he overwhelmed an opponent; the object was to point out to them their lack of proficiency, not to show off.

'I am curious, Mr Pearce, where you learnt your skill,' Neame said, as they ate their dinner.

He could have said anything, but the truth would be best. 'There is an army barracks in Paris called Les Invalides. I went there for instruction in swordsmanship, shooting and riding.'

'Paris?' declared the purser, through a mouthful of salted beef and sauerkraut, as though it was some kind of mortal sin.

'Yes, Mr Ottershaw. I spent more than two years there, until the beginning of this year and the start of the present war.'

There was a temptation to go on, to tell them all, even how pleasant the French capital had been if you ignored the smells that were the affliction of every city, still full of elegant and interesting people. To tell what it was like to a young man growing up surrounded by that, his entry to salon society guaranteed because of the esteem in which his father was held as a radical and honest man. But then he would also have to describe how it changed; how the spiral of decline began that led to the present mayhem, and to the consequences his father suffered for being as truthful with those who took power. That was not a place John Pearce wanted to go, so he changed the subject.

'I believe the next harbour we raise will be Ajaccio.'

CHAPTER TWENTY-THREE

Ajaccio looked a dull and uninteresting place, with a small fort in a sorry state of repair and no shipping bar fishing boats off the beaches, so they headed on south. Putting up their helm, they sailed through the Bouches de Bonifacio, but on a wind that was now dead foul and reinforced by the tunnel effect of the narrow straits between Corsica and Sardinia, dominated by forbidding rocky escarpments and a fortress similar in design to that of Calvi. That changed as they cleared the east of the islands, sailing inshore of Les Iles Lavezzi. Judging by the number of boats, good fishing ground lay between the islands and the high southern cliffs, and sick of salted beef and pork, Pearce sent Harbin off in a boat to purchase some fish from the tiny smacks that seemed reluctant to come close to a strange warship.

'And see what they know of matters on the island, Harbin.'

'What do they speak, sir, the locals?'

'According to an old friend of my father's, no language known to man. The island has been Greek, Carthaginian, Roman, Genoese, and finally it was bought by the French, who are not much loved by the original Corsicans. Try a jabbing finger.'

The eight-oared cutter was obviously less of a threat and, after a long hard pull, and what seemed like a lot of talking and arm waving, the boy returned with enough fish for both the wardroom, the gunroom and Benton's dinner. But Harbin brought more than just food; without any knowledge of the Corsican tongue, he had managed to extract some startling news.

'Sir, they convinced me that a French warship is moored in a bay to the north, which I think they called Porto Vecchio, though the tongue was so barbarous I cannot be sure. It seems that she is not manned. The fishermen indicated that the crew are ashore.'

'There is an anchorage by that name, Mr Pearce,' said Neame, who had been studying the charts of the east coast. '*Golfo di Porto Vecchio* in the Italian, a deep bay and a port that goes back to ancient times, though not, I suspect, of much use now.'

'How did they manage to convince you of this?'

Harbin's explanation, related with an excited air, took nearly as long as the original telling. The fishermen had drawn the coastline with wetted fingers, pointed north with much simulation of banging guns and waving of their small anchor, and repeated the name over and over again. Pearce could see the way Harbin's mind was working; the boy saw adventure, saw himself leaping over enemy bulwarks sword in hand, but it was not his decision to believe or disbelieve what he had been told, or that of his temporary premier.

'This is information, Mr Harbin, that has to be reported to the captain.'

Which it duly was, to a man who seemed burdened by the information. Harbin was dismissed, leaving Pearce alone with Benton. 'If this is true, and there is an unmanned French warship there, what are we to do?'

'It is up to you, sir, to decide the best course of action.'

'I would value your opinion, Mr Pearce.'

Why did he feel he was being asked to take, or at the very least share, responsibility? Was it something in Benton's orders, which he had been very reluctant up till now to fully communicate?

'I think, sir, that no opinion can be advanced until we have seen what is and what is not accurate. With a trio of tongues to choose from, young Mr Harbin might have got the whole thing wrong.'

Benton stared at his temporary second-in-command for a long time, his bloated face expressionless. 'Please ask Mr Neame to give us an estimate of how long that will be.'

'On this wind, Mr Pearce, a true Levanter, I reckon we will raise Porto Vecchio well before last light.'

His calculation was close, but with the sun having dipped behind the central Corsican mountains throwing the whole eastern coastline into shadow, it was too near twilight to be fully certain of what they observed. But there was a ship, a sloop slightly larger than their own, of fourteen guns, moored in a small, hill-enclosed bay to the north of the main approach to Porto Vecchio, and no sign of activity could be seen, either on her decks, or between ship and shore.

'Would it be a good idea to send in a boat, sir?' asked Pearce.

For once Benton spoke as a normal human being; no growl, no disdain, and Pearce realised that he appeared to be completely sober. 'That would only serve to alert anyone either on the ship or ashore. No, Mr Pearce, we must make our decisions based on what we can now perceive.'

They stayed, hove to, telescopes trained on the silent and still ship and the sloping hills that surrounded the bay, until the light faded completely, and twinkling lanterns could be seen from the town itself, at the deepest part of the gulf, a good mile away. At this point, Benton, having seen his own ship's lanterns ignited, invited Pearce to join him in his cabin, that after issuing an order to the master.

'Mr Neame, set us back on our previous course, I would wish anyone watching to see us sailing away northwards.'

Sat either side of his desk, Benton did not speak for a full minute, and when he did his voice was low and muted. 'My orders were quite specific, Mr Pearce, and I am going to share them with you. I am not to indulge in any action which threatens the ship, or to chase after anything I might see as a potential prize. I am to reconnoitre the island, look out for suitable fleet anchorages, and report back to Admiral Hotham.'

'Which presents an awkward dilemma.'

'Precisely. Yet here we have before us what seems like a tempting prospect, an enemy vessel seemingly unmanned. Would I be forgiven for passing up such an opportunity?' Since Pearce declined to answer, Benton went on. 'I think not.'

'I doubt your orders anticipated such a possibility, sir.'

'That is true.' Another long silence followed, until Benton said. 'Do you not find it strange that a warship is so moored and without a crew?'

'I think what has happened in Toulon, sir, tells us that these are strange times. There could be any number of reasons for the lack of a crew in a climate in which loyalties are uncertain. They may have deserted.'

'I dare not take *Weazel* right into the bay, Mr Pearce, for fear that, without charts, I might run her aground, but I have the added complication of having no marines on board, which is a limiting factor in a cutting-out expedition.'

Benton looked really glum, a man damned if he did and damned if he did not, but Pearce was also damned if he was going to say so, for it seemed clear that was what the captain was looking for, words that would make up his mind, but also words that could be quoted in his defence if he faced censure. Pearce knew that Benton would have to cut out that ship; advancement in King George's Navy did not come from sailing on reconnaissance and disobedience was always a second cousin to success with a nation that loved their Wooden Walls. Take that sloop and he would be hailed throughout the fleet; leave it and heads would shake in wonderment, perhaps even the powdered wigs of senior admirals.

'I must put myself in Admiral Hotham's place,' said Benton.

'Admiral Hood's, as well,' Pearce replied.

He had said that without giving the notion much thought, but it had an electrifying effect on Benton, who slapped a decisive hand on the table. 'Hood would not hesitate, would he?'

The implication that Hotham might was telling, but best left unsaid. Suddenly Benton was all animation, a man from whom a burden had been completely lifted by the mere thought of approval from the Commander-in-Chief.

'Mr Pearce, I want us off the bay at first light, with the boats ready and over the side. We will come upon them, stern lanterns out and hope they suppose us gone. You will take the jolly boat and Mr Harbin, and carry out an assault over the stern, I will take the cutter and come aboard over the bows. Mr Neame and the other two mids can have charge of our ship.'

There was a temptation to dampen Benton's sudden enthusiasm with an observation that it was not a captain's job to lead such an assault, but then, if Benton did not, Pearce would have to, and he felt that, with his lack of experience, that was probably a bad idea. It was only much later, when it was too late to say anything that would not sound like an expression of cowardice, that John Pearce realised he should have declined to have anything to do with the affair. What was he doing putting his person at risk?

* * *

The crew, from mids, through warrants to seamen had been waiting with bated breath for a decision, and when it came it was clear they were pleased, for a ship like that fourteen-gun sloop, taken whole, was certain to be bought into the service, so there was money to be made. The hours of darkness were spent sharpening knives and cutlasses, in sorting out who would go over the bows with Pearce and who would assault their quarry over the stern, but it was reckoned that muskets would be a bad idea – an encumbrance to men unused to them – though pistols would be allowed. The activity stopped Pearce from dwelling on what might happen, for as the premier he was kept busy organising everything, from the issue of weapons to the sailing of the ship.

Ghosting along, yards braced right round, Neame kept their speed in check so as to arrive at their destination just before dawn. It was a clear night with a half moon in the sky, which at sea tended to look like full daylight, but it was hoped that any lookout posted on the rocky hills surrounding the bay would be too tired to pay proper attention in the last hour before dawn. They sailed slowly into the bay under topsails, backing them to slow progress. The tide, only a few feet in the Mediterranean, was still rising so the master could let her drift in slowly, and moor when action had been joined. This way they would avoid attracting attention either by the noise, or the phosphorescent splash that a dropping anchor would create.

The crew clambered into the boats as the eastern sky began to show the first trace of a clear dawn, with many a command to keep silent. Benton was sober too, apparently not having touched a drink since the previous day, and Pearce had to admit a degree of excitement and wondered at it. The boats formed up and headed in towards the land, rowing slowly and quietly. As the light increased they saw the outline of the mast tops emerging in the gloom to form a silhouette above the dark backdrop of the surrounding hills. No lights appeared, no shout announced their approach and it looked as though the information Harbin had gathered was correct.

Benton's arm waved and the boats split up, he going to the bow, Pearce to the stern. Still no shout came to warn of their approach, and Pearce, who had been tense, began to relax. He heard the faint scrape of Benton's boat as it touched and in the increasing light he could see the sailors swarming aboard, and soon he too was leading his men over the taffrail, seemingly without anyone aware of their presence.

The sun hit the horizon, a gold-sliver that turned into a fiery orb, spreading a golden glow as he and Harbin walked across to join Benton. The captain turned to him, his eyes glowing in the increasing light.

'The ship is deserted. Not even an anchor watch. They must all be sleeping ashore. I have never heard of such luck. Let's cut the cable and get some men aloft.'

Pearce was never quite sure which came first, the crack of the shot, or the way the side of Benton's face seemed to explode. He was aware, as the captain was whacked over, of the musket balls around him, whistling through the morning air. He heard voices shouting for the cable to be cut, and he felt the rush of men as they made for the ratlines to run aloft and let go the sails, but he did not move, because, in shock, his feet seemed stuck to the deck. Moments passed, as he saw the boats pulling back to their mother ship in panic, and another volley cracked in his ear, which dragged his gaze away from Benton's shattered head, the body crumpled on the deck, one good eye staring straight ahead in death.

Turning, he saw the hillsides surrounding the ship dotted with the puffs of smoke from dozens of muskets, and then a cannon boomed, creating a much greater cloud of billowing black and the yards were swept with grapeshot. Men who had been climbing to let fall the sails were swept from the yards and plunged screaming either onto the deck or into the water alongside. The rest froze, trying to use what they could to shield themselves from another salvo.

It was a trap. They had been waiting for them, allowing them to come aboard before opening fire, and while he and Harbin had been targets, as they stood there, very obvious in their blue coats, most of the execution had taken place aloft as well as with a party trying to cut the forward anchor cable. Pearce came alive, and shouted for everyone to get themselves and any wounded down behind the inshore bulwark, with one fellow close to a hatch diving below. He then crawled along the side of the ship, past the bowsed cannons and the cowering men, to the bows. Two were dead, lying with their axes in their hands, but Pearce could see that they had done good service before being shot; the cable was nearly through and he shouted at the remaining pair.

'We've got to cut that through!'

That got a knowing look at the two dead bodies, one that silently imparted the notion that, it being suicide, if he wanted the cable cut he had better stand up and get on with it. Yet it was the obvious solution; they had deliberately come in on the top of the tide and it was about to turn. If they could cut that cable and the one securing the stern, they might drift out of the bay, slowly certainly, but if they kept their heads down, perhaps they would survive. Aware that whatever happened had to be co-ordinated, he crawled back along the deck to the stern. Harbin sat below the bulwark and Pearce looked into his face, recognising in the boy's expression a wish to be told what to do from the man who was now in command. That knowledge partly explained the sweat Pearce felt on his brow, the other being more prosaic; the sun was now fully up and it was beginning to get warm.

The muskets were trying to pick off the remaining sailors in the rigging, while their only thought was to get down to the safety of the deck. Every time they moved the muskets banged and another volley swept over their heads. It seemed to him when one weapon fired they all did, that there was no one in control, and that gave Pearce his idea, though he knew that it took no cognisance of that damned grapeshot-firing cannon, which made him hesitate, but since there was no alternative he could think of, it had to be risked.

'Harbin, I am going up to the bows, where I am going to tell them to stand up and chop at the cable till it parts. I will allow three swings of their axes, and then they will get under cover again. As we go down, get your men to stand up and hack away, the same number – three cuts – and then get down again. That will deny them time to take proper aim. Understand?'

'Aye, aye sir.'

And if they have shifted the aim of that cannon, thought Pearce, one of us is likely to die.

He scurried back to the bows, stopping halfway to shed his coat, and gave his orders, waiting till another volley swept the rigging. Trembling slightly he stood with his sailors, who got in two good hacks and a feeble third before he commanded them to get down, just in time to avoid a fusillade, in his heart thanking Providence for the lack of cannon fire. At the stern a now-coatless Harbin stood up, and his men did the same – and still the cannon stayed silent – ducking down at the right moment, thus allowing Pearce and his party to go again. The first swing parted the thick forward cable, so now it was only secured at the stern, and Pearce realised Harbin would have to be quick or the ship would start to swing round. Stern on to the shore, they would be exposed to the fire from the hillsides with no protection.

'Come on, Mr Harbin,' he yelled.

Pearce admired the way the boy obliged, even though he

must have known the ruse would not work a second time, knew that the chances of that cannon remaining silent were slim. He stood with his men and regardless of the shots whizzing around – fortunately only muskets – encouraged them as they hacked away. One sailor went down before the cable parted, but there was one positive; the men in the rigging had taken advantage of the respite to get back on deck. With both cables cut, Pearce waited for the ship to start drifting, but nothing happened. He couldn't understand it; the prize was as stationary as it had been before.

Harbin shouted, and looking towards the stern, Pearce saw him pointing aloft. He squinted against the glare of the sun, seeing nothing to justify the call, as one of the crew, who he recognised as one of the Gunner's mates, emerged from below and crawled towards him, getting himself to safety just as a well-aimed musket ball hit the planking behind his feet. Clearly the enemy had a weapon trained on the space between the hatchway and the side.

'There's nothing to drink below and the magazine is empty, your honour.'

'What?'

'The magazine, your honour, there's no gunpowder. There be shot in the locker but we can't turn their guns on them, since we have nothing to fire them with.'

That thought had not even occurred to Pearce, for which he cursed himself. Harbin shouted a second time, a hand again pointing towards the top of the mizzenmast, and finally Pearce saw what he was on about. The gunner's mate saw it too as Pearce looked to the mainmast to see that what Harbin had spotted was replicated there.

'The bastards have cables from the mastheads to the shore, your honour.'

Cutting the cables had not freed the ship, and it would not move until those cables aloft were cut as well. Aware that he had little notion of how to solve that, Pearce sat down, leaning against the side of the ship, as Harbin crawled down to join him.

'Do you have any orders, sir?'

'Orders?' Pearce replied with a grim smile. 'We need to get a party together, under someone reliable, to get aloft and cut those cables on the masts.'

'I'll go myself, sir,' said Harbin.

Was it bravery or stupidity that made the boy volunteer for something so deadly? Pearce did not know, he only knew that it was admirable, just as he knew that if he ordered the men aloft they would go. And why had that cannon not fired again? It seemed obvious; they knew ashore what had to be done, had probably reset their aim, and were just waiting for them to attempt it.

'Getting killed is not part of your duties, Mr Harbin, and we have already seen what happens to the anyone caught in the rigging.' He explained his thoughts about the cannon, then added, 'We will need to contrive some other scheme. Perhaps we can get our boats back and get clear.'

'I fear they would suffer many casualties, sir, just to get to us, as we would going over the side.'

'Which we will also do if we stay put. The sun is rising, and I am informed there is nothing to drink aboard, this while the route of escape is on the other side of the ship. Our opponents have thought this out well.'

He knew it would be better to get the men below; at least there they would be safe, but there was a risk in just getting them down as well as the very obvious fact that getting them back on deck in numbers would be even more risky, and if he could not do that he could not do anything. Rack his brains as he might, Pearce could see no other way out of this trap than by cutting the cables aloft and that could not be done from below. Did he have the right to get killed the half dozen hands it would take? Not unless he risked his own life; there was no way John Pearce could order men to climb the shrouds with axes, the only thing that could save them, while he sat safe behind his bulwark. He too would have to go, knowledge which concentrated his mind. Could he contrive a distraction of some kind?

He was gnawing on that when he heard a loud bang offshore, saw a ball arc over his head, which he followed, risking musket fire to see a shot strike the hill face. *Weazel* had joined in; Neame had anchored her fore and aft, and run out the guns. Would it answer, or would it take too long, for the deck was getting damned hot? If they could not move they would have to stay here all day, in the sweltering glare, while Neame traded gunfire. They then needed a cloudy, moonless night, unlikely since right now there was not a cloud in the sky, and that would only help if the men ashore made no attempt to retake the ship.

Weazel fired again and again, seeking to dislodge the musketeers from the hillside, but given they were well concealed and he was having to fire over the French ship it was a forlorn hope. But the real problem was that of the cannon and its grapeshot. Bodies lay around the deck, while another was hanging from the rigging, and that took no account of those who had hit the water. Benton's corpse was crumpled in the centre of the quarterdeck, like a broken doll, his blood, now dark like the wine he had been so fond of, staining several yards of the planking. Along the bulwark the wounded were being made as comfortable as possible, which was, judging by the moaning, not comfortable enough.

Harbin joined him again. 'I have had an idea, sir. If we could rig some way of signalling to the master we could direct his fire.'

'Explain.'

Harbin grinned, all freckles and teeth, then crawled

away. He managed to get to the signal locker by the binnacle without attracting attention, and there he set to, trying to sort out the flags so that he could compose signals that Neame would understand. This took quite a time and the heat, the silence, added to the fact that he had been up all night, was extremely enervating. Pearce closed his eyes, and was day-dreaming of a cool dip in the sea when he was alerted by the sound of more shots caused by Harbin running to the signal halyard, having sorted out which flags he could use. The boy was busy, using the mast itself as cover, bending on a message, one that the master, with the aid of the signal book, might understand. He extended the halyard lines to reach into the protected bulwarks, and then, flags under his arms, dived for shelter alongside his superior.

'All's ready sir. The first signal will read, "Can you understand our signals?" Might I suggest, sir, that our first task should be to get their fire to silence that cannon?'

'That seems the obvious course, Mr Harbin. You see to the signals, and I will deal with the cables.'

'Right, sir. I will ask them to acknowledge with the signal gun.'

He hoisted his first message, which attracted a lot of useless gunfire from the shore. Harbin left it for a moment, and hoisted another, on sight of which *Weazel* fired a gun. They had communication, so there followed a complicated running up and down of flags which made no sense at all to Pearce, but a quick glance offshore showed him that *Weazel* had shifted her position to get a clear shot at the hillsides. Pearce issued his orders, and at the right moment called out, setting he and his party running towards the mast. As soon as they got there they flung themselves on the deck, this, as a great swathe of grapeshot passed over their heads, after which Pearce had them scurrying back to safety.

After a pause, there was a rolling broadside from *Weazel*,

followed by another, then a third, which brought forth a great clanging sound which echoed round the bay, that in its turn followed by a faint cheer from out at sea. Harbin, who had been raising and lowering his head throughout, called to say that the cannon, having given its position away by firing, had, he thought, been dislodged by the sloop's long nines. The possibility was encouraging, but that did nothing as regards the musketry, and Pearce was reluctant to expose his men to that either.

'Mr Harbin, is it possible to signal *Weazel* to load with grape?'

'I can try, sir.'

While the midshipman set about that, Pearce called to the gunner's mate who had told him about the lack of drink and gunpowder. 'Are there any hammocks below?' A quick crawl got the man below, with another musket ball scarring the same part of the deck as previously.

'Don't come back,' Pearce yelled, 'just shout.'

The wait was only a minute, but it seemed longer before a rolled up hammock was thrown out, that too attracting a single shot from the shore, this as Pearce reached out for his coat, relieved that the notion he had had seemed a sound one.

'Right, lads, what we are going to do is to make a dummy that our enemies will take to be a sailor, and since it needs to be perceived to be an idiot it better be an officer.' It was a feeble joke, but it got a laugh. 'We must find something to fly the dummy so as to draw their fire. That, Mr Harbin, is when we want grapeshot from *Weazel*, as they are reloading. It may not kill them, they could be too well concealed, but it will keep their heads down and spoil their aim and by the time they have been swept twice I hope we shall have cut ourselves free.'

'Is there enough in the tide to take us out of danger?' asked Harbin.

'What makes you doubt it?' asked Pearce, unsure of the answer.

'As you know, the Mediterranean don't rise an' fall much, sir, only a couple of feet, and with no steerage way we can't keep her beam on to the shore.'

Pearce looked aloft, to where the sails were clewed up, realising that instead of risking only a proportion of the boarding party, he was going to have to risk them all. 'Then we must also send men up to drop the topsails, those left on deck are going to have to sheet them home, and some poor soul is going to have to manage the wheel.'

'Might be a job for an idiot, sir,' suggested a voice.

'Then I'd best volunteer,' Pearce replied, to a gale of laughter, which had him wondering if they could hear that ashore, and if they could, what they would make of it.

It took time to signal *Weazel*, time enough to allow them to fully dress the dummy as a naval lieutenant. It looked like nothing close to, but from a distance it might pass for a man. Nothing but use would tell and they could only hope that Neame fully understood what was required with the gunnery. Harbin waved that he was ready, and the crew crouched beside the useless guns, preparing to leap for the ratlines. One man had the dummy tied to a whip, one he had found that went all the way to the upper yards. Pearce nodded, the man pulled, the hammock rose, and a fusillade of shots cracked over them, none of them striking the dummy.

'Now!' shouted Pearce.

The men ran as fast as they could, scrabbling for their footholds in the ratlines as they raced aloft. Mentally, making his way towards the wheel, Pearce went through the loading of a musket. He had just levelled the gun in his mind's eye, and was ducking down, when *Weazel* opened up with a blast of grapeshot and suddenly the air was alive with the whistling sound of hundreds of small balls. Shots flew from the hillsides, but faced with a salvo of deadly grape and ricocheting rock, they flew wide.

Within a minute the men were in the tops, letting go the sails as their mates went even higher. Pearce moved from safety and ran to grab the wheel, feeling just as exposed, and waited until he could see that the upper yardsmen had cut them free from the restraining cables, which fell from the masts with a loud splash, this while those left on deck stood to sheet the sails home. He was congratulating himself on getting away without more casualties when a sailor fell from the yards into the sea, just at the moment the sloop had life.

'Get a rope to that fellow, quick,' he called to the wounded men, some of whom had the ability to move, humbled by the way they obeyed, hobbling to the task and managing to get a line into the fellow's outstretched hand.

There was not much wind but the sloop was taking it and getting under way, groaning and creaking, towing the man in the water, but still puffs of powder smoke were erupting from the rocks, braving the continued fire from *Weazel*. Muskets had a poor range, no more than a hundred yards at best if the user wanted accuracy, and Pearce reckoned they must be getting beyond that now, so it would have to be a very lucky shot that would hit anyone. When it did, jarring his arm, the shock killed any pain; that would come later. He looked down to see where the bullet had cut through his shirt and grazed his right arm. He also saw the bright blood well up from the wound, but he took a tight grip and the ship stayed steady, seen out of the bay by the sound of loud cheering.

Arm bandaged, Pearce sat in Benton's cabin, writing a report on the action, an absolute necessity and a task best carried out when everything was fresh in the mind. The owner of the quill in his hand was laying on the deck, already sown in canvas, with some joker suggesting that it should be weighted with his store of wine rather than a cannon ball. The jest was not cruelly meant, and it had some truth to it when Pearce discovered just how many bottles and pipes Benton had brought along; ten dozen of his blackstrap unconsumed and two pipes of port bought in Lisbon, and that was without his supply of brandy. It was just the natural morbidity of seamen, and in truth too many of their mates had died or taken a wound in that bay, too many lay alongside Benton on the deck, for the men not to be downcast and in need of some humour. Alongside was the ship they had taken, called *Mariette*, with the *Weazel*'s warrant officers crawling all over her to establish her condition, her guns, stores and the like, all guessing at what she might be worth.

'Mr Harbin,' he said, as the midshipman entered.

'Sir.'

Pearce did not reply at once. Instead he re-read what he had written, particularly about this young man. Finally he looked up at the midshipman standing rigid before him. 'Mr Harbin, I want you to take command of our prize, and ask Mr Neame to provide you with a decent master's mate. Choose what crew you need to sail her in safety, though you are to stay in our wake.'

The boy seemed to physically swell. 'Thank you, sir.'

'I want you to know that I have said in my report that without your intelligence and your efforts we would all have either died or been taken prisoner.' Now Harbin blushed and began to protest that it was not true. 'Please, Mr Harbin, cease your protests, and go and take command of your ship.'

The two sloops sailed in line ahead, up the east coast of Corsica, the flag of the Union flying above the tricolour on the mainmast of *Mariette*. Abreast of the fortified town of Bastia, in the early afternoon, having surveyed the good landing beaches to the south, Mr Neame had a request to the man walking on the windward side of the quarterdeck, who had just issued orders to hold their course, the anchorage off the town being empty of shipping.

'I'd like your permission to fire a signal gun, sir.' Responding to a quizzical look, the master added, pointing to yet another citadel and gun-bristling fortress, 'We would not want them French buggers in Bastia not to see the arrangement of Mr Harbin's flags.'

Pearce thought of the crooked-faced gunner, and his miserly husbanding of powder, who had been fussing like a mother hen over the state of his guns after the depredations caused by Neame's actions, blacking the muzzles and painting the trunnions. The chance to beard him was too good to miss. He looked at the shore, where there seemed little sign of any activity.

'I think a broadside would be in order, Mr Neame. I am given to understand that people in hot climates sleep at this time of day. Let us make sure that their slumbers are disturbed.'

No balls were fired, just powder, and Harbin responded to the loud bangs by dipping the tricolour and jerking the Union Jack. As the smoke swept aft, Neame said, 'I wonder what they will make of this in Toulon, Mr Pearce.'

Pearce grinned. 'That, Mr Neame, makes two of us.'

AUTHOR'S NOTE

Like most writers I am often asked where my ideas come from. The truth, in many cases, is that my imagination is the only spur, but that would not suffice if it was not based on some solid foundations.

The actions of HMS *Brilliant* off Toulon are fictitious, though the French ships involved did exist and the actual surrender of the port was as is stated – dramatic license notwithstanding. Added to that the terms which allowed Lord Hood to take over the port were negotiated by an English Naval officer who was taken as a prisoner by Admiral St Julien, only to be released by Baron d'Imbert.

Then there is the final battle in this novel, which takes place in the Golfo de Porto Vecchio. That is taken from a true account of an action involving the Royal Navy. Only the time at which it occurred and the use of my fictional characters depart from that which was real.

a&b

WWW.ALLISONANDBUSBY.COM

For more information and to place an order, visit our website where you'll also find free tasters, exclusive discounts, competitions and giveaways. Be sure to sign up to our monthly newsletter to keep up-to-date on our latest releases, news and upcoming events.

Alternatively, call us on
020 7580 1080
to place your order.